A THING IMMORTAL

A DARK FANTASY

BARRY K GREGORY

PULPTROPOLIS

Sign up for our mailing list at https://barrykgregory.com/

Copyright © 2023 by Barry K Gregory. All rights reserved.

Published by Pulptropolis Media.

The characters and events in this book are fictitious. Any similarity to actual persons, living or dead, is purely coincidental and not intended by the author.

No portion of this book may be reproduced in any form without written permission from the publisher or author, except as permitted by U.S. copyright law.

*For Jennifer.
It's always for Jennifer.*

One

The Wing-Thief

The wing-thief stared down the shaft of the nocked arrow, the black tattoos that lined his arms and wrapped around his back dancing with each muscle twitch. The bowstring was pulled to full extension, sunlight glinting off the obsidian arrowhead. He knelt on one knee, bracing himself against a sturdy aspen in the thick grove behind the trapper's shack. The sun slid below the snow-capped peaks to the west, shadows stretching long, blanketing the ground and darkening the gaps between the trees.

The holy man squatted behind him and leaned close, gently brushing Black Wing's hair behind his ear with a finger. "Tell me what you see," whispered the holy man, his lips inches from Black Wing's ear, his breath hot on the wing-thief's cheek.

"The same thing you see," answered the wing-thief, ignoring the holy man's provocations.

"Not likely," said the holy man Antelope Eyes. His voice rose, a gentle lilt to his tone. "Look closely and tell me exactly what you see."

"I see a girl being menaced by a naked man."

"Describe the man."

"I just did."

"More detail, please."

Black Wing sighed. The holy man often exasperated him. "You can see the man as well as I."

"Oh, I see him all right. I see far more than you do, I assure you. But I don't have an arrow pointing at his heart. I'm not the one who is a twitch of the finger away from killing him. I know what I see. I want to know what *you* see."

"He is a white eye," said Black Wing.

"Is that why you want to kill him? Because he is a white eye?"

"I do not want to kill him."

"Really? It certainly seems to me you want to kill him."

"No. But I am prepared to kill him if necessary."

"Interesting," said Antelope Eyes. "Tell me more about this man. What do you see when you look at him?"

"Please stop."

"Humor me."

The wing-thief sighed. "His movements are sluggish. Lethargic. As if he is intoxicated."

"Very observant. Is he tall?"

"No. He is short. Hirsute. His beard is scraggly, streaked with gray."

"What animal does he most resemble?"

"He has the face of a weasel."

"And his body?"

"He looks like a small, shaved bear."

The holy man twirled a lock of Black Wing's hair with his finger. "You said he was menacing."

"You don't find bears menacing?"

Antelope Eyes snickered. "Actually, I find bears can be quite charming, so long as they are well-fed and do not feel threatened. Tell me why you have an arrow pointing at his heart."

"The cruelty he shows the girl is not explanation enough for you?"

"We're not talking about the girl just yet," said Antelope Eyes. "We're still talking about the shaved bear." He paused, then said, "Can you see his manhood?"

Black Wing sighed again. "You know I can."

"Describe it to me."

"I am not describing his cock to you."

"Is it erect?"

"We can both see that it is."

"Do you know this man?"

"I've seen him before," the wing-thief said through gritted teeth. "He sets traps on the mountainside. Iron abominations that crush the legs of wolverines and badgers."

"You do not like the man?" asked Antelope Eyes.

"He sets traps that crush the legs of wolverines and badgers," the wing-thief repeated.

The holy man smiled, whispered in the wing-thief's ear. "So you have decided to kill him, then?"

Black Wing's eyes narrowed. "No. He will decide if I kill him."

"Interesting. And how will you know when he has made his decision?"

"When he moves to harm the girl."

"Ah. So you are protecting the girl then, are you?"

"I grow weary of this game," said the wing-thief

"Then end it. Release your arrow. Kill him."

"I meant your game, not his."

"They are one and the same. So if you want to end the game, then kill him and be done with it."

The wing-thief hesitated.

"So perhaps you do not want the game to end just yet. Very well, then. Since you brought up the girl again, we will talk about her now. Describe her to me."

"We both see her," said Black Wing, frustration in his voice.

"You are angry with me? This is for your benefit, not mine. If you won't describe her, then tell me what she is doing."

The wing-thief took a breath. "She is clutching a rooster to her breast."

"Why is she doing that?"

"For protection. She is attempting to maintain a buffer between herself and the drunkard."

The holy man reached beneath Black Wing's arm, his fingers sliding across the wing-thief's chest until he found the medicine bundle Black Wing kept tied in a pouch around his neck. He cupped the pouch gently. "If you are so interested in protecting the girl, there is a more direct route than your bow. Use your medicine. You are a wing-thief, are you not? Swap bodies with the rooster. A rooster's spur is sharp enough to injure the man badly. You could blind him. You could slit his throat."

"And if he caught the rooster, he could just as easily wring its neck."

"This is true. Tell me, what do you think would happen to a wing-thief if the bird were to die while the thief was inside it?"

"I don't want to find out," said Black Wing. "That's why I'm still in my own body."

While the wing-thief and the holy man watched, the naked man escalated the situation, lunging awkwardly at the girl. She dodged easily enough, sidestepping and throwing the rooster in his face, before turning and sprinting up the hillside and into the trees. The startled rooster flapped its wings madly, talons raking across the man's chest and arms. The naked, hirsute man grabbed the bird's head and did as Black Wing had suggested he might. He wrung the rooster's neck and dropped the limp carcass to the ground.

Black Wing kept the arrow trained on the man, waiting for him to follow the girl into the woods. But the man only staggered about, yelling after her, calling her vile names, and ordering her to come back. The girl ignored him. The man spewed threats, but still the girl did not come back. When the man ran out of threats, he spit in his hand and began masturbating.

"Kill him," whispered Antelope Eyes, his hand still holding the wing-thief's medicine bundle. "Release your arrow."

Black Wing hesitated.

"End this."

"Why are we here?" the wing-thief asked. "Tell me the truth. Why did you bring me here? Was I meant to kill him? Was that your intention?"

The holy man smiled. He released the medicine bundle, then reached forward, pressing down gently on the wing-thief's bow arm. "No. He is not the reason I brought you here. He is no one. An insignificant fool who will be dead before the next moon. But not by your hand."

Black Wing eased the tension on the bowstring and lowered the nocked arrow. "Then we are here to rescue the girl from him?"

"No." The holy man pointed to an aspen trunk a few feet away from them. "If you were more observant, then you would have noticed that."

The wing-thief looked and saw a small carving on the tree, a series of cuts and slashes underscored by a looping mark.

Antelope Eyes smiled. "I told you, I see more than you. If you were to look closely, you would see that there is a similar ward carved into the trunk of many trees encircling the trapper's shack. You and I can get no closer than we are now. Your arrow, had you released it, would have dropped to the ground almost as soon as it left your hand."

"The wards would keep us out?"

"Yes. Just as they keep the girl trapped inside."

The naked man finished with a shudder, then yelled once more after the girl, before turning and staggering back inside the shack.

Black Wing was relieved to know the little man would be dead soon. "If we cannot cross the wards, if I cannot kill the man, nor rescue the girl, then why did you bring me here?"

The holy man smiled again. "Do you still see her?"

The wing-thief scanned the trees until he found her, squatting behind a moss-covered boulder jutting from the hillside. "Yes."

"Describe her to me."

"Must I? Have you not made your point?"

"Have I? Describe her."

Black Wing sighed. "She has dark hair."

"How old is she?"

"Perhaps twelve summers."

"More detail. What does she look like? What do you see?"

"She is pretty."

"Do you like pretty little girls?" Antelope Eyes said.

"You and I have established what I like," said the wing-thief.

The holy man smiled. "Is that the best description you can give me? Dark hair and pretty?"

"She is frightened."

"Why do you think this little white-eyed girl is frightened?"

"She is not a white," said Black Wing.

"Ah, you *do* see," said Antelope Eyes. "Perhaps you are not as hopeless as I feared. If she is not a white-eye, then look closely and tell me, who are her people?"

"I do not know. She does not look as if she belongs to any of the people of the plains."

"Does she have medicine?" asked the holy man.

Black Wing paused. "Yes."

"How do you know that? Can you see it?"

"How does one see medicine?"

"When your eyes have been opened, you will see. How do you know she has medicine?"

"I don't know." Black Wing turned his head, looked at the holy man. "You know this girl. Who is she?"

Antelope Eyes pointed. "There is something else you should see."

Black Wing saw the eyes first. Great yellow orbs emerging from the shimmering golden leaves of the aspens, glowing and sparkling like the afternoon sun. As he watched, the shadows seemed to expand, taking on volume, flowing upward from the ground and coalescing around the eyes. The collective darkness morphed into a massive silhouette and the shadowy thing stepped into the light, revealing itself.

An impossibly large wolf, black as midnight and taller than a horse, stood in front of the crouching girl. To the wing-thief's surprise, the girl did not seem afraid. It was as if the wolf's presence comforted her. The giant wolf lowered its head, a submissive gesture inviting the girl's touch. The girl got to her feet, bracing herself against the boulder, and held out a tentative hand.

The wolf placed its head beneath the girl's hand. The girl scratched the top of the wolf's head, her fingers disappearing into the thick tuft of black fur.

The holy man leaned closer to Black Wing, whispering in his ear. "First time you've seen a god?"

Two

The Gunslinger

THE OLD GUNSLINGER GAZED up at the night sky, billions of stars staring back at him as he waited for sleep to take him. An odd feeling rolled over him. The night was eerily silent, still as death. No breeze, no insects chirping or singing. No lonesome owl calling out for companionship. Hamish Frost realized he was frozen, unable to move. The old man didn't recall having lain down, nor even having made camp for the evening. Yet there he was, lying on the grassy plains, staring up at an ocean of stars. The milky, spiral nebulae hovered over him, swirling like a slow-spinning pinwheel, seeming so close he could almost reach up and scrape the stars with his fingertips or swat away a streaking comet.

As he watched, the constellations above began to rearrange themselves. Stars slid across the sky, miraculously avoiding collision as they repositioned themselves. Condensing and coalescing, the stars took on form and volume until a new shape appeared. Striding through the sky above him, a sparkling woman made entirely of star-stuff stood alone against a black void. Between her breasts, a single pulsing star flared and burned with the brightness of the midday sun.

I'm having a vision, he realized.

The star woman reached down, holding out a hand, motioning to the old gunslinger, beckoning him to leave the ground and fly up to her. Frost felt compelled to do just that, but the heat from the blazing star at her breast kept him at bay. The brightness grew so intense that he was forced to cross his arms in front of his face, shielding his eyes. He waited for what seemed an eternity before he felt the blinding light fade and then disappear.

As his sight returned, he found the star-woman gone and the night sky back in its proper place. He, however, was no longer on his back in the grass. He was standing atop a wide, but narrow plateau high in the craggy mountains. Evergreens a hundred feet tall sprang from the sloping mountainside, casting soft shadows over the entire plateau.

Ahead of him, the old gunslinger could see a lonely tipi, the flap open and welcoming. Puffs of white smoke wafted through the vent at the top. On the ground, a trail of lush blue moss led all the way from where he stood to the flap of the tipi. A stiff but cool breeze pushed against his back, whipping his long, stringy white hair into his eyes and prodding him down the mossy path. He took one step forward and then...

...the old man opened his eyes and sat up. The night sky had been replaced by enormous billowing white clouds set against an expanse of cerulean blue, the sun rising steadily in the east. To the west, the craggy snow-capped peaks sparkled with an unnatural whiteness.

His fire had gone cold in the night, leaving only faintly smoldering embers. His painted horse grazed quietly on thick grasses in the near distance.

Hamish Frost had lived a long, long life. He had the wrinkles and the scars to prove it. He had learned many years ago to recognize the difference between dream and vision and to understand the importance of that difference. Dreams were meaningless and random. A jumble of nonsense, conjured by the unconscious mind. Visions, on the other hand, were encoded messages. Missives from a sender, a riddle to be deciphered. Often a warning.

The old gunslinger sensed he was not alone. He reached for his six-guns and they appeared in his hands as if by magic. Twin revolvers, polished steel with elephant ivory handles, his thumbs on the hammers, index fingers on the trigger of each. The old man's speed with the guns had not diminished with age. Hamish Frost was reputed to be the fastest there ever was and he had the kills to prove it.

A giant shadow came to life in front of him. Glowing amber-colored eyes set against an immense mound of fur as black as coal. The old gunslinger lowered his guns and smiled. *"Stiffen the sinews, summon up the blood. Disguise fair nature with hard-favored rage,"* he said with a theatrical flourish. *"Then lend the eye to a terrible aspect. Let pry through the portage of the head like the brass cannon, let the brow o'erwhelm it as fearfully as doth a galled rock o'erhang and jutty his confounded base."*

The Shadow Wolf stared back at him, eyes aglow.

"I suppose the time has come to see the old woman again, huh?"

With a swipe of one massive paw, the Shadow Wolf spread dirt over the remains of Frost's campfire.

"I was about to do that."

The Shadow Wolf lowered its massive head, then swung its neck to the west, towards the distant mountains.

"I know," said the old gunslinger. "She sent me a vision. Any idea what she wants?"

The Shadow Wolf only stared at him.

"Now don't be impatient." The old man stood, stretched, and yawned. His skin was almost as pale as his white hair, his eyes a shade of violet. "It will take us at least a few days to get there. She can't be in that much of a rush. You can wait while I have some breakfast. Won't take that long."

The Shadow Wolf turned and began walking westward, the swaying grasses seeming to part ahead of each step.

Frost sighed. "Seriously? No breakfast? You're not even going to let me have a proper morning shit, are you? Can you at least wait long enough for me to pull on my boots and saddle my horse?"

The Shadow Wolf kept walking and was almost out of sight by the time the old gunslinger saddled up and followed after it.

Three

The Manhunter

Ozymandias Hayes suppressed a rising sense of foreboding as he surveyed the landscape. The sun hung low on the immense horizon abutting the plains, painting the sparsely clouded sky in shades of red, orange, and purple. Hayes twisted in the saddle and looked over his shoulder, the long shadows cast by the horses stretching into the distance.

"This is not a good spot," said Hayes. "We should keep moving."

His partner Jacob Hutchens scoffed. "Nonsense. It's an ideal spot."

Hayes shook his head. "We've got at least an hour until sunset. We can find better."

"Better than ideal?" Hutchens sat ramrod straight in the saddle, shoulders back, chest out. He pointed toward a ridge near a small creek where the plain undulated like a cresting wave on the ocean. "That little rise there will block our campfire from view and the cottonwoods behind it will mask any cast shadows. Our pursuers would be damned hard-pressed to see us there. And with the bluff to the north, you couldn't ask for a more secure spot should our prisoner's gang somehow chance upon us in the night."

Hayes looked at their prisoner. Enoch Munn sat on a horse next to Hutchens, his hands tied behind his back. His head lolled, his chin on his chest, a shock of red hair falling over a face left in ruin by a severe bout of chickenpox. Munn's eyes were closed, but Hayes knew he was feigning sleep, biding his time, waiting for an opening. Any chance — no matter how small — to escape his predicament.

"If his gang catches up to us in the dark of night," Hayes said, "we need to be sure we see them coming long before they see us. That bluff guarantees we won't."

Hutchens dismissed the argument without consideration. "No. I'm exercising my prerogative as your superior. This is the spot. We make camp here."

Hayes had long since concluded that Jacob Hutchens was a blustering fool. He needed no further evidence, but the man continuously provided it. "The topography here — that ridge over there — works against us. We'll be somewhat hidden, that's true, but when night falls, we won't be able to see anyone approaching until they're practically on top of us. And the cottonwoods will hinder our line of sight in the opposite direction. This is a dangerously poor spot for a camp. We'd do better to put some distance between us and the bluff, find a clear, flat area with a three-hundred-sixty-degree view, and forego the campfire altogether. Even a small fire would be like a beacon on these plains."

"Camp out in the open? Totally exposed? No fire? With a gang of murderous outlaws pursuing us? I think not." Hutchens laughed derisively. "I thought you negroes didn't cotton to the cold." He smiled, having amused himself with the double entendre.

"Nee-gro." Enoch Munn lifted his head, grinning devilishly, his buck teeth on display. "Nee-gro. Is that the same thing as a nigger? Don't tell me I been sayin' it wrong all this time?"

"Shut your mouth," barked Hutchens.

"Nee-gro," Munn laughed again. "That's the funniest fuckin' word I ever did hear."

Hayes gave Munn a stone-faced stare. Munn only winked and smiled back at him. The look made Hayes' skin crawl.

"I'll book no further argument," said Hutchens. "We camp here. You square away our prisoner and get the fire started while I hobble the horses and do a little surveillance."

Hayes bit his tongue, deciding against pointing out to Hutchens that it wasn't necessary to hobble horses when there were trees to which they could be tied off. He climbed down from his horse and attempted to assist Munn off of his.

"Don't touch me, nigger!" Munn hocked and spit, a large wad of phlegm landing squarely between Hayes' eyes.

Hayes calmly wiped away the spittle with the back of his glove, then grabbed Munn by the arm and snatched him from the saddle, making no effort to ease Munn's fall. A gasp escaped from Munn's lips as he landed flat on his back, the air vacating his lungs on impact. Hayes took a coil of rope from his saddle while Munn was still struggling to reclaim his breath. Hayes grabbed a fistful of red hair and dragged Munn across the ground to a cottonwood. He lashed the outlaw to the tree trunk, then yanked Munn's filthy kerchief from his neck, wadded it, and shoved it in Munn's mouth.

Hutchens adopted a leisurely pace, taking care to be sure that Hayes did most of the work in setting camp. Hayes built the fire from the driest wood he could find, keeping the fire small and tight. Fast burning with as little smoke as possible.

"I've been monitoring the trail behind us," Hutchens said.

Hayes took off his gloves and made a show of warming his hands near the flames. He didn't want the fire, knew it was a mistake to build it, but thought it wise to placate Hutchens. At least for the nonce. "See anything?" he asked.

"Looks clear," said Hutchens.

"I'll take first watch." Hayes volunteered, knowing that trusting his safety to the watchfulness of Jacob Hutchens was unwise in the least.

Hutchens acquiesced with a nod, retrieved his bedroll, and shook it out on the ground. "Wake me in the early a.m." He pulled off his boots and lowered himself to the ground, rolling onto his side, his back to Hayes. Inside of two minutes, Hutchens was snoring fitfully.

Hayes immediately kicked out the small campfire. The temperature would drop precipitously as the night wore on, but a fire was a terrible idea. The night wasn't dark enough to keep the smoke from giving away their position and the circle of light would not only illuminate them but would also prevent their eyes from adjusting enough to see past the ring of shadows at the light's terminus.

And Hayes knew Munn's gang was out there somewhere. Following them.

With the flames faded to smolders, Hayes used the toe of his boot to reassemble the embers, making it appear as if the fire had simply burned itself out. In the morning, he would explain to Hutchens that, in the dark, he'd been unable to restart the fire. A needful lie, but Hutchens would know no different.

Hayes next removed the hobbles and led the horses to the trees. If they needed to make a quick getaway in the night, untying the horses' reins from the trees would be much quicker than removing hobbles.

Hayes stole a glance at Enoch Munn. The prisoner watched him closely, eyes narrowed, mercifully silent thanks to the gag in his mouth.

Should've done that at least a day ago, thought Hayes.

After two weeks on his trail, Hayes and Hutchens had found Munn sleeping in a hollowed log on the banks of a river. In taking him into custody, Hayes discovered they had underestimated the limits of Munn's atrocities. In a satchel Munn was using as a pillow, Hayes found seven scalps, hair as black as ink, all of which, based on the closeness of the crown to the hairline, Hayes knew had come from children.

Jacob Hutchens had wrinkled his nose and shrugged. "At least he didn't scalp white children."

Hayes ground his teeth at the remark but managed to hold his tongue.

"What are these?" Hutchens asked, shaking from the satchel three dried, shriveled, fleshy things into his palm.

Munn chuckled. "Peckers. I collect 'em. I'll be adding both of your'n to my collection when my boys catch up to you. I ain't never cut off a nigger pecker before. I'm lookin' forward to that."

Jacob Hutchens struck Munn in the mouth with the butt of his pistol, then pulled back the hammer and aimed at Munn's head.

"No," said Hayes. "We're taking him to the fort. Alive."

"The handbill says 'Dead or Alive,'" said Hutchens. "Dead suits me just fine."

"Dead or Alive is not a sanction of murder," Hayes reminded him.

"Says who?"

"I say." Hayes paused. "The law says. And I'll not have you murder a man in front of me."

"You know what will happen to us if his gang catches up to us with him in our custody?"

"Same thing that would happen if you were to execute him here."

Hutchens grumbled but relented. He gathered up Munn's satchel, the scalps, and the mummified phalluses and tossed them all in the river. "Nobody needs to see Indian scalps and a bunch of dried-up peckers. This fucker's going to hang with or without that shit. If I don't kill him before then."

For the first time since they'd been traveling together, Hayes noted Hutchens was probably right.

After an hour of listening to Hutchens snore, Hayes stood and patrolled the perimeter of the campsite. He kept low to the ground, careful to avoid silhouetting himself against the light of the moon. He spied a herd of several dozen mule deer moving quickly across the distant plains, not stampeding but traveling with haste, clearly spooked. Curious, he watched for a few minutes, expecting to see a pack of wolves pacing the herd. But there were no wolves. Instead, he saw another herd of... something. Of what exactly, he couldn't be sure. He saw only a silhouetted mass, packed tightly together and moving at a steady, unified pace.

A cold shiver ran down Hayes' spine and the hair on his arms rose as if drawn by a static charge. He struggled to make sense of what he was seeing. The mass resembled nothing more than people lumbering in lockstep. But that made no sense. None at all. He had seen the red men approach a target stealthily under cover of darkness, but that was not what he was witnessing now. There was no stealth in what he was seeing.

Was this Munn's gang? No. They would be on horseback, not walking. And at most, the gang would comprise five or six men. If this awkward mass was indeed people, there were dozens of them.

Thankfully, whatever he was seeing was moving away from his campsite, which suited Hayes just fine. Time permitting, he would check the tracks in the morning and see if that added any clarity to the mystery.

He watched until both the deer and their pursuers disappeared over the horizon. Hayes checked the position of the moon. It was past time he woke Hutchens. An equitable watch would have ended a few hours earlier, but fairness was not Hayes' guiding concern. His chances of surviving the night were increased if he spent more time on watch duty than Jacob Hutchens. If the dawn arrived without further event, he could still manage about three hours of sleep. Not enough, of course, but he had functioned on fewer.

Movement in his periphery caught his attention. Hayes spun, sidearm drawn. Standing on the crest of the ridge was a woman. Naked and startling in her beauty, slim with full breasts and wide hips. Her long dark hair billowed about her head as if buffeted by strong winds, even though the night was still and the winds almost nonexistent.

Hayes froze. The woman made no effort to cover her nakedness. She stared at Hayes, a Mona Lisa smile on her lips. She did not speak, only stood there, as if waiting for him. To do what, he did not know.

Hayes opened his mouth to speak, but the words were sidetracked somewhere between brain and tongue. The woman's form shimmered in the moonlight, almost as if translucent. Hayes thought he could see the shape of the bluff behind her, through her, as if she were a mirage of some sort. She made a motion with her hand as if summoning him to her. Hayes took a step forward. The woman motioned him closer. He took another step.

And then she was no longer there.

Hayes blinked, rubbed his eyes, and looked all around him. There was nowhere for the woman to have gone, but she had disappeared. Vanished into the air.

Had he just seen a ghost?

Ozymandias Hayes was an educated man and never one to put stock in the supernatural, but how else to explain what he had just seen?

Had he been dreaming? Had he allowed himself to fall asleep on watch? He didn't think so, but that would provide an explanation. Certainly a better explanation than his having seen a phantom. It would also explain the silhouetted mass he had watched pursuing the herd of deer.

But he knew that wasn't so. He had not been sleeping. It wasn't a dream.

Was he hallucinating then? Was his exhausted, sleep-deprived mind showing him things that were not there?

He looked over at Enoch Munn tied to a tree behind him. Perhaps the outlaw had seen something as well. But Munn's head was down, red hair in front of his face. Whether sleeping or feigning sleep, this time didn't matter. Munn would be no help in determining whether the vision had been real or conjured.

Hutchens awoke with a start when Hayes prodded him. He reached immediately for his sidearm, but Hayes had expected this and rested his own hand over Hutchens' pistol before attempting to rouse him.

Satisfied that Hutchens had shaken off his slumber, Hayes gave him a brief report but mentioned nothing of the naked, spectral woman or the mule deer and their mystery pursuers.

Hutchens was not happy about the fire having gone cold. He rolled up his blankets, set them aside, and turned his attention to restarting the campfire. Hayes knew that his succeeding was unlikely. He retrieved his own bedroll from his saddle and stretched out on a grassy spot he had cleared of sticks and debris earlier in the evening. Sleep came quickly and deeply. But did not last long.

Hayes' eyes snapped open. The sun had broken over the horizon, its splintered rays spraying the morning sky with bands of light. To Hayes' surprise, Hutchens had somehow managed to restart the fire. It took him a few seconds to realize the sound that woke him was a gunshot. Jacob Hutchens was sitting across from him, head slumped over, asleep and snoring.

"Hutchens!" Hayes said as loudly as he dared. "Wake up!"

Hutchens' whole body jerked, his head snapping up and to attention.

"Someone's shooting at us." Hayes scrambled to his feet, keeping low to the ground, and pulled his pistol.

Hutchens looked around and then stood up.

"Don't stand, you fool!" Hayes' words came in almost perfect unison with the second gunshot.

Hutchens grimaced and clutched his chest. He crumbled, landing face-first in the fire.

Hayes leaped over and grabbed Hutchens' shoulders, pulling him from the flames as quickly as he could. For all the good it did. The fire had blistered Hutchens' face, his hair all singed away, but he was beyond feeling any of it.

Hayes scrambled for the cover of the trees. Another gunshot rang out, and he felt as much as heard the bullet whizz past his head. He dove behind the cottonwood tree where Enoch Munn was lashed. He got to his feet, flattening himself against the trunk. He lifted his pistol to eye level, then peered carefully around the tree, scanning, searching for the source of the gunshots.

He could see no one.

From somewhere behind him, Hayes heard a heavy footstep and a twig cracking. He spun around, gun arm extended, leveled, and ready to fire, only to take the full brunt of a rifle butt in the face.

Four

The Wing-Thief

The wing-thief glided silently to a perch in the upper limbs of a sassafras tree on the banks of a dark, deepwater lake. A retreating glacier had gouged the land, creating the lake eons ago. From the air, Black Wing had spotted the holy man floating on his back in the shallows along the opposite shore of the lake. The moonlight glistened on the still waters, casting the world in a soft blue glow. The holy man's head was staring up into the sky. With graceful strokes, he rotated his arms back and over, pulling himself along steadily in the water.

Black Wing could see the holy man's mouth moving as he swam. At first, he thought Antelope Eyes was singing but as he watched more closely, he could see the way the holy man's lips moved, the forming of words, the pausing as if listening to another voice, then responding.

He wasn't singing. He was talking.

The wing-thief watched in silence as the moon rose, slowly crossing the star-filled sky. Still, the holy man swam and talked. Only when at long last the edges of the eastern sky grew lighter, did Antelope Eyes finally turn and swim for shore.

Black Wing watched him as he climbed naked from the water and sat on the grassy bank by the boulder on which his clothing rested. The holy man closed his eyes and Black Wing could see his chest expanding rhythmically, his breath measured as he meditated. He sat there for some time, letting the rising sun's rays dry him. The holy man had been in the water for so long that his fingers and toes had pruned and his member had shrunk back into his body for warmth. After a while, he stood and pulled on his leggings. After putting on his tunic, he reached for his beaded necklace, but paused and looked up into the tree where the wing-thief perched.

Black Wing could tell he had been spotted. Antelope Eyes was one of only two people he knew who could recognize him when he wasn't in his own body. The holy man cupped his hands around his mouth and did his best to hoot like an owl. Antelope Eye's attempt at mimicry was so poor Black Wing wished he could have laughed.

Antelope Eyes smiled. Even waterlogged and goose-pimpled from the cool breeze, Black Wing saw the holy man as beautiful.

Antelope Eyes adopted a leisurely pace as he walked back to their camp, stopping from time to time to run his fingers along the flaking bark of an aspen tree or bending to smell wildflowers, even picking a few and weaving them into his hair. Black Wing took flight and followed him, but had to perch often to keep from getting ahead. Even having to circle back once when Antelope Eyes sat and waited rather than step over a tortoise crossing his path.

The sun was well up into the morning sky by the time Antelope Eyes finally reached their camp. He plopped down on the buffalo fur they used for sleeping and munched some pine nuts while he waited as Black Wing returned the borrowed owl's body and reclaimed his own.

The holy man had already broken camp and readied the horses by the time Black Wing climbed down from the top of the tall oak tree where he had stashed his body the night before.

"Took your time," said the holy man, smiling.

"My legs were asleep," answered Black Wing. "I couldn't climb down until I got the blood flowing again."

"You spent the night in two different trees." Antelope Eyes laughed.

"I was worried about you. We are in a dangerous country. You brought me on this spirit quest to protect you. You shouldn't go off in the middle of the night without me."

The holy man smiled. "I didn't bring you to protect me."

"If not to protect you, then what is my purpose here?"

"Perhaps I just enjoy your company."

"If it's my company you desire, then don't get out of our bed in the middle of the night."

Antelope Eyes shrugged. "Don't be angry. I just wanted to go for a swim."

"At night?"

"I like night swimming."

"And you, of course, knew precisely where to find a lake, even in the dark?"

"It wasn't that dark and there are lots of lakes and rivers about. I knew I'd find something sooner or later."

"I was worried about what might find you."

The holy man smiled, waving a hand dismissively. "You need not worry. I have known the day and the place of my end for a long time. It is not here and it is not today."

"So you say. But that is no reason to throw caution to the wind. The future is not set. You have told me that many times." Antelope Eyes had not been trained as a warrior. He did not see the world through the same eyes that Black Wing did. He didn't perceive threat or take caution in strange places as a warrior would. The wing-thief was torn between admiring those traits and being angered by the naivete implicit in them.

"I apologize," said the holy man. "I will exercise more caution in the future."

Black Wing didn't believe him. His words were the same placating pablum he always offered. "What did the fish have to say?"

Antelope Eyes furrowed his brow. "Hmm?"

"In the water, I saw you. You were talking."

"Ah yes. So I was, but not to fish. Fish are poor conversationalists. One sentence or two is the most you can hope for before something shiny catches their attention and off they go."

Black Wing wasn't in the mood for jest. "Who were you talking to?"

The holy man sat down on the grass and patted the ground, motioning for Black Wing to join him.

"I'll stand."

"No," said the holy man. "You will sit and I will explain. Owls have powerful eyes, that is known, but they do not see all."

Black Wing sighed but obeyed. He crossed his legs and sat staring into the holy man's dark, doe-shaped eyes. "So explain."

"You are asking the wrong question," the holy man said. "Who I was talking to is not what you should concern yourself with."

"Then what should I concern myself with?"

Antelope Eyes smiled. "That's a better question."

"How about an answer then?"

"It's a better question, though still not the right question. The question you should ask of me is what were we talking about."

"Fine. What were you and the fish talking about?"

"I told you, not fish."

Black Wing sighed. "What were you and some invisible person — that no one but you could see — talking about?"

"Just because you do not see, does not mean *all* do not see. Your eyes have not yet been opened, but when they are, you will see. Ask your question again. But more respectfully this time."

Black Wing spoke slowly. Haltingly. "What...were...you...talking...about?"

Antelope Eyes smiled. "You," he paused. "We were talking about you."

"Me?"

"Yes."

"You were talking about me?"

"That is what I said."

"So why were you — and this invisible person — talking about me?"

"You don't believe you are a good subject for conversation?"

"I don't think I'm a good enough subject for a conversation that went as long as yours did."

The holy man went silent for a moment, then said, "Why are you here?"

"You know why I am here."

"I do, but it seems you do not."

"I am here to protect you while you are on a spirit quest."

"No." The holy man shook his head. "I told you that is not why I brought you. You are not here for my protection. So I ask you again... why are you here?"

"Enough with the games. Just tell me. If not to protect you, then why am I here?"

The holy man walked to his horse, pulled himself onto the horse's back, and positioned himself on the small blanket. He ran a hand along the length of the horse's neck, then patted the animal just above the shoulder. "A spirit quest is a search for answers in places one has never looked. It is known that answers sometimes hide in strange and unfamiliar locales. Sometimes the answers come before we even know the questions. We go where the spirits lead us. We find what they want us to find, see what they want us to see, learn what they would have us learn. Sometimes answers greet us openly, sometimes they hide themselves, disguise themselves. We must be wise enough to see through their subterfuge. Do you understand?"

"Not particularly, no."

"Then you should try harder." The holy man put his heels gently to the horse's flanks and the animal began to trot.

"I lied to you," said Black Wing.

"Oh?" Antelope Eyes tugged on the horse's mane, stopping it as he looked over his shoulder.

"Not by commission, but by omission. Back in the mountains. At the trapper's shack. You asked if that was the first time I had seen a god. I let you believe it was, but the truth is, I have seen the Shadow Wolf before. In the company of Whiteskin."

"You know Whiteskin, do you?" asked Antelope Eyes.

"We have crossed paths before. The Shadow Wolf traveled with him. I thought it was an unusual creature, but I did not know it was a god."

Antelope Eyes smiled. "You assume I was talking about the Shadow Wolf."

Black Wing's eyes went wide. "The girl...?"

The holy man turned away from him, urging the horse forward. "I lied to you as well," he said without looking back. "And in the same manner. By omission. You knew this was a spirit quest and I allowed you to believe it was mine. That you were my guide and helpmeet. That is not the case. This is not my spirit quest. It is yours."

Five

The Girl

THE GIRL HAD WANTED desperately to escape the buffalo hunter. She thought that anything would be better than being tied to a tree, naked all the time, sleeping as close as she could to the fire so as not to freeze at night, and then having him do all those things to her. Anything would be better. Anyone would be better.

But she was wrong. The fur trader was worse. Much worse.

She didn't realize that would be the case, not at first. Where the buffalo hunter had been a large, imposing man with thickly muscled arms, the fur trader was a smallish, weak-looking man with a narrow, pointed face that reminded her of a rat. He wore animal skins for clothes.

The fur trader gave the buffalo hunter a tiny nugget of gold that he claimed was worth at least ten dollars. The buffalo hunter bit down on the nugget like that was supposed to tell him something he couldn't know just from looking at it. The buffalo hunter nodded his head and, just like that, the transaction was complete and she had been sold.

The fur trader untied the rope from the tree, grabbed the girl by her hair, and dragged her to his mule. When the girl didn't move as quickly as he would've liked, the fur trader slapped her with the back of his hand so hard, she fell down in a daze. She could taste blood in her mouth as he picked her up, flung her across the back of his mule, trussed her up like she was a deer he'd just killed, and took her to his shack way up in the mountains.

She'd been there ever since.

The fur trader, like the buffalo hunter, would go off every day and leave the girl alone inside the small shack. There were no windows, and there was a latch on the outside of the door that kept her from leaving. With the door latched, the girl could only sit in the darkness and wait for the fur trader's return.

Unlike the buffalo hunter, the fur trader did not keep her naked. He gave her a poorly stitched smock made of deer leather and a pair of fur shoes. He gave her a small bucket so she wouldn't have to do her business on the dirt floor of the shack and sometimes he would remember to leave another bucket with fresh water for her to drink, but most of the time she would have to go thirsty while he was away. He seldom ever left food for her and when he did, it was some dirty root or dried mystery meat that tasted worse than the root.

She had no way of knowing how much time passed while the fur trader was away or how long he might be gone each time, but she knew that as soon as he returned she'd get a beating first and then he'd do those same things to her that the buffalo hunter did. Even with the hunger and painful thirst, she treasured the solitude, the times when she didn't have to put up with the fur trader's beatings or his sweaty gruntings.

The fur trader's bed took up most of the floor space of the shack. It wasn't an actual wooden bed like the one she remembered sleeping in as a small child. Instead, it was a stack of animal skins resting on top of a pile of pine needles. There was a fireplace in one corner, a crude chimney of stacked stones that directed the smoke through a narrow hole in the roof and out of the shack.

Of course, the girl didn't know how to start a fire and even if she did, there was no wood to burn inside the shack. The floor was dirt and too cold for sitting, so she would sit on the fur bed and wait. She once made the mistake of falling asleep there while the fur trader was out. He came home and found her on the bed and gave her the worst beating she'd ever gotten in her life. Worse than any beating the buffalo hunter ever gave her. Her eyes swelled shut and stayed that way for what seemed like days. So long that the girl thought maybe he'd beat her blind, but eventually the swelling went down and her sight returned.

The fur trader didn't mind leaving her alone in the darkness, but he himself clearly didn't like it. He would keep a fire burning in the fireplace, even on nights when it wasn't so cold out. And one day he brought home a box of lucifer matches and a fancy-looking kerosene lamp with a glass chimney. He would light the lamp anytime it grew dim in the shack. He would turn the flame up and keep the interiors of the shack as bright as he could. When the kerosene ran low or the wick was close to burning out, the fur trader would disappear and come back with more oil and a new wick. The girl wasn't sure where he got them.

One day when he left, he didn't latch the cabin door behind him, leaving the door wide open, almost like he was inviting the girl to escape. She waited until the fur trader had been gone a while, then took a few tentative steps outside the cabin, looking all around her and making sure that the fur trader was nowhere to be seen. Then moving as quickly, cautiously, and quietly as she could, she made her way down the mountain, the whole time scared to death that as soon as she lost sight of the shack, the fur trader would descend on her with a fury and give her a beating so bad as to make that time her eyes had swollen shut seem like a pleasant memory.

She was little more than half a mile from the shack when she saw the carvings on the trees, strange-looking symbols with dashes and slashes. The closer she got to a carved tree, the stranger she felt. Dizzy and wobbly. Her head throbbed and her stomach churned and cramped. She felt a wave rushing up from the pit of her stomach and she bent over and violently dry-heaved. If she'd eaten anything in the past couple of days, it would surely have come pouring out.

She straightened, wiped her mouth with her hand, then took a few deep breaths, trying to steady herself. She tried to walk past the tree again, forcing herself to ignore the headache and the cramping, but some unseen force knocked her back, slamming her to the ground. She lay there for a moment, dazed, then crawled a few feet backward and away from the carved tree. She found the headache and the cramping lessened with distance from the tree.

She changed directions. If she couldn't go past those trees, she'd go around them. But only a few feet away, she saw more trees with almost identical carvings. Approaching those trees, she felt the same cramping in her gut and the pounding in her head. Again, she tried to ignore the pain and walk past, but once again she was knocked backward and driven to the ground.

She looked around and saw yet another tree with the carvings. And another just past that. Then another. The carvings ringed the entire area around the shack, creating an invisible barrier that she couldn't seem to get past. She worried that the fur trader would return and find her outside the shack, so she returned to await the beating he would deliver on his return.

The fur trader never latched the door again after that. She tried a few more times, probing the ring of carved trees, searching for a spot she could slip through. She found none. She came to realize the reason the fur trader had stopped latching the door was that it was no longer necessary. He had placed the carvings there to keep her from leaving and it had worked. She wasn't going anywhere.

The appearance of the giant black wolf in the trees behind the shack had given her a brief comfort, if not hope. She never saw it again after it disappeared into the shadows.

So she spent her days in the shack. She watched the fur trader come and go and she endured his beatings and gruntings. She resigned herself to the fact that her life was no longer hers. It belonged to the fur trader. Her only escape would be that day when a beating went too far and he killed her. Then and only then would she be free.

And that was what she believed right up until the day she saw the old man with the stringy white hair and the tattered buckskin long coat come riding up to the shack on a painted horse.

SIX

THE MANHUNTER

OZYMANDIAS HAYES ENDURED THE kicks and punches for as long as he could before losing consciousness. When he awoke, he found himself sitting on the back of a horse, stripped naked, hands bound tightly behind his back with a leather strap. His head throbbed, a dull pounding that kept both focus and concentration at bay. One eye so swelled as to be completely shut, but the other allowed a sliver of vision through a narrow slit that remained open. Blood dripped from his nose, running over his lips and down his chin. Every breath brought a jabbing pain into his side, like the sudden poke of a sharp stick. A wayward rib impacting a lung, he assumed.

They had tied a rope around his neck, the knot behind his head and against the base of his skull, almost in line with the spine. When the horse bolted from beneath him and the noose bore the full weight of his body, his neck would not break. He would dangle until he asphyxiated. It would be a painful way to die.

To his left, he could see the body of Jacob Hutchens sprawled on the ground not twenty feet distant. Flies buzzed about his dead partner's head and Hayes could see — not to mention smell — that someone had taken a shit on Hutchens' face. They had moved the body, dragged it away from the fire. Hutchens' suspenders had been cut away and his breeches were bunched around his ankles. The front flap of Hutchens' longjohns was opened, blood smeared all over the exposed skin and seeping into the fabric. His manhood had been cut off.

Hayes could see three men sitting around the still-burning fire. He didn't know how long he had been unconscious, but clearly long enough for the bandits to help themselves to his bacon and to brew the last of his coffee. Enoch Munn, grinning broadly, stepped into Hayes' field of vision. The outlaw's hands were slicked with blood.

"Well," Munn said, "It ain't much to look at, but I got a new pecker for my collection. Had to start all over since your partner threw my last ones in the river."

Munn held up an oversized skinning knife, sunlight glinting off of the blade. "I'm about to add another one. Just like I told you I would. What do you think about that, nee-gro?" Munn laughed heartily. "Goddamn! That's a funny word!"

"Move the knot," Hayes croaked, not realizing until that moment how much damage they had done to his throat during the beating.

"You want me to move the knot?" Munn's grin spread across his face.

Hayes nodded to the degree the rope would permit. "In front of my ear, just below the corner of my jaw."

"Shit." Munn spat on the ground and laughed. "You think I ain't never strung nobody up before? You think I don't know where to put a fuckin' knot? You think I'm stupid?"

"I think," Hayes said with difficulty. "There's evidence to support that hypothesis."

"I put the knot where I put it because I want to watch you kick, nigger. I want to watch your fuckin' face go from black to blue. I want to watch your eyes bug out of your head and see you bite your fuckin' tongue off."

"Move the knot," said Hayes. "Kill me quick or I'll take you with me when I go."

Munn snickered, then snorted, then laughed out loud. Laughed so hard he doubled over, holding his belly. He turned to the men sitting around the fire. "Y'all hear that? He goan take me with him. We goan die together. Me and the nee-gro, here."

Munn turned back to Hayes. "What happened to all yo' high and mighty talk? You goan take me to the fort. You goan let them decide my fate. You ain't goan allow a man to be murdered in front you. You remember sayin' all that shit? 'Cause I remember hearin' it. I don't think I imagined none of it. Did I?"

When Hayes didn't answer, Munn reached up and jabbed his knife into Hayes' ribs, sinking the blade halfway to the hilt, and left it there. Hayes grunted, the pain so intense he almost blacked out.

Munn stomped away, walking in a half-circle and then coming back to the spot he had been standing. "You see what you made me do?" said Munn. "You made me fuck up my own plan. I was goan cut your pecker off before I hung you. Cut it off while you was still alive and show it to you. But now I can't do that. I pull my knife out and you goan bleed to death in about three seconds. You see my dilemma?"

Munn shook his head, pushed the red hair out of his eyes. "If you still plannin' to take me with you, you better get to figurin' 'cause you ain't got long."

Munn slapped the horse on the rump. The animal whinnied and bolted. The rope pulled taut and it snatched Hayes from the back of the horse. It felt like a mule had kicked him in the throat. But his neck did not break. He dangled from the rope, his feet kicking out involuntarily, his toes six inches above the ground. The rope tightened with each movement, crushing his windpipe. His lungs were on fire. He could feel the darkness encroaching, a blackness on the edge of his periphery rushing towards him.

Time lost all meaning. He could feel his eyes bulging, eardrums popping as his jaw worked violently, trying in vain to gulp down air. His head jerked side to side, muscle memory fighting back against the constriction of the rope.

Somewhere in the back of his mind, he realized that he'd stopped kicking. His swaying was purely inertial.

Hayes looked to the crest of the ridge and saw the woman standing there again, spectral, translucent, just as she had when he had seen her the night before. Her raven hair swirled about her head as if of its own accord. The woman looked at him, stretched her arms out toward him. Hayes felt a sense of calm and then everything went black.

He had expected death to be a state of nothingness. Nonexistence. Instead, Hayes experienced a spark of consciousness, followed slowly by the return of cognizance. No sight, no sound, no pain, no sensory input at all that he could discern. But he was aware. Aware of himself floating in the blackness. Blackness like the bottom of a well at midnight.

The sudden appearance of the light startled him. Dim and distant, shimmering like a lantern on the opposite side of a lake, a wavering of brilliance against a sea of darkness. Feeling drawn to it, Hayes walked towards the light. As he grew closer, a silhouette appeared from out of the darkness. The woman again, framed in the circle of light, her hair so black it almost melded into the surrounding shadows, making it impossible for him to tell where the hair stopped and the blackness began. She held a torch in her right hand, illuminating a rocky wall behind her and revealing a river of slow-moving black water lapping gently at the muddy ground on which she stood. A birch-bark canoe rested, half in the water, on the shore by her, a carved wooden paddle against the hull.

She smiled at Hayes.

"Who are you?" he asked. "Where am I?"

"Where do you think you are?" she answered. Ozymandias Hayes spoke three languages with fluency — English, French, and Spanish. He knew enough words in at least seven native tongues to be conversant. The woman spoke no language he had ever heard, yet somehow he understood every word.

"I'm dead," he answered. "Is this Hell?"

"You don't believe in Hell, Mr. Hayes. Heaven either. You never have."

"So am I dead?" Hayes asked.

"It's more complicated than that, I'm afraid."

"What does that mean?"

The woman smiled again. "I give you a choice, Mr. Hayes. If death is what you desire, step into the canoe, push off into the river, and paddle downstream."

Hayes peered into the blackness around the canoe. "Where does the river lead? What's downstream?"

"I can't tell you. That's something you'll have to discover on your own."

"And if I choose not to get in the canoe?"

The woman lowered the torch, held it to her side. Hayes saw a large clay bowl on the banks of the river only a few steps away from the canoe. A dark liquid inside the bowl, stained streaks marring the bowl's exterior.

"You may instead choose to return to the world you know. For a time at least."

Hayes hesitated.

"It is a difficult decision for you?" asked the woman.

"I wasn't expecting a choice."

"Dip your fingers in the bowl," said the woman. "A little is all you need."

"What is in the bowl?"

"My blood," said the woman.

Hayes wrinkled his brow.

"If you want to return," said the woman. "If delivering justice to the men who wronged you is your desire, then you will need my help."

"What makes you think that matters to me?"

"If it doesn't, then you are not whom I believed you to be, and the canoe awaits you."

Hayes reached down, swiped his fingertips along the inside of the bowl.

The woman opened her mouth and mimed licking her fingers. As she did, Hayes noticed her deformity for the first time. The little finger on her left hand was missing from just below the first knuckle.

Hayes looked back at his own hand, at the dark, almost black liquid quickly congealing on his fingertips. He brought the fingers to his lips and tasted the blood.

Seven

The Wing-Thief

ANTELOPE EYES SLID FROM the horse's back, his feet touching lightly on the ground. The grassy arroyo they'd been following for the past several hours abruptly ended, leveling with the surrounding land. Something on the thick prairie had caught the holy man's eye. He knelt, fished through the grass, and lifted a stone about the size of a chipmunk. The sandy-colored rock fit easily in the palm of his hand.

"Is that chalkstone?" asked Black Wing, bringing his horse to a halt where the holy man knelt.

"Shhh," said Antelope Eyes. "I can't listen to both of you at the same time."

The wing-thief sighed, leaned back, crossed his arms, and waited. Antelope Eyes would let him know when the rock had finished speaking.

After a short while, the holy man stood and, holding it out like some great, hard-won prize, showed the rock to Black Wing. It was indeed chalkstone, but not chalkstone like any he'd ever seen before. One side of the rock had been polished smooth, almost glass-like, with all the rough edges and porous texture ground away and buffed until it shined like still waters at sunrise.

"How did it get that way?" asked the wing-thief. "I've seen rocks polished smooth by rushing waters, but never chalkstone. Too soft. Too porous. It would crumble and disintegrate. I wouldn't have believed that chalkstone could be polished like that."

"Water can not polish it. Only heat can do this."

"Heat?" Black Wing shook his head. "I've used chalkstone to ring a fire. Many times. But I've seen nothing like that. Not once."

"It takes heat much greater than your campfire can produce."

"How do you get hotter than fire?"

The holy man smiled. "When your eyes have been opened, you will understand."

More riddles, thought Black Wing.

Antelope Eyes went to his horse and, still holding the stone with great care, took a piece of soft leather buckskin from his saddlebag. He wrapped it around the stone, then put the buckskin-encased stone back into his bag.

The wing-thief jumped down from his horse and looked at the ground all around them. He kicked through the grasses but saw no other similar rocks. No rocks at all anywhere around them. "We're a week's ride west of the Chalkstones and the arroyo flows from the west to the east."

"Meaning?"

"Meaning that rock shouldn't be here."

Antelope Eyes smiled. The holy man's eyes did not seem to narrow. They remained wide, oval, like the eyes of the creature for which he had been named. "Yet it is here."

"How do you think it got here?"

"How do *you* think it got here?"

The wing-thief shrugged. "Someone must have dropped it."

"Yes."

"But why? If someone had gone to the trouble of polishing a chalkstone, then it must have some significance. Why bring it all the way out here, drop it, and not pick it up? Or not come back for it when they realized they no longer had it? It wasn't hard to find. It glinted in the sunlight."

"There is a more simple explanation."

"Not that I can think of," said Black Wing.

The holy man smiled. "The great spirits left it here. They left it for me to find."

The wing-thief was skeptical. "Why would they do that? And if this is my spirit quest, not yours, then shouldn't it have been left here for *me* to find?"

"Did you find it?"

"No."

"Who found it?"

Black Wing sighed.

"Besides," said the holy man. "You would not have known what it is or what to do with it. I do. That is why they left it for me."

"Then what is the stone's purpose?"

"You'll know soon enough," said Antelope Eyes. "Ready our camp and see to the horses. I have to gather a few things before we can put the stone to its proper use."

"We should camp closer to the treeline," said the wing-thief, pointing to a copse of aspens a short walk from the end of the arroyo. "Not here in the open."

"No," said the holy man. "We must camp where the stone was found."

"Why?"

"Because that is what the stone said we should do."

"Why didn't you just ask the stone how it got here?"

"I did. How did you think I knew?"

"The stone told you how it got here and what its purpose is?"

"No. I knew what it was. The stone told me only how it got here."

Black Wing rolled his eyes. While he removed what gear they had from the horses, the holy man took a walk into the trees.

"Wait!" said the wing-thief. "Let me make sure it's safe before you go wandering off."

The holy man waved a dismissive hand. "I go where the gods will have me go. I told you, I know my end and my end is not today."

"At least be careful," called Black-Wing. "We do not know this land."

"You do not know this land," Antelope Eyes answered. "I have seen it many times."

"You've been here before?"

"No," the holy man said, and kept walking.

Black Wing shook his head and unrolled the thick buffalo fur they used as a bed, spreading it on the ground. He then found a small spring not too far away and let the horses drink.

Antelope Eyes returned a short time later with a few cattails, some thin branches he'd chopped from a cedar tree, and several small sage plants he had pulled up by the roots. He broke the cedar branches into kindling and fashioned small mounds just past each corner of the buffalo skin. He put a leafy sage plant on top of the cedar kindling and then harvested the dry fluff from the cattails and placed that on top of each mound. He took a piece of flint from a pocket in his tunic and, holding the flint over the fluff, scraped his knife against it. Sparks flew from the flint and landed on the cattail fluff. The fluff ignited. The holy man cupped his hands around the fluff and blew gently. In seconds, flames danced atop each mound, the burning cedar and sage filling the air with their aromas.

With each of the bundles burning, Antelope Eyes went to his saddlebag and retrieved the buckskin-wrapped stone. He removed the stone from the leather and placed it gently in the center of their buffalo skin bed.

The green cedar branches gave off considerable smoke as they burned — too much for Black Wing's comfort. Already, they were camping in a disadvantageous spot and now they were creating copious amounts of aromatic smoke. He feared the attention the smoke might bring on them, but the holy man did not seem concerned.

"The stone says that you worry too much," he said.

"The stone doesn't have to concern itself with strangers slitting its throat and taking its scalp."

Antelope Eyes smirked. "I agree with the stone."

The holy man pulled his tunic over his head, careful not to dislodge the feathers in his hair, and laid it on the grass a few feet away. He then slipped off his moccasins, stripped off his leggings, and placed them each atop the tunic. Naked, he sat crossed-legged on one side of the buffalo skin, the stone now between him and Black Wing. He looked up at the wing-thief.

"We're waiting," he said.

"What are we doing?"

The holy man shook his head and spoke slowly, as if speaking to a child. "I am going to show you the purpose of the stone. What did you think we were going to do?"

"I don't know. That's why I asked."

"Strip naked and sit."

"Why do I have to strip?"

"Because the stone said for you to."

"Why does the stone want to see my cock?"

Antelope Eyes shrugged. "Why wouldn't it?"

The wing-thief sighed, stripped off his breastplate, moccasins, leggings, and breechclout, then stepped through the smoke and sat on the buffalo skin facing the holy man. "Now what?"

Antelope Eyes pointed to the stone, laying polished side up on the buffalo skin between them. "This is a truthstone."

"A truthstone?"

"Yes."

"You just made that up, didn't you?" said Black Wing.

The holy man ignored the jibe. "Touch the stone," he said, "but do not lift it."

"Why?"

"Because that's what I asked you to do."

Black Wing reached out, placed three fingers on the stone. "So what is this supposed to accomplish?"

Antelope Eyes didn't answer that question. Instead, he asked one of his own. "How did you get the scar above your eye?"

"When I was a child, a raider rode me down and split my head open with a club made from a buffalo's femur."

The wing-thief snatched his fingers away from the stone as if it were a hot clay pot. The answer he had given to the question was the truth, but the words had flowed from his lips unbidden. He had never told a soul the story of the day the raiders came to his village. The day he became an orphan. The day he became a thief. The day he did the unthinkable. The unforgivable.

"How did you do that?" he asked.

"It is not my doing," said the holy man. "That is the power of the stone."

"I don't want to play this game."

"We are not playing a game. Put your fingers back on the stone."

"No," said the wing-thief.

"Put your fingers back on the stone," Antelope Eyes repeated.

"Please don't ask that of me."

The holy man locked eyes with the wing-thief. "I know the story. The stone has already told it to me."

"Then you don't need to hear it from me."

"Yes," said the holy man. "I do. Put your fingers on the stone."

"Please, don't. Don't ask that of me."

"I am not the one asking."

Black Wing reached out, extending his fingers tentatively. His hand shook as he felt the cold of the stone. He looked up at the holy man and began to speak.

"I was little more than a boy. I had a different name then —"

"You are Black Wing now," Antelope Eyes interrupted. "Your birth name is of no consequence."

Black Wing closed his eyes. The day, that terrible day, he had spent a lifetime trying unsuccessfully to forget, played across the stage of his mind. He could hear the horses' hooves thundering toward him. He could see his hand, the tiny hand of a child, barely ten summers old, reaching for the flap of his father's tent. He stepped from the tent and stood there frozen, dumbfounded, unable to move a muscle as the raiders charged into the camp. He saw the warrior's arm drift from his side, saw him swinging the bone club.

"The club almost missed. It skimmed the side of my head and ripped open my scalp. The momentum of the raider, more than the force of the blow, knocked me off my feet."

Black Wing could see himself, face down in the mud, blood gushing from the gash on the side of his head. Had it not been for the mud, he would certainly have bled to death. As it was, the mud created compression, stanching the blood flow. He lay there unmoving, terrified, certain the raider who had ridden him down would realize that he was not dead and return to him. Return and rain down more blows from the bone club. But that never happened.

"I awoke the next day with a grackle pecking at my head."

He could see the bird's long beak pulling at small smatterings of tissue stuck to his exposed skull. The boy he had been reached up and tried to shoo the grackle away. The bird protested but took flight as he got wobbly to his feet.

"The raiders had long since departed, but in their wake, bodies lay scattered in the mud all around me. My tribe, my people. Everyone I knew. Flies fluttered about in great swarms and more buzzards than I had ever seen in one place had converged for a feast."

He staggered through the bodies, searching through the dead. "I looked for my parents, my sisters. I found only my father. He was lying on his back, barely twenty steps from where I had fallen. The buzzards had gotten to him before I did. The raiders had bashed his head and all that was left was a mass of purple and black stuck to the insides of his shattered skull. No face. No eyes. No nose. No mouth. I recognized him only from his clothes."

Black Wing wanted to take his fingers from the stone, but the stone would not permit it. It was as if his fingers were glued to the smooth surface. "My mother and my two sisters were nowhere to be found. All the young women and girls were missing. The raiders had murdered everyone else. All the old women, all the men and boys."

"Not everyone," said the holy man.

"No. Not everyone."

"I am not referring to you."

"I know," said Black Wing. He tried again to lift his fingers from the stone, but the pull of the stone was greater than he could overcome. "Buzzards leaped about and took flight as I walked past. I searched the bodies, one by one, looking for anything that might help keep me alive. I took a knife from the body of an old man named Laughing Deer, a kind widower who used to carve us toys from wood."

"And then you found her."

Black Wing nodded. He closed his eyes again. He could see the old medicine woman lying on the ground in front of her tent, her silver hair mussed and matted to her face. The feathers she so carefully wove into a braid over her ear were bent and broken. A tomahawk chop had bitten deeply into the crook between her shoulder and neck. A great dark bloodstain covered the front of her tunic. In her gnarled hands, she clutched a small buckskin pouch, holding it close to her breast.

"She had lost so much blood. Her face was pale, her lips blue. I thought she was dead when I found her. But then she opened her eyes and looked at me. She tried to speak, but no words would come."

Black Wing paused, swallowed hard. He didn't want to continue, didn't want to confess what he had never admitted to anyone, but the truthstone would not relent.

"I knew what it was that she held in her hand. I had seen her use it before. It was the thing she prized above all things. She knew that if she held it to her heart as she died, it would come with her into the world beyond this life. She looked at me with pleading eyes. She knew what I was going to do. I ignored her pleas. I had made my decision."

Black Wing looked down at the truthstone.

"I pried her fingers from the pouch. I was small, but she was old and dying. Weak. I took it from her. I pulled a leather string from the stitching of her apron and tied the pouch around my neck. She stared at me in disbelief for a brief moment. Then she went still, staring at me through dead eyes."

Black Wing exhaled. A long, slow, stuttering breath escaped from his lungs. "I robbed her. I stole her medicine bundle. I stole that which was most precious to her. I stole her wings. She would not fly in the world beyond this life. I robbed her of that."

The holy man nodded. "Stealing a medicine bundle is a great offense. But stealing from the dying, stealing from the world beyond, is unforgivable. One who does so is damned."

"I know."

"Do you believe you deserve damnation? Do you believe that justice demands that your death be the death that ends? That you never see the world beyond this life?"

"Yes," said the wing-thief.

"Truly?" said Antelope Eyes. "You would condemn such a desperate child, one who has just lost all that he has ever known? No matter his circumstances? No matter his will to live? No matter the man he will grow to be? Do you believe the gods would be just in passing such a sentence?"

Black Wing didn't answer.

"Tell me what happened after that?" asked the holy man.

"Do you not already know? Has the stone not told you?"

"It has. But you have to say it."

Black Wing hesitated as long as the stone would permit before speaking. "I wandered away from the camp, from the massacre, leaving my father unburied. I stopped at a river and looked at my reflection. I was covered in mud, my face streaked with blood. A large flap of skin was dangling over my ear. I washed the wound. The pain was so intense I had to bite down on a piece of driftwood to keep from crying out. I packed the wound with soft river mud, as I had seen the old medicine woman do to wounded warriors. Then I tore a strip from my breechclout and tied it around my head to hold it in place. The wound was never stitched. And that is why I have this," said Black Wing, pointing to the scar above his eye.

Antelope Eyes tilted his head to the side and stared unblinking at Black Wing. "You don't think my question was actually about the scar, do you?"

"No. But you asked and I am compelled to answer."

"You taught yourself to use her medicine?"

He nodded. "Over time, yes." He looked at the tattoos on his arms. "Her marks — her wings — appeared on my arms and my back as I became proficient."

The holy man nodded. "And your mother and sisters? What became of them?"

"I don't know."

"Did you ever see them again?"

The wing-thief shook his head.

"We're going to change that," said the holy man.

"What?"

Antelope Eyes passed a hand over one of the burning bundles, held it there, and let the smoke roll over his fingers. He closed his eyes and breathed in deeply. When he exhaled, smoke infused with cedar and sage flowed from his nose and mouth until the entire area was covered in a thick, gray haze.

"Keep your fingers on the stone," said the holy man, "and I will show you your mother and sisters."

EIGHT

THE MANHUNTER

OZYMANDIAS HAYES FELT THE heat of the sun pressing against his eyelids, like iron pulled from a forge and laid atop an anvil. A cacophony of men's voices, horses snorting, wind whistling through buffalo grass, crows calling in the distance, the musk of horse lather, and the odor of unwashed bodies overwhelmed his senses. He felt the sucking void in his lungs, the vice of the rope constricting his throat.

He opened his eyes and saw Enoch Munn nearly shit himself. Munn staggered backward, his jaw hanging slack, eyes so wide they nearly popped out of their sockets. Munn's lips quivered. He tried to speak, but the words lodged in his throat, never making it to his mouth.

Before Munn could react, Hayes bent at the waist, swinging his legs up, over, and around Munn's head. The assault staggered Munn. Hayes twisted, brought his knees together with all the force he could muster, pressing into Munn's throat and squeezing. Munn gasped, tried desperately to pry Hayes' legs from around his throat, but lacked the strength. Seeing the skinning knife still protruding from Hayes' side, Munn gave up on extricating his head from Hayes' grip and reached for the knife.

Hayes wrenched his shoulder, stretching his tied hands enough to get his fingers around the hilt of the knife before Munn could grab it. Hayes pulled the knife from his side, twisted the blade, sliding it inside his bonds, and sliced them cleanly in half. His hands were free.

Hayes reached above his head, the knife sawing through the rope. With the release of the rope's tension, the full weight of Hayes' body crashed down on top of Enoch Munn. When they hit the ground, his knees were still around Munn's throat.

Hayes heard Munn's neck snap on impact with the ground, the vertebrae twisting, bone shattering into splinters. Munn stared up at Hayes with unmoving eyes, blood oozing from the corners of his mouth.

The noise of the scuffle quickly drew the attention of the rest of Munn's gang. The first of the men to get to his feet charged towards them, reaching for his sidearm as he ran. Hayes flipped the knife, switching his grip from the hilt to his fingers, squeezing the side of the blade, and flung it. The ten-inch blade buried itself in the man's chest. The man froze, eyes drifting down in bewilderment to the knife hilt. He dropped to his knees, then fell over into a fetal position and lay unmoving.

Before the other two men could react, Hayes rolled, releasing his knees from Munn's head. He pulled Munn's pistol from its holster and came up firing. Two cocks of the hammer, two pulls on the trigger. Two headshots before either of the remaining members of Munn's gang had even cleared leather.

Hayes stood and looked all around. Enoch Munn's jaw hung slack, head turned at an impossible angle, his shock of red hair hanging over his forehead. His eyes remained open wide, staring blankly at the sun.

The two men he'd headshot lay on the ground unmoving, blood and grey matter pooling around their heads. The man with the knife in his chest squirmed on the ground, his boot heels digging in the dirt, fingers clawing at the blade. The man was in the same circumstance that Hayes had been in the seconds before Munn had sent the horse scurrying from beneath him. Hemorrhaging internally, lungs filling with blood. Hayes bent over and pulled the knife free. Blood poured from the man's chest, spreading and soaking into the fabric of his shirt. The man looked down at the gushing wound, then raised his head, gazing blankly in Hayes' direction, eyes wide, his face a mask of confusion. Hayes wiped the blade on the man's sleeve. The man coughed, spraying a geyser of blood into the air. He spasmed and then rolled his head to the side and didn't move again.

Hayes brought the knife up to his neck, slid the point of the blade under the noose still cinched tightly around his neck. With a flick of his wrist, the razor-sharp edge sliced through the rope. Where the rope had been, a three-inch wide friction burn, raw and bleeding, ringed his neck, bisecting a deep, purple bruise along his throat. Hayes' breath came in shallow, excruciating gasps. Already he could feel his airways expanding, his ruptured trachea repairing itself. His ribs ached with each breath and a steady trickle of blood dribbled from the gash in his side, but the flesh had already begun stitching itself back together, slowly creating a scar where a mortal wound had been.

Hayes took the bacon off of the fire and set the cast-iron pan on the ground. The handle blistered his palm, but that too, he knew, would quickly heal. He moved the coffeepot from a stone on the fire ring to the ground nearby. The smoky, herbal scent of the roasted beans filled his nostrils. He badly wanted to pour himself a cup, but he knew his throat needed more time to repair itself before he could again swallow.

He located his bedroll. One man he'd headshot had fallen partially over it. Hayes rolled the body clear with his foot. Without bothering to dress himself, he sat down naked on the blood-splotched blanket. Exhausted, spent, and in dire need of rest.

He set Munn's pistol and knife on the ground beside the bedroll, keeping both within easy reach. He would sleep now. He knew his body needed a long, deep, dreamless slumber to restore itself. He would decide what to do about the bodies of Munn and his gang when he awoke. He lay back on the blanket and stared up at the sky. It was wider and more blue than he remembered. He took as deep a breath as his throat and lungs would permit, then closed his eyes. He felt sleep coming for him, rapidly, like a stallion in full gallop.

He thought of the woman on the banks of the river in that expanse of blackness, the birch-bark canoe resting on the edge of the water. Perhaps he'd made a mistake. Perhaps he'd allowed the woman to goad him into a return he didn't really want. Perhaps he should have climbed into the canoe, pushed off into the darkness, and followed the river to wherever it led. Before he could ponder it further, his consciousness slipped away.

Nine

The Girl

THE GIRL STOOD IN the doorway and watched the old man on the painted horse ride through the trees and all the way up to the front of the trapper's shack. His long white hair flowed from beneath a floppy hat, an iridescent, blue-green magpie feather tucked into its leather band. The old man had a short, scraggly excuse for a beard and skin almost the same shade of white as the hair on his head and the whiskers on his face. He wore a faded buckskin long coat with fringe on the sleeves and around his waist was a leather gun belt with two holsters, a strap of rawhide securing them to each leg. The girl could see matching ivory-handled six-guns protruding from each holster. His boney, gnarled hands held the horse's reins loosely.

As he got closer, the girl could see the old man smiling. His teeth seemed more yellow than they likely were compared to his alabaster skin. His eyes were a pale violet the girl had only seen before in wildflowers. The old man took off his hat and shook his hair free.

"Here's ado to lock up honesty, and honor from th' access of gentle visitors," he said, his voice resonant, theatrical. Not loud, but it projected and seemed to float on the air. If the fur trader had been there, thought the girl, he would have come running with rifle in hand. Lucky for the old man, the little rat-faced mountain man was off again, checking his traps or such.

When the girl said nothing in response, the old man gave her a wink. "You must be the lady of the house."

The girl didn't know what to make of the old man. His appearance was odd, unlike that of any man she'd ever seen, but his presence was strangely comforting. A sense of strength and calm seemed to exude from him, but there was something more as well, the girl realized. It was the way he sat the saddle. His face and his hair and hands told the girl he was an old man, but his posture — his back ramrod straight with no stoop at all, his shoulders round and not sloping — belied a man of youth and vigor.

In spite of herself, the girl wondered if he might be her salvation. No. She couldn't allow herself to think that way. She had once dared to hope that when the buffalo hunter sold her to the fur trader that her circumstances might improve. They had not.

"I mean you no harm, child," said the old man. "To whom do I have the pleasure of speaking?"

The girl remained silent. She guarded her face, keeping all expression from it.

"I just want to know your name," he said.

"You don't need to know my name."

The old man pursed his lips, considered this, then nodded. "You might have a point. Names are powerful things. Valuable things. If you think about it, they are the only thing we truly own in this life. I've known medicine men who believe that knowing an enemy's name can give them power over their foe. I don't subscribe to that notion myself, but I don't doubt the power in a name."

"You want mine, but you ain't told me yours."

The old man smiled again. "And that is rude of me. I apologize. I tend to assume my infamy proceeds me and that appearance gives away my identity. I should have realized that a young lady of your tender years might never have heard of me. The people of the plains call me 'Whiteskin', among other less flattering appellations, but my name is Hamish Frost. And I'm at your service."

He bowed his head and held his hands out in a gesture of curtsey.

The girl stared at him, clearly confused.

"The customary thing to do," he said, "would be for you to respond in kind."

The girl narrowed her eyes.

"I'm not trying to trick you, child. I just want to know to whom I'm speaking."

"Maybe I don't have a name."

"You have no name? Now, how is that possible? Names are the first thing given to us. Everyone has one whether you want it or not."

"Maybe I gave it up. Maybe I don't need one no more."

The old man again seemed to ponder this. "Perhaps you think so. Perhaps you believe you don't need a name, but so long as there's another who wants to know you, I'm afraid you do."

"Ain't nobody wants to know me."

"That's not true, child. I'm here and I want to know you." He smiled. *"O, how I faint when I of you do write, Knowing a better spirit doth use your name, And in the praise thereof spends all his might."*

"You talk funny," said the girl.

"Not my words," said the old man. "Those were the words of the greatest poet ever to draw breath and stand on this globe."

"I don't want to talk to you. You need to leave."

"I think you very much would like to talk to me," said the old man. "You're just afraid of what might happen if you should."

The girl could feel her hands shaking and hid them behind her smock.

"I am not here to hurt you, child. I've come looking for a man who lives in this shack. A trapper and animal skinner who goes by the name of Shadrach Brown. He still resides here, does he not?"

The girl gave a slight shrug.

"You don't live here alone, do you?"

The girl gave her head a subtle shake.

"Does a man live here with you?"

The girl nodded.

"You've made it clear that you don't want to give me your name, but surely you have no compunction against giving me his?"

"I don't know his name."

"But you do know the man. Is he inside the shack?"

"If he was, he'd have killed you by now."

"Somehow I doubt that. If he's not here, where is he?"

"He don't share his comings and goings with me."

"So, who are you to him? Daughter? No? Wife perhaps?"

The girl didn't answer.

"You're not his kin at all, are you?"

"Are you here to kill him?" the girl asked.

The old man scratched his chin. "Does he need killing?"

The girl didn't answer. She realized she had probably asked a question better kept to herself.

"I can see you'd like to have your question back, but I'm afraid I can't pretend I didn't hear it. So what's the reason you asked me that? Why are you wondering if I'm here to kill him?"

"I don't know."

"Oh, I think you do."

"He ain't nice," said the girl.

"Well, that's hardly a reason to want a man dead. I've killed more than a fair share of men in my day and, I must say, whether he was nice was one of the least considerations in my decision to pull the trigger. I ask myself if this man has done something so vile as to forfeit his right to draw breath. I ask myself if his continued existence can be justified. I ask myself if there's a soul on this planet whose life would be worsened by his absence. I have never concerned myself with whether he greets strangers with a frown."

The girl looked down at her feet.

"Does he do worse than greet strangers with a frown?"

She didn't answer.

"You're not his daughter. Not his wife. Not his kin," said the old man. "Are you his slave?"

"I don't know what that means."

"Are you free to leave? Can you come and go as you please?"

"He don't latch me in the shack no more when he leaves," said the girl.

The old man looked away, sighed audibly. "Is he raping you?"

"Is that when he lays on top of me and puts his thing — "

The old man held up a hand, indicating she need not finish the sentence.

"You've tried to run away, I'm sure. But you can't get past the trees, can you? The trees that are all carved up around the mountainside here. You've tried, haven't you?"

No answer.

"Those carvings are called wards. There's power in them, what the people of the plains call 'medicine'. The wards keep folks out. In as well, in your case."

"They didn't keep you out."

"No, they did not. Wards like that aren't powerful enough to keep me out. Do you have any family to whom you could go? Someone who'll look after you until you're all grown?"

The girl shook her head. "My ma's dead. The buffalo hunter killed her."

"What about your father?"
"Don't have one. Never did."
"Do you have any kin at all?"
The girl shook her head.
"Well, I suppose, we could just stand around here jawing and waiting for Shadrach to come back and shoot me or we can go find him and get this over with."
"I don't know where he is."
"I can find him. He's not exactly subtle in his movements these days."
"Then why do you need me to go with you?"
"I don't *need* you to come with me. I *want* you to come with me."
"I can't."
The old man smiled. *"My book, wherein my soul recorded the history of all her secret thoughts."* He paused as if the words needed time to seep into the air. "Look at me, child."
The girl lifted her chin, looked into the old man's eyes.
"I know why you won't give me your name," he said. "I know the truth. You didn't surrender it. It's there. In your heart. In your soul. Your name means the world to you. It's all you have left. You didn't give it up. You've locked it away in a secure spot. You're protecting it. Hoping desperately that someday, you'll be free of this place, free of all the men who've taken advantage of you and held you against your will. Then, and only then, will you take that name out of its locked box. Until then, you'll keep it hidden, secreted away. Until then, you'll pretend you gave it up and forgot all about it. But that's not the truth, is it? Your name is your hope. It's what you cling to. The only thing you've held onto through thick and thin. You struggle through your days in the hope that sometime, somewhere far from here, you'll get to speak your name aloud once again. That you'll get to introduce yourself to a stranger and hear them say your name back to you with kindness in their voice."
The blood drained from the girl's face, her flesh nearly as pale as the old man's. "I can't leave. He'll beat me bad if I try to leave again."
"There's only one way down from this mountain, child. Only one way you'll ever get past those trees. Only one way you'll ever get to take your name out of that box. And that's if you come with me. Right now. I can get you past the trees. It won't be easy, but we can do it."

"I don't know you. You might be as bad as him. I thought nobody could be as bad as the buffalo hunter, but he's worse. He's worse!"

"*O villain, villain, smiling, damned villain!*"

The old man put his floppy hat back atop his head. He climbed slowly down off his horse and took two careful steps towards the front door of the cabin. He held out a hand, palm up, inviting the girl to take it. "My name is Hamish Frost and I swear to you on my name and on what honor I may have, I am not like those men. I don't hurt children. I don't hurt anyone who doesn't have a hurt coming to them. Come with me, child. I will guarantee your safety. Shadrach Brown will never lay a hand on you again."

The girl stood there in the shadows of the doorway for an interminable time. She looked closely at the old man in the faded, fringed buckskins. She looked at the magpie feather, shifting colors in the sunlight that filtered through the trees. She looked at the guns on his hips. His long white hair, his purple eyes, and his strange pale skin.

"*Nothing will come of nothing,*" the old man said. "Come to me, child. It's now or never."

The girl hesitated, trembling all over. Slowly, she stepped from the shadows of the doorway. With quivering fingers, she reached out and tentatively took the old man's hand.

The girl had half expected his pale, white flesh to be cold and cadaver-like, but his hand enveloped hers with a comforting warmth. The old man gave her hand a gentle squeeze.

"Once *more unto the breach, dear friends, once more; Or close the wall up with our English dead. In peace there's nothing so becomes a man as modest stillness and humility; But when the blast of war blows in our ears, then imitate the action of the tiger.*"

"I don't know what that means," said the girl.

The old man narrowed his eyes. "It means it's time for me to kill the son of a bitch that's been keeping you here."

Ten

The Wing-Thief

The wing-thief coughed as the aromatic smoke wrapped around him, enveloping him like an ethereal blanket. He closed his eyes and when he opened them again, he was no longer seated on the buffalo skin. Instead, he stood on the crest of a small hill overlooking a verdant valley. Aspen trees, their yellow-gold leaves tinkling in the wind, lined the hills sloping down to the valley floor. The clear blue sky was a domed ceiling overhead. In the valley below, he could see a bustling camp. Buffalo hide tipis wrapped around cut lodgepole pines, more than sapling but not yet mature, and arranged in a conical shape. Children hooted and hollered, playing naked in a babbling stream that snaked along the edge of the camp while women and girls washed pots and kept a close watch on the children.

Suddenly noticing his own nakedness, Black Wing dropped to the ground and crawled on his belly to a bushy shrub atop the hill. Hiding behind the shrub, he studied the camp.

"Tell me what you see," came Antelope Eyes' voice.

The wing-thief turned and looked all around him, but the holy man was nowhere to be found.

"Where are you?" he whispered.

"I am on the buffalo skin," said Antelope Eyes. "Where else would I be?"

"Where am I?" asked Black Wing.

"Your body is here with me, but I have sent your spirit on a small journey."

"How is this possible?"

"I would think a wing-thief might be accustomed to having his body in one place and his eyes in another."

"This is not the same. I have not borrowed the body of a bird. I can see my body. Here with me. I can feel my body, but I can still smell the cedar and sage. It is as if I am in two places at once."

"Perhaps you are," said the holy man. "Look closely. Tell me what you see."

"A camp. Children playing, women washing. Other women are roasting a deer over a spit and cooking vegetables in pots over the fire."

"And the men?"

"I see no men. Only women and children."

"Whose camp is it?"

"I don't know."

"Look closely."

Black Wing studied the tipis. Colorful paintings made with dyes from copper ore and phosphates of iron adorned them. Scenes of warriors on horseback, holding the heads of their enemies and brandishing bone clubs.

The wing-thief felt a lump in his throat, tried to swallow it down, but it lodged, threatening to cut off his breath and suffocate him. He felt a moment of panic.

"Is something wrong?" asked the holy man.

Black Wing forced the lump down but felt his jaw quivering as he spoke. "Raiders," he said. "This is the camp of the raiders who murdered my father and stole my mother and sisters."

"Is it?" the holy man feigned surprise. "Look again at the women cooking the deer."

Black Wing turned his head slowly, his heart racing. They were older, of course, but now he recognized the faces. His mother and his sisters.

Other women came from the tipis and joined them, working with them to prepare the meal for the rest of the camp. The women were all laughing and smiling as they worked. Even his sisters. Even his widowed mother. Laughing.

The naked children came splashing from the stream and his sisters left the deer roasting on the spit and intercepted the children before they could reach the cooking fire.

"Tell me what you see," said the holy man.

But Black Wing remained silent, his eyes locked on the children. He saw now the familiar traits in the faces, the thin noses and high foreheads, the cheekbones sharp enough to cut. It was like looking at younger versions of his own face. He saw them for who they were. His nieces and nephews, his new brothers and new sisters.

"How does this make you feel?" asked Antelope Eyes.

"I am angry."

"Why?"

The bitter sting of betrayal brought a tear to his eyes. He wished for his tomahawk that he might charge into the village, kill his mother and sisters for their treachery. For abandoning him and dishonoring the memory of his father. But he had no tomahawk, no weapon at all. He lay naked on the grass above the camp.

"My father's bones lay in a rut while they spread their legs and take the seed of the butchers who bashed in his skull."

"Your blood boils at this," said Antelope Eyes. "You would see them dead for their offense?"

"Yes."

"Soon, the men will return from their raiding. Would you like to see your mother's new husband? The man who sired your new siblings? The men who took your sisters as their brides? Who gave you nieces and nephews?"

"No. End this. I do not wish to see."

"Are you sure?"

Black Wing clenched his eyes tightly closed. "Yes. I want this to stop. I want to forget them. Forget them all. My mother and sisters do not deserve to be remembered. They deserve oblivion. To be wiped from existence, as if they had never been. I do not wish to waste another thought on them ever again."

"I thought you wanted them dead. Which is it? Do you want them dead or do you just want to forget they exist?"

"Why did you show this to me?" asked the wing-thief.

"Open your eyes," said the holy man.

"No. I don't want to see any more. Bring me back from this place."

The holy man's words were soft, but commanding. "Open your eyes."

Black Wing did as he was told. The hill overlooking the verdant valley, the tinkling aspens, the camp, the naked children, his mother, and his sisters were all gone. Once again, he sat on the buffalo skin across from Antelope Eyes. The smoke from the burning cedar and sage stung his eyes. The truthstone lay on the hide between them.

"Touch the stone again," said the holy man.

"No."

Antelope Eyes reached across and took Black Wing by the wrist, pulling his hand to the stone. "Touch."

Black Wing's fingers brushed the smooth surface of the stone.

"No more questions," said the holy man. "No more smoke. No more visions. I want you only to think. Think of your mother. Think of your sisters. And see them with your new eyes."

"What new eyes?"

"Shh," said the holy man. "Be quiet and see the truth. See what you have not seen before."

Black Wing took a deep breath, cleared his thoughts. Unbidden and unwelcome, images formed in his mind. He saw himself, a defenseless child in the killing field that had been his home. He had stolen a knife from the corpse of a kindly old man. And worse, much worse, he had robbed an old woman of her medicine bundle, stolen her wings as she lay dying. He had crippled her spirit, ensured that she would never fly in the world beyond this one, and damned himself by so doing. He had done this and many more terrible things in the days that followed because that was what survival had demanded of him.

Epiphany hit him harder than had the raider's bone club.

His mother and sisters had surrendered themselves to their captors, not because they had betrayed him and his father, but because that was what survival had demanded of them. They were taken by the raiders during the massacre, taken as slaves. But they had endured. They had done what survival demanded they do.

He had left his birth name in the mud with his father's bones. He had stumbled away from the killing field, leaving all that he had been behind him. He had become another. A wandering warrior. A nomad with stolen wings. Survival had demanded it of him, and he had determined to survive.

His mother and his sisters had left their names in the mud that day as well. They had seen his small body lying there near his father, had assumed he was equally as dead. They could not know he lived, and even if they had, there was nothing they could have done. They had been dragged away against their will. Stolen. Taken as slaves. They had faced a simple choice, survive or die. And if they chose to survive, then they would have to do what survival demanded they do.

Perhaps their children had been forced upon them. Or perhaps not. It no longer mattered. His mother and sisters had chosen survival. And in so doing, they had risen above their circumstances. They had been taken as slaves, but they were slaves no longer. They were survivors. And Black Wing had seen from his perch on the hilltop overlooking their camp, they no longer had captors. They had husbands. They had children. They had families. They were what he had never been. They were happy.

"Your eyes have been opened," said Antelope Eyes. "Let them never be closed again."

Black Wing looked at Antelope Eyes. He could see a faint violet glow surrounding the holy man, pulsing and shimmering like the rays of the rising sun. He looked at the truthstone and saw a similar glow.

"I see your medicine," he said.

The holy man smiled.

Black Wing felt the tears flowing from his eyes. Not out of pain, or anger, or sorrow, but from joy. Joy that his mother lived and had found happiness. Joy for his sisters. His nieces and nephews and his young brothers and sisters that he would never know.

He shuddered, freed from a great weight that he had not known had been pressing down on him for these many years. His head lolled forward, and he fell over onto the buffalo skin, his face inches away from the truthstone. He curled into a fetal position, making no effort to curb his tears.

Antelope Eyes reached out a hand and stroked the wing-thief's hair. Gently. The holy man began to sing, his voice soft, barely above a whisper.

Black Wing cried himself to sleep.

Eleven

The Manhunter

OZYMANDIAS HAYES PUSHED OPEN the heavy wooden door and heard the oiled, ancient hinges squeak as the springs expanded. He took a quick look behind him at the rows of stacked and cataloged tomes, the oaken tables, and empty chairs. It was an unseasonably warm afternoon in early October, his second year at law school. The breeze through an opened window in the library had been teasing him, taunting him to shelve his books, abandon his studies, and join the rest of the city in the out of doors until, at last, he could no longer resist its call.

Stepping through the doors, he turned his head, dodging an enormous sycamore leaf, brown and curled, floating past and carried on the wind. But for that, he might not have seen her. She sat on a wrought-iron bench near the blood-red roses in the park across the road. A thick book lay open on her lap. Two young, sandy-haired children played in the grass near her feet.

Hayes crossed the street as she looked up from her book. Their gazes locked. A gentle smile crossed her face, accentuating high cheekbones and a perfectly formed nose. Her eyes were the woody green of willow leaves and her skin cafe au lait. She wore a yellow-gold dress with a small, matching hat pinned and sitting askew atop a mound of reddish-brown curls.

Somewhere in the back of Hayes' mind, he knew this was a memory. He had been here before, had lived this moment. Had lived all the moments to come after it. He knew how the story ended.

He bowed as he approached her and reached up to doff a hat that he belatedly remembered was still on a hatrack inside the library. Undeterred by his clumsy faux pas, he introduced himself.

"The king of kings?" she said, looking up at him with a playful grin.

"You've read Shelley?" said Hayes with a cocked eyebrow.

"*In Egypt's sandy silence, all alone, Stands a gigantic Leg, which far off throws The only shadow that the Desert knows: — 'I am great Ozymandias,' saith the stone, 'The King of Kings; this mighty City shows 'The wonders of my hand'.*" She smiled at him. "Shelley is my favorite."

Hayes returned her smile. "You have my name, mademoiselle, but I'm afraid I do not have yours."

"That's because I didn't give it. To be quite honest, I haven't decided if I'm going to give it. While I do admire your boldness, Mr. Ozymandias, you are a stranger, and by introducing yourself to me directly rather than allowing a mutual acquaintance to introduce us, you've shown a significant disregard for decorum."

"In my defense, when in the presence of such beauty, a gentleman's sense of propriety can sometimes fail him. My apologies. It was not my intent to give offense."

"Clearly," she said. "For all you know, sir, I could be a married woman."

"You wear no ring and are much too young to have borne these children playing at your feet. I believe I may safely assume that you are their au pair and, as such, unwed."

"Bold as well as skilled in deductive reasoning," she said. "But there is another possibility that you have not considered. I am unwed, that's true, but perhaps I am betrothed."

Hayes couldn't stop smiling. "Engagements can be broken."

"Bold, reasoned, and *presumptuous*, Mr. Ozymandias."

"Ozymandias is my Christian name," he said. "Hayes is my surname."

She gave him a look that let him know she would call him whatever she chose to call him. She closed her book, stood, and motioned the children to her side. They protested, but she quelled their simmering disobedience with a tilt of her head and a stern look. Together, they took to the sidewalk and began to walk away from him.

Hayes watched her go. He remembered what happened next.

She stopped and looked over her shoulder at him.

"Cora Arrington," she said.

"I beg your pardon?"

She rolled her eyes. "You asked for my name and against my better judgment, I am giving it to you. My name is Cora Arrington."

Hayes smiled. "May I see you again, Miss Arrington?"

"That, Mr. Ozymandias," she said with a note of playful mischief in her voice, "Shall be entirely up to you."

She walked away down the sidewalk, hand in hand with the two children, the little yellow hat atop her head, her auburn curls spilling from beneath it, falling to her shoulders, her book tucked under her arm. She did not look back again.

Hayes knew this was a memory. Knew he would see her again. Knew how it would all end.

He opened his eyes. The fire had burned itself out during the night, the ashes gone cold. He sat up slowly, looked to the horizon, and saw the sun cresting, spires of light splayed in a one-hundred-and-eighty-degree arc. It had been late morning when he'd laid down on the blood-spattered bedroll. Now it was morning again, but just after dawn. He had slept for most of a full day.

The swelling in his eyes had gone down enough that he could see through both again. His pain had subsided notably, but his ribs still ached. Dark mottled bruises covered his chest and abdomen, compliments of the beating he'd received at the hands of Enoch Munn's gang before they had lynched him.

He ran his fingers along his throat. The friction burn had scabbed but was still tender to the touch. He found his canteen not far from the bedroll. He uncorked it, pressed it to his dry lips. The water tasted stale, acidic. He held it in his mouth for a few seconds before attempting to swallow. When he did, it didn't go well. His crushed throat fought back, pushing the water up and into his nasal passages. He hacked, retched, and had to spit it out.

He had a powerful thirst, but his throat needed more time to heal before he could drink. Hopefully, he wouldn't dehydrate before then. He considered lying back down, resting for another day, giving his body more time to heal, but there was no time for that. The dead bodies surrounding him were already ripening. Scavengers would arrive soon.

He stood up and looked for his clothing. He found them scattered on the ground behind the cottonwoods where Munn's gang had beaten and stripped him. He shook the dirt from his undergarments and was about to pull them on when he noticed the thin stream of fast-flowing water on the other side of the trees.

He went to the stream and stuck in a toe. Cold, but not so cold he couldn't withstand it. He stepped in, squatted down, and scooped water in his cupped hands. He released the water over his head, let it trickle down his face and over his chest. He splashed water under his arms and on his chest, on his groin and his backside. He stood slowly and let himself drip dry in the sun.

He dressed as quickly as his aching body would allow. He found his coat ripped, destroyed beyond repair when they'd torn it off of him. He was going to need a new one. Jacob Hutchens would provide it. The body lay not far from the cold remains of the fire. He'd had no love for the man, had thought him a blustering fool whose poor decision-making had led them to this point. It was Hutchens' ineptitude that had facilitated his murder. Both of their murders. Even so, Hutchens had been his partner and deserved better than the indignities done to his corpse.

Rigor mortis had set in, locking Hutchens' limbs in the positions they'd been when he fell. With difficulty, Hayes removed Hutchens' leather duster. The coat was of an expensive make, precision tailored with soft, well-tanned leather and a plush sheepskin collar and cuffs. Hayes pulled it on. The coat was an ill-fit. Hutchens had been a heavier man than Hayes, plus there was the matter of the prominent bullet hole and large bloodstain. But neither of those things would hamper the coat's ability to shield Hayes from the cold.

Turning back to the camp, Hayes was pleased to discover the horse he had been perched on prior to his lynching, had returned of its own volition and was grazing on buffalo grass. He took the reins and tied the horse off to a cottonwood limb. He shuffled through his saddlebags. He found the rolled handbills, printed drawings of men's faces and reward details for the capture or killing beneath the likenesses.

The resemblance to Enoch Munn on his poster was clear. His unruly hair, freckles, and buck teeth had given the artist a lot with which to work. The likenesses of Munn's gang had been less precise. Still, there was enough of a resemblance that Hayes could identify each man. All were wanted on the same counts as Munn. Robbery, rape, murder, and horse theft.

With the outlaws all identified, Hayes now had the problem of what to do with them. He was one man traveling alone and, including Jacob Hutchens, he had five bodies, all in a state of advanced rigor. He knew the rigor would fade in time, making the bodies more pliable, but he didn't have the time to wait it out. The outpost was a good hundred miles away, and he needed to get started.

He had three horses. His own, Hutchens', and Munn's. Presumably, there were three more somewhere nearby. Munn's gang hadn't caught up to them on foot. He found the horses in a small ravine, barely a quarter-mile upstream. They were hobbled and grazing. Hayes removed the hobbles and led the horses downstream to the campsite. With six horses, he could tie the reins of each horse to the saddle of the one in front, create a daisy chain of sorts. It would be slow going and after a couple of days, the stench from the rotting bodies would be near overpowering. Hayes considered his options. He had the knife that Munn had jammed to the hilt in his ribs. He could saw off the heads, bundle them in a bedroll, and leave the bodies where they lay. He considered it only briefly. Ozymandias Hayes was many things, but one thing he was not was a goddamn butcher.

He retrieved Hutchens' body from the stream and, with effort, managed to position him atop his horse. He retrieved from the cottonwood the rope with which he'd been lynched and secured the body to the saddle. The rigor did not make it easy. He cut the remainder of the rope and used it to tie the outlaws to their horses. Enoch Munn's neck was twisted at an impossible angle, his head facing away from the horse, his dead eyes staring up at Hayes. Hayes re-broke Munn's neck, twisting it around, forcing his head toward the horse's flank.

Better, he thought.

Hayes searched through the outlaws' coats and clothing for anything that might be of use. He took their weapons, some ammunition, a few strips of jerky, and a half-drank bottle of whiskey. He stashed the weapons in his saddlebags. The whiskey and jerky he put in the pockets of Hutchens' coat. One outlaw had a sombrero, a much better hat than the one Hayes had been wearing, but fearing lice, he left the hat behind.

He washed his hands in the creek, then filled his canteen, as well as the one that had previously belonged to Jacob Hutchens. Back at the campsite, he forced himself to eat some of the cold bacon and beans the outlaws had cooked the night before. He took tiny bites, chewing thoroughly before attempting to swallow. Painful, but he forced it down. He ate as much as he dared. He needed food in his belly for the long ride ahead of him. Hayes was a poor hunter and unless he could catch some game unaware, those few strips of jerky were all that stood between him and starvation.

The bacon and beans had opened his constricted throat enough that he could take a few sips of the whiskey. He thought the alcohol, unlike the water he had tried and failed to drink, might soothe his throat. It didn't. Rather, it burned all the way down. He took one last sip anyway, before corking it, and putting it away.

He gathered his bedroll and secured it. He tied the reins from the harness of Hutchens' horse to his saddle, Munn's reins to Hutchens' saddle, and on until he had created a train of corpses and horses.

He took one last look at the severed noose lying on the ground by the remains of the fire, then set off for the outpost.

Twelve

The Gunslinger

"How long have you been here?" Hamish Frost asked as he walked beside the girl through the trees behind the trapper's shack.

The girl had shown a good deal of backbone in agreeing to come with him, but she had been resolute about walking and not riding. So Frost tied off the horse to a tree near the shack and walked with her. She'd ride when she was ready to ride. Not a second before.

"I don't know," she said. "Don't have no way to know."

Frost nodded understandingly. "Of course. It was a thoughtless question on my part. A poor attempt to keep the conversation from lagging."

"I'm used to the quiet."

"The silence, often of pure innocence, persuades where speaking fails." Frost gave the girl a smile. "I should heed the bard's advice. I can be a loquacious bastard, in love with the sound of my own voice. Forgive me, child."

The girl looked up at him, her brows knit in confusion. Frost's instinct was to explain himself, but he held his tongue and kept the silence for as long as he could. They rounded a jagged rock jutting from the hillside and began working their way down a game trail leading to a stream fed by icy mountain runoff.

"Was he always afraid of the dark?" asked Frost.

The girl stopped in her tracks. "How do you know about that?"

"The instruments of darkness tell us truths; Win us with honest trifles, to betray's In deepest consequence." Frost paused. "My assumption is he developed the aversion to darkness sometime after he took you captive. You said he used to latch you in the

shack, but stopped doing so after a while. This was when you discovered the wards carved into the trees, yes?"

The girl nodded. "The dark didn't bother him none at first, but after a while, he started to keep a fire burning most all the time. Or else he burned a lamp. He never let it get full dark in the cabin again."

"And you? Does the darkness frighten you?"

The girl shook her head.

"Not even a little?"

"I don't like it, but I ain't afraid of it."

"What *are* you afraid of?"

The girl didn't answer, so Frost answered for her.

"You're afraid I'm not what I say I am. You're afraid you've made a grave mistake in coming with me. You're afraid Shadrach Brown is going to kill us both. Is that what frightens you?"

"No. I'm afraid he's going to kill *you.* He'll do a lot worse to me."

Frost turned and continued down the game trail, speaking out in his best theatrical voice.

"Fear no more the heat o' the sun, Nor the furious winter's rages; Thou thy worldly task hast done, Home art gone, and ta'en they wages; Golden lads and girls all must, As chimney-sweepers, come to dust.

Fear no more the frown o' the great; Thou art past the tyrant's stroke: Care no more to clothe and eat; To thee the reed is as the oak: The sceptre, learning, physic, must All follow this, and come to dust.

Fear no more the lightning-flash, Nor the all-dreaded thunder-stone; Fear not slander, censure rash; Thou hast finished joy and moan; All lovers young, all lovers must Consign to thee, and come to dust.

No exorciser harm thee! Nor no witchcraft charm thee! Ghost unlaid forbear thee! Nothing ill come near thee! Quiet consummation have; And renownéd be thy grave!"

Frost smiled at the girl. "We're all going to die one day, child, but today is not that day. Not for you. And not for me."

If the girl took solace from his words, she gave no indication. They walked in silence for a few moments before she said, "Why were you asking me if I was afraid of the dark?"

Frost sighed. "I need you to do something for me. I want you to recall one of those times he left you alone in the dark of the shack. I want you to think on that. Put yourself back in that space. Remember what it felt like."

"I don't want to."

There was fear in the girl's voice. Frost reached to take the girl by the shoulders, offer a comforting touch, but thought better of it and let his hands drop to his side. "I know it was unpleasant. I know it was frightening, but I ask you to recall it for a purpose. Just close your eyes and think on it for a moment."

The girl hesitated.

"Just for a moment," he said. "I'll watch over you while you do so."

He could see her body trembling. She closed her eyes. "How long do I have to do this?"

"Keep them closed a little longer. Think about being in the dark of the cabin. Alone."

The girl's trembling turned to fearful shaking.

"Open your eyes, child."

When she did, he could see the tears welling, forming in the corners of her eyes. "That's the last time I want you to hold that thought in your head. Do you understand me? The last time. Never think on it again. Your days of captivity have ended. No one will ever lock you up again. Not ever. I'm sorry to have forced that recollection on you, but I had a question that needed answering, and this is one of those rare instances wherein words alone would not have sufficed."

"What was the question?"

Frost nodded grimly. "Doesn't matter. I have the answer now. Let's pick up the pace, child. We're burning daylight and a task most unpleasant awaits."

Frost managed a better job of keeping his tongue still as they wound down the hillside and neared the mountain stream. He halted suddenly, holding a hand out in front of the girl. He put a finger to his lips, then pointed to a boulder resting at the stream's edge.

The mountain man named Shadrach Brown squatted in front of the great rock, his faded furs creating an almost perfect camouflage. He had his back to Frost and the girl, his hands working furiously at a task they could not discern from their vantage point.

"You stay here, child," Frost said. He took off his buckskin long coat and floppy hat, handing them both to the girl. "Hold onto these for me, if you will. But come no closer than you are now. I'm sorry you have to see this, but belief would ever elude you if you did not."

As if on cue, the little mountain man pivoted and looked directly at them. A dead beaver lay on the ground in front of him. The beaver had yet to be skinned, but it had been ripped from ass to throat, its sternum cracked open and all its innards dumped into a bloody pile on the ground. All the innards, except the ones that Shadrach Brown was busily shoving into his mouth. Face and fingers smeared with dark red blood, bile trickling from his lips and off his chin. He smacked noisily as he chewed, swallowing in great gulps. He stuck his chin in the air, nose held high, sniffing as if more trusting of his sense of smell than the sight that met his eyes. His face looked less than human. Feral, animalistic.

The girl stared, dumbfounded.

"I take it you've never seen him like this?" said Frost.

The girl shook her head.

"That's Shadrach Brown's body, but he's no longer in control of it. The thing inside him is driving the wagon now."

The rat-faced fur trader stood up awkwardly and hissed at them, a guttural growl escaping his lips. He took one step toward them, but before he could take another, Frost stepped in front of the girl. In one fluid motion, his hands moving so fast the girl's eyes couldn't track them, he had pulled both pistols from their holsters. Thunder boomed from both barrels as his hands leveled.

Shadrach Brown's body jerked, spasming as the bullets tore into him. A frothy, red mist sprayed from his mouth, but he did not go down. Instead, he lurched forward, stutter-stepping, then sprinting toward Frost and the girl. The guns roared again, bullets striking Brown's torso. Or rather, striking the torso that had once belonged to Shadrach Brown. The mountain man's body seemed to shrink, his fur clothing falling away, and his flesh, pallid and gray, sloughed off like a snake shedding its skin.

Frost kept firing, emptying both cylinders. Each bullet struck their target but had no effect. Shadrach Brown's body was beyond feeling. His flesh bloodlessly falling from his withered muscles as what remained continued charging at Frost and the girl.

Frost shoved the girl off the path of the game trail as the animated remains of the mountain man slammed into him. Frost crashed to the ground, but rolled with the impact and came up on top of the fleshless carcass, straddling it. Empty of bullets, his revolvers became clubs in his hands, pistol-whipping what was left of the mountain man about the face and head until the carcass stopped moving and lay still.

Frost tossed the revolvers aside and grabbed Brown's upper palate in one hand and the lower mandible with the other. He yanked hard, hands pulling in opposite directions, and the jaw broke with a popping sound as it tore away from its hinge. Frost shoved his fist into Brown's gaping, lipless mouth, forcing it down the throat. His fingers punched through the stomach lining, searching, probing until they found and grabbed hold of the squirming thing hiding in the bowels of the mountain man's carcass. The thing tried to escape, but had nowhere to go. Frost held tight, retracting his hand, pulling it back up Brown's esophagus and ripping the thing from its hiding place.

Frost held a squirming, bloody thing by a thrashing, lizard-like tail. The thing was roughly the size of a weasel and resembled nothing so much as a stout but tiny, hairless man with a long, thick tail and nubby, almost vestigial arms. The thing spun on Frost, opening its mouth so wide that the top of its head seemed to disappear. In its wide maw was row upon row of sharp, jagged teeth, swirling down the throat. The mouth snapped closed on Frost's forearm, needle-like teeth burying themselves in his pale flesh.

Frost groaned in pain. He snapped the tail like a whip, forcing the creature's jaws to release its grip on him. The squirming creature's head slammed into the trunk of the nearest tree. The creature rebounded, lunging and snapping at Frost once again, the teeth raking his arm but finding no purchase this time. Frost whipped the tail again, bashing the creature's head into the same tree once more. A spray of red and a dozen or more teeth were left embedded in the bark. The creature dangled limply from Frost's hand. He dropped the thing on the ground.

"That was inside of him?" The girl stood next to Frost, looking down at the stunted creature.

"It was."

"Is that what made him do the things he did to me?"

"No. He did those things to you because he was a vile sonofabitch long before this thing took up residence in his gut. But Shadrach Brown's been dead for some time. This lived inside him, kept his body alive, controlled it, while it feasted on him. It used his hands to carve the wards into the trees that trapped you here and kept others out."

"They didn't keep you out."

"No, they did not."

"You're hurt," said the girl, pointing to Frost's arm.

Blood oozed from a vicious, three-inch gash just above his wrist. A few of the creature's yellow teeth remained embedded in the old man's arm.

"So I am," he said.

The girl pointed at the creature. "I don't think it's dead."

Frost looked down just in time to see the thing jump up and take off, running down the game trail with surprising speed. Its ruined head and broken neck flopped from side to side as it sprinted.

Frost sighed and shook his head. He looked off into the trees and shouted. "You want to hear me say it? Fine. I was wrong. I misjudged the little fucker. You can gloat and watch it get away or you can manifest yourself and solve the problem."

As Frost and the girl watched, something formed in the shadows of the trees. A wolf taller than a horse and as black as the shadows around it emerged from the woods as if suddenly stepping from nothingness into existence. The Shadow Wolf stood directly in the path of the escaping creature. The creature tried to stop, to change course, its little legs spinning as it fought its own momentum, tail dragging in the dirt like a rutter. The Shadow Wolf dropped its massive head, jaws clamping over the creature. When the wolf raised its head, the creature was nowhere to be seen. The wolf snapped its jaws. Frost and the girl could hear the crunch of bones and then the Shadow Wolf swallowed.

Frost turned to the girl, saw her staring transfixed at the giant wolf. "Don't be frightened, child," he said. "The wolf's with me."

Thirteen

The Wing-Thief

Black Wing woke to find an enormous flock of passenger pigeons pecking through the thick grasses of the surrounding plain. Tens of thousands of birds, perhaps a hundred thousand, blue-gray heads and backs, bright peach-colored breasts, and long blue tail feathers feasting on prairie grass seed, transforming the flat plain of green grasses into an undulating sea of blue-gray with splotches of orange.

"Friends of yours?" asked Antelope Eyes, propping himself up on his elbows.

The wing-thief sat upon the buffalo skin. "Of mine? You're the one who talks to beasts."

The holy man pulled his knees to his chest. "Yes, but you're the one who flies. Birds are your thing."

Black Wing stared at the flock. He found it impossible to focus on a single bird. The movement of feathers, the shifting of colors, would not allow his eyes to linger, but kept them jumping from one bird to another, making the flock seem like one enormous organism. It was a defense mechanism, confusing predators when the flock was on the ground.

"Would you like to know a secret?" asked Antelope Eyes.

"I don't know," Black Wing said with hesitation. "Do I?"

"Perhaps not. It is a sad secret, but nonetheless true."

"What is the secret?"

Antelope Eyes stretched out his arms in an expansive gesture. "These birds will be dead and gone in a mere fifty summers."

Black Wing laughed. "Of course, they will. Birds don't live as long as men. A few summers at most and they die."

"You misunderstand me." The holy man's face was somber. "I don't mean this flock. I mean the pigeon. All will be gone. Forever."

Black Wing shook his head. "That's not possible. There are too many. I've seen flocks so large they fill the sky, blocking out the sun and casting the whole land in shadow."

"I wish it were not so, but I have seen it. The whites will come west. They will bring their guns and their crops and they will kill all the pigeon. All of them."

"How could you know this?"

The holy man only shrugged.

"No. Don't do that. Answer my question," said the wing-thief. "How could you know things that have not yet happened? Things that may not happen for many summers to come? How can you speak of them with certainty?"

"I have been shown."

"How? By whom?"

"I cannot say."

"Cannot or will not?"

"Does it matter? You have heard me speak often of having seen my own end. Is it so hard to believe I have also been shown other things to come?"

"Yes. Yes, it is hard to believe. When I don't know how you have been shown or by whom. Was it in dreams? Visions? Have you journeyed into the future and come back with all the knowledge that entails? How is that you know these things?"

"That's not important."

"Meaning that you don't want to tell me?"

The holy man pursed his lips. "Yes, that's what it means. Does that anger you?"

"Of course it angers me! You ask me to believe, but you won't give me reason to!"

The holy man looked out at the flock. A gentle wind blew a lock of hair across his face. He looked down at the truthstone, still lying on the buffalo skin. "I have opened your eyes. I have shown you gods who walk among men. You know I speak the truth. I have given you ample reason to believe my words. That is not what angers you."

"Oh? Then tell me why I am angry."

"You dislike when I mention my end. That is what angers you."

"I do not like talk of death. I see no point in it."

The holy man nodded. "I know. But you are wrong. We talk of death to remind ourselves that it comes for all and that we should live while we can."

"If you truly know your end, then tell me and I will prevent it."

"No."

"Why not?"

"Because you cannot prevent it."

"Tell me."

The holy man shook his head. "You would not believe me if I told you."

"Try me."

Antelope Eyes smiled. "Let's talk about something else."

"I do not want to talk about something else."

"Because you are angry." The holy man reached out a hand, placed it gently on the wing-thief's cheek. "I do not want to see you so angry."

"What do you want then?"

Antelope Eyes smiled. "I want to see you fly."

"You've seen me fly."

"No, I've seen a bird fly after you've borrowed its body. But I've never seen how you do it. Show me. I want to see it all."

"There's nothing to see," said Black Wing. "It just happens."

"Show me."

"For what purpose?"

"The purpose of letting me see you fly."

Black Wing sighed. "It's nothing. You're going to be disappointed."

"Show me."

The wing thief shook his head. "Fine." Black Wing scanned the flock, patiently waiting. Holding his focus was difficult amongst the motion and the shifting colors of plumage, but at last, he locked onto a single bird. He felt a wave of disorientation, the familiar but ever-frightening moment of panic at leaving his body.

He looked back at the buffalo skin, at his own body lying there next to the holy man. The violet aura around Antelope Eyes, the glow of his medicine, was more pronounced, more vibrant, when seen through the bird's eyes. The same held for the truthstone. It pulsed a fierce purple light. His own body, however, had no aura. He looked at the gray tips of the pigeon's wings and saw that his medicine had followed him into the bird's body.

"Are you going to fly or not?" The holy man called out.

Black Wing stretched his wings and lifted off the ground. He flew to Antelope Eyes, circled around his head a few times and then landed on the buffalo skin. He stole a glance at his own body, still unmoving except for the eyes, which flitted back and forth. With medicine and practice, a wing-thief could learn to control a bird's body, but a bird who suddenly finds itself inside the body of a man can only move the eyes.

Black Wing shifted back to his own body. The pigeon flopped around on the buffalo skin for a few seconds before taking flight and rejoined the flock.

The wing-thief looked at the holy man. "I told you it would be disappointing."

"I wanted to see you fly," said Antelope Eyes.

"You just did."

"No. I saw you take a bird and flit about without going higher than I can reach. I want to see you fly. Take to the skies and soar. Touch the clouds before you return to earth. I want to see you fly."

"Why?" asked Black Wing.

"Humor me," said Antelope Eyes.

Black Wing relented. He took the body of another pigeon and flew straight up, higher and higher, faster and faster, until he pierced a low floating cloud. He looked down as the cloud slid slowly past. He realized he had flown too high, so far above the earth that the buffalo skin was little more than a speck of discoloration amidst the green of the plain and the gray of the pigeon flock.

It occurred to him it was not wise to be so far above the ground, alone in a pigeon's body. Without the protection of the flock, the pigeon would be an easy target for a bird of prey. He could never outfly a hawk. And he wasn't sure if he could swap bodies with the predator should one appear. He had never tried to jump from one bird to another without first returning to his own flesh.

He had done what the holy man had asked. He had flown higher and faster than he should've. He had touched the sky. Now it was time to return to his body and return the pigeon to his flock.

As he returned to the earth, something in the distance caught his eye. Several miles to the south, a shallow river wound through the plains. On the banks of the river, he could see a wooden settler's wagon. Swooping lower, he could see the wagon had overturned and all the contents had been scattered along the riverbank. Clothing and cookery, woodworking tools, and books. He could see four bodies, three of them children, the other a woman wearing a bonnet and a long dress, lay unmoving on the bank. A dead mule bobbed in the river, its belly and hindquarter above the surface, its head and legs below the waterline.

A large creature, half again the size of a man, sat on the rocks by the edge of the river. The same luminous violet glow Black Wing had seen around Antelope Eyes enveloped the creature. It had a broad, angular head that sloped into a beaked mouth, reminding the wing-thief of a snapping turtle. The creature had entirely too much skin, folds of mottled, blue-black flesh hanging loosely from its arms and upper body. Black Wing could see great thorn-like spurs running the length of the creature's spine. Similar yet smaller spurs lined its forearms from elbow to wrist. In its misshapen hands, it held something large and fleshy.

Black Wing flew closer, landing atop the overturned wagon. He could see the woman and children on the ground, their skulls crushed and heads mashed to pulp. The fleshy thing the creature held was the limbless upper body of another settler. The creature's beak-shaped mouth tore off the head from the torso. Its powerful jaws crunched flesh, muscle, and bone alike. It swallowed without chewing. Dark crimson dribbled from the creature's mouth.

Black Wing noted the creature's hands. More human-like than its head or body, though lacking in symmetry. One hand was narrow, with long fingers and sharp nails, while the other was meaty, with thick, sausage-shaped fingers and cracked, jagged fingernails. The creature's feet were similarly human-shaped and equally mismatched.

The angular head rotated in Black Wing's direction. Narrow, yellow eyes stared from unblinking slits. The air around the creature's head shimmered, the purple aura fading momentarily. The grotesque, turtle-like head disappeared. Atop the creature's sloping shoulders was the head and face of a man. Peach-colored skin, brown hair, blue eyes, and a thick beard not yet gone to gray.

The wing-thief blinked, nictitating membranes sweeping across his eyes, but the visage before him remained unchanged. The creature still wore the settler's head melded onto its massive body. Black Wing knew the creature was looking at him, knew it saw through his disguise, realized he was not a bird, but a man borrowing a bird's body. He expected it to come for him, but the creature made no move. It remained still, staring. After a long moment, the creature raised its mis-matched hands, lifting the bloody torso to its mouth. The brown-haired head and bearded face disappeared as the broad, turtle-like head that had previously sat atop the creature's shoulders returned. Its beak opened and clamped with frightening suddenness, ripping away another chunk of man-flesh from the settler's corpse.

Black Wing had seen enough. This was bad medicine. Such a vile thing should not exist. The wing-thief would fly back to their camp, release the bird and reclaim his body. Then he would return to this place with his weapons. He would fill this obscene creature with arrows, then chop it into pieces with his axe, and leave the remains for the wolves. He pushed off the wagon and took flight.

When he arrived back at the campsite, he found the entire flock of pigeons had moved on without him. His body lay unmoving on the buffalo skin, the eyes still rolling about the sockets in panic. The mounds of sage and cedar that had yielded so much smoke the night before had long since gone cold and ceased their smolder, leaving only wisps of the violet aura still dancing flame-like atop them.

The holy man was nowhere to be found.

Fourteen

The Manhunter

The bodies smelled so rank after three days, that Ozymandias Hayes had to cut little swatches from his bedroll to plug his nose. The horses too were clearly bothered by the smell and had grown more difficult to control, slowing down what had already been a slower-than-expected journey. Buzzards circling overhead had followed him from the time he left the campsite and had grown more bold each day, sometimes landing within a few feet during Hayes' infrequent stops for rest or to water the horses.

Each night when he stopped, Hayes would build a much larger fire than he would in any other circumstance. He would remove the bodies from the horses and pile them near the flames, and hope that the fire was enough to keep the wolves at bay. The good news, slim though it might be, was that at least the rigor had faded, allowing him to more easily move the bodies when necessary.

He slept little, only as much as he dared. From the first night, he could hear howling in the distance, getting closer with each succeeding night. On the fourth night, he awoke unexpectedly sometime after midnight. A buzzard was perched on the corpse of Enoch Munn pecking at his eye socket, the eyeball dangling over the cheek by a thin gray strand that might once have been a nerve or perhaps a blood vessel. Hayes shooed the bird away with a torch he kept on the edge of the fire pit, only to turn around and see a large, gray wolf with yellow eyes standing not thirty feet away.

Hayes waved the torch in the wolf's direction. The wolf bared its teeth and let out a low, guttural snarl. It paced side to side but did not advance. He waved the torch again, moving toward the wolf, but the wolf held its ground.

Hayes pulled his pistol and cocked the hammer. "Don't make me kill you," he said to the wolf. "Do not make me kill you."

The wolf continued pacing, snarling. Hayes felt the hackles rise on the back of his neck. Something was behind him. He spun to see three more gray wolves approaching from the other side of the fire. The one in the forefront reached the pile of corpses ahead of its companions, burying its teeth in the pant leg of one outlaw. The wolf jerked its head from side to side, trying to dislodge the corpse from the pile, pull it away from the fire.

Hayes shot the wolf dead, then fired again, this time into the air, hoping the sound would scare the others into a retreat. It didn't. Instead, the two wolves sprinted around their fallen pack member, charging at him. Hayes shot them both in rapid succession.

He spun, trying to find the wolf that had distracted him, drawn his attention away while the others advanced on the corpses. From his periphery, he saw a gray blur moving fast. Hayes dodged to his left, but the lead wolf collided with him, taking him off his feet, knocking him to the ground. The wolf tumbled off balance, rolling over Hayes, skidding past the ring of stones and into the fire.

The wolf kicked hard, pushing itself out of the fire and over the ring of stones, rolling across the prairie grass. Its fur was singed and smoking in spots, one ear blackened and hairless. The wolf never looked back as it high-tailed away from the camp.

Hayes reloaded quickly, then got to his feet. He scanned in all directions, but the lead wolf had disappeared. He looked at the three dead wolves on the ground around him. Four was a small pack, he knew. Too small, in all likelihood. Hayes suspected there could be maybe another dozen nearby. He gathered the horses and began loading the outlaws' bodies onto them as quickly as he could, not even bothering to tie them down. Hutchens' body was the last to go atop a horse.

Get some distance, he thought. *Let the sun rise, then you can stop and secure the bodies.*

He kicked dirt into the fire but didn't bother to extinguish it fully. He'd ringed it well and was confident there was no chance of the fire escaping. He tied reins to saddles, recreating the chain, then threw his saddle onto his horse, cinched it tight, and flung himself onto the horse's back. He snapped the reins and put heels to his horse's flank. From somewhere behind him, he heard a wolf howl but didn't bother to look over his shoulder for it.

You know they're out there, he told himself. *Just keep moving and don't look back.*

For about the dozenth time, he questioned his decision to transport bodies to the outpost, rather than just severed heads. It was a question that kept recurring as he rode throughout the days. Hayes fought it back each time.

I will not cut off heads. That is not what I am. That is not what I do.

He stopped a few hours later by a small, shallow river to let the horses drink. The sun's rays broke over the horizon. Morning had arrived. He took a few moments to tie down the bodies to the horses, then refilled his canteen and ate the last small bite of the jerky he'd been rationing. His throat had healed. He could swallow with only minimal discomfort. He uncorked the whiskey bottle he'd taken from the dead outlaws and took a good, long pull from it. Drinking on an empty stomach was probably not the wisest thing to do, but the encounter with the wolves had left him disconcerted and he needed to calm his nerves.

Mounting his horse, he thought he saw movement in the distance. He counted nine dark shapes moving in formation, trying to flank him. He kicked his horse in the ribs, prodding the animal forward. The wolves hung back, just out of range of his pistols, almost as if they knew what that range was. Hayes dismissed the thought. *They're animals, not men. They act on instinct, not reason.* Even so, he knew they'd likely learned from the last encounter.

Next time, they would be patient. They would pace him, wait for him to slow down or make a mistake, then they would attack. Hayes resolved that would not happen. He would not make a mistake. He would not slow down. He would ride day and night until the wolves gave up or until he got to the outpost. Whichever came first. And if the wolves did come closer, if the wolves did attack, he would kill them. Kill them all. Or at least as many as he could before they got him.

For the rest of the day, the wolves were never out of sight, always loping along behind Hayes' caravan of corpses, always just on the outer edge of pistol range. Hayes was tempted to take a shot several times. Even if they weren't close enough to hit, perhaps the sound would frighten them away or at the very least put them off the trail for a while. Each time, he decided against it. His warning shot last time had little effect. The pack had followed him this far. He didn't see them giving up until they got theirs and he didn't want to waste a bullet that he might need later. If only for himself.

The thought occurred to him that putting a bullet in his own head might be a waste of a bullet. The woman with nine fingers had sent him back after Munn's gang had murdered him. Who's to say what would happen if he died again? If the wolves got him or if he took his own life, would he find the cold embrace of death he'd expected earlier? Would he find himself back on the banks of the dark river, the canoe waiting for him? Or would he simply awaken on the plain again, his body healing from the ordeal? He didn't know. And wasn't eager to find out.

As the sun sank on the cloudless horizon, Hayes rode on. Darkness fell and the moon rose, waxing gibbous. At the very least the night was bright enough that he didn't have to worry about a horse blindly stepping into a prairie dog hole and breaking a leg.

He did, however, worry about staying awake. Since the night Munn's gang had attacked, Hayes hadn't slept more than a dozen hours total. Since the wolves had attacked, he had not stopped to sleep at all. He would doze in the saddle, but had not stopped to rest. He was exhausted. The horses were exhausted. If he kept pushing them like this, he was going to ride them to death. But he had no choice. The wolves remained close. So he willed himself on, willed the horses on, staying just ahead of the pack.

Hayes lost track of time as he rode. He felt himself drifting, his eyelids heavy, a struggle to keep them open. He jerked in the saddle, eyes going wide as he realized he had nodded off. For how long, he couldn't be sure. Up ahead of him, looming large on the horizon, he could see a series of huge chalkstone formations, bluffs jutting hundreds of feet into the air, the remnants of an ancient inland sea floor. Moonlight glinted off the Chalkstones, making them seem almost luminescent.

Hayes glanced over his shoulder. He could see dark shapes following. More than he had seen previously. The pack had swelled from nine to more than two dozen. And closer than they had been since that night they'd attacked. If he fell asleep again, even for a little while, if the horses stopped, the pack of wolves would be on him in moments. And there would be no fighting them off this time. There were too many of them.

Hayes slapped himself across the face. Hard. Again.

Stay awake. Damn you. Stay awake.

He put heels to the horse's flanks, urging it onward, to pick up the pace. It worked for a while, but soon the horse slowed again. It was too tired. Hayes was riding it to death. He jerked to attention, sat up straight in the saddle. He had drifted. Dozed again. He realized with a sense of dread that he wasn't going to stay awake no matter what he did. His body had crossed a line that not even its need for survival could pull back from. His body craved sleep and had reached the point of involuntarily taking it. All this time, he had feared the loss of a horse, but it was his own body that was betraying him. This was the end of the line. He could no longer outrun the wolves. They had him.

Give them a body.

The thought came unbidden. Hayes tried to force it away. He had stubbornly refused to behead the corpses earlier, refused to leave the bodies for the wolves. There were things he simply would not do. He'd killed men in combat, but he'd never murdered a man in cold blood and he'd never desecrated a body.

Give the wolves a body. The voice in his head grew more insistent. *Give it to them before they take it from you. Before they take it and more.*

Hayes leaped down from his horse, letting the reins drop to the ground. He ran to the last of the horses, pulled the knife from his belt, and cut the rope holding the corpse to the saddle. He grabbed the body and threw it to the ground. He hadn't realized which body he'd chosen until he saw it lying at his feet. Enoch Munn, buck-toothed and pockmarked, one eye flopping from the socket, stared blankly up at the night sky.

Hayes sprinted back to his horse, launched himself into the saddle. He looked back at the pack closing in, moving faster, yellow eyes glowing in the darkness. He snapped the reins and his horse lurched forward, the other horses following with an urgency.

Lead by the wolf with the singed fur and the blackened, naked ear, the pack tore into Munn, a frenzy of white teeth and yellow eyes. Hayes glanced over his shoulder. The pack had lost all interest in pursuit. Men were led by guile, animals by instinct. They wanted a meal, not mayhem.

After fighting for days, Hayes had given in, surrendered. He should be repulsed by what he had done. He should be ashamed of his weakness, but all he felt was relief. The thought of Munn's satchel with the scalps of children, the glee on Munn's face when the horse bolted from beneath him and the rope tightened around his neck, was all he needed to keep the shame at bay.

He rode on for a short distance, until his burst of adrenaline was swallowed up by his drowsiness, until the feasting wolves were no longer in sight. He dropped his head and slept in the saddle.

Fifteen

The Girl

The girl stood, frozen in place. A gust of wind whipped a strand of dark hair across her face. After a moment, she lifted a hand and tucked the strand behind her ear, but her feet remained fixed. Unmoving. She stared forward at the fur trader's shack where she had long been held prisoner.

From a few steps behind her, the old man watched. He had torn a swath of cloth from the bottom of his tunic to bandage the wound on his arm, but the blood still seeped through. The Shadow Wolf stood beside him, its enormous head on a level with the old man's shoulder. The girl had stood there for so long the old man began to wonder if perhaps she had slipped into a state of stupor.

"*What seest thou else, In the dark backward and abysm of time?*" he said.

The girl showed no sign of acknowledgment.

"Child?"

She did not answer him.

"We should get a move on. The trees await and I'd like to be down the steepest part of the mountain before nightfall. I know a good spot there to camp, but we need to be going if we're going to make it by sundown."

"I have to go inside. There's something I need." The girl's eyes remained glued to the shack, her back to the old man and the Shadow Wolf.

"Are you sure? Is there anything in there that you can't do without? There's a town through the hills aways. When we get there, I'll buy you a new dress. Get you out of that filthy smock. I'll buy you a hairbrush. New shoes. You can take a hot bath. Let's leave this place behind."

"I need to go inside."

"Let me go in with you."
"I don't need you to come in."
"I'm sure you don't. But let me do it, regardless."
"No. Just me."

The old man sighed. "Fine then. See to your business. We'll be right here. Be quick about it."

The girl said nothing more. She walked slowly, almost trance-like, to the door of the shack, pulled it open and stepped inside. She remembered when the fur trader first brought her to this place, how tiny and confining the shack had seemed. But over time, as she came to realize that she would likely never leave, she ceased to notice how cramped it was. It became neither spacious nor constrictive. It simply was. But now, with her freedom at hand, assuming the old man could get her past the warded trees as he had promised, the shack had reverted to being claustrophobic. She looked at the crude bed, covered in animal skins. The bed where the fur trader, or whatever that thing inside him had been, had violated her on an almost daily basis.

On the floor next to the bed was the fur trader's kerosene lamp. She picked up the lamp, twisted off the glass chimney and threw it on the dirt floor. The glass shattered on impact.

"Are you all right in there?" the old man shouted.

"Yes." was all she said.

She pulled out the wick, then held the lamp upside down. The kerosene poured out, soaking the pelts. She tossed the lamp onto the bed and found the box of lucifers near the fireplace. She struck one, scraping it across the crudely cemented pile of rocks that passed for a smokestack, and threw the flaming match onto the kerosene-soaked pelts.

She stepped back and watched the flames quickly reaching the low ceiling and blackening the rough-hewn beams that supported the roof. Smoke filled the shack, but the girl refused to move. She stood there, watching the flames dance.

When the old man saw the smoke billowing out of the shack, he sprinted for the door. He bumped into the girl as she walked calmly from the flaming shack, accompanied by an angry cloud of black smoke that swirled around her.

"Are you hurt, child?" he asked.

The girl didn't answer. She walked past the old man and straight to the giant black wolf. Silently, she burst into tears and leaned into the wolf, burying her face in its thick fur. She never looked up, not even when the roof, consumed by the flames, collapsed in on what was left of the shack.

The Shadow Wolf lay down on its belly and the girl grabbed handfuls of fur and pulled herself onto the wolf's back. She put her arms around its neck and held tight. The Shadow Wolf stood, the girl straddling it like it was a horse, and ambled off down the hillside. The girl leaned forward, laid her head on the thick mane of fur at the wolf's neck, and closed her eyes.

"You're going to let her ride you like that?" the old man called out incredulously.

The old man shook his head and walked from the burning shack to where his horse was tied off to an aspen tree. He loosed the reins and mounted the horse. There was something here he wasn't privy to. *Who is this girl?*

He turned the horse and caught up to them as they reached the ring of carved trees.

"The wards are still in force," said the old man. "With their maker dead, their power will wane over time, but there's no telling how long that might be. Could be years."

"I can't get past them," said the girl. "I've tried. I can't."

"Our doubts are traitors, And make us lose the good we oft might win, By fearing to attempt." The old man smiled at the girl. "We'll get you past. Just stay on the wolf and hold tight."

"Will it hurt?" asked the girl.

"It won't be pleasant, but if you trust me and persist, the pain will be temporary."

"I'm scared."

"I know. Hold tight to the wolf and keep your head down."

The old man led the way, hand atop his floppy hat, holding it to his head. As the force pushing against them grew, his painted horse balked. The animal stamped its feet, whinnied, and seemed on the verge of rearing, but the old gunslinger calmed the horse with whispered words and forced it forward into the line of trees. A silent wind whipped against his long coat, but if the wards had any effect on him, the girl couldn't see it. In a moment, he was past the line of trees. He sat up straight in the saddle, adjusted his floppy hat, the magpie feather still in place. He looked back at the girl.

"Action is eloquence." He held out a hand toward her. "Come now, child. Come to me."

The girl swallowed hard, fighting back her fears. She put her head down, her arms around the wolf's thick neck, clinging tightly. She rested her face against the black fur and closed her eyes. The Shadow Wolf moved forward.

Her head throbbed as if someone was boring the tip of a knife into each temple. She winced and cried out. She could feel the tears welling in her eyes, her insides being twisted into knots. Gale-force winds buffeted her from all sides. She held tight to the wolf's neck, squeezed her knees to its ribs, clinging with all her might.

The winds intensified and she could feel her grip slipping. As her hands were forced apart, she grabbed at the wolf's fur, desperate to hang on, but her fingers could not grab hold. She felt herself lifted from the wolf's back, nothing but air beneath her. The winds spun her around and slammed her to the ground. The air rushed from her lungs and each attempt to refill them brought a wracking wave of agony.

Dazed from the impact, she struggled to get to her elbows, only to see that the Shadow Wolf had crossed the plane of the tree line. It was on the other side, standing next to the old man and his painted horse. She looked up and saw the wards gouged into the trees. The crude carvings crackled with energy. She had failed. She was still the prisoner of the trees.

She could not hold back the bitter tears that flowed from her eyes. "You lied to me!" she yelled at the old man. "You told me you could get me across! You lied!"

The old man climbed down from his horse, walked to the invisible line made by the warded trees. "No, child. I did not. You merely failed the first attempt. Get to your feet. The wolf and I will come back for you."

"No," she said, standing. "I don't need you. Go away! You lied to me!"

"We must awake endeavour for defence; for courage mounteth with occasion." The old man extended his hand. "Take my hand, child. I'll pull you through."

The girl stared at him, her eyes drifting down to his outstretched, bone-white hand. "It hurts. It hurts so bad."

"I know, but I'm not leaving you. Take my hand."

The girl wavered.

"Do it now, child."

The girl stepped forward. She could feel the power of the wards pushing against her, feel the crushing pain in her head, her intestines churning, knotting. She reached out a hand and the invisible wind slapped it back at her.

"Don't stop," said the old man. "Try again. Take my hand."

She took a step. Then another. The force of the wards pressed against her, shoving her backward. She put her head down and kept moving her feet. She could feel the power of the wards trying to lift her from the ground, slam her down again. Her insides burned as if her bowels were being pulled through her skin.

"Your hand, child! Give me your hand!"

The girl reached out, her fingers inches away from the old man's. The wards pushed, trying to force her back, but she refused. Her fingertips brushed his. She stretched, felt his hand wrap around hers, and then...

The force pressing against her was gone. The pain in her head and the horrible cramping inside her was gone. She stood on the other side of the ring of warded trees.

"You pulled me through," she said, looking into the old man's violet eyes.

"You pulled yourself through."

The girl smiled, but her smile quickly faded. Something wasn't right. Again, her insides churned. Pain making her double over.

But she was past the trees, past the wards! How could this be?

She felt bile rising fast in her throat. She turned her head, opening her mouth wide, retching violently, and repeatedly vomiting on the ground. She stepped back, dizzy, her footing uncertain. And then she saw it. There, in the midst of the stomach contents she had sprayed on the ground, was a small squirming creature just like the one the old man had pulled from the fur trader.

Before she realized what she was doing, the girl was stomping on the creature. Screaming at the top of her lungs as she brought the heel of her foot down again and again. Until what remained of the squirming thing was indistinguishable from the matter around it.

The old man took the girl by the shoulders, pulled her into an embrace. She wrapped her arms around him, burying her face in his buckskin long coat, and sobbed until she was all sobbed out.

When at last she broke the embrace, the old man walked her over to the Shadow Wolf and helped her onto its back. She held on tightly and lay her head against the wolf's neck. The old man gave her a wink, but, uncharacteristically, said nothing.

He climbed onto his horse and they made their way down the mountain, not stopping until the shadows grew long and the sun began to slip beneath the mountain tops.

While the old man gathered wood and built a fire, the Shadow Wolf lay on the ground, and the girl curled up against it. With the warmth of the wolf at her back, the fire roaring in front of her, the birds chirping in the trees, and the old man with the pale white skin sitting across from her, the girl felt a peace she hadn't known in longer than she could remember. She took a deep breath, held the mountain air in her lungs. It felt different, cleaner than it ever had before. She had a strange feeling, a feeling she had forgotten existed.

Hope. She felt hope.

The old man reached into a pocket of his long coat and brought out a handful of purple berries he had picked while gathering wood. He held out his hand to her, and she took the berries.

She looked at him. At his heavily lined face and purple eyes. At his stringy white hair and flesh completely lacking in color.

"Are you all right, child?" he asked.

"Ana," she said with a smile. "My name is Ana."

The old man returned her smile. "It's nice to meet you, Ana."

Sixteen

The Wing-Thief

WHERE HAD THE HOLY man gone now?

Black Wing zoomed over his own body, lying on the buffalo skin, the truthstone glowing violet beside it. Some distance up the arroyo, near a copse of golden-leaved aspens, he found the holy man lying on his back in the grass. His arms were stretched out to his sides, palms up as if holding an invisible offering to some unseen god. He looked so still, unmoving. The wing-thief feared the worst, but on landing near him, he could hear Antelope Eyes humming softly. The holy man's eyes were closed, but behind his lids, his eyes twitched furiously as if he were deeply dreaming or perhaps in a trance-like state.

A wave of relief flooded over Black Wing, but the relief was short-lived. Two painted warriors wearing bone armor and war bonnets emerged from the trees, moving stealthily for the spot where the holy man lay. One warrior's face was coated with white clay, streaks of brilliant blue from powdered lapis lazuli running diagonally across his eyes and nose and down his arms. The other sported red paint with a black vertical streak bisecting his face. The former held a club fashioned from the jawbone of a horse. Red Face carried a large flint knife with a hilt made from elk antler. The blade's edge glistened in the light of the morning sun as the two warriors silently approached the sleeping holy man.

Black Wing leaped onto Antelope Eye's chest, scratching and pecking at him, trying to wake him, but the holy man did not respond. Black Wing took flight, veering sharply and flying with as much speed as the pigeon's wings could muster. He had to reach the buffalo skin and reclaim his body, then hope that he could somehow make it back and intercept the painted warriors before they could murder the holy man.

He could see the end of the arroyo, his body on the buffalo skin. Just a little closer and then...

Black Wing, back in his own body, sat up. He could see the pigeon fluttering, struggling to regain control of its airborne body. It narrowly avoided a collision with a tree, scattering leaves as it shot upward.

Black Wing vaulted to his feet and ran to his horse, leaping onto its bare back. He grabbed the horse's mane and kicked its ribs, spurring it forward. No time to grab his tomahawk or his bow. The seconds it would take to gather weapons might be the difference between getting to Antelope Eyes in time or getting there to find the painted warriors holding the holy man's bloody scalp. So he rode, unarmed, to battle two heavily armed, painted warriors.

The horse's legs churned and Black Wing pushed the animal harder. With the painted warriors in sight, the horse stumbled, tripping over a gopher hole. As the horse went down, Black Wing released its mane and jumped. He hit the ground rolling and came to his feet. He didn't have time to worry if the horse was injured. He had to get to the holy man. That was all that mattered, all he could concern himself with.

He sprinted for the painted warriors. Both warriors diverted their attention from the holy man to him. If either had a bow instead of hand weapons, he would be dead already. The painted warriors shook their weapons in the air and hooted as they ran for him. As the distance between them disappeared, Black Wing dropped and dove for the warriors' legs. His shoulder caught Red Face just below the knees, flipping him forward and crashing him into the ground. Black Wing whipped his legs around, striking White Paint in the meaty part of his thighs. White Paint's momentum was halted, and he stumbled forward but did not leave his feet.

Black Wing rolled to his feet and delivered a heel kick to the ear of Red Paint. The painted warrior's head spun with the force of the kick, his war bonnet shifted and fell in front of his eyes. Black Wing stamped down hard on Red Face's knife hand, driving his heel into the carpal bones. Red Face's fingers released and the flint knife slipped from his grasp.

The wing-thief wanted the knife but knew it had landed too far away for him to grab without leaving himself in a defenseless position. Sensing White Paint behind him, he kicked the knife away with his foot, pushing it just out of Red Face's reach. White Paint swung the bone club at the back of his head, but Black Wing dodged, twisting away. The club landed a glancing blow, scraping the side of his head and tearing a chunk from his ear. White Paint swung the bone club again, this time a back-handed motion aimed at Black Wing's face. He ducked, and the club sailed over his head.

With the backhand swing failing to connect, White Paint was off balance. Black Wing kicked out, sweeping White Paint's legs from under him. White Paint hit the ground face first. Black Wing rolled to grab the knife he had kicked aside, but he was too late. Red Face had already reclaimed it and gotten to his feet. But the knife was in Red Face's left hand, not his right as it had been earlier. The painted warrior cradled the right hand close to his body. Black Wing's stomp had broken Red Face's preferred hand. Red Face swiped with the knife, more adept with the left than Black Wing had expected. The blade opened up a red seam between Black Wing's wrist and elbow. Thick crimson seeped furiously from the wound.

Red Face swung the knife again, the blade arcing across the wing-thief's chest and opening another bloody seam. As Red Face's arm swept past him, Black Wing grabbed his wrist and spun the warrior around, extending the momentum of the swipe. White Paint had by that time gotten to his feet. He had the bone club raised overhead, prepared to deliver a blow that would have shattered Black Wing's skull. If only he had been able to deliver it. Instead, the bone club slipped involuntarily from White Paint's hands.

The painted warrior looked down to see his bloody bowels spilling from a gash across his midsection. The flint knife jointly held by Black Wing and Red Face had sliced him nearly in half. White Paint staggered backward. His knees gave way, and he flopped to a seated position, a dazed look on his face as he watched his intestines ooze from his belly.

Black Wing used the leverage he still had over Red Face to drive the painted warrior to the ground, his war bonnet flying from his head as he crashed down. The wing-thief landed atop Red Face, both of them struggling for control of the knife. Black Wing drove his knee into Red Face's groin. Again. And again. Over and over. Blood gushed from the cuts on the wing-thief's forearm and chest as the two wrestled. Black Wing used the blood to his advantage, letting it drip into Red Face's eyes. The painted warrior closed his eyes and turned his head, trying to shake the blood from his eyes. He bucked hard and rolled, coming up on top of Black Wing. The wing-thief's hands, slick with his own blood, kept slipping. He realized with a sense of growing dread that even with his preferred hand broken, the painted warrior was stronger than him. He was not going to be able to wrest the knife from Red Face. The painted warrior was going to win this fight. Red Face was going to kill him and then he would murder the holy man as well.

The painted warrior forced the point of the blade into the side of Black Wing's head. The wing-thief pushed back, but he could feel the knifepoint boring into his temple. His blood was now dripping into his own eyes. He felt weakened, light-headed. The loss of blood from the gashes in his arm and across his chest was draining his strength. A few seconds more and Red Face would overpower him.

Black Wing turned his head. He wanted to see the holy man one last time before the painted warrior drove the blade into his skull. Antelope Eyes lay unmoving in the grass, still entranced, his eyes closed. Black Wing would like to have looked into the holy man's eyes one last time. To carry the memory of that perfect face, those doe-shaped eyes, with him into the next world, his only comfort in the certain damnation that awaited him. But it was not to be.

His right hand slipped from Red Face's wrist. The blade broke through the skin of the wing-thief's temple. He could feel the tip grinding against bone. Black Wing brought his free hand up, a desperate swing of his fist at Red Face's head. He felt something cold and solid in the palm of his hand, something that should not be there. The solid thing in his hand slammed into the back of the painted warrior's head.

The pressure of the blade against Black Wing's temple eased. Red Face was stunned by the blow. The wing-thief swung his hand again. He heard the crack of bone. Red Face dropped the knife, the elk antler hilt bouncing off of Black Wing's shoulder. The painted warrior slumped, the weight of his body resting atop the wing-thief. Black Wing hit him again. And again. The painted warrior did not fight back.

Black Wing pushed Red Face off of him, the body lay beside him in the grass. The wing-thief rolled to his feet. Looking down, he saw the painted warrior on his side, convulsing on the ground. The back of his skull was crushed in, blood and brain matter oozing from the wound. Red Face soiled himself and the smell of shit hung heavy in the air.

Black Wing looked down at the cold solid thing in his right hand, but he knew what it was before he saw it. The truthstone, pulsing with a violet glow. Blood and tiny flecks of white bone covered its smooth, heat-forged surface. He didn't know how the truthstone had gone from laying in the middle of the buffalo skin blanket at the end of the arroyo to suddenly being in his hand at the moment he desperately needed it. Had he summoned it somehow? Or had it come to him on its own? As if it were not a rock, but a living thing with the power to act and move of its own accord?

The stone turned from cool to hot. Hot like it had been pulled from a fire. Black Wing dropped it, but the truthstone never touched the ground. Somewhere between his hand and the prairie grass, the stone disappeared. Black Wing looked around his feet, but the stone was nowhere to be seen.

He heard the sound of incoherent mumbling and turned to see White Paint sitting a few feet away. Still somehow alive, still staring numbly at his bloody bowels and the red chasm from which they'd fallen out. Black Wing picked up Red Face's flint knife. He snatched the war bonnet off of White Paint's head and threw it aside. He slid the blade of the flint knife quickly across the painted warrior's throat.

Black Wing took a deep breath, then dropped the knife. He looked down at the crimson seeping from the slash across his chest. He could feel blood trickling down the side of his head, dripping from his jaw. Both hands were slicked with red.

"Why didn't you get your bow or your axe?" The holy man had risen from his trance, walked up behind him. "This would've been over more quickly and with a lot less mess if you'd just taken a second to get your weapons."

"I didn't have a second to spare," Black Wing said without turning to face him. "They were coming to murder you."

"You did cut it pretty close," said Antelope Eyes.

"What were you doing just lying there like that? Why didn't you stand up and run? You didn't even try to save yourself."

The holy man shrugged. "I knew you were coming."

"I was unarmed. I nearly died."

"Looked to me like you had things under control."

Black Wing turned and looked at the holy man. "That's what control looks like to you?"

"Control comes in many forms."

"When I thought I was going to die, when I thought I couldn't stop the red one from sticking his knife into my brain, the only thing I could think of was you. Of the times you had told me of seeing your own end. You telling me I could not prevent it." The wing-thief paused. "I thought that time had come and you were right. Your end had come. You were going to be murdered and I could not prevent it because I was going to be murdered first. I had failed you. I hadn't been able to save you. And I knew that when we were both in the world beyond this one, you would avoid me, not just because I was damned, but because I had proven so unworthy of you. That was what I was thinking as Red Face stuck the point of his blade into my head."

The holy man said nothing.

"But this was just another of your tests, wasn't it? You knew this wasn't your end. You knew those warriors were there. You didn't try to get away because you were testing me. Again."

The holy man turned, motioning for Black Wing to follow. "Come. You need stitching and rest. You've lost a lot of blood."

"Why? Why are you doing this? What more do I have to do to prove myself to you?"

"Can we talk about this downwind of here?"

"No, we can't. We're going to stand here and enjoy the smell of shit until I get an answer from you."

Antelope Eyes waved a hand in front of his nose. "Just a few steps that way?"

"Why do you keep testing me?"

"I am not the one testing you."

"What does that mean?"

"You need stitching. Come. I have catgut and needle in my saddlebag."

"What do you mean by you are not the one testing me?"

Antelope Eyes reached down and plucked an eagle feather from White Paint's bonnet and poked it through his top knot. "You're going to bleed to death if you don't get stitching. Come with me and I will answer your questions."

Seventeen

Interlude One

For days, he followed the dark-skinned man and his caravan of corpses across the plains. The herd trudged behind him in silence, pausing when he paused, stopping when he stopped. Feeding when he fed. The herd protected him. Sustained him. His long imprisonment had sapped him, robbed him of his power. But the power was returning. Growing with each day. Soon he would hide no longer.

He had been careful to avoid the dark-skin's notice ever since the dark-skin had seen him earlier. Seen him and the herd on the night when the witch appeared before the dark-skin. The dark-skin intrigued him, piqued his curiosity. He had wondered why the witch had come to the dark-skin. Wondered how the dark-skin had conquered death that night. Had the witch helped him? Or was the dark-skin himself a god? One he had forgotten during his long confinement? Had the dark-skin conspired with the witch against him? Was he her ally now?

If the dark-skin was a god, why had he let him pass without attacking? Had the dark-skin not recognized him? Or had the presence of the herd dissuaded him?

Was the dark-skin assembling his own herd? Was that the purpose of the corpses he traveled with? Then why had he not raised them? Why did they not walk at his side? Why carry them upon the backs of beasts? Did he lack the power? Was he truly a god?

No. He was not. He had given a corpse to the wolves. The dark-skin was no god. He feared the wolves. He fed them to save himself.

If he was no god, then what was the witch's interest in him? What was the source of his power? The dark-skin had power.

He was certain of that. Had the witch given it to him? Was he her assassin? Was this a trap? Was that why the witch had not come for him? She knew he had returned. She would have to know he had escaped. Was she conspiring with the dark-skin to lure him into a conflict before his power had fully returned?

He needed answers. So many questions. So few answers.

Patience, he reminded himself. The solstice was yet some time away. Time had not defeated him, could not defeat him. It only served him.

He watched the dark-skin and his caravan of corpses hurry away into the distance. He walked into the circle of feasting wolves. He had no fear of them. Unlike the dark-skin, he was a god.

The wolf with the naked ear and singed fur tore a chunk of flesh free of the corpse's leg. Sensing his presence, the wolf dropped the meat. It crouched, pulled back its lips and bared its teeth, snarling at him. The other wolves left their feast and circled him, prepared to attack as a pack.

He moved with a speed the wolves could not have anticipated. He grabbed the naked-eared wolf by the scruff of its neck, finger bones digging deeply into fur and flesh. He lifted the wolf into the air, snapping its spine, and whipping the body with a force that nearly decapitated the wolf.

The dying wolf's life turned to energy, flowing from it and down his arm. Flowing into him. Feeding him.

He dropped the wolf's shriveled husk and grabbed another, claws scraping and ripping the hide from the wolf's back. He tore the wolf in half, its entrails spilling onto the ground. He shuddered as the wolf's death fed him.

Instinctively, the remaining wolves attempted to flee, but the herd surrounded them, encircling them, and blocking their escape. They howled in frustration, clawing and snapping at the herd. But the herd contracted the circle, pushing the wolves to him.

When he finished feeding, he felt stronger than he had since escaping his confinement. The life he drained from the wolves energized him more than had the collective lives of the humans who had become his herd. Wolves were stronger than men. More full of life.

He reached a hand down, and the shriveled remains of the wolves began to tremble, reanimating. The naked-eared wolf was the first to rise, its head hanging limply. The wolf he had ripped in half was next, the two halves coming together, dead flesh melding, stitching itself together again. The rest followed, and the reanimated pack joined his herd.

He looked down at the body of the man on which the wolves had been feasting. Orange hair, scarred face, grotesque teeth. The nose, lips, ears and one eye had been eaten away. The abdomen was shredded, soft organs all removed. One leg had been chewed to the bone below the knee.

He held out a hand, calling to the body, and the body answered, rising and joining the herd.

He walked in the direction the dark-skin had ridden. The herd followed behind him.

Eighteen

The Girl

AHEAD OF THEM, THE terrain leveled to a grassy plain. In the middle of the plain, the Chalkstones loomed on the horizon. The gnarled rock formations and sheer cliffs jutting white from the sea of buffalo grass like the skeletal remains of a mountain-sized giant.

It had been three days since Hamish Frost, the girl named Ana, and the Shadow Wolf had forced their way through the warded trees on their way down the mountain from the trapper's shack where Ana had been held captive. Frost, on his painted horse, rode at the girl's side as she sat atop the Shadow Wolf, riding the giant creature as one would ride a bareback horse. Frost noted that she and the wolf had been inseparable since it had manifested from the shadows outside the trapper's shack.

"What is that?" she asked, pointing to the massive rock formations ahead of them.

"Of his bones are coral made; Those are pearls that were his eyes; Nothing of him that doth fade, But doth suffer a sea-change Into something rich and strange."

Ana wrinkled her brow, looked at Frost.

The old man with snow-white skin and eyes the color of lilacs smiled back at her. "They have many names among the people of the plains," he said. "The Chalkstones is perhaps the most common. Albeit incorrect."

"My mother talked about seeing the Chalkstones when she came west."

It was the first time Frost had heard the girl mention her mother, mention anything regarding her life before it had been hijacked by men like the mountain man named

Shadrach Brown. The girl went quiet as if brought to silence by the memory of her mother.

Frost looked at her and felt a surge of empathy for this child whose well-being he had taken on. His fringed, long coat was draped around her shoulders. He had given it to her when he'd seen her shivering around the campfire on their first night down the mountain. She'd slept with it as a cover that night and never given it back.

"They're actually limestone, not chalk," he said in an attempt to wrest her thoughts back to the moment. "The remains of an ancient undersea mountain."

The girl looked at him curiously. "How did they get here if they were under the sea?"

"They've always been here. It's the sea that went away."

Frost shifted in his saddle. He pulled the brim of his floppy hat lower, shielding his face and eyes from the sun. He winced as he lowered his hand. The wound on his arm, the gash given him by the squirming thing he had ripped from inside the mountain man, was festering. He had rinsed the wound in a mountain stream, torn a swatch from the bottom of his tunic, and wrapped it tight, but still the gash oozed a foul-smelling, ochre-like pus.

"Does it hurt?" asked the girl.

"Pain pays the income of each precious thing." When Ana continued looking at him uncomprehendingly, he added, "It's unpleasant, but I've endured worse."

"You should clean it again."

"Won't do any good," Frost said. "Let's pick up the pace. I'd like to make camp on the north face tonight."

He shook the reins, urging his painted horse forward. The Shadow Wolf and the girl followed. They skirted the edge of the cliffs as they rode, keeping their distance from the rock face. The old man pointed to an accumulation of white rocks along the base of the Chalkstones. "Not unusual for pieces of the cliff to break free. We need to keep clear. Be a shame to come this far only to get our skulls crushed by a stone from the sky."

The girl looked up. She saw no falling stones, but she did see small, black shapes circling high above, contrasting sharply against the stark white of the cliffs.

"What kind of birds are those?" she asked, squinting as she pointed upward.

Frost didn't need to look up to know of what she spoke. "Not birds. Bats. The cliffs are full of caves and the caves are full of bats. They'll fill the sky by the time the sun goes down."

"I can hear them now," she said. Clicks and chirps not too dissimilar to birdsong.

"Do they frighten you?" he asked.

"No. Should I be scared?"

"After what you have endured, child, little should frighten you."

They rode on in silence, the sun fading as it slipped slowly toward the horizon. The girl looked up often, watching the circling bats grow in number.

"What do they eat?" she asked after a long while.

Frost didn't answer her question. She considered asking again, assuming the old gunslinger had not heard, but then realized his lack of an answer had nothing to do with her question. He pulled back on the reins, bringing his horse to a stop. The Shadow Wolf stopped beside him.

She saw the wagons ahead, on the north-facing side of the Chalkstones where the old man had spoken of making camp. Dozens of covered wooden wagons parked in defensive rings of concentric circles stretched out across the grassy plain. Inside the centermost ring of wagons, they could see dozens of single-poled, white canvas tents. The wagons and tents were enough for dozens, perhaps a hundred or more people, but the camp seemed empty.

"Where are — " The girl cut off her words mid-sentence when Frost held up a hand to silence her. The old gunslinger leaned forward, resting his hands on the horn of his saddle, and listened intently. The whistling of the wind, the rustling of the deep grass, and the clicking of the bats were the only sounds that reached their ears.

"There's no people," Ana said.

"No, there is not," answered the old man.

"Where are they?"

The old gunslinger turned and faced the girl. "*Be wary then. Best safety lies in fear.* You stay here with the wolf."

"You're not leaving me." A command, not a question.

"You'll be safe with the wolf," the old man said. "Safer with him than you would with me. I'll be back directly."

"Where are you going?"

"To see where all the people went."

Nineteen

The Gunslinger

Hamish Frost climbed from the saddle, letting the reins drop to the dusty ground. His painted horse stood motionless and would remain so until he retook the reins.

Stepping lightly, the old gunslinger breached the outer ring of encircled wagons. He saw no people. No oxen or horses to pull the wagons. No livestock. No life of any kind. No birds. Not even insects. The stillness and unnatural silence that greeted him within the abandoned pilgrim camp was unsettling. Even the chirp of the circling bats at the top of the Chalkstones did not reach his ears. The smell of death hung in the air, like a fog that would not lift. He pulled his bandana up over his nose, but it did little to curb the stench.

He pushed back the canvas covering of a wagon and peeked inside. Save for some folded bedding and blankets, the wagon was near empty. Pilgrims had been its cargo. He pushed aside the blankets and found some cookware beneath. Cast-iron pots and skillets. The next wagon was similar. Some bedding, cookery, but also books of scripture.

In the second ring of wagons, he found more blankets, as well as saddles, bridles, and various leatherworks. An anvil, hammers, tongs, and other blacksmith's tools. Saws, chisels, and planes for woodworking. Another contained what looked to be parts of a machine, a printing press perhaps. Still no sign of people or livestock.

Within the innermost ring, he found the pilgrims' food stores. Wagons filled with dried fruits and vegetables. Salt pork and venison jerky. Sacks of flour and ground corn. Barrels of water and jugs of distilled spirits. Beehives dripping with honey, but no bees living or dead.

He moved on to the canvas tents inside the third ring of wagons. The tents had been set up in groupings of five. There were easily two dozen groupings. This wagon train had accommodated at least a hundred souls moving westward. But none seemed to be here now. Where had they gone? What had befallen them?

Inside the tents, he found more blankets. Clothing. Boots and shoes. And weapons. Pistols and long guns left laying on the blankets. Loaded. Extra ammunition nearby.

He found the cold remains of what had been a campfire in the center of the circle of tents. The fire had burned itself out a long time back. Whatever had happened here happened days ago.

On the ground beside the dead fire, he found a child's doll. Corncob body, a dress of painted husks, and corn silk for hair.

Frost couldn't make sense of the scene before him. The unmistakable stench of death was in the air, but he had yet to find any bodies. Where had they gone? And why had they left behind all their supplies? All their food? Why abandon their weapons?

Wagon trains were often attacked by raiders, but this one had been positioned with defensive precision. They had weapons to repel attackers, but there was no sign the weapons had been used. No sign at all of an attack. If raiders were responsible for the disappearance of the pilgrims, then the scene before him would look quite different. Arrows and spears would've shredded the tents and covered wagons. There would be blood. On the ground. In the tents. In the wagons. On the blankets. Bodies would be scattered like leaves beneath a sycamore tree. The men, boys, and older women would all have been slaughtered. Scalped and tortured. Their hearts ripped from their chests. The girls and the younger women would have been taken as prizes. Slaves. The children would have been taken for food. Younger bodies were softer, the meat more tender.

The camp would have been ransacked, perhaps burned. Certainly looted. An anvil and a printing press wouldn't have garnered interest, but no raiding party would have left behind the blankets and the honey. The dried meats and grains would have been taken. All the food wagons would likely have been driven away. And raiders would've never left weapons — loaded guns — laying on the ground.

Frost's introspection was interrupted by a flash of motion from a nearby tent. His hands moved so quickly his sidearm revolvers seemed to appear magically in his grip. He stood motionless, searching with his eyes, but saw nothing. He slipped silently around the side of a nearby tent. He found the spot where he had seen movement but could see no tracks on the dusty ground.

The smell of death intensified as if growing closer. Frost circled around another tent and saw the movement again. A small, indistinct shape drifting through the white canvases. He adjusted his angle of pursuit and picked up his pace. He rounded another tent, revolvers leveled and ready to fire.

A young child stood in the open space inside a circle of tents. A girl. Much younger than the one he had rescued from the mountain man. Fair-skinned with flaxen hair and pale freckles dotting her nose. She was barefoot and wore a simple cotton shift. Night clothes. Cradled in her arms was the same corncob doll Frost had seen on the ground by the remains of the fire.

The girl looked up at him, large cerulean eyes full of palpable sadness.

Frost holstered his weapons with exaggerated slowness. He tugged the bandana from his nose, letting the girl see his face. "I mean you no harm, child. Where are your people?"

The girl stared at him in silence.

"Where did everyone go?"

The girl's lips parted and her mouth moved, but the words lagged. As if they rolled from her tongue and circled the globe before finding their way to Frost's ears. The girl's mouth was closed by the time he finally heard the words.

"Vi er døde. Vi er alle døde."

The girl's visage flickered. Frost blinked, and the girl faded from view as if she had never been there at all. The corncob doll lay on the ground.

"She said 'We are dead. We are all dead.'"

Frost spun around, revolvers again in his hands.

Standing behind him was a trail-weary man in a dusty long coat. A light-skinned black man, perhaps a mulatto. His face was haggard, his eyes alert but heavy-lidded from too many days on the trail and too many sleepless nights. He had a six-gun holstered on his right hip, a large knife in a sheath over his left, and a rifle slung over his shoulder. He stood in front of a chestnut-colored horse, the reins in his hands. Five other horses were tethered to the chestnut. One unencumbered, but four of the five had the body of a dead man slung across their back.

"Ay, but to die, and go we know not where," said Frost. He holstered his weapons and gave a nod of greeting to the man. "Ozymandias Hayes. Didn't know you spoke the Nordic tongue. Was that Swedish?"

"Norwegian," said the black man. "And thank you for not killing me."

"You'd be wise not to sneak up on me like that again."

"I didn't think it was possible to catch Hamish Frost unawares."

"I'm getting old," said Frost. "What brings you to the Chalkstones, Mr. Hayes?"

"Headed to the cavalry outpost."

"Bold of you to shortcut through forbidden lands alone."

"Time is of the essence. Felt I had little choice."

"What's the hurry? Your bounties aren't getting any deader. All this time I thought I was smelling dead pilgrims, but I see now that was just your cargo. Who've you got there?"

"Enoch Munn's gang."

"You took them all yourself? That's impressive."

"Not without a price. They killed my partner."

"Short time seems long in sorrow's sharp sustaining." Frost doffed his hat. "My condolences."

"Thank you. He was a poor manhunter and even poorer companion, but we rode together and that means something."

Frost could see the manhunter looking at the wrapped wound on his arm, the pus seeping through the fabric. "A small scratch," the old gunslinger said. "It'll heal."

Hayes nodded.

Frost noted the scarred-over rope burns surrounding Hayes' throat. "You are well, I take it?"

"Weary, but well," said Hayes. "Forgive a beggarly question, but you wouldn't happen to have any food on you? I haven't eaten in days."

"I have none, but there are wagons full of salt pork and jerky. Help yourself to all you can carry. Hell, hitch your horses and take a wagon full. If the ghost child spoke true, the pilgrims won't be coming back for it. You didn't happen across any bodies, did you?"

"My search has been cursory, but I've seen none. It's as if they've turned to dust and blown away with the wind."

"That's as good an explanation as any." Frost sighed, scratched his beard. "I always took you for a man of science, yet you don't seem too taken aback by the apparition or her dis-corporation in front of our very eyes."

"Recent experiences have shifted my perspective."

The old gunslinger nodded but didn't ask him to elaborate. "Experience has a way of doing that. Forgive me, but curiosity has always been my weakness. May I ask why you travel with bodies? The heads alone would have sufficed to claim a bounty. Even if the stench would be only slightly lessened."

"A question I've asked myself often over the past week. The truth is, I couldn't bring myself to behead them. It seems I found my limits."

Frost considered this. *"The will is infinite. The execution confin'd.* I'm surprised you've made it this far and had no problem with wolves."

"They menaced me for days." Hayes tilted his head toward the unencumbered horse. "But not after I fed them the fifth. My only regret was it occurred in the dark of night and I couldn't see which body I had given them until it was too late. Had I planned it better I would not have given them Enoch Munn. His bounty was twice the others combined."

Frost smiled. "At least the bastard met a fitting end. I would have done for him long ago should our paths have ever crossed."

"What of your wolf?" asked Hayes.

"He is not mine. I have no say in the Shadow Wolf's comings and goings. But he's here. On the other side of the Chalkstones. With a girl we liberated from a mountain man named Shadrach Brown."

"I know of this man."

"He had a bounty?"

"Indeed. But your use of the past tense tells me it will go uncollected."

"Didn't occur to me he might've been wanted until just now," said Frost with a smile. "But, as it turns out, there was little left of him in the end. Certainly not enough to collect on. The wolf got him."

The manhunter looked off into the distance. "Where are you headed, Mr. Frost?"

"Denver City. Don't care for the place. Little more than a jumped-up miner's camp, but I should be able to put the girl on a coach there. The plains are no place for a child alone."

"She has no kin?"

Frost shook his head. "None she knows of. I have friends back east who'll see to her care."

"If you can stomach the smell, you're welcomed to travel with me until our paths diverge."

"A kind offer, but I'm afraid we have a stopover 'tween here and there. A brief sojourn, I hope, though the length of stay is beyond my control."

"There's something beyond the control of Hamish Frost?" Hayes said with a smile.

"I told you, I'm getting old."

Hayes looked around the camp. "Seems we'll have no answer to the mystery. It saddens me to think they came all this way for a better life. Left their homeland, crossed the ocean, walked hundreds of miles behind a wagon, only to disappear and never be heard from again."

"They didn't leave here by choice," said the old gunslinger. "They didn't walk away from their food, their tools, their weapons. Didn't leave all their worldly possessions behind. Not after bringing them all this way. *'O wretched state! O bosom black as death!* Something befell these pilgrims. Something dark and full of malice crossed their path. There's bad medicine here."

Twenty

The Wing-Thief

Black Wing approached the overturned wagon, tomahawk in hand. He stepped lightly, stealthily, prepared for combat, but the hulking creature was nowhere to be found. The scattered belongings of the settler family remained where he had last seen them, but their bodies were gone. Torn bits and pieces of their clothing and dark wet stains seeping into the soil were the only sign they had ever been there at all. The dead mule that had floated in the water's edge had vanished as well.

Among the chaotic tracks that peppered the soft ground, the wing-thief could discern two deep, yet mismatched, footprints near where each of the bodies had lain. He followed the tracks back to the river's edge, could see where they disappeared into the water.

"Where are the bodies?" he asked, more to himself than to the holy man who stood silently behind him.

Antelope Eyes surveyed the scene, his face absent of emotion.

"There were five of them. And a mule," said Black Wing.

"It ate them."

"Nothing could have done that in so short a time."

"Yes," said Antelope Eyes. "It could."

Black Wing turned, looked at the holy man. "You know more than you have said. You know this creature, don't you? You knew I had seen it before I ever mentioned it to you. This was the reason you told me to fly. You knew it was here. You knew I would see it. You wanted me to see it."

The holy man walked to his horse, vaulted onto its back. "Get back on your horse. We need to move. Where there are two painted warriors, there are likely more. It is not safe to tarry."

"Answer my questions."

"I heard no questions. Only accusations."

"Did you know I would see this creature?"

"Get on your horse."

"I did ask a question that time, but I heard no answer."

"Get on your horse. That is my answer."

"If you had seen this creature, seen what it was, what it had done, what it was doing, then you would want to kill it as badly as I do."

"I have seen the creature, but it is not here now and we are wasting time."

"We have nothing but time."

"You are a fool if you believe that."

"Enough of your games! Enough of your tests! Tell me what you are hiding from me!"

"Get on your horse. We need to leave here."

"You leave. I am going to find and kill this vile creature."

"How? How will you find it?"

"I can track it."

"The tracks lead into the river. Will you track it through the water?"

"I will borrow a bird. I'll follow the river. It has to come out of the water sometime."

"Upstream or down?" asked Antelope Eyes.

"Down."

"Are you sure?"

"The current is too strong upstream."

"For a man, perhaps," said Antelope Eyes.

"Then I will fly upstream and down until I find it."

"And then what? You find the creature and then you will kill it while in the body of a bird? Scratch it to death? Peck it? No. You'll fly back and claim your body, your weapons, then hurry to the spot and the creature will have disappeared once again. This is the errand of a fool. Get on your horse. We need to leave here."

"You know this creature," said Black Wing with certainty. "You wanted me to see it, but you won't tell me why."

"What I want is for you to get on your horse."

"And now that I have seen it, you wish me to leave it alone. Why? What is this creature?"

Antelope Eyes sighed. "I will answer the questions that I can, but only if we leave this place now."

The wing-thief looked around. "Is the creature still here? Somewhere hiding? Watching us? Is that why you want us to leave? You don't want me to see it again? You don't want me to kill it?"

"I want to leave because people shit themselves when they die and I have a sensitive nose. The bodies may no longer be here, but their stink lingers. It smells even worse here than it did back at the arroyo with the dead warriors."

"Then leave," said Black Wing.

"I will. Follow if you wish." The holy man put his heels to his horse's flank, and the horse took off away from the river, away from the overturned wagon and the residue of murder.

Black Wing watched him riding away. He looked back at the overturned wagon, the settlers' scattered belongings, the river. He wondered if he had guessed correctly. Was the creature still there, lurking just beneath the surface of the murky water? Watching him? He stared into the water, searching for any sign of movement at or beneath the surface. He saw none.

He lifted his tomahawk, shook it at the water. "If you are watching me, beast, know that I have not forgotten you and if I should see you again..." He let the words trail off without finishing the sentence. He waited a few moments more, then mounted his horse and hurried after the holy man.

As the sun sank low in the afternoon sky, they reached sloping hills dotted with boulders and heavily forested with spruce, pines, and aspens. Just before sunset, they found a ravine with a sparkling stream fed by runoff from the melting snows of higher elevations.

"We'll camp here," said Antelope Eyes. It was the first words he'd spoken since they'd ridden away from the overturned wagon.

Black Wing found a rocky overhang that would provide them shelter for the night. He gathered some fallen tree branches, made a small fire, then spread the buffalo skin on the ground while the holy man watered the horses in the stream. The sun slipped below the tips of the distant peaks and the long shadow cast by the steep edges of the ravine enshrouded them in darkness even before the sun had fully set.

Antelope Eyes sat and warmed his hands by the fire, staring into the flames. The wing-thief joined him, sitting across the fire. The holy man stared into the flames for so long, Black Wing wondered if he had entranced himself.

After a long silence, the holy man lowered his eyes, looked away from the dancing flames.

"It is called Wechuge," he said.

Black Wing looked at him. "The creature?"

Antelope Eyes nodded. "That is its name. Wechuge. It is ancient. As old as the gods. Perhaps older. A creature that climbed into our world through a crack in the rock that separates us from the night world."

"The night world, monsters that climb through the cracks, those are just stories told to children."

The holy man smiled knowingly. "Your eyes have been opened. You are allowed to believe that no longer. Your eyes saw it."

"No. The pigeon's eyes saw it."

Antelope Eyes nodded. "Yes. And that is why you are here now. Why you are still alive."

"Explain."

"You confused it. Had you been in your own body and not the body of the pigeon, then you would not have seen Wechuge's true form."

"True form?" asked Black Wing. "It can appear in other forms?"

"It takes many forms. It can appear as anyone it has slain."

"Is that why it killed the settlers? To steal their appearance?"

"No. It killed because it was hungry. It killed to eat. It kills to sustain itself."

Black Wing considered this. "I saw its head change. One moment I was looking at the creature's head, the next there was a white man's head on the creature's body. It looked at me, then it changed back."

"As I said, you confused it. It saw through your disguise. It knew you were more than a pigeon, but it could not tell if you were a man who had borrowed the body of a bird, or a bird who had borrowed the spirit of a man. When its appearance shifted, when the white man's head appeared as it did, that was a reflex of sorts. It did not know how best to appear to you. It killed the settlers and their mule for food, but once digested, they became a part of Wechuge. The creature can now appear as any of them. It can now be seen as the mule or any of the settlers. Wechuge eats more than the body. Wechuge eats the soul. It consumes all. Bodies, faces, memories, voices. All that its victims were, become a part of Wechuge."

"But its true form...?"

"Is what you saw. What no one else sees and lives to tell."

"Why did you want me to see it?"

"Not me. The gods. The gods wanted you to see Wechuge. Want you to understand it. What it is. Why it does what it does."

"It kills. It eats. It steals souls."

Antelope Eyes looked into the flames again. "You saw the tracks by the river, yes?"

The wing-thief nodded. "They were mismatched. One was larger than the other. Shaped differently."

"Wechuge is not of this world. Its body cannot survive outside of the night world. It exists in a state of perpetual rot. Limbs, hands, feet, everything except its head, rots and falls away. Wechuge must replace them. Often. Or it will die."

"Replace? How does it replace a limb?"

"It eats. Wechuge is a patchwork creature. A mass of dead and decaying parts. That is why its feet, its legs, its arms, and hands were mismatched. It is a melange of those it has killed and consumed."

"And it can appear as anyone it has eaten? In face and voice?"

"Yes."

"Memories? It gains the memories of those it eats?"

"Yes."

"Then how would one know? How would you know if you ever saw it? In the morning, how would you know I am me, and not Wechuge appearing as me after murdering and eating me in the night?"

Antelope Eyes smiled weakly. "It is best not to think about it too much."

But that was all the wing-thief could think about. "Why wouldn't you let me kill it?"

"Are you so sure you could?" said Antelope Eyes. "Even if you found it. Even if you could see through its disguise and recognize its true form, what makes you think you could kill it? Wechuge is not of this world. It is ancient. It has killed tens of thousands in its long life."

"Then why show it to me? Why show me the creature? Why explain what it is and then tell me to put it out of my mind?"

"Best not to think about it."

"No. There is more you are not telling me. You don't want me to kill it, do you?" said Black Wing. "You wanted me to see it, to know what it is, but you don't want me to kill it. You didn't even want me to try. Why is that?"

The holy man said, "There are many things you do not know. Some you will learn. Some you will never know. I reveal what the gods tell me to reveal. All else, you must learn for yourself."

Antelope Eyes said no more. He ate some venison jerky, then lay down on the buffalo skin, his back to Black Wing, and fell quickly asleep.

The wing-thief sat by the fire, watching the flames dance, hoping to see what the holy man had seen there, but he saw only fire and smoke. He stood and kicked out the fire. He gathered his tomahawk and sat down on the buffalo skin beside the holy man. He let his eyes adjust to the darkness while listening to the flowing stream, the insects in the trees. The moon had risen, casting a bluish glow and creating deep shadows in the ravine. Black Wing looked to the horses, then all around him, identifying each rock, each tree, each tuft of grass. He accounted for every shadow.

He did not sleep that night.

Twenty-One

The Gunslinger

HAMISH FROST HELPED THE manhunter Ozymandias Hayes load his cargo of corpses into the back of a wagon and then hitch his horses to the wagon's rig. Hayes gathered some salt pork and jerky, filled a couple of canteens from the barreled water, and helped himself to a jug of distilled liquor.

"I have a long ride ahead," said the manhunter. "And enough daylight remaining to put a few miles between me and this place before I have to make camp for the night."

"Then don't let me hold you up," said Frost.

Hayes nodded and shook the old gunslinger's hand. "Would that it were under better circumstances, but it was good to see you again, Mr. Frost."

The old man doffed his hat. *"And whether we shall meet again I know not. Therefore our everlasting farewell take: For ever, and for ever, farewell, If we do meet again, why, we shall smile; If not, why then, this parting was well made."* He brushed the stringy white hair from his pale face. "Safe travels, Mr. Hayes."

The manhunter shook the reins and the wagon filled with the bodies of outlaws lumbered away. Frost watched for a moment, then considered his next move. The mystery of what befell the pilgrims still called out for an answer. The girl Ana would be fine under the protection of the Shadow Wolf and the old woman wasn't going anywhere. She'd chastise him for taking so long to answer her call, but once he explained, she'd be as interested in the bad medicine afoot here as he was.

The old gunslinger mounted his horse and rode the perimeter of the camp in ever-widening circles, searching for some sign of the pilgrims' passing. This many people walking away from their camp en masse should have left a trail any greenhorn could follow, but he saw no evidence of that. At last, he found a faint trail leading away from the campsite, one he almost dismissed at first. Then he realized at what he was actually looking. One hundred-plus pilgrims, barefoot, had marched away from the camp in a single file line, each stepping precisely in the tracks left by the one in front of them, leaving only a single faint set of prints on the hard-packed prairie floor.

His curiosity piqued, the old gunslinger followed. A few miles north of the campsite, the trail led to a large spot of heavily trod, discolored ground, a muddy stain seeping into the prairie floor. Flies buzzed about in great swarms and dozens of buzzards pecked about in confusion, attracted by the smell of blood but unable to locate the carrion that should be accompanying it. The coppery tang in the air was so pronounced and the stain on the ground so large, Frost could only surmise that every man, woman, and child in the wagon company must have bled out on this spot. He realized he had perhaps misjudged the timeline of events. He had assumed from the state of the camp that it had been abandoned for days, perhaps weeks. But the stain on the ground was wet, the blood relatively fresh.

The sheer volume of blood spilled here confirmed the ghost child's proclamation. They were all dead. But who or what had killed them? And why had they marched in formation to their deaths? Frost wrinkled his nose, catching a whiff of another scent carried on the air. Faint compared to the blood stench, but unmistakable. Ammonia. He climbed down from his horse. On the ground, almost invisible against the wet-stained earth, he found dark, elongated pellets. Guano. Bat-shit. And a lot of it.

He looked back at the Chalkstones. The sun had dipped lower. Night would fall fast. The bats were already pouring from the limestone caves atop the chalkstones, darkening the sky. Had the bats been feasting on the blood of the pilgrims?

The old gunslinger got back on his horse and followed the tracks. There was no single file this time, but rather a trampled mass of prints leading from the stain. The sun set and then slid below the horizon. A new moon rose in a cloudless sky, casting the prairie in a pale blue light. He rode on through the night, following the mass of tracks. As best he could tell, they had marched without rest. Or if they'd rested, they'd done so standing in place, for the tracks showed no sign of slowing down.

He lost the trail the next morning when he came upon a freshly churned swath of terrain almost a mile wide. A massive bison herd had passed this way, their stampeding hooves trampling vegetation and completely obscuring the tracks he had been following. On the other side of the bison's passage, the trail went cold. He searched for another few hours, but unable to pick the track back up again, he decided it was time to turn around and reunite with the girl and the Shadow Wolf. The mystery of the pilgrims would remain unsolved.

Halfway back to the Chalkstones, Frost saw the boy. Shirtless and sitting all alone on the plain. The boy wore only a breechclout that looked in dire need of a washing. His inky black hair, greasy and unkempt, was coated with a liberal spattering of reddish-brown dust. His face was smudged with dirt and a stream of snot ran from both nostrils, dribbling over his lips. He didn't seem to care or notice. The boy sat, knees bent, legs tucked beneath his body in front of a large hole, the entrance to a labyrinth of prairie dog tunnels.

Between the boy and the hole leading to the tunnels sat a large toad, doing its level best to escape the boy's machinations. But with each movement the toad made, the boy would drop a hand to block its path or swat its hindquarters, rolling it over onto its back.

Frost recognized the boy, even though he hadn't seen him in many years. He knew to approach with great care. He reined in, bringing his painted horse to a halt more than two dozen paces from where the boy sat. Frost flung a leg over the saddle and dismounted. He let the reins drop, but the paint wasn't so willing to stand in place this time. Its legs twitched and hooves danced, almost as if fighting the urge to bolt. Frost patted the animal on the neck and made soft, soothing sounds in a hushed voice. The horse lowered its head in submission, though Frost could see the tension remained in the animal's legs.

Without taking his eyes off of the boy, he unbuckled his gun belt, leaving the twin six-guns with the elephant ivory handles holstered, then draped the belt over his saddle. He doffed his floppy hat, shook out the long, white hair falling just past his shoulders, and placed the hat on top of the gun belt. Hands up, palms open and fingers splayed, he walked slowly, deliberately towards the boy.

The boy never looked up. If he knew Frost was there, he seemed completely indifferent to his presence. Frost paused, stood in silence, watching the boy mistreat the poor toad. The morning sun bore down hard and bright. Except for the Chalkstones in the distance, the prairie was flat as a flapjack, stretching to the horizon in all directions. A flock of passenger pigeons appeared in the east, darkening the sky for a few moments as they passed overhead. Pleased to have a brief respite from the sun, Frost watched the flock disappear into the distance. The boy seemed oblivious to the passing shade. He continued his torturing of the toad.

Frost shuffled his feet, then softly cleared his throat.

"I know you're there, Whiteskin," said the boy. "I just don't care."

"You looked busy," said Frost. "I didn't want to disturb you."

"So you were just going to stand there all day with your dick in your hand?"

"How poor are they that have not patience," said Frost.

"I think you quote Shakespeare just because you know it annoys everyone," said the boy. He looked up from the toad for the first time since Frost had arrived. "Sonofabitch, Whiteskin! You got old as shit!"

"That happens to us mere mortals," said the old gunslinger.

"Still pretending you're one of those, huh?"

"Just because I'm not dead yet, doesn't mean I won't be someday."

"Where's your wolf?" asked the boy.

"He's not *my* wolf. He comes and goes as he pleases with no leave from me."

"I forget sometimes which one of you is pet to the other."

Frost let the insult go unanswered. The last thing he wanted was to provoke the boy. He had gone to great pains to avoid that circumstance.

"Okay, I'll bite," the boy sighed. "Why are you here?"

Frost chose his words carefully. "I was surprised to see you."

"Why?" asked the boy. "You've always been able to see us."

"I meant only that I hadn't *expected* to see you, but now that I have, I believe this might be a propitious meeting."

"How so?"

"I was following the trail of some pilgrims who wandered away from their campsite. They would have walked right past here. You didn't happen to see them, did you?"

The boy shrugged. "You white eyes all look alike to me."

"I have reason to believe they could be dead."

"Yeah, well, shit happens. And you're boring me," said the boy, returning his attention to the toad. "It was probably raiders who killed them."

"Under normal circumstances, I would be inclined to agree with you. But there are circumstances involved here that go far beyond the normal. There were no bodies left behind and none of their goods or gear was taken."

"You think all red men are thieves?"

"I think all murderers are thieves. Taking possessions pales next to taking a life. If this were a raider attack, they wouldn't have left the camp unransacked. And they wouldn't have killed them all when there were women and slaves to be taken."

"What makes you think they're all dead?" asked the boy.

"Because I found enough blood to paint a small town."

"I'm confused. You said you were following them. That they would have walked past here. Now you're saying they died at the campsite. Which is it? Are they dead, or did they walk away?"

"Both, I fear," said Frost.

The boy laughed. A string of mucus stretched across his open lips. "I think you got old and now you're touched in the fucking head."

"I found bat-shit all over the ground where they bled out. I've never known bats to be blood-eaters, but that seems to be the case here. Would you know anything of that?

The boy looked down as Frost spoke, turning his attention back to the toad. It lay on its back, immobile, four feet in the air. The boy's hands rested palms down on the ground, one on either side of the toad. After a long moment, Frost realized the boy was not moving, frozen in place. The toad squirmed, trying to flip back over and escape. Still, the boy remained unmoving. Frost noticed a puddle of urine spreading from between the boy's legs, soaking into the dusty ground.

"Did you just piss yourself?" Frost asked.

The boy looked up quickly as if snapped from a deep trance. Tears flowed from his eyes and rolled over his dust-covered cheeks. He picked up a hand and slammed it down with great force on the squirming toad. Then scooped up the dead toad and popped it into his mouth, swallowing it whole. Frost could see the boy's throat expand unnaturally wide as the bulge of the toad slid down his esophagus.

The boy's eyes changed from deep brown to yellow-orange, his pupils — almost invisible against the dark of his irises before — were now narrow vertical slits. Nictitating membranes blinked across his eyes. Scales spread across the boy's skin as his arms pressed against his sides, fusing with his torso. A thin, forked tongue flicked across his lips, wiping away the snot that still streamed from his nose. The boy's legs melded together as his body undulated from side to side, leaving the soiled breechclout behind on the ground.

In one fluid motion, the boy who was no longer a boy, bent at the waist and dove headfirst into the hole in front of him. The last thing Frost saw of the god the people of the plains called *Snake*, was the repeating diamond pattern of his scales and the great bone-colored keratin rattle — almost two dozen buttons long — at the end of his tail, disappearing into the shadows of the hole.

Twenty-Two

The Wing-Thief

The wing-thief and the holy man made camp in a small open area amidst a copse of pine and oak along the river they had been following. Black Wing tied off the horses, gathered some dry wood for the fire, and scraped some pine bark for kindling. Antelope Eyes sat on the buffalo skin they shared for a bed and watched the wing-thief work.

With the fire roaring, Black Wing stood and stared up at the millions of milky stars twinkling in the vibrant canopy overhead.

"I'll take the first watch," said the wing-thief.

"We need no watch tonight," said Antelope Eyes. "Come lay with me."

Black Wing raised an eyebrow. "No watch? Do you know something I do not?"

"I know many things you do not."

"We are in unfamiliar country. We just fled from painted warriors who tried to kill us, and there is a creature roaming about that wears the bodies of those it eats. But we need no watch while we sleep? That is your contention?"

"You killed the painted warriors, remember?"

"There could be more."

"Bah," said the holy man dismissively.

"And what of the creature?"

"The creature will do what the creature will do."

Black Wing stared at him, mouth agape. "The creature will do what the creature will do? What is that supposed to mean?"

Antelope Eyes smiled. "I told you before, the future has been shown to me. I have seen my end. There is no need for a watch. It is a beautiful night. We can both sleep well."

"Is this more of my test from the gods?"

The holy man shrugged. "I'm tired and would like to sleep. I would enjoy your company, but do as you will."

Antelope Eyes rolled over, giving his back to the wing-thief, and pretended to sleep. Black Wing had learned to tell the difference between when Antelope Eyes was actually sleeping and when he was only pretending. The pronounced rise and fall of his chest as he drew breath, the unconscious twitching of his fingers, the movement of his eyes beneath his lids were all absent when he pretended.

Black Wing suspected the holy man was waiting for him to lie down and drift off to sleep so that he might take another midnight walk or perhaps a night swim. Black Wing was determined to prevent that or at the very least be certain that the holy man did not walk alone. He lay down next to Antelope Eyes, believing that when the holy man did inevitably arise in the middle of the night, he would sleep lightly enough to wake and follow after him. But the days spent riding and the nights watching over Antelope Eyes were catching up to him. His light sleep quickly turned to deep slumber.

When he awoke some time later, he found — as he knew he would — the holy man no longer lying on the buffalo skin. Black Wing searched the surrounding darkness, scanning the shadows of the trees. He could see no sign of the holy man. He listened, but heard nothing out of the ordinary. He wasn't sure how long he had been asleep, but reasoned, based on the state of the fire, it could not have been long. He would not need to borrow the body of a bird. Antelope Eyes could not have gotten far and the night was bright enough that Black Wing could track him.

His expectation was to find the holy man near or perhaps swimming in the river, but to his surprise, the tracks led in the opposite direction, over a small, grassy hill lined with boulders to the south. At the base of the hill was another thicket of tall, lodgepole pines. Black Wing followed the holy man's tracks into the thicket and found him standing in a small clearing. The starlight illuminated the gap in the trees and the holy man stood enveloped by the lavender glow of his medicine. But he was not alone.

A woman, tall and raven-haired, barefoot and wearing only a long tunic stitched from tanned buckskin, stood in front of the holy man. The winds were still in the pines, but the woman's hair shimmied, flowing as if tossed about by winds that did not exist. A pale purple aura surrounded her.

Black Wing slipped behind a tree, craning his neck to look around the trunk. The woman was startlingly beautiful; her face both familiar and strange at the same time. Black Wing could hear their voices as they spoke, but he could not understand their strange language.

After a moment, the woman stopped speaking and extended her hand, gently tracing her fingertips along the side of the holy man's face. A gesture of tenderness and high regard. The woman dropped her hand and Antelope Eyes bowed his head, standing before her in silence. The woman spoke a few more words of the strange language, then smiled. A heartbreakingly wistful smile. Her aura intensified and she slowly faded from view, like a mist evaporating when the sun breaks through the clouds.

The woman had long disappeared by the time the holy man lifted his head. He turned slowly, looking directly at Black Wing as if he had known the wing-thief was standing there the entire time.

Black Wing stepped from behind the tree and faced Antelope Eyes. "Who was she?"

The holy man shook his head. "You're still asking the wrong question."

"We've played that game. Just tell me who she is."

"You will know who she is when she introduces herself to you. You do not need to know now."

"Why not?"

"Still the wrong question. What is the question you should be asking?"

"Just tell me," said Black Wing in exasperation.

"Ask the question."

Black Wing sighed. "I don't need to ask the question. I know the answer. It's me. You were talking about me."

The holy man smiled, a smile not unlike the one on the woman's face as she faded from view. He walked to the wing-thief, reached out a hand, placing his palm softly against Black Wing's cheek, just as the woman had done to him moments earlier.

"No," said Antelope Eyes. "Not this time. We talked about you the last time she and I spoke. This time, we were talking about *me*." The holy man dropped his hand, lowered his eyes, and walked past Black Wing without another word.

The next morning, they broke camp and continued following the river upstream. Late in the afternoon, the trees grew ever thicker and taller until they came upon a spot where beavers had dammed the river, controlling the flow and flooding the forest, creating a large but shallow lake.

"We'll camp here," said the holy man. "Perhaps tomorrow we'll see if we can find a spot upstream for us to cross."

Black Wing tied off the horses and was gathering wood for the fire when he heard a loud shout from Antelope Eyes. Fearing the worst, he rushed back to the campsite only to find the holy man doubled over laughing.

"What's so funny?" he asked.

Antelope Eyes pointed to a nearby cluster of squat, bushy trees, heavy with small, maroon-colored berries. "Chokecherries," he said, still laughing.

Black Wing had eaten more than his share of chokecherries in his younger days as a scrounging wanderer, though he had never liked the taste. Too sour and sometimes bitter. For the holy man, however, chokecherries were candy, a treat he could never resist.

After picking and eating his fill, he waddled over and laid down on the buffalo skin while Black Wing built a fire. "I left a few for you," Antelope Eyes said, rubbing his belly. "But you should hurry. I'm going back for more as soon as my stomach settles."

"You can have them all. Just remember this when you're shitting liquid for days."

The holy man waved a hand dismissively and laughed. "I would eat every chokecherry on earth if I could fit them in my belly."

"We can pick a few handfuls to take with us." To the wing-thief's surprise, Antelope Eyes didn't acknowledge the offer. Instead, the holy man tucked his hands behind his head and stared up at the darkening sky.

"If the lake is not too shallow, I think I will go for a swim later tonight. I would ask you to join me, but I know you do not care for night swimming."

"Thank you for the warning this time," said Black Wing. "At least I will know where to look for you tonight when I wake up and you are not there."

Antelope Eyes laughed again and sat up. "Well," he said slowly, "since you will not swim with me, then you must sing me a song."

"Are you all right?"

"I have never been better. I have a belly full of chokecherries and now I want to be entertained. Sing for me."

"You have never asked me to sing before."

"I am asking now."

"I am not a good singer," said the wing-thief.

"You sing when you are in the body of a bird. Sing for me now."

"The birds sing. Not me. Birds sing. They fly and they sing. That is them, not me."

"I'm waiting."

"I know no songs."

"Everyone knows at least one song, and I'll decide if you are a good singer."

Black Wing protested. "I don't know any songs. You forget, I am a wanderer who never had the benefit of a tribe to teach me songs."

"I forget nothing. And you are not being truthful. Everyone knows a song. Everyone."

"I don't."

"You do. Now sing."

The wing-thief lowered his head and sighed. He cleared his throat and began to sing. Softly, barely above a whisper.

"Louder please."

Black Wing raised his voice, but only a little.

The holy man closed his eyes and listened. After a few moments, he joined in and sang along with the wing-thief. His voice was rich, melodious, and the song that came from his throat drowned out Black Wing's whispered bleatings.

When the song was finished, Antelope Eyes opened his eyes and smiled at Black Wing. "You were right. You are not a good singer." He laughed heartily. Then said, "But it is a good song and I thank you for singing it to me."

"Should I be surprised you knew the words?"

"I know many songs. Tell me the story. How did you come to know this song?"

"When I was younger and in need of food or shelter, I would sometimes barter with people I would come across. I would borrow the body of a bird to help hunters locate deer or elk or mountain sheep. When the hunts were successful, they would sometimes ask me to stay for a while. I would hear the women teaching songs to the children. That song of friendship I heard so often I couldn't help but memorize it."

"A good song and a good story." Antelope Eyes stood. "Now I have something for you." The holy man went to his horse and fished around in his satchel. He brought out a canteen made from a deer's bladder. He carefully untied the end of the bladder and took a sip, then offered it to Black Wing. "Here. Try this."

Black Wing suspected he knew what was inside the canteen, and one sniff confirmed it. Holy men sometimes kept with them for ceremonial purposes a fermented drink made from wild plums and honey. Black Wing had avoided strong drinks ever since that time as a boy when he stole a bladder of dark beer from his father and drank it with his friends. It made him sicker than he had ever been and caused him to stay up all night vomiting.

When the wing-thief hesitated, Antelope Eyes helped himself to another hearty swallow. "Last chance or I drink it all," said the holy man, once again holding out the bladder for Black Wing.

The wing-thief took a small sip, but he found it — like the chokecherries — too bitter for his tastes.

The holy man laughed again. "It's an acquired taste, I suppose. Take another drink, see if you can acquire it."

Black Wing did as he was told. His throat burned as he swallowed and his head swam like he had spun around too quickly.

"Another," said Antelope Eyes, laughing.

The wing-thief took one more sip. His vision blurred, then went double. Time seemed to slow as shapes danced in and out of his vision. Antelope Eyes leaned closer to him, talking to him, but the words were garbled and unintelligible. Black Wing tried to speak, but found his tongue thick, unwieldy and incapable of forming words. While trying to figure out what had happened to his senses, why his eyes, ears and tongue were failing him, he realized he was no longer standing. He lay on his back with the world spinning all around him. It was a strange sensation, he thought, and then everything went black.

Twenty-Three

The Manhunter

Ozymandias Hayes was ordered to stop as he approached the outpost's front gate. A wall of lodgepole pines ringed the circumference of the outpost, serving as a fortified barrier against attack or invasion from raiders or aggrieved native peoples whose territory had been appropriated in the outpost's creation. The pines were cut to a uniform height, stripped of bark, chiseled to sharp points at the top, and driven deep into the prairie soil. In the distance, Hayes could see jagged, snow-capped mountain peaks rising above the heavily forested foothills. A dense fog had settled at the base of the trees; the haze making it impossible to tell where the plains ended and the rolling hills began.

A steady, uneventful morning of bouncing along in the buckboard he had commandeered from the abandoned pilgrim campsite had brought him at long last to his destination. He had gotten six blessed hours of sleep on a patch of soft ground and tender grass beneath the wagon the night before. Then a breakfast comprising the last of the pilgrim's salt pork, washed down by a hearty slug of their liquor, had gone a long way toward reviving him. He still carried an enormous sleep debt, which he had every intention of paying down over the next few days.

A sentry dressed in cavalry blues appeared on the balcony at the top of the gate, staring down through the spear points of the lodgepoles. "Halt and state your business," the sentry shouted at him.

"My name is Ozymandias Hayes. I've got bounties."

"Am I supposed to be impressed?" the sentry shouted back. He was a short man with bad skin, sandy hair, and a scruff of a beard.

"No, but you're supposed to open the gate and let me in."

"Where are the bounties?"

"In the wagon. I have the paperworks in my satchel."

"You been riding around with dead men in the back of your wagon?"

"I'm a manhunter. That's what we do. We deliver bodies."

"We don't pay no bounties here. This is a cavalry outpost."

"Since when?"

"It's always been a cavalry outpost."

"I know that. Since when do you not pay bounties?"

The sentry shrugged. "I don't know. I don't make those decisions."

"Who's your commanding officer?"

"Why?"

"Because I want to appeal to him. Please, let me in. I've been traveling for more than a week to get here."

"How do I know you're who you say you are? You could be some runaway slave and them could be the bodies of your master and his men."

"I have handbills bearing the likenesses of these outlaws. Your commanding officer could verify that. And I'm a free man. I have emancipation papers in my pocket."

"I can't read 'em if they're in your pocket."

"Open the gate, let me in, and I'll happily show them to you."

When the sentry hesitated still, Hayes said, "Tell your commander I have the bodies of Enoch Munn's gang."

"Never heard of him."

"Your commander will have. He has access to the same handbills I have."

The sentry sighed loudly enough for Hayes to hear. Then motioned to someone inside the fort that Hayes couldn't see. "Wait here," he called down to Hayes.

"Why can't I wait inside the fort?"

"Wait here," said the sentry, emphasizing each word. He turned, speaking in whispered tones and exaggerated hand motions to his unseen compatriot, then disappeared behind the wall.

Hayes waited. Then waited some more. The sentry returned to his position, but offered Hayes no further guidance.

"Are you sure someone's coming?" he called up to the sentry.

"I said wait!"

Hayes waited another few minutes, growing more impatient by the second. Exasperated, he climbed down from the buckboard's box and walked around to the back of the wagon. He grabbed the closest outlaw's body, dragged it to the lip of the wagon, then hoisted it onto his shoulder and walked it to the front gate, where he dropped it unceremoniously.

"What are you doing?" The sentry called down.

Hayes didn't answer. He went back to the wagon, grabbed another body, carried it to the gate, and piled it on top of the first.

"I said 'What are you doing?'" The sentry yelled.

"What does it look like I'm doing?"

"You can't do that!"

"Is that a fact?" said Hayes.

"Stop that. Stop that right now." The sentry pointed a rifle at Hayes.

Hayes didn't stop. He removed the third outlaw's corpse from the wagon and dropped the body on top of the other two, directly in front of the main gate.

"I'm telling you to stop that!" yelled the sentry.

"I damned near killed myself to bring these bodies here. I'm done with them. Let me in or don't. They're your problem now."

The sentry's face grew red. He put the rifle to his shoulder, drew a bead on Hayes. The manhunter stared him down. The tension hung in the air for a few seconds, then the sentry quickly dropped his weapon and stood at attention.

Slowly, the gate rolled back. A short man with mutton-chop sideburns and a sharply receding hairline stood just inside the opening. He wore the dress blues of an officer, the twin golden oak leafs inside the gold sardine box insignia of a major on his shoulder. His uniform was an ill-fit, as if sewn for a heavier man, which Hayes figured he had likely been before being assigned to the outpost. He carried his hat, like a possession too prized to be used for its rightful purpose, in white-gloved hands.

The stub of a cheroot between the man's teeth seemed to be getting chewed more than smoked. A thin, bespectacled lieutenant of about the same height as the major flanked him on the right. The cavalry, Hayes knew, had an unspoken preference for shorter men.

The major stared at the pile of bodies on the ground in front of him. He narrowed his eyes and moved the cheroot to the other side of his mouth without touching it. He offered no comment on the sight, but stepped around the pile, approaching Hayes.

"Major Anderson McKinney. Company G, Sixth Infantry. I understand you've requested an audience with me."

The major pointedly did not offer his hand, but then Hayes had not expected him to do so.

"Ozymandias Hayes," the manhunter said with a slight nod of his head.

"I'm told you have papers confirming your status as a freeman?"

Hayes reached for the papers in his pocket, but the major waved him off.

"You killed all these men?"

"Only those on the ground," Hayes said. He tilted his head toward the wagon. "The remaining body is that of my partner, Jacob Hutchens. Enoch Munn killed him."

"One of those bodies there is Munn?"

"No," said Hayes. "I killed him, too, but wolves took the body from me on the way here."

"Far be it from me to tell a bounty hunter how to conduct his business, Mr. Hayes, but the heads alone would've provided proof of death and positive identification. You didn't need to bring bodies."

Hayes clenched his jaw, but elected to not explain himself. "I have the wanted posters in my satchel."

"We don't pay bounties here," said the lieutenant.

The major turned his head in the man's direction. A silent, but effective rebuke, a subtle gesture to reclaim his authority. The lieutenant dropped his chin, eyes looking down at his boots.

"My lieutenant spoke out of turn, but he spoke the truth," said the major. "I appreciate you ridding the plains of these outlaws, but I'm afraid we are no longer authorized to pay bounties. I can reward your efforts only with my gratitude."

"Actually," said Hayes. "There is a way you can help me. A letter from you stating that I delivered the bodies to your custody, bodies which you identified and disposed of, would satisfy the bounty's requirements. I could use that letter to submit my claim to the authorities in the next settlement I come across."

The major chewed his cheroot and nodded. "What of your partner?"

"If you have a chaplain and are willing to extend me the use of a shovel, I'll see to his burial."

Major McKinney nodded. "I can't spare any men to help, but there's a preacher inside. He's not our chaplain, but I don't suspect that really matters in this instance. We haven't yet established a cemetery here, so you've got your pick of any spot outside the gates. Mind the distance and keep clear of any demarcated trails. Be sure to mark the gravesite well."

Hayes nodded.

The major looked at the ragged, but now fully healed scar around Hayes' throat. "What was the cause of that?"

"A poorly positioned knot."

Major McKinney paused and narrowed his eyes. He puffed on the cheroot, chewed for a few seconds. He looked to his lieutenant. "Find the preacher. Then draft the letter for Mr. Hayes and bring it to me for my signature. And find him a shovel."

Hayes nodded. "Thank you."

Still addressing the lieutenant, McKinney said, "Tell the sentry Mr. Hayes has leave to come inside the gate after he's buried his man. Inform the quartermaster that we have a guest and arrange lodging." He turned back to Hayes. "Temporarily."

"Understood," said Hayes. "A good night's sleep, a hot meal, and I'll be on my way."

The lieutenant saluted and turned.

Before he could walk away, the major added, "After he buries his man, have the wagon brought inside, and see to his horses. But first, get these bodies out from in front of my gate."

"Should we bury them, sir?" asked the lieutenant.

"Fuck no!" said McKinney. "Drag them a few hundred yards away from the gate and leave them for the damn coyotes."

The lieutenant saluted again and scurried away.

"I'll retrieve the handbills," said Hayes. "The likenesses were passable when the bodies were more fresh."

"Are they who you claimed they were? Are they Munn's gang?" asked the major.

"They are."

"Then I trust they are who you say they are."

"You don't want to see for yourself?"

The major glared at him without speaking. He had been courteous to Hayes, but clearly saw the manhunter as beneath his station, and did not appreciate having his word questioned.

"The preacher should be out directly." And with that, the major turned and went back inside the fort.

While Hayes retrieved Hutchens' body from the wagon, several enlisted men emerged from inside the gate, one mounted on a chestnut gelding. While the mounted man barked orders, his fellow soldiers struggled with the task of securing the bodies of the outlaws, before finally managing to get them all tied together by the feet and the rope affixed to the gelding's saddle. The mounted man spurred the gelding forward and, with the other enlisted men jogging along behind, the corpses were finally dragged away and abandoned half a mile from the fort.

Hayes watched the entire comedy of errors without uttering a word. He looked back to the fort and saw a thin man in a well-worn dark suit walking toward him. The man carried a shovel in one hand and a bible in the other.

As the man came closer, Hayes noticed a pronounced limp in his gait. Closer still and Hayes could see the hand holding the bible was heavily scarred, the fingers twisted and gnarled, barely capable of closing enough to hold the book without dropping it.

The man stopped in front of Hayes and offered a crooked smile. Half of his face was frozen in place, the skin scarred by fire. He was missing an eye. A polished, painted stone rested in the socket where the eye had once been. He had long, black sideburns flecked with gray and a thin strip of hair framing his temples and bordering his forehead, but the entirety of his scalp was missing. Not bald, but removed. Deep scars on the top of his head formed an irregular box-shape, the skin so thin the bumps and ridges of his skull seemed on the verge of poking through.

"Good afternoon," said the scalped man. "My name is Josiah Cooley. I understand we have a body to inter and a soul to send to our Lord."

Twenty-Four

The Gunslinger

The Shadow Wolf ambled up to Hamish Frost as he unsaddled his horse at the base of the near-vertical cliff. The girl named Ana sat atop the giant wolf. The late afternoon sun framed the rocky mesa, creating a golden glow at the edges, and splintering the light into rays that splayed over the land.

"What are you doing?" the girl asked.

Frost took the saddle from the horse's back, set it on the ground. *"The quality of mercy is not strained."*

"I don't understand you when you talk like that."

He took the blanket from the horse's back, laid it over the saddle. *"Ignorance is the curse of God; knowledge is the wing wherewith we fly to Heaven."*

"Like that. That's what I mean."

He removed the bridle, dropped it on the blanket. "Where we're going," he said, "Would be impossible for my old paint to go. We'll leave him and the saddle here and trust that both will be waiting for us when we come back down."

The girl looked to the top of the mesa. "We're going up there?"

"We are indeed."

"What's up there?"

"Someone who's requested an audience with me."

"Somebody lives up there?" Ana asked incredulously.

He smiled at her, then stretched his arms over his head, locking his fingers and twisting his back until he heard a popping sound. He twisted in the opposite direction, then bent over and touched the top of his leather boots, leaving his fingers there for a few seconds. He then squatted so low his backside almost touched the ground.

Ana watched him go through his calisthenics. "Why are you doing that?"

"Just limbering up the old joints. There are few things worse than cramping up when you're dangling from a cliff face. Take my word for it."

"You're climbing up that?"

"Can't fly. And I don't know another way to the top."

"I can't climb that. Can I just wait here with the wolf? Like before?"

"No ma'am. You're coming with me."

Concern bordering on fear flashed across Ana's face. "I'll fall. I can't climb that."

"You won't have to climb. The wolf is sure-footed. He'll have little trouble navigating the incline. You'll just have to hold on tight. I'll do my best to keep up."

"I'm going first?"

"Only by means of circumstance. The wolf is going first. You'll be his passenger. Don't fret. He knows the way. And I'll be right behind you." He paused. "Well, perhaps not directly behind, but I'll be along shortly."

"Are you sure you can climb that?"

"I've done it before, though it's been some time since last I was here."

"When are we...?" She let the words trail off.

He smiled at her.

"We're not going to camp here tonight and start in the morning? We're doing this now?" The concern etched on her face ratcheted up.

"Make mountains level, and the continent, weary of solid firmness!" Frost winked at her. "No time like the present."

He reached above his head and slid his fingers along the rock until he found purchase. "Just hold tight and he'll do the rest," he said, pulling himself up and securing another finger hold as he dug his boots into the rock wall.

"I don't want to go up there."

"You don't get a vote, I'm afraid. I don't either. The old woman has requested an audience with me and I know better than to refuse such a request."

"Who is the old woman?" She asked.

Frost didn't answer.

The Shadow Wolf placed its front paws on the rock face, coiled its haunches, and sprang upward. Its feet took to the incline and, with little effort, the giant wolf walked up the cliff face as casually as it did across the level plains. Fighting back a wave of disorientation, the girl buried her face in the scruff at the base of the wolf's neck and held on tightly.

"I'll see you at the top," Frost called after her.

The climb had gotten no easier in the time since last Frost made it. And he wasn't getting any younger. As he neared the top of the cliff, his back and shoulder muscles ached with each reach for a new handhold. His legs quivered and he could feel his calves tightening almost to the point of cramping. His heart skipped a beat every time he dislodged a rock and sent it cascading down the cliff. When he finally reached the top and pulled himself onto the plateau, he rolled over onto his back and breathed deeply. The air was crisp and cool in his lungs. He savored it, exhaling slowly. He refilled his lungs, closed his eyes, then let out a long, deep sigh.

"I can no other answer make, but, thanks, and thanks," he mumbled.

When he opened his eyes, he saw Ana standing over him. The Shadow Wolf stood just behind her. Frost sat up. *"Mistress, what cheer?"*

The girl wrinkled her brow, then turned and pointed into the distance. "Is that where we're going?"

Frost's eyes narrowed. He looked in the direction the girl had pointed.

A wispy trail of white smoke escaped through the vent of a tipi, well-tanned buffalo skins wrapped around a framework of thin pine poles. The tipi abutted a large boulder amid a stand of gnarled, short-needled pines and tall quivering aspens. The trees offered shade and blocked the harsh winds that buffeted the mountain at such high altitudes. Frost never found the tipi in the same place twice. It, like everything atop the mesa, was subject to the old woman's whims and wishes. The tipi was visible to Frost because he had been summoned. Absent the old woman's consent, he would never have found it.

"What do you see, child?" He asked Ana.

The girl looked confused. She pointed directly at the tipi. "That thing right there. You don't see it?"

"I see it," said Frost, without taking his eyes off of the girl. "But I don't know how it is that *you're* seeing it."

"I'm not blind. It's right in front of me."

The old gunslinger got to his feet. "Come with me, but say nothing unless you're asked directly. Do you understand?"

She nodded. "Is something wrong?"

"Wrong? I don't know. But something is, for want of a better word, *off.*"

Frost led the way, the girl and the Shadow Wolf walking a few steps behind. As they passed through the shadow of the trees, the wolf slowed.

"Don't be alarmed, child," said Frost. "He does this sometimes."

The girl turned and looked at the wolf. "Does what?"

The shadows flowed on the ground, reaching for the wolf, or perhaps the wolf reached for them. The wolf's form shimmered, then stretched. Its blackness seemed to lose definition. With each step, the wolf and the shadows became more entwined, melding together, making it impossible to separate them. A few steps more and the wolf disappeared into the darkness. The shadows retracted, returning to their position on the ground. The yellow-gold glow of the wolf's eyes lingered for a few seconds before floating up into the canopy of the aspens. The girl lost sight of them amidst the quivering leaves. "Where did he go?" She asked.

Frost smiled at her. "Don't fret, child. He'll be back."

As they neared the tipi, they found a large circle of polished, sand-colored stones ringing the outer perimeter. Inside the ring of stones, a thick carpet of plush blue-green moss blanketed the ground.

"Who lives here?" asked Ana.

"No more talk," said Frost, softly but sternly.

He paused at the ring of stones and stood silently. After a few moments, an ancient, gnarled hand pushed back the flap of the tipi. A thumb and three fingers. Where the end finger should have been was a scarred nub. A stooped old woman dressed in well-worn deerskins hobbled out. She leaned heavily on a wooden walking stick as she shuffled forward, her back so bent with age that she leaned almost parallel to the ground as she walked. She looked up at Frost and squinted. Her eyes nearly disappeared within the folds of the heavy wrinkles on her face.

"Who's making all the racket out here?" she said in a shrill voice.

"Is that any way to greet a guest?" said Frost with a cautious smile.

The old woman's expression remained completely neutral. She tilted her head, turning her milky eyes to Ana.

"You have my permission to be here, Whiteskin. This whip of a girl does not."

"My name is Ana."

Frost held up his hand in front of the girl, reminding her of his admonition to remain silent. "I apologize. The girl doesn't know any better."

"If she's going to travel with you, then you should teach her better," said the old woman.

"I can easier teach twenty what were good to be done, than to be one of the twenty to follow mine own teaching."

The old woman sighed. "Spare me the Shakespeare. Why did you bring her to my house, Whiteskin?"

"I had little choice. I chanced across her after I'd already received your summons. She was in need of my help."

"Did you help her?"

"I'm in the process of so doing."

"Are you?" The old woman looked down at the polished stones. "She passed through the warded trees without your help. Did she not?"

Ana stepped closer to Frost. "How did you know about — ?"

"Quiet, child," said the old gunslinger, without looking at Ana. He held a hand out to his side, a caution for her to come no closer.

"If she crossed through the wards on her own, then what did you do to help her?" Asked the old woman.

"He killed the trapper," said Ana. "He killed the man who took me."

Frost tensed, but before he could rebuke the girl for speaking out of turn, the old woman looked at Ana and addressed her directly.

"No, girl. He did not. The gnome killed your captor. That squirming little thing that was inside him killed him. Its larvae climbed up his ass while he was taking a shit in the woods and dug its spurs into his intestines. It anchored itself there while it grew. It ate him from the inside. The gnome killed your captor. Not Whiteskin."

"He killed it," said the girl. "He killed that thing that came out of the trapper."

The old woman shook her head. "No. The Shadow Wolf killed the gnome. What did you do, Whiteskin?"

"I found her," he answered.

"No," said the old woman. "What did you do, Whiteskin?"

"I brought her here."

The old woman smiled. "Yes. That is what you did. She didn't need you to escape the wards. She didn't need you to kill her captor or the gnome. She didn't need you at all. You could have just left her to her own devices, but you brought her to my home. That is what you did, Whiteskin."

"That's not true," said Ana. "I *did* need him."

The old woman stared at her. "Did you, girl?"

"Yes," said Ana with steel in her voice. "I needed him. I would never have been strong enough to leave without him. If he hadn't come along, I'd still be there. In that shack. With one of those things in me. Eating me from the inside just like it did the trapper. I don't know who you are, but you're being mean to him and he don't deserve it. He got me out. He saved me. I'd be dead without him." She paused. "And he's been kind to me." She spoke the last words as if Frost's kindness had been the thing that mattered most to her.

The old woman stared at her in silence, then turned her head toward Frost. Her gaze bore holes in him. "You know better than to bring the uninvited to my home."

"*When a man's verses cannot be understood, nor a man's good wit seconded with the forward child understanding, it strikes a man more dead than a great reckoning in a little room.*"

"Shakespeare again," said the old woman with a sigh.

Frost smiled. "You knew. That's why you summoned me in the first place. I didn't find her. You sent me to her. This was all a part of a plan. You knew I would bring her here."

The old woman turned her back to them and walked to her tipi. She lifted the flap and said, "Come with me, Whiteskin. The girl stays outside the circle."

Twenty-Five

The Wing-Thief

The sun had long since set when Black Wing awoke. A field of stars covered the sky, thick swirls of distant nebulae giving color to the void of space. His head throbbed, a dull pounding like fists striking the inside of his skull. His throat was parched, his tongue swollen and alien in his mouth. His thoughts were a muddle and, try as he may, focus and concentration escaped him. He lay on the buffalo skin, feeling the world spin beneath him.

Slowly, he sat up and looked around. He was alone. Antelope Eyes was not next to him, nor anywhere he could see.

Black Wing struggled to his feet, finding his legs wobbly, his knees weak. He staggered a few paces from the campsite, feeling a sudden rumble in his belly, then a rush of bile erupting from deep within him. He doubled over and retched, spraying the contents of his stomach onto the ground. He retched again and again until it seemed he was empty inside. He straightened slowly, fearing another surge, but none came. He wiped his mouth with the back of his hand, tried to swallow down the bitterness in his mouth.

He heard a twig snapping from somewhere behind him, then the sound of heavy footsteps. Instinctively, he reached for his axe, but it lay on the ground by the buffalo skin. He turned, expecting to see a bear or perhaps more painted warriors, but it was only Antelope Eyes walking through the trees toward their camp. The holy man was naked, his skin glistening in the soft blue glow of starlight. Water dripped from his hair and rolled down his chest. The violet aura that had surrounded him since Black Wing's eyes had been opened shimmered, pulsing in waves as if the night swim had somehow strengthened the holy man's medicine.

Black Wing sighed with relief. "At least you didn't make me search for you this time." Or rather, that's what he tried to say. The words came out somewhat garbled, his tongue still thick in his mouth.

"I told you I was going for a swim," said Antelope Eyes, seeming to have understood nonetheless. "You should have joined me."

The wing-thief took a moment, forming the words in his mind before he spoke. "Your wine has left me out of sorts," he said slowly, pausing between the words. "My head is pounding, my senses are dull. My arms and legs are so heavy. I feel dizzy just trying to stand. And you can see what has become of yesterday's supper."

The holy man smiled. "It's my fault you can't hold a strong drink? Go back to sleep. My swim is over. My night walking is done. You can rest now."

"And why should I believe you this time? When so often it has not been true?"

"Because this time is different."

"Of course it is," said Black Wing with sarcasm. "What makes this time any different?"

The holy man stood there unmoving, looking at Black Wing with a strange expression. Longing, sadness, and something else. An expression that sent a shiver down the wing-thief's spine.

"Is something wrong?" asked Black Wing.

Antelope Eyes smiled, but did not answer.

"There is something wrong, isn't there? Tell me."

A silent tear rolled down the holy man's cheek, dripping from his jaw to his naked chest. "Run," he said.

Black Wing wasn't sure he'd heard him correctly.

"Run," said the holy man again.

Black Wing's eyes followed the teardrop, then drifted to the ground on which Antelope Eyes stood. A trail of wet footprints led through the soft, mulch-covered floor of the thicket and back to the beaver's lake. Heavy, mismatched prints that sank deep into the ground. One print notably larger and wider than the other.

Black Wing's heart dropped. His knees buckled and he nearly collapsed. Words he had heard the holy man say many times previously echoed in his mind. *I have seen my end.*

"No," he said, barely above a whisper. He felt the bile rising fast and again he retched, but he had nothing left inside him.

He looked back at Antelope Eyes in time to see the holy man's mouth distort, opening wider than should have been possible. The top of his head almost disappeared from view. Rows of jagged yellow teeth flashed in the blue starlight and the mouth lunged forward, jaws snapping.

Instinctively, the wing-thief moved, narrowly dodging the snapping jaws. He slipped on the soiled grass and fell, but rolled to his feet. He looked back at Antelope Eyes, but the holy man was gone. Replaced by a creature with a wide, flat, misshapen, turtle-like head atop a hulking mass of bloated, mismatched body parts blackened with rot and decay. Tiny eyes glowed within the hard edges of the creature's head, malice radiating in waves.

Wechuge.

The creature stood on the buffalo skin, the bed that Black Wing and Antelope Eyes had shared for weeks as they traveled together. Black Wing saw his axe on the ground near the bed. He dove, rolled past the creature's feet, reaching for the axe.

Wechuge swung a massive, mottled arm, the clump of a hand at the end the size of a bear's head as the wing-thief rolled by. The blow would have crushed Black Wing's skull, but it missed his head and slammed into his back. The force knocked the wind from the wing-thief's lungs and sent him tumbling into the fire.

Black Wing rolled through the flames and came to his knees, his hair singed, skin splotched with soot and ash. He looked to his right hand. Somehow, his fingers had found his axe as he rolled. He gripped the shaft of the weapon and swung in a wild arc. The blade sliced through the monster's thigh, a spurt of black blood gushed from the wound. Wechuge roared, a sound like boulders crashing against each other in a rockslide.

Black Wing swung again, but he swung wide, missing. Wechuge kicked out at him, the grotesque foot thudding against his chest with the force of a horse's kick. Black Wing flew backward, landing hard, the air forced from his lungs on impact. The axe flew from his fingers as he fell, thudding to the ground a few feet away. He struggled to refill his lungs as the monster lumbered toward him. He reached for the axe, but it was beyond his grasp.

Wechuge's shadow fell across him. Black Wing looked up as the creature's mouth opened. Row upon row of jagged teeth flashed as the head plunged downward. Black Wing closed his eyes and waited for death.

But he felt nothing. After a second or two, he realized death was not coming. At least not yet. When Black Wing opened his eyes, Wechuge was gone and in the creature's place stood Antelope Eyes. The holy man's face trembled, his body shook.

"Run. Now," Antelope Eyes pleaded. "Leave while you still can. Go before it kills you."

"No!" said Black Wing, grabbing his axe and bounding to his feet. "I will kill it!"

"Leave!" shouted Antelope Eyes. "I don't know how much longer I can hold it back! You must leave now!"

"I can't," said Black Wing. "I can't leave you."

"Run."

"It ate you." Black Wing tried to make it a question, but his words came out as a simple statement of heartbreaking fact. "You knew this would happen! You knew it would kill you! Eat you!" He raised his axe, hand trembling, shaking with rage and anguish. "You should have let me kill it when I first saw it! Why didn't you let me kill it? I could have saved you! I could have stopped this!"

"You must go! Go now! Run! Please. I beg you!" said Antelope Eyes.

Black Wing shook his head and mumbled, "I can't. I can't leave you."

Antelope Eyes' body rippled, his form shifting. The holy man disappeared and the monster Wechuge returned. It lunged, reaching for Black Wing. The wing-thief swung his axe. The blade struck the creature's arm, severing it just below the elbow. The stub of blackened flesh and massive, twisted hand landed at the wing-thief's feet. Wechuge roared in pain, its fetid breath forcing Black Wing to stagger back. He brought the axe up, but before he could strike, Wechuge disappeared again.

Antelope Eyes stood before him, cradling the stump of his arm against his bare chest. There was little blood, but Black Wing could see exposed bone.

"I hurt you," said Black Wing.

"Run," the holy man pleaded again.

"No."

The holy man looked at him one last time, eyes beseeching. Black Wing stared back, feet planted firmly.

"Do not follow." Antelope Eyes turned and walked briskly through the trees, toward the lake. Away from the campsite. Away from Black Wing.

The wing-thief ignored the holy man's words and followed after him. "Is it you?" he called out. "Tell me! Is it you? Am I talking to you or am I talking to that thing pretending to be you?"

Antelope Eyes kept walking briskly towards the lake.

"Are you in there?" screamed Black Wing in anguish. "Can I free you? Can I bring you back?"

Antelope Eyes didn't answer. Black Wing stumbled through the trees, catching up to the holy man by the lake's edge. "Please, tell me. Is this you? Are you in there? How can I save you? How do I get you back?"

The holy man waded into the lake.

"Is there any part of you left? Have I lost you forever? Answer me! Have I failed you? Have I lost you?"

Antelope Eyes ignored him. Waded deeper, the water at his thighs.

His hand shaking, Black Wing lifted his axe and took aim at the center of Antelope Eye's back. "If I throw my axe, do I kill the creature or do I kill what remains of you?"

The water reached the middle of Antelope Eye's back. Black Wing drew back his hand, prepared to throw the axe. But his feet slipped from beneath him and he tumbled down. He tried to stand, but his feet slid from under him again. Something was on his hands. He looked down. Dark blood coated his fingers, smeared across his arms and chest. Down his legs. All around him was a great slick of dark red blood, slowly soaking into the mossy lake bank.

The holy man's blood. The blood of Antelope Eyes.

The holy man's clothing lay scattered all about, torn and shredded. One of his braids, still attached to a flap of scalp, lay near the wing-thief's hand.

Black Wing recoiled. He struggled to his feet and splashed into the lake, following. The water was at the holy man's shoulders.

Black Wing knew he could still deal a killing blow, even from this distance. He had only to throw the axe. He knew he might never get another chance to kill the monster Wechuge. He had only to throw the axe.

But it wasn't Wechuge at which he would throw the axe. It was the holy man. It was Antelope Eyes.

Black Wing hesitated.

Throw! Throw now! A voice inside his head screamed. He shuddered, an ache building in his soul. *Throw! Throw! Throw!*

But he did not throw the axe.

Throw! The voice pleaded again, but Black Wing knew he would not throw the axe.

He lowered his arm, held the weapon limply at his side. The water was at the holy man's ears.

The wing-thief watched in silence as Antelope Eyes' head disappeared beneath the water. He continued to watch as the water rippled in the starlight, then grew still, erasing all evidence of the holy man's passage beneath the surface.

Twenty-Six

The Manhunter

Ozymandias Hayes realized he was staring at the scalped man's disfigured face and scarred head. He turned away, tried to divert his eyes, hoping the preacher had not taken notice.

"It's alright, son," said the Reverend Josiah Cooley. "No need to look away. I know the sight I present. One can't help but stare."

"My apologies," said Hayes, with a slight bow of his head.

"Not necessary." The scalped man placed a hand on Hayes' shoulder. In any other context, such a gesture might have carried condescension and Hayes would have bristled. "I suppose I could wear a hat to avoid the stares. An eyepatch as well. But I choose not to do so." Cooley lifted his hand from Hayes' shoulder and tapped the side of his head, touching his scarred face. "This was a gift given to me by the natives of this wild land."

Hayes' eyebrows raised. "A gift?"

Cooley smiled. "When I was a young man, I went among them to preach the word of God. I was full of righteous zeal and youthful vigor. Truth be told, I was more full of myself than anything else. I found the natives, or rather they found me, and I set immediately to the task of convincing them of their heathen ways. I called on them to humble themselves, repent of their savagery, reject their false gods, and be baptized in the light of our Lord. The natives didn't take kindly, to say the least. But they taught me a valuable lesson. A life-altering lesson. They taught me the power and grace of my God. By that power and grace, I survived. I am aware that most who face what I did do not. I choose to display my wounds so that men may see what faith in Christ can accomplish."

Or what your god allows men to do to one another, Hayes thought,

Then, to Hayes' surprise, Cooley extended his left hand, not his maimed right. They shook. Hayes feared gripping the scalped man's hand too tightly but he needn't have worried. The preacher's grip was surprisingly firm.

Cooley pointed to a stand of maple trees about a hundred yards east of the fort.

"Contrary to what the good major believes, we do have something of a cemetery here. There are a dozen or so buried right over there by the trees. Settlers on their way westward. Their infant children who were too precious for this world and the mothers who did not survive the birthing. We can bury your friend there as well."

"He was my partner, not my friend," said Hayes. The truth, but it seemed a cruel distinction, and he regretted having voiced it the moment it left his lips.

Cooley nodded. "Come then, dear brother, let us get about the interring." He ambled toward the trees, using the shovel as a walking stick.

Hayes followed, holding the reins of the horse bearing Hutchens' body. As they neared the stand of maples, he said, "Forgive me for not knowing the answer to this question, but is there a certain honorific by which I should address you, Mr. Cooley? I'm afraid my religious education ended with the forced Bible readings of my childhood."

"You may call me Josiah, if you wish. Or if that's too informal for you, I suppose Reverend Cooley or just Preacher, would suffice. May I call you Ozymandias? Or would you prefer Mr. Hayes?"

"I will answer to either."

"Were you named for the Shelley poem?"

"Yes," said Hayes with a forced smile. In truth, he only assumed such was the case. The man who had sired him -- the plantation owner who had repeatedly forced himself on a twelve-year-old slave girl until she found herself with child -- had chosen the name. Whether the choice of name had originated from the poem, or from antiquity, or from some other source, Hayes did not know. He had never spoken to the man. Not once.

When they reached the makeshift cemetery, Cooley lifted his twisted arm and extended the shovel to Hayes. "I'm afraid I won't be of much use to you in the excavation. The Lord may have healed me, but did not see fit to fully restore me. Would you mind if I read from the Good Book while you dig?"

Hayes nodded. He chose a spot close enough to the trees to be in the shade, but distant enough, he hoped, to be free of the root system and began digging.

He had assumed the preacher intended to read silently, but that turned out to not be the case. Cooley read from selected passages in an almost stream-of-consciousness manner, letting the words of one verse spark his recollection of another. He seldom looked at the page from which he recited. Hayes suspected the reverend had the entirety of both Old and New Testaments memorized and used the book only as a prop.

Cooley had a flair for the melodramatic and a knack for choosing the wrong words to emphasize, but Hayes let the preacher speak without interruption. Aside from his chance meeting with Hamish Frost, he had spent two weeks in the company only of corpses and wolves. Conversation, one-sided as it might be, was appreciated.

Cooley paused, wiped sweat from his brow with his sleeve, then continued "... found the stone rolled away from the sepulchre. And they entered in, and found not the body of the Lord Jesus. And it came to pass, as they were much perplexed thereabout, behold, two men stood by them in shining garments: And as they were afraid, and bowed down their faces to the earth, they said unto them, Why seek ye the living among the dead? He is not here, but is risen: remember how he spake—"

Hayes stopped digging. He turned and looked at the preacher.

"Something wrong, son?"

"What you just read..."

"Luke Chapter 24. The resurrection of our Lord Jesus Christ," said Cooley.

"How did that work?"

"I'm not sure I follow your question."

"He was dead, yes?"

"Crucified by the Romans and laid to rest in the tomb of Joseph of Arimathea."

"But then he was alive again?"

"Yes, resurrected in the flesh. With angels of God bearing witness when the stone was rolled back to reveal an empty tomb."

"How?"

"I beg your pardon?"

"How was he alive again?"

"He was resurrected."

"But how? How is it that one can be dead and then be restored to life?"

"Only by the grace of God," said Cooley. "Through the blood of Christ, we shall all be restored to the flesh. I am the resurrection, and the life: he that believeth in me, though he were dead, yet shall he live."

"Only a god has that power? The power to raise the dead, to restore life?"

"There is only one god, Mr. Hayes, and his name is Jesus Christ."

Hayes paused a moment, then nodded and resumed shoveling.

It took Hayes almost three hours to dig the grave. He was drenched in sweat by the time he finished the task. His back and shoulders ached, muscles burning. The Reverend Cooley went back inside the gates for a while, but returned later with a canteen of water and some johnnycakes. Hayes wondered if this was a courteous offer of refreshment or if the preacher was surreptitiously giving him communion. Water for wine. Johnnycakes for wafer. Regardless, Hayes climbed from the hole, drank the water and ate the cakes. Cooley then helped Hayes lower Hutchens' body into the grave. Hayes took Hutchens' bedroll from the horse and laid it over the corpse.

Cooley bowed his head and gave a long, rambling, take-the-soul-of-this-good-man-into-thy-bosom sort of prayer. As the words all ran together, Hayes stared at the back of the preacher's head. He traced the scars with his eyes, envisioning what the attack must have been like. A fierce, painted warrior standing over him, knife in hand. Or perhaps a tomahawk. The dread and the feeling of absolute helplessness. Then the first cut, fingers burying themselves in the hair, gripping, tearing, the flesh ripped away. Blood flowing down his face, into his eyes. The sensation of sunlight and air touching raw, exposed muscle. The sharp, stinging, debilitating pain.

Hayes realized the preacher has stopped speaking. He looked away and muttered a quick, "Amen", then grabbed the shovel and began filling the hole back up again. Cooley excused himself and went back inside the gates of the outpost.

It took Hayes only a fraction of the time to fill the hole that it had taken him to dig it. He reflected on the reverend's words.

There is only one god, and his name is Jesus Christ.

Hayes had been dead. Enoch Munn had lynched him, murdered him. Hanged him from a tree. He remembered the crush of the rope around his neck. The weight of his own body pulling it ever tighter until he had felt — literally felt — his life slip away. He had been dead. Dead for some time. Enoch Munn had been shocked when Hayes had opened his eyes and reached for him. No. More than shocked. The outlaw had been frightened. The terror on his face was palpable. A man he had murdered had come back to life. Hayes had not seen Reverend Cooley's god during the time he had been dead. He had not been restored by faith. He had none. The force that had restored him to life was not the grace of a Hebrew god or the blood of an ancient Judahite.

It was the woman with flowing, raven hair. The woman with nine fingers. The spectral, ghostly woman he had seen on the plains shortly before Enoch Munn's gang attacked his campsite. The woman with a ball of lightning who had greeted him by the shores of the black water river. The woman who had shown him the canoe and given him a choice — paddle the canoe into the darkness and discover the mysteries of the next life or return to the world he had known, the world of the living.

Reverend Cooley's god might indeed have the power to restore the dead to life. His grace and his power might have healed Cooley's broken body, preserved his life. But he was not the one who had resurrected Ozymandias Hayes. He was not the only god. He was not the only one with such power.

The woman with nine fingers had greeted Hayes in the land of the dead. She had given him a choice by the banks of the river. She had the power to make such an offer, the power to make his choice a reality. The power to bring the dead back to life.

The woman with nine fingers was a god.

Twenty-Seven

Interlude Two

THE SNAKE GOD WAS in his human form, sitting on the blackened stump of a tree felled by lightning. The shattered trunk lay in hunks and splinters all around his feet, exploded by the force of the strike.

The Snake God wiped his nose with the back of his hand. The constant flow of mucus from his nasal passages was one of the few things he disliked about taking on human form. Gods should be immune from allergies, he thought, but to whom could he appeal? The old woman? Hardly. She had long since abandoned his kind. The old woman wanted nothing to do with him or his brothers and sisters. Except for the wolf, of course. The fucking wolf. The rest of us she cut free, but the wolf still danced at the end of her strings.

The Snake God sniffed again. Allergies were a petty punishment, but also a small price to pay to occasionally escape his serpentine form. Even that though he had had to learn on his own. All of them had. The old woman hadn't taught them. It was only through the sheer force of his will that he could shift between snake and human form. To come out of the holes in the ground and walk about on legs.

The Snake God didn't like humans, detested them in truth, but he enjoyed wearing their form. Or rather, he enjoyed the form he had chosen. He liked being a boy. He enjoyed the small, sleek, hairless body. Hairless except, of course, for the dense black mop atop his head. If not for that — and the allergies — the form would be perfect.

He was eating a tortoise he'd spent the morning torturing. He'd flipped it over, left it helpless, exposing the softer underside of its shell. Feet and nub of a tail in the air, wagging helplessly. He'd torn the tail off first. Eaten it whole, bones crunching in his mouth. The legs had come next. One at a time. He'd twisted each leg, ripped it from the socket, tearing, shredding muscle and flesh. He ate slowly, savoring each bite. With the legs devoured, he broke open the bottom of the shell and scraped the meat from inside it. He saved the tortoise's head for last. Tearing off the head would kill it, and he wanted it alive for as long as possible.

That had been his plan, at least, but he noticed while pulling a bloody morsel from deep inside the shell that the tortoise had stopped squirming. The head lolled to the side. The eyes rolled back.

Shit, he thought. The little fucker died too soon.

He picked up the shell and bit off the tortoise's head. While he crunched on it, he looked up and saw an indistinct mass on the horizon. Fear shot through his body. Yes, gods could know fear. When facing what he saw moving toward him, fear was the only reaction. He could see the black dots swirling above the mass. Bats. Fucking bats. They'd found him.

Oh fuck. Fuck, fuck, fuck.

He pissed himself again, urine puddling at the stump of the shattered tree. He dropped the shell and looked about for a hole in which to hide.

In the days since he'd encountered old Whiteskin near the Chalkstones, he'd spent most of his time underground. Moving and hiding. The old pale-skinned bastard might not know what had been unleashed, what had escaped the inescapable prison, but he did. He knew. And he had determined he wanted nothing to do with it. He would hide as best he could. Stay away and let the old woman deal with it. It was her mess, after all. She should clean it up. Leave him the fuck out of it.

He'd hidden in the ground during the days, popping up at night to survey his surroundings and move to his next hiding place. Slithering along in the shadows. Staying out of sight. Today was the first day since he'd seen old Whiteskin that he'd felt safe enough to emerge in the sunlight, to take on human form. He had grown tired of the darkness, of eating only rats and mice for sustenance. He wanted to feel sunlight on his skin, to eat something more substantial. And he wanted amusement. He craved amusement. When a god has lived for eons upon eons, amusement is sometimes the only thing one has to look forward to.

But now he had been found. Fuck.

He squatted low to the ground, arms and legs fusing to his torso as he shifted back into his true form. He found the burrowed hole he'd crawled out of when he'd seen the tortoise plodding by. He slipped into the burrow, coiling in on himself, keeping his head to the shadows, and hoped the horde would pass him by.

He heard the cacophonous chirp of the bats, could see them swooping ever lower in cyclonic swirls, searching for him. He stilled his tail, held it completely motionless. It was in his nature to rattle it when confronted with danger, but to do so now would mean certain doom.

He heard the trudging, lumbering steps of the horde. Growing ever louder, ever closer, until he could see stained and dust-covered trousers, tattered skirts. Diseased and rotting feet. Green buzzing flies and other insects swarmed around them. The horde had once been human, but no longer. They were revenants now. Slaves to The One Who Had Returned.

He tried to retreat deeper into the hole, but the hole would not permit. He could retreat no further.

The horde came closer, gathering in front of his hole. He watched, tongue in his mouth, barely breathing. The horde suddenly parted, and he saw another walking toward the hole. One unlike those in the horde. Not human. Not revenant.

A large fleshless hand, muscle and bone exposed, reached into the hole and grabbed for him. He lashed out defensively, sinking his fangs into the back of the hand. Or rather, he attempted to do so. His fangs failed to penetrate the hand, instead snapping off, breaking free from his mouth, falling and disappearing into the shadows of the hole. He could see his venom, thick amber liquid, dripping from the fleshless hand.

Giant fingers wrapped around him, just beneath his head, snatched him from the hole.

The One Who Had Returned held him high in the air, squeezing him. The Snake God's tail whipped about impotently. The One Who Had Returned lifted his other hand, touched a forefinger to the Snake God's soft underside. Then plunged the finger into flesh, dragging it downward. Ripping and shredding, opening his belly.

The One Who Had Returned found the Snake God's heart, wrapped fingers around it, and plucked it free. He showed it to the Snake God, then opened his lipless mouth and ate the heart, chewing noisily. The Snake God's blood oozed from the mouth of The One Who Had Returned. The Snake God could feel his life, his power fading, yet still he lived. For a time. He watched as The One Who Had Returned swallowed. All of the Snake God's power, his medicine, had transferred to The One Who Had Returned. He could see The One Who Had Returned grow in stature and strength as the last of his own life essence slipped away.

The One Who Had Returned tossed the Snake God's husk on the ground at the feet of the horde. They bent, kneeled, and fed. Eating until all of the Snake God was consumed.

Twenty-Eight

The Gunslinger

Hamish Frost felt a charge, like the pop of released static electricity, when he stepped over the ring of polished medicine stones circling the old woman's tipi. He looked back at the girl named Ana.

She stood alone on the mesa, the shadows of twinkling aspen leaves playing across her face. Worry flashed in her eyes. "You're going to leave me out here?"

"You'll be as safe as you were with the wolf at the Chalkstones."

"I'll be all alone."

"Thus weary of the world, away she hies, And yokes her silver doves; by whose swift aid Their mistress mounted through the empty skies In her light chariot quickly is convey'd; Holding their course to Paphos, where their queen Means to immure herself and not be seen." He smiled at her. "The woman in that tipi might look old and frail, but she could bring down this whole mountain range if she were of a mind to do so. You're under her protection here. No harm will befall you in this place, child."

"Who is she? And why does she only have nine fingers?"

"To the latter, I've never inquired. To the former, well, that's a story for another day." He reached for the flap of the tipi and smiled at her again. "I'll be out directly."

Frost found the old woman sitting on a bearskin across from a smoldering fire pit. The tipi was notably larger on the inside than seemed possible from the outside. The headless carcass of a large rodent sizzled on a spit over the flames. The old woman stoked the fire with a stick, stirring and rearranging the coals. Without looking up at Frost, she motioned for him to sit. There was no fur rug on his side of the fire, but Frost found the same plush moss covering the ground outside of the tipi growing inside as well. If the old woman could move the tipi's location by whim, could hide the entire mesa from any eyes she didn't want to see it, then growing moss without sunlight was child's play for her.

Frost sat and crossed his legs, watching the old woman prodding the fire. He looked at the nub on her left hand where a pinkie finger should be, at the scar tissue crisscrossing it. It occurred to him the girl had a legitimate concern. If the old woman was as powerful as he knew her to be, how had she allowed something to take her finger?

Without looking up from the flames, the old woman said, "You want to ask me about the girl."

"Can such things be; And overcome us like a summer's cloud, Without our special wonder?"

"You can't help yourself, can you? Quoting Shakespeare is like breathing to you, isn't it?"

The old gunslinger smiled. "I would indeed like to know about the girl. There's clearly a lot more to her than meets the eye. But there is also another matter that needs to be discussed."

"What's the other matter?"

"We found an abandoned wagon train at the Chalkstones. Pilgrims walked off and left everything. I found a spot some distance away where they were slaughtered, but it seemed their bodies kept walking even after they'd been exsanguinated. I followed their track for miles before I lost them."

"You find walking corpses unusual, do you?"

Frost forced a smile. "Found an inordinate amount of bat shit, too. Then I came across Snake. He went into a panic when I asked him about it. Pissed himself."

"He does that," she said.

"I take it none of this has escaped your notice?"

She nodded. "It wasn't a panic. Snake has always scared easily, but this time, it is justified."

The old woman took the rodent from the spit and tore a hind quarter off of the carcass and began eating. Grease ran down her chin and dripped onto the bearskin rug.

"Are you hungry?" she asked.

He shook his head. "Rat meat gives me gas."

"All the same. It's not very good. Greasy and gamey. It tastes like shit, but I'm old and slow and rats are all I can catch anymore."

Frost laughed. "Have you worn the body of an old woman so long that you've begun to think of yourself as one? There are no rats on this mesa. The only animals here are the ones you summon. That rat climbed the wall just like I did. You called it because you got hungry. You could've made a mule deer climb that wall if you'd wanted venison."

The old woman chewed noisily. "You've gotten impertinent in your old age."

"I've always been impertinent. It's why they ran me out of England."

The old woman reached beneath the bearskin and pulled out a small leather pouch. She tossed the pouch to Frost. "Eat those."

Frost caught the pouch, emptied the contents into his palm. Half a dozen tiny, dried mushrooms. He looked up at the old woman. "Why do I have to eat these?"

"Because I told you to."

"Is this necessary?"

She nodded. "Eat them."

"They smell like horseshit."

"What do you think they grow in?"

"Are they poisonous?"

"Of course. What good would they be if they weren't?"

Frost took a deep breath, then tossed the mushrooms into his mouth. The taste was beyond foul. Acrid and bitter and growing worse with each successive chew. He gulped, forcing them down, wishing he had something to drink. Water or rum or, better yet, a cold tin of buttermilk. The taste lingered long after he had swallowed.

The old woman could have provided a drink for him, but she had offered him nothing. Which told him she did not want him to dilute the potency of the mushrooms. Within moments, his lips went numb and his tongue felt swollen, too big to stay in his mouth. He opened wide and let his tongue loll. His eyelids grew twitchy. His eyes watered. His head felt lighter, his sense of equilibrium failing.

For fear of passing out and falling into the fire pit, he lay back on the moss and rested his head. His hands tingled. He held them up and saw that his fingers were growing, elongating, turning into ribbons of flesh that rolled and drooped from his hands. His heart raced, pounding so that he could feel each beat slamming against his rib cage. He closed his eyes, forced himself to take deep, calming breaths.

Time passed, though whether seconds or days, he couldn't be sure. The only thing of which he was certain was that he was no longer in the tipi.

He didn't recall opening his eyes. Curiously, he wondered if perhaps somehow, in some way, they weren't actually open. A stiff wind blew, sending goose pimples all across his skin. He looked down and saw that he was naked. He was standing, staring out across lush green plains, tall grass swaying in the wind. Wildflowers bloomed all around him and the plains teemed with wildlife, some familiar, some strange. He saw great herds of elephants with long shaggy fur and curling tusks half the length of their bodies. Massive bison, larger than any he had ever seen. Stalking lions with knives for teeth and enormous bears with squashed, shortened faces.

In the distance, he saw great hills composed entirely of ice. The ice hills moved, inching slowly in a northward retreat, scarring the land, and leaving massive gouges in their wake. He looked up at the sun and saw it racing across the sky. The sun set and then rose, raced across the sky and set again. The cycle repeated in a dizzying blur. Months, years, passed in seconds as he stood watching. He saw seasons change, the grasses browning and turning to hay, then back to green and flowering. Again and again.

He saw the arrival of people. Not the European settlers, nor even the people of the plains he was familiar with. But a primitive people, new to the land, dressed in animal skins and carrying crudely made weapons. Men hunted antelope and prairie fowl while the women gathered nuts and berries, eggs and hatchling birds. Dark-haired, smiling children ran underfoot.

And amid these primitive people, Frost saw a shaman, face-painted white with a pigment made from powdered rock. The shaman preached of a great god who visited him in dreams, a god who promised the people plenty in their hunts and gathers and protection from the lions, bears, and wolves who came at night. He spoke of a benevolent god who wanted only the adoration of the people and a frequent sacrifice to prove their devotion.

As winter approached, the nights grew long and the winds ever colder. The northern lights danced in the sky and reflected their ghostly green glow on the mountains of ice. Frost saw the shaman choose a girl for an offering to this new god. The girl was an orphan and had no one to speak for her. No one to object to her being chosen as sacrificial tribute.

Frost looked at the girl. Thin and pretty, with high cheekbones and almond eyes. A face that seemed familiar, though attempts to study it only made the face less distinct, as if his eyes lacked the ability to focus on it

The shaman took the girl to a rock altar built atop a formation of pale yellow cliffs carved into towers by the retreating glaciers. The Chalkstones, he realized.

The shaman and his followers stripped the girl naked. Then, while his followers held her, the shaman took an obsidian blade and sliced the girl's arms and legs. The shaman coated his hands in her blood, then smeared the blood all over the altar. He prayed to the new god. Prayed for the rest of the day while the girl's wounds oozed blood.

As the sun sank low on the horizon, the shaman took the girl and stuffed her into a small cavity in the rock. Frightened and freezing, coated in her own blood, tears streaming down her face, the girl pleaded for the mercy of a quick death. The shaman ignored her. His followers sealed the hole with large, heavy stones. The shaman and his followers left the Chalkstone cliffs, leaving the girl to die in the sealed cave.

Frost watched time speed up again. Snows fell, then melted. Grasses greened and wildflowers bloomed. When spring arrived, the shaman and his followers returned to the Chalkstones to extract the girl's bones from the cave. But when the stones were removed, they found the girl still alive inside the small cavity. The cuts on her arms and legs had healed and scarred over.

The shaman and his servants took the girl from the cave and bathed her. They dressed her in the finest, softest leathers, fed her the sweetest fruits, and choicest cuts of meat. They built her a soft bed that she might sleep under the stars and never know captivity again. All spring, through the summer, and into the fall, the girl lived in great comfort. By the shaman's command, she did no work and had no responsibilities. She did not join the women in the daily gatherings. Each day she was fed and bathed, her hair brushed with a bone comb and her skin perfumed with oils extracted from wildflowers.

Each night, the shaman would come to the girl's bed, but he laid no hands upon her. Instead, he would gently stroke her hair and sing her to sleep. On the night of the winter solstice, the shaman came to the girl's bed and sang to her one last time. Then his followers lifted the girl from the bed and took her back to the top of the chalkstone cliffs.

They stripped her naked and bound her, hand and foot, with grass ropes. They looped the rope over a rocky outcropping a dozen feet up and hoisted the girl into the air, her feet dangling. The shaman placed a wide clay bowl beneath the girl's feet.

Frost heard a sound from behind him, a cacophony of high-pitched squeals. He looked away from the girl and saw the stars in the night sky disappearing, winking from view as massive dark clouds spread rapidly from the horizon, filling the expanse.

No, not clouds, he realized. Bats. Millions and millions of bats flying in tight formation. The bats shifted, creating a series of intersecting circles, a hovering, swirling vortex. One column of bats broke off from the larger vortex and touched down on the ground in front of the girl like a leathery dust devil. The shaman and all his followers prostrated themselves on the ground. Only the girl remained upright.

The column of bats spun faster and faster, swirling into a blur, making it impossible for Frost to separate one from another. He could see only a cyclone of black. The swirling mass coalesced into a vaguely man-shaped form. As the vortex dissipated, Frost saw a giant with an elongated torso, long slender arms, fingers that melded into claws. The giant's head was more bat-like than human.

The shaman raised his head. Adoration bordering on ecstasy flashed across his face as he found himself in the presence of his god. Tears of joy welled in his eyes, but the tears that rolled down his cheeks were anything but joyous. The shaman cried out in anguish as his bones shattered. Shards exploded through his flesh, ripping and tearing, blood flowing from each puncture. He opened his mouth to scream, but no sound came from him. His body shook, then went still. Dark blood pooled beneath him.

The giant tilted his bat-like head to the side, looking at the girl through his tiny eye slits. He lifted a hand and caressed her face, fingers lingering on her cheek before sliding down her chest, between her breasts. The giant's fingers traced across her mid-section, sliding gently across her abdomen. The girl shuddered.

Then the giant raked his claws across her mid-section, opening four dark seams. He tugged and her bowels came tumbling out in a spray of dark arterial blood.

Her intestines landed in the clay bowl at her feet. Blood flowed like a river from her wound, down her legs, pooling into the clay bowl. As the girl's blood overflowed the bowl and dripped to the rock floor, the earth shook. The Chalkstone cliffs shuddered and chunks of rock broke away, raining down.

A great fissure appeared at the giant's feet. The crack in the rock opened and expanded, revealing a void that mirrored the stars overhead. The clay bowl teetered on the edge of the hole. Blood spilled into the void.

The giant took the girl's body in his arms, grass ropes snapping and tearing free. The giant stepped into the void as if walking down a staircase. Frost watched the giant carry the girl's body away, both disappearing into the darkness. The ground shook once more, and the bowl tipped over, fell into the fissure after them.

As Frost watched, the rupture in the rock floor stitched itself back together, swallowing up the giant creature, the girl, and the bowl of her blood. The gap in the rock floor disappeared so completely Frost could no longer tell where it had been.

Frost stared at the girl's blood spattered across the rock and puddled on the stone floor. The shaman's followers fled down from the top of the rocks, leaving the bloody corpse of their leader behind.

Frost looked up at the sky. The stars were spinning, accelerating and then giving way to the sun's recrudescence. The morning light bathed the Chalkstones.

Frost looked at the spot where the fissure had been, where the girl's blood had been spilled. The shaman's broken corpse lay a few feet away. As he watched, a thorn bush wormed its way from inside the rock, springing into existence fully formed. A single wildflower bloomed, crimson petals as red as blood.

Frost sat up, breathing heavily. He was back inside the tipi.

Twenty-Nine

The Manhunter

Ozymandias Hayes felt the light of day on his eyelids. He opened his eyes slowly, the mid-morning sun streaming through a curtained window. He squeezed his eyes closed again, tried to blink away the crusted sleep that had accumulated, cementing his lids together. His sight returned as blurred blocks of grey and splotches of yellow-white light. His slumber had been profound, deep and dreamless.

He was lying on soft, freshly laundered sheets atop a cotton-stuffed mattress. Beneath his head was a pillow filled with goose down. He couldn't remember the last time he had slept in such a bed, in such comfort.

Hayes had long since grown accustomed to the crude sleeping conditions his employment mandated. As a free man of color, he was often denied lodging in homes or hotels, even in the states where slavery had been outlawed and his status went unquestioned. Sleeping on a pile of hay in a stable or on the hard-packed prairie dirt underneath a canopy of stars had become almost the expected for him.

His fuzziness of thought left him unsure of where he was, how he might have gotten there, how long he had slept, or on some metaphysical level, who he was.

He remembered delivering the bodies of Enoch Munn's gang to the outpost, burying Jacob Hutchens in the shade of a maple tree beyond the outpost's gate with the help of a scalped and maimed preacher. He remembered the quartermaster provided him with only a canvas hammock, for which he had been grateful. Compared to the cold, rocky soil on which he'd been sleeping, the hammock would be like lounging on a cloud.

But he wasn't in the hammock now. He was in a soft, warm bed.

"I was wondering how long you would sleep."

The voice belonged to a young woman. There was a hint of an English accent, faded now, but once more prominent. Soft, lilting playfulness escaped from her every syllable. It was a voice that had ingrained itself in Hayes' heart, in his soul, and then gone silent for so long he had almost forgotten the tenor of it. Almost.

He forced himself to his elbows. His arms were sore to the bone. His chest tight, the muscles constricted and knotted, as if he had taken the beating of his life. He ignored the stiffness and craned his neck, searching for the source of the voice.

He saw her and his breath caught in his throat. His heart stopped, completely stopped beating, then abruptly raced. Pounding, thumping so hard in his chest that he could almost feel it slamming against his sternum.

He blinked. Blinked again.

Are you still sleeping? Dreaming? Your subconscious conjuring images that couldn't be, shouldn't be?

Across the room, Cora sat in an oaken rocking chair. A fire crackled in the fireplace to her left.

"I'm sorry," she said with a small laugh, full lips pursed and the corners of her mouth curling upward into a smile that broke Hayes' heart all over again. "I thought you were awake. I didn't mean to startle you."

Cora.

Cora Hayes, née Arrington.

His wife.

Her eyes were large, doe-shaped, the green of willow-leaves. Her lashes long, her brows naturally thin. Her skin café au lait, smooth and flawless. Her hair was pulled back away from her face, long, coppery tresses tied with a purple ribbon. The sight of her made Hayes' soul ache far more than any of his muscles.

"I was afraid you were going to sleep the day away," she said.

She wore a white gown, unbuttoned to the navel, the sleeves draping off her bare shoulders and bunching around her elbows.

She cradled the baby in her arms. The child nursed noisily, sloppily, at her breast. Cora ran her fingers over the infant's scalp, making little swirling motions in the fine hair. She bent and kissed the top of the infant's head, pausing and breathing in the child's scent.

"She's missed you," Cora said without looking up from the child. "I've missed you."

Hayes' eyes panned the room. He didn't want to take them off of Cora, but the desire to ascertain his whereabouts was overwhelming.

He was in a small, but well-furnished room with high ceilings and papered walls. Crown molding abutted the ceiling. Hayes remembered affixing the trim himself. Sanding it, painting it, tacking it into place.

He was home. His home. Their home. The one-room brick house in Illinois that he had purchased with an advance from the firm on his hiring. The new home they had moved into shortly after they were married, the wedding present that he had surprised her with when he brought her to Chicago from Boston.

"Are you going to say anything?" she said, still smiling, almost teasing. "I had hoped you missed us as much as we had you."

"How long have I slept?" he asked. It was not what he had wanted to say, but the words came unbidden to his lips. Almost as if somewhere inside him, the questions he most wanted to ask were being suppressed for fear of the answer. In their place, he had only mundanity.

"A while," she said. "A long while. Are you rested?"

"I think so. But I feel... odd."

"Odd? How so?"

"I don't know. I'm confused. I'm having trouble thinking clearly. I don't remember coming here, don't remember going to bed."

"My poor dear," she said, tilting her head to the side and looking at him. "It's all that unpleasantness you went through in the west, isn't it?"

Unpleasantness? In the west...

"Please, Ozymandias, tell me that business is over and done with and that you are here to stay. Tell me you will stay with us this time. That you'll never leave us again."

Had he left them? He knew — in some hidden compartment of his mind — the answer to that question, but the door to that compartment was blocked.

"You came here to practice law," she said. "Didn't you? And if the firm doesn't appreciate your value as a barrister, then you can start your own practice. Hang a shingle. Isn't that what they call it?"

"I don't know," he said, his mind still grasping for answers. "I can't remember. Can't remember where I left things... what I've done, what I was trying to do. I can't remember how I got back here. I'm sorry, Cora. My head is so... muddled."

Cora smiled. "Your recall will return in time, my love. You just need more rest. More sleep."

"Perhaps you're right," he said. Again, words that came unbidden. Sleep was the last thing he wanted. He wanted to stay awake forever, didn't want to take his eyes off of Cora ever again. He was afraid that if he slept, she might not be there when he next awoke. He was afraid that he might not remember her face, might forget the sound of her voice. Might forget that she was his and he was hers. Might forget that she had borne a child, his child. Their child. Might forget that they had been happy together, had forged a life together. He knew it was an irrational, inexplicable fear. How could he forget his wife's face? Her voice? How could he forget their child?

What kind of man could do such a thing?

You did. Or at least you tried. God, how you tried.

Hayes spasmed, his body jerking involuntarily. His eyes snapping open. Against his most fervent wishes, he had nodded off. Fallen asleep while Cora was talking to him. He glanced in her direction, terrified that he might no longer be in the home they had made together, that Cora and the baby and the soft bed might have all been a dream, that she might no longer be there at all.

But she was. Still looking adoringly at him. Still smiling. Still cradling the nursing baby.

"Charlotte," said Hayes. "Her name is Charlotte. We named her for your... your..."

"My great aunt," said Cora.

"Yes. Your great aunt. In London. She sent you to America, financed your voyage, arranged your employment as an au pair."

Hayes looked at Cora, his wife, the woman he loved with his whole soul. Why had they ever been apart? Why had he gone gallivanting all over the country when she was here, waiting for him? Why was he out west, killing vile men, transporting their bodies to outposts across the plains, when Cora and Charlotte were here? Why was he neglecting his duties as a husband and father?

"I'm sorry," he said.

"For what?" she asked.

"I-I don't know."

Cora stood. She shifted baby Charlotte from one hand to the other and let her sleeping gown slip over her hips and fall to the floor. Naked, her breasts full and heavy, milk still dripping from her nipple, she walked to the bed and sat on the edge next to Hayes. Gently, she placed Charlotte on Hayes' chest.

Hayes reached up and put a supportive hand on the child's back, cupping her head. The baby girl mewled, flexed her arms and legs and began as if to squall, then just as suddenly stopped and, to Hayes' surprise, grew content. In seconds, Charlotte was sleeping fitfully. Her little chest rising and falling with each deep breath.

Cora looked at Hayes, holding his infant daughter, and smiled. He returned the smile. Cora leaned close, touching him for the first time since he'd awakened. Her fingers played across his cheek, then lifted his chin. She kissed him, softly. Slowly. Lingering.

How could he have forgotten the feel of her lips against his?
Because you forced yourself to forget.

Cora slipped into the bed next to him. They lay there in silence for a long while. Hayes with his tiny daughter sleeping in his arms and his wife nestled beside him. He felt a surge of contentment, a joy so profound as to be overwhelming. He had a family.

You've always had a family. You just forced them from your thoughts.

Hayes felt the tears welling in his eyes. He turned his head away from Cora, tried to free a hand to shield his eyes from her view, to brush the tears away. Cora sensed what he was doing and gently blocked his hand. She turned his face back toward her.

"Don't hide, Ozymandias. You never have to hide from me."

She smiled, then kissed him again. Without another word, she got out of the bed and lifted the sleeping baby from his chest. She walked across the room to a bassinet, laid Charlotte gently inside, then extended the linen hood. As she turned back toward Hayes, she reached up and pulled the purple ribbon from her hair. She gave her head a small shake, letting her locks fall halfway down her back.

She returned to the bed, and they made love. Slowly, gently, but with a passion that made him forget about the ache in his joints and the soreness of his muscles. Hayes stared into her eyes the entire time. She was his and he was hers.

When they finished, he held her close to him. Desperately close. A sliver of recall had returned during the lovemaking, as if the passion had jarred it loose. He had been here before. This was a memory. All of it. Cora. Charlotte. The little house in Chicago. It was a memory.

This is all a memory.

He had just returned from the Kansas territory. The firm had sent him there to obtain a signature on a land deed. There had been trouble on the stagecoach. An attack by raiders. A man on the coach was killed. Hamish Frost had saved the rest of them. It was the first time he had met the old gunslinger.

Unpleasantness in the west.

This is a memory. You know how the story ends. That's why you forced yourself to forget.

He held Cora tightly. Knowing the moment he let go would be the moment she would disappear. Charlotte would disappear, their little house, their happy life together, would all disappear.

She lifted her head, looked up at him.

"Don't go back, Ozymandias," she said softly. "You don't have to go back. Stay here with us. With Charlotte. With me. We can be a family again. You can watch her grow. Don't go back."

Hayes was confused. This wasn't part of the memory. She hadn't said that.

He kissed her forehead and brushed the hair from her face. She looked away, buried her face in the crook between his neck and shoulder.

Hayes could hear her sobbing, feel her body trembling softly. He didn't know what he had done to upset her. Not knowing what to say, he said nothing. He continued to hold her close, his face resting against the top of her head, and waited for her crying to stop.

"You're not staying," she said, barely above a whisper. "You could have been with us. You only had to get in the canoe, Ozymandias. Why didn't you get in the canoe? That's all you had to do."

"What?" he said. "What did you say?"

But Cora was not there to hear his words. She had disappeared. Charlotte had disappeared. Their little home had disappeared. All that he had ever had and lost, he'd had and lost all over again.

Ozymandias Hayes was alone, lying in a hammock in a dark, windowless room in a tiny outpost where the plains met the mountains.

The door to his room opened and the bespectacled lieutenant who had met him at the front gate stepped in.

"The major wants to see you in his office," he said.

Thirty

The Gunslinger

THE OLD WOMAN PLACED a firm hand on Hamish Frost's naked chest and pushed him back to a prone position. He still found himself frozen, unable to move, speak, or resist the old woman's manipulations. He lay naked on the bearskin inside the tipi. The fire that had smoldered in the pit when he took the mushrooms had been rebuilt and now blazed with blue-white flames. His eyes drifted, following the smoke as it escaped through the vent at the top of the tipi. Through the swirls, he could see milky stars against the blackness of space. It had been midday when he entered the tipi.

Where had the time gone?

The old woman reached down, took his hand, turned his wrist, and inspected the festering wound on his arm. She poked and probed the jagged cut where the gnome's teeth had torn his flesh. Frost felt nothing. Yellow pus oozed at her touch, pooling, then dripping from his arm. The old woman tsked him, shook her head.

"Sloppy, Whiteskin," she said. "Very sloppy. You're getting old. Letting a fucking gnome do this to you. This is bad enough. You're lucky you don't have one of those little fuckers growing inside you. Eating you from the inside."

She dug a long fingernail into the flesh at the crook of his elbow, burrowing in, slicing deeply, then dragging the nail downward, creating an incision that ran from his elbow to his wrist. Still, he felt nothing.

She burrowed her fingers into the cut and scraped out a handful of bloody pulp. She held it up for him to see. Brown and necrotic. Speckled with a black, moldy substance and crawling with long, pale yellow worms. She flung the diseased flesh into the fire. The fire hissed and the flames danced. She scraped away more dead muscle. Less mold and fewer worms this time, but more blood. Into the fire, it went, sizzling and smoking as it was consumed.

Frost could see into her incision. See his exposed arm bones, all the muscle stripped away. The old woman inspected the wound, more poking and prodding. She shook her head and sighed.

"That's all the worms and mold. All the dead tissue." She exhaled, looked at him sternly. "You've got to be more careful, old man. Just because you're still alive three hundred years after you were born doesn't mean you can't be killed. Immortality is only good until it isn't. The wolf won't always be there to save you, and I won't always be around to fix you. Our day has come. Our end is near. The day of the gods is over."

She reached into the fire, scooped up white-hot coals, and withdrew her hand unburned. She cupped the coals between her palms and pressed, grinding the coals together, crushing them into powdery embers. She opened her hand, the embers in a pile that sparked and glowed. She poured the crushed coals into Frost's opened wound, then ran her fingers over the powdered embers, spreading and smoothing them, filling the space where the muscles of his arm had been. Frost knew there should be pain, searing pain from the heat of the embers, but again, he felt nothing.

The old woman pulled the flaps of his skin together, pressed them against the coals. She reached back into the fire, held her hand there until flames covered it, dancing along her fingers and flattened palm. When she withdrew her hand, it glowed with the same white-hot intensity as it had in the fire. She ran her fingertips over Frost's wound. His flesh sizzled and popped, melting and fusing, closing and suturing the wound. She lifted his arm to her face, watched the bubbling flesh for a moment, then exhaled a puff of breath, as if blowing out a candle. In seconds, Frost's flesh had cooled, and no sign of the wound remained. The alabaster skin of his forearm was like a polished stone, smooth and unmarred.

"Good as new," said the old woman, lowering his arm.

Frost's eyes drifted from his arm to the old woman's face. For a moment, he saw not the old crone, but the void of space in the shape of a woman. Distant stars twinkled where eyes should have been. Nebulae swirled in hues of magenta and blue, and in the center of her chest, where her heart should be, a blindingly bright red orb pulsed.

He blinked and the woman made of stars disappeared, but the old woman did not return. In her place was a younger woman. Beautiful, with a thin nose that ended in a button shape. Coal-black hair fell halfway down her back, shimmering with a glow from the firelight and seeming to move and sway as if it were a living thing.

Frost blinked again, tried to stir, but the mushrooms' effect prevented him from moving and held his tongue immobile, keeping him from speaking.

"Shhh," said the Beauty, placing a forefinger to Frost's lips. He counted the fingers on her hand, could see that her small finger ended in a scarred nub before the first knuckle. "You have questions. More than you had when you entered the tipi. They'll be answered. All of them. In time. But not now and not by me."

She stood, let the buckskin shift she wore slip from her shoulders and fall to her feet. Her breasts were small, but full. Her hips wide and a thatch of dark hair covered her pubis. She pushed the shift aside with a foot and leaned over Frost.

He felt a sensation he hadn't known in many a year. His eyes moved down his chest, past his waist. His manhood stood at attention, pointing straight up at the sky. The Beauty climbed on top of him, straddling and easing him inside her.

Frost couldn't remember the last time he had been with a woman. He hadn't always been an old man, but the young man he had once been seemed at best a distant memory. The pleasures of the flesh were so far in his past as to be something he no longer concerned himself with. To find himself in this position now was more than surprising. At least, the mushroom-induced paralysis freed him from the obligation of performing. All he could do was lay there and watch her move atop him.

The Beauty said nothing, made no sounds. She placed her hands on his chest and worked her hips rhythmically. Her breasts were high and so firm they barely moved as she rode him. Slowly, almost methodically, her pace quickened until Frost could see that she was close to climax. Suddenly, she stopped and looked down at his face as if waiting for him to catch up. Frost was looking into her eyes as the two of them finished together.

Afterward, she rolled off and lay beside him, resting her head on his chest, breathing softly, haltingly. Frost still could not move.

After a few moments, she said, "Take the girl to the settlement and put her in the coach headed east. Your obligation to her, your obligation to me, will then be fulfilled."

What obligation to you? He wanted to ask, but could not.

"Find the trickster," she said. "He has the answers you seek."

Frost waited for her to say more, but she did not speak again.

Why could she not give him his answers? Why must he go to another? How long would the paralysis rob him of his ability to speak?

All this and more, he wanted to ask, but could not. Spent and paralyzed, he could only lay there, staring at the smoke rising through the vent in the tipi. He could feel sleep encroaching, and knew he lacked the power to resist.

He lowered his eyes, looked down at the Beauty sleeping atop him. Her hair was as black as raven feathers, shimmering with hints of blue and purple. Her eyes were closed, but he could see her face, her cheek resting against his chest. She was a mature woman, not the girl she had been when the bat-headed giant had murdered her, disemboweled her, sent her blood splashing, cascading down her legs, and overflowing the clay pot at her feet.

Thirty-One

The Wing-Thief

Black Wing was lying face down in the mud on the banks of a river when he felt strong hands grab him. Long fingers wrapped around his biceps, gripping, lifting, then rolling him over. The wing-thief didn't even open his eyes. He didn't care who had found him. A part of him hoped it was a painted warrior. Hoped that the next thing he would feel was the cold kiss of an obsidian blade against his scalp or his throat. He hoped a warrior's knife would do what he had lacked the courage to do.

He had lost track of the days since the holy man Antelope Eyes had been murdered by the creature called Wechuge, since he had followed the creature — wearing the body of the holy man — to the water's edge. He could have killed the creature, but he did not. He could have killed Wechuge days earlier, but the holy man had not allowed it. The holy man had known that the creature would end him, murder him, consume him, but he had done nothing to escape his fate. He had let it happen.

Black Wing did not understand. He had sat at the water's edge for at least a day and night, staring at the spot where he had last seen the holy man, the spot where the holy man's head had disappeared beneath the water. He wondered if there was any way to free the holy man's spirit from the creature. If he had killed Wechuge, would he have freed Antelope Eyes, allowed his spirit to go to the nightlands?

Or would he, by killing Wechuge, have killed what remained of the holy man, as well? Was Antelope Eyes gone forever?

When at last he rose from the riverside, he went to their horses, untied them, and set them free. He went back to the water and followed the river upstream for days on end, wandering, searching for any sign of the monster's exit from the water. Then, finding none, he turned and followed back in the direction from which he had come, studying every spot of the muddy shore, every blade of grass along the banks of both sides of the river. It was pointless, he realized. The monster had disappeared.

Days blurred together. At some point, exhaustion overtook him and he collapsed, lacking the will to get back to his feet. He had nothing left to live for, no reason to fight. He surrendered to despair.

The hands dragged him into the river, forced his head beneath the water. He did not resist. He could feel the current rushing past, melting away the mud caked on his face. Before he could take the water into his lungs, the hands lifted him. Dragged him to the bank. He lay there, coughing, shuddering, and sputtering his way back to consciousness, back to awareness of the world around him.

When he opened his eyes, he saw a tall, broad-shouldered brave, his face painted for war, but the brave held no weapon. His axe was tucked into a belt around his waist. Black Wing counted seven others in the war party standing behind the tall warrior. All staring at him.

Black Wing looked into the tall warrior's face. He knew him. He was a war chief named Bull Elk, the younger brother of the holy man Antelope Eyes.

"I know why you have come," said Black Wing. "I don't know how you knew, but I know why you are here. I am sorry. I'm sorry I couldn't save him. I am ashamed I have not avenged him. Do with me as you will. I will accept your justice."

To Black Wing's surprise, the war chief offered a slight bow and a respectful nod. He reached down a hand and helped the wing-thief to his feet. He stared Black Wing in the eyes.

"Before my brother left on this spirit quest with you, he came to my mother and me. He told us that the gods had shown him his end and that he would not be returning."

"You knew?" Black Wing said incredulously.

Bull Elk nodded. "He insisted we tell no one. Particularly, that we not tell you. We said our goodbyes that day. My mother cried for many days after you two rode away."

"Did he tell you how...?"

Bull Elk shook his head. "He said the gods had permitted him to know, granted that he might bid us farewell, but we were not to know the circumstances and we were not to follow. He said we were not to fault you."

"You knew?" Black Wing said again.

"My mother said he appeared to her in her dreams the night of his death and reminded her it was the will of the gods. He told her that you were blameless, that you could have saved him, but the gods would not allow it. She said she felt the moment he was taken. Like an arrow piercing her heart."

Black Wing was speechless.

"I have not come to kill you," Bull Elk said. "I am not here to avenge him."

Black Wing looked at him curiously. "You wear war paint. You have a war party at your back. Why have you come to me?"

"Antelope Eyes was my brother, and I loved him as one brother loves another. And he loved you. In my eyes, that makes you my brother, as well. Do you accept me as your brother?"

The wing-thief nodded. "Of course."

"My mother stared into the flames of her scrying fire for many days, searching for you. She told me where I would find you." The war chief looked down at the ground. When he looked up again, his eyes were rimmed with tears. "I need your help. And I ask you, as one brother to another, for the love we both shared for Antelope Eyes, will you help me?"

"Tell me why you have come," said Black Wing.

"One of my wives, her name is Snow Cloud, has been taken, stolen by white raiders while she was washing pots in the river. We have searched, but we cannot find her." He paused. "From the sky, with the eyes of an eagle, you could find the men. You could find Snow Cloud."

"How do you know she was taken by white raiders?" asked Black Wing.

"Come," said Bull Elk, turning and motioning a young warrior to step forward.

The boy's name was Slow Rabbit. He was about fourteen summers, but tall for his age. Almost gangly, thought Black Wing. He had a wound on the side of his head, bandaged with a poultice of soap and honey. He spoke with a slight stutter. "Th-there were three of th-them," he said. "White m-men in furs, riding horses. When they saw me running after them, they sh-shot me."

"The bullet grazed his head," said Bull Elk. "Tore his scalp."

"Trappers? Mountain men?" asked Black Wing.

The boy nodded.

Taking a woman from her camp was a bold act, bordering on reckless. In Black Wing's experience, mountain men were often violent and dangerous and not above stealing women.

"That is helpful," he said to Slow Rabbit. "It eliminates the need to look eastward. We know they are in the mountains." To Bull Elk, he said, "When did you lose the track?"

The war chief looked down as if ashamed.

"I'm trying only to determine how far they could have traveled. I don't want to waste time looking in places they could not have reached."

"I was on a hunt when she was taken," said Bull Elk. "With many of my warriors. Slow Rabbit came for us as quickly as he could. The raiders had half a day's head start on us when we found their track. Then we lost the track two days ago."

Two days was not good. The field of search would have to be wide and already Black Wing knew he would have to stay closer to the ground in areas where the trees created a canopy. This could take a long time, longer than Snow Cloud might have. If he could find her at all.

"We have located an eagle's nest for you," said Bull Elk. "There are hatchlings in the nest, so we know the eagle must return soon."

For the first time since the monster Wechuge had killed Antelope Eyes, the wing-thief had a purpose. Had Bull Elk not found him and forced him to his feet, he would still be laying there in the mud, waiting for oblivion to claim him.

Antelope Eyes might have been lost to him. The one he had loved and had failed to protect, failed to save, might be gone, but he could still serve the holy man by helping Antelope Eyes' family. He could help Bull Elk find his lost wife.

"An eagle is good," said Black Wing. "Take me to it."

Thirty-Two

The Manhunter

OZYMANDIAS HAYES LOOKED BACK at the Reverend Josiah Cooley sitting awkwardly in the saddle and wondered if he had made a mistake. The wind whistled around them, swirling in gusts that pushed back against their progress on the high-altitude plain. If nothing else, the wind swallowed the sound of the reverend's constant chatter. So much so that after a while, he'd given up and gone silent. For which Hayes was grateful.

He'd had no reason to acquiesce when the major had asked him to take the Reverend Josiah Cooley with him to Denver City. Truth be known, the major hadn't asked. He'd ordered and hadn't appreciated when Hayes reminded him he was a private citizen and not under the major's command.

"May I ask why you've rejected him as chaplain?" Hayes had asked.

The major chewed the end of his cheroot. He wasn't a man accustomed to being questioned. He narrowed his gaze and sat back in his chair. "You have eyes, do you not, Mr. Hayes? One more than the reverend has, at the very least. Do you not see the man? He's a grotesquerie." The major paused, shifted the cheroot from one side of his mouth to the other.

"I am in command of the cavalry's westernmost outpost. I have two hundred men behind these walls. Two hundred men to hold the line against the savages out there who outnumber us a thousand to one. Do you know what the men see when they look at him? They do not see a godly man who can offer them comfort and spiritual guidance. No, they see their worst fears. They see a reminder of the fate that awaits them if the savages take them while on patrol or if, God forbid, these walls should ever be breached. They look at that man and they see the horror of getting scalped and burned and buggered. They see the tortures they'll endure if they're taken out there. They see God is impotent. That he does not even protect his own from the savages. That man's appearance — his existence — frightens them, scares the fuck out of them, frankly, and the last thing I need out here is frightened men."

Hayes looked down at the dirt floor. "What would you have me do?"

The major told him and Hayes agreed to his request.

The major handed him a folded paper. "This is the letter you requested, attesting to you having delivered the bodies of the outlaws to me."

Hayes took it with a nod.

"I'll give you back your pick of the horses you brought here," said the major. "One for you, one for him. I'm commandeering the remainder. The wagon as well. We'll chop it up and use it for firewood when the nights get colder. The quartermaster will provide you a map, some rations, and fare for Cooley's passage on a coach headed back east. Given the wind, the terrain, and the changing altitude, the ride should take you four days, though I suspect your companion will slow you down more than a bit."

The major stood, indicating their meeting was over, and it was time for Hayes to be on his way. The major did not offer to shake Hayes' hand.

"I bid you good journeys, Mr. Hayes. I don't believe you're the sort to murder him along the way and steal the coach fare for yourself, but that's a chance I'm willing to take."

Hayes glanced over his shoulder at the reverend. He'd had to slow his pace to allow the scalped man to keep up. Josiah Cooley was not a man who belonged on the frontier. The ordeal that had left him disfigured and disabled and somehow shockingly still alive was ample evidence of that. Major McKinney's rejection of him as chaplain had been both an act of cruelty and mercy at the same time. Cooley belonged back in the east, not on the frontier. Cooley had a compassionate heart, but a zealous spirit. Both were liabilities out here.

As the sun sank over the distant mountaintops on the first day of their journey, they had not covered the distance that Hayes had hoped they might. But it was clear the reverend could go no further. They reached a clear, level spot that allowed them a good view in all directions. They'd have little protection from the winds and might be unable to keep a fire burning, but Hayes didn't see a better option. They had to stop and make camp for the night. Weather permitting, they would try to make up the time tomorrow.

With the horses hobbled and their bedrolls laid out, Hayes set about trying to gather enough fuel to build a fire. There was little wood to be found and the buffalo grass was too green to burn.

"I think we may have to forgo a fire tonight," he said, returning to the campsite. Darkness was fast approaching.

The reverend smiled. "Perhaps not," he said, holding up a huge clump of dried dung. "I found this buffalo scat just right over there."

Hayes looked at it.

"You don't seem pleased with my discovery," said Cooley.

"That's not buffalo dung. It's bear shit."

The reverend dropped it and looked around, as if expecting to find a grizzly just over his shoulder.

"Don't be alarmed. We knew there were bears here," said Hayes. "And it'll burn as well as buffalo dung. Though you might want to pluck the chokecherries out. Save them for later, should our rations run low."

"Are you being serious?"

Hayes nodded. He'd eaten worse things he'd found in bear shit.

The reverend offered to take the first watch, but Hayes declined. "Get some rest. I'll wake you later."

The scalped man curled up in his bedroll and Hayes could hear him muttering a long prayer. He caught bits of the twenty-third Psalm -- 'Yea, though I walk through the valley of the shadow of death' -- before the reverend went silent and Hayes realized the scalped man had fallen asleep.

Hayes dug a handful of dried chokecherries from the bear shit and put them in his pocket. He cleared a spot for the fire and managed to light the bear dung, but as he feared, the wind kept extinguishing the fire. He gave up after the second attempt to reignite it. He wrapped his blankets around his shoulders and sat on the ground, staring up at the expansive sky. It was a bright, cloudless night. A three-quarters moon hung overhead amidst a sea of milky stars.

Hayes let the reverend sleep through the night, calculating that having the man well-rested -- even at the expense of his own restfulness -- would speed their journey.

Sunrise came without incident and Cooley woke with a prayer on his scarred lips, thanking the Lord for the new day and beseeching him to guide their steps in the light of morning.

When he finished the prayer, he looked at Hayes. The horses were unhobbled, Hayes' bedroll already secured to the back of his saddle. "You let me sleep through the night?" Cooley said.

"I saw no need to wake you."

"Did you sleep?"

"I dozed," Hayes lied. "Seemed safe enough. We should get to riding."

The swirling winds died down as the day wore on, becoming little more than a stiff breeze. As the elevation increased, the terrain grew more rocky and forested. Pines and quivering aspens with their leaves of golden yellow lined their path.

Despite Hayes' hopes, Cooley continued to slow them down. His crippled arm prevented him from holding the reins properly and without guidance, his horse persistently strayed off course. After a while, Hayes decided it was time to take the reins out of the preacher's hands.

According to the map they'd been given, their path would soon lead them along narrow, winding ledges with steep drop-offs. One false step could prove disastrous. Hayes called a stop and explained his plan to Cooley. He would take the same tact he had used with the caravan of bodies on the plains, tying the reins of Cooley's horse to his own saddle. That way, Cooley's horse would be forced to keep pace and the reverend could focus on simply staying in the saddle.

Hayes cinched the reins, then climbed back onto his horse. After a few steps, the reins pulled taut and Cooley's horse trotted to keep pace, gradually adapting to the new circumstances and following along at enough of a gait to keep just a bit of slack in the reins.

Cooley seemed to like the new arrangement, placing a hand on the horn of his saddle and saying, "Oh, that's much better. Much easier."

They rode through the rest of the afternoon and, as evening approached, Hayes pointed to a rocky outcropping ahead of them, a narrow ledge cutting into the side of the steep, wooded hill.

"Our path takes us there," he said, pointing. "It will be dark soon, but we should keep riding at least for a few more hours. We have a lot of time to make up, and if the night is as clear and as bright as the evening past, we should be able to travel safely."

"Is that wise?" asked Cooley.

"It's not without risk, but it's a risk we should take. We'll be cautious. We'll travel more slowly than we would in the light of day. But if the map is correct, we still have a lot of ground to cover."

"I will defer to your judgment." Cooley mumbled yet another prayer, the shortest Hayes had ever heard him speak, "Lord, guide our steps as darkness falls."

They rode in relative silence for a time, then Cooley said, "You are not a believer, are you, Mr. Hayes?"

"I am not," he said, hoping that this avenue of conversation would go no further.

"That being the case, it strikes me as curious, your questions regarding the resurrection of Christ."

"Merely indulging my own curiosity," said Hayes, wishing to speak no more on the subject.

"What exactly spurred your curiosity?"

Hayes recalled the moment the spark of life -- his soul? -- had returned while his body dangled from the tree, the strange sensation of being alive... again.

"I don't remember. It's nothing," said Hayes.

"Were you born a slave?"

"I beg your pardon?"

"Was that too intimate a question? If so, I apologize."

Hayes shook his head, dismissing the question. "I was."

"Hmm. You mentioned to me you were named for the poem by Shelley. I assumed by your answer that you are a learned man, or at the very least, literate."

"I can read, if that's what you're asking."

"Is it not unusual for a slave to be taught to read?"

"My circumstances were..." Hayes struggled to find the right word and, failing that, said simply, "different from most."

Josiah Cooley nodded. "Your master was also your father."

"You are an astute man," said Hayes.

Cooley smiled. "The Lord grants me wisdom, but I hardly needed that in this instance. You are clearly a mulatto. Had you been sired by an overseer or anyone less than the master of the house, you would likely not have been educated. I assume your father acknowledged your parentage?"

Hayes was silent for a while.

"Forgive me if I have overstepped," said the scalped man.

"I was granted certain privileges," said Hayes. "Education among them, and upon his death, I was given my freedom. But the man never spoke word one to me and the only time I ever knew his touch came at the end of an overseer's strap."

"And what of your mother?"

"Scarcely remember her. She died when I was a small child."

"We have orphanism in common," said Cooley. "When my parents were taken by the pox, I turned to the Good Book to ease my sadness. I found great comfort in the word of God."

"I envy you then. I'm afraid the book had no such effect on me."

Cooley nodded, as if understanding. "Your sadness was in evidence from the moment I met you, Mr. Hayes. But I believe it goes much deeper than the loss of your mother and a father who did not acknowledge you. Why are you here?"

"I'm taking us to Denver City to catch a coach back east."

"I meant here on the frontier? Why is an educated man reduced to hunting down outlaws for his wages?"

"It's my profession."

"It is now, but it wasn't always, was it? You were someone else once. You had another life, but something happened to bring you to this place. Something unpleasant upended your circumstances. You wear your sadness like a garment. Tell me, Mr. Hayes, what is the source of your great sadness?"

Hayes didn't answer.

"There is comfort to be found in the words of the Lord. A comfort that can relieve all pain, all sadness. I speak from experience. I would like to share that comfort with you. I would have you know the peace that fills my heart," Cooley said. "Will you let me help you?"

Before Hayes could answer, he heard a whistling sound, not the whistle of the wind that had accompanied them on their first day from the outpost, but a whoosh of air. A jarring thud vibrated up his legs to his spine. His horse bucked, jerking beneath him. Hayes could see an arrow sticking all the way through the horse's neck. Blood streamed from the wound. The horse staggered in shock, its life fading, its steps taking it ever closer to the edge of a ravine. Hayes peered over the ravine's edge. The drop was at least fifty feet and near-vertical.

Hayes' first thought was to leap from the horse before it fell, but then he saw Cooley behind him, remembered that the reins of Cooley's horse were tied to his saddle. The reverend was desperately clinging to the horn of the saddle with his one good hand. Hayes knew that if his dying horse went over the edge, Cooley's horse would be pulled over with it.

Hayes reached to his boot and pulled the knife he had taken from the outlaw Enoch Munn. Another arrow whizzed past his head, so close he could see the obsidian arrowhead, the striations in the feathers at the arrow's end. He slipped the knife beneath the reins tethering Cooley's horse to his and brought the blade up quickly. The leather strap split and the two horses were bound to each other no longer. Cooley's horse staggered backward, away from the cliff's edge.

Hayes' horse — with Hayes still in the saddle — tumbled over the edge.

Thirty-Three

The Gunslinger

When Hamish Frost awoke again, he found the morning sun beaming through the tipi's vent, the golden light warm on his face. He sat up, looked around. The fire had grown cold and neither the old woman nor the beauty who had taken her place were inside with him. He was alone.

He looked at his arm, wiggled his fingers. He had thought there was a chance he had hallucinated the old woman opening the wound and filling it with hot coals, melting the skin back together, but his arm appeared as good as new, with no trace of the wound given him by the dire gnome.

He stood, found his clothes, and dressed. The paralytic effects of the mushrooms the old woman had given him had faded. He had full control of himself again. Felt better, stronger, than he had in some time.

He threw back the flap of buffalo hide and stepped out of the tipi. The morning sun sat in a cloudless sky. The girl Ana was lying on the moss, asleep in the shadow cast by the tipi and nestled against the abdomen of the giant Wolf, who lay curled around her. Neither stirred at his appearance.

Frost stepped around to the backside of the tipi and peered into the stand of aspens, their golden leaves making a jangling sound as they quivered in the breeze. He looked from one end of the plateau to the other, but saw no sign of either the old woman or the beauty.

He walked back around to the front of the tipi, looked at the slumbering girl and the wolf.

"We are such stuff as dreams are made on, and our little life is rounded with a sleep," he said

Ana stirred, opened her eyes and sat up, her arms wide as she stretched. The wolf opened its amber eyes, but did not move.

"I thought you said you weren't going to be long," said the girl.

"So I did," said Frost. "Seems I was wrong about that."

"Where'd the old woman go?"

"You've seen her?"

The girl shook her head.

"Then how did you know she's not in the tipi?"

The girl wrinkled her brow. "I don't know. But she's not, is she?"

Frost looked at her curiously. "No. She's not. When did the wolf come back?"

"The first night."

"The first? How many nights was I in there?"

"Four."

Frost was stunned. "I was in there for four days?"

The girl nodded.

"And you just stayed out here the entire time?"

"What else could I do? You told me not to cross the stones. You said I'd be safe while you were in there, so I just waited."

"What did you do for food? For water?"

The girl shrugged. "Didn't think about it."

"You went four days without food or water and you didn't think about it?"

"I suppose not."

"The wolf's been with you the entire time?"

She nodded.

Frost pursed his lips. The wolf had sustained her. That was the only answer. His presence had kept her free from hunger and bodily needs.

"I would that she were here to see us off," he said. *"Parting is such sweet sorrow,* but I suppose our business here is complete. Let's head down the mesa and be on our way."

Frost took a step toward the girl, but as his foot passed over the medicine stones, his toe breaking the plane of the circle, there was a flash of lightning and a deafening burst of thunder. Frost was lifted off his feet and hurled backwards. He slammed into the tipi, shattering the bracing poles and collapsing the structure on top of him.

Dazed, he untangled himself from the buffalo hides and pushed aside the splintered poles that had landed on top of him. His vision was blurred, fuzzy spectral clouds floating in front of his eyes. His hearing was likewise compromised, a discordant thrum accompanying the ringing in his ears. His first thought was that had it not been for the tipi, he would've sailed over the edge of the plateau, but then he realized it was more likely he would've been hit by another bolt of lightning when his flailing body tried to cross the opposite edge of the circle.

Slowly, he got to his feet. With his vision clearing, he gave himself a quick look over. He could smell burnt hair and assumed his eyebrows, at the very least, were singed. His clothes were likewise blackened and smoking in a few spots, but as far as he could tell, he wasn't on fire, which was always good to know. No bones seemed broken and aside from a trickle coming out of his nose, there was no blood. All in all, it could have been a lot worse, considering he'd just been hit by a literal bolt from the blue.

Ana was staring at him in disbelief. Her mouth was moving, but the pulsing in his ears prevented him from hearing any of her words. The Shadow Wolf sprang to its feet, head down, canines bared, pawing at the ground. Frost saw what was about to happen. He held up his hands to stop the wolf, but it was already too late. The wolf bounded forward and tried to leap over the medicine stones. There was no explosion this time, no thunder or lightning. Instead, the wolf collided headlong with an invisible wall aligned with the plane of the circle. The wolf slumped to the ground in a heap.

So hard was the impact that Frost feared the wolf had broken its neck. After a moment though, the wolf found its feet. It growled and pawed at the invisible wall, slipping and sliding like it was trying to run across black ice. The wolf stopped the pawing and loped around the circumference of the circle of stones, sniffing and searching for a weak spot. Finding no obvious vulnerability, the wolf lowered its great head and began digging in front of the stones, as if trying to tunnel underneath the barrier. Dirt and moss flew, but the soil at the top of the small plateau was shallow and less than two feet down, the wolf hit stone.

"Stop," yelled Frost. The ringing in his ears was fast subsiding. "You can't dig me out. She gave me permission to enter, but it seems I don't have permission to leave. You can't enter and I can't exit. I need her consent to cross the stones."

The girl looked at him with wide eyes. "They're like the trees," she said. "The trees that trapped me and kept me from leaving the shack."

Frost sighed. "Somewhat, yes. Only stronger. Because the one who created this circle is vastly more powerful than the thing that was inside your captor."

"Then you're trapped. She trapped you."

"I don't think that's what's happening here."

"I do," said Ana. "She trapped you in there. Just like the fur trader trapped me."

"It's not an apt comparison."

"How is it different?"

"It's vastly different," he said.

"How?"

Frost sighed. "Perhaps it was in my approach," he said. He reached down and plucked his floppy hat from beneath a pine pole. He straightened the magpie feather and placed the hat atop his head. "Let's try this again."

He reached a cautious hand out towards the circle of stones, probing. From a foot away, he could feel an electric charge dancing along his fingertips, the hair on his arms standing up and at attention. He dropped his hand. Any closer, he knew, would bring another explosion, another bolt of lightning. He exhaled harshly.

"You can't get out, can you?" Ana said.

"That would appear to be the case. For the nonce, at least."

"When the fur trader trapped me, at least he brought me food and there was a stream I could draw water from. You don't have food or water in there, do you?"

"I don't need it. Not for a while. You won't either. The wolf's medicine will sustain you. Like it did for the last few days. Food and water are not a concern."

"I would've died if you hadn't gotten me past the trees."

"Don't overreact, child. I won't die. I'm tougher than you know. I can handle a while without food or water. And she'll be back. She'll grant me leave. And then we'll be on our way."

"I don't think she's coming back."

"She will. You don't know her as I do."

"I know she trapped you. I know you can't get past that circle of stones. I know you got struck by lightning the last time you tried. And every time you try, it'll happen again, won't it?"

"She has a purpose for everything she does. We may not understand it, but she has a purpose. She summoned me. She gave me instructions for what to do when we leave here." He held up his arm, showed her that his wound was gone. "She healed me. Why would she do that if she meant for me to die here? That would serve no purpose. And she has a purpose. I'll get out. She'll let me out. We just have to be patient."

Ana looked down at the ring of polished medicine stones. "I won't let you die in there."

"Listen to me, child. There's no cause for that kind of talk. No one's dying here. Not me. Not you."

Ana knelt in front of the medicine circle.

"Stay back! Do not touch the stones."

The girl ignored him. She reached down, wrapped her fingers around the edges of one of the polished stones. There was no bolt of lightning. No invisible wall to push back against her.

Frost's mouth hung open. Words failed him.

Ana twisted the stone back and forth, prying it from the dirt and moss. She tugged, hefting the stone, and it came free of the ground. She straightened, got to her feet, holding the stone in her hands. She looked it over, then tossed it aside as if it weighed no more than a pine cone.

Frost stared at her, dumbfounded. The girl had broken the circle. She had broken the old woman's circle. The old woman made of stars, the most powerful being Frost had ever encountered, had built a medicine ring around her tipi. Lightning struck him when he tried to cross it. Even the Shadow Wolf had slammed headlong into an invisible wall when it had tried. But this girl had simply reached down and removed one of the stones. This girl had broken the old woman's circle.

Ana smiled at him. She reached a hand over the bare spot of ground where the stone had been, held it out palm up, inviting him to take it.

"I wasn't going to let you die," she said.

Frost took her hand and stepped across the broken circle.

Thirty-Four

The Wing-Thief

Through the eyes of the eagle, from high above the heavily forested foothills, Black Wing watched the rider expertly weaving his way down the mountainside. The wing-thief circled, watched a while longer, then, still curious, swooped downward, spreading his wings to catch the wind and slow his descent. He took perch in the top of a blue spruce at the edge of a small clearing, a rocky field strewn with small boulders.

The wing-thief watched as the rider emerged from the trees and entered the clearing. Black Wing had believed the rider to be alone, but seconds after the rider entered the clearing, he realized he had been wrong. Like a shadow come to life, the giant black wolf stepped from the treeline and trotted briskly behind the rider. In spite of its enormous size, the Shadow Wolf had been undetectable, almost invisible, as it moved through the trees. But the Shadow Wolf was not alone, either. Riding on its back was a girl. Black Wing recognized her instantly. She was the same girl he and Antelope Eyes had watched throw a rooster into the face of the naked, rat-faced trapper. The girl who had hidden in the boulders not far from the warded trees. The girl to whom the Shadow Wolf had appeared while the wing-thief and the holy man watched from a short distance.

The girl now clung to the wolf's back, her arms wrapped tightly around its neck as it glided through the clearing. Black Wing could see a violet aura shimmering around both of them. Each was possessed of powerful medicine. A similar aura enveloped the rider, though not as vibrant as that around the girl or the wolf.

The rider reined in, bringing his painted horse to a stop. The Shadow Wolf paused behind him. The rider shifted in his saddle, then angled his head upward and looked directly to the top of the blue spruce.

Black Wing had known only one, other than Antelope Eyes, who could recognize him when he wore the body of a bird. And that was the wizened old man with purple eyes and skin as white as his hair, the ancient-looking, strange-talking gunfighter named Hamish Frost, whom the people of the plains called Whiteskin. The very man who sat on the painted horse in the clearing. The man who looked up at an eagle in the top of the spruce, and saw not a bird, but a wing-thief, a warrior borrowing the body of a bird.

Black Wing had heard tribal elders, men with leathery, wrinkled skin and spines curved by age, claim that Whiteskin was the oldest man alive, that he had been old when their grandfathers were children. Yet despite his years, Whiteskin sat tall in the saddle, his chest out, his shoulders back. No stoop at all to his posture.

Whiteskin doffed his floppy hat and shook out his long, stringy hair. He smiled and gave Black Wing a wave of his hand.

"*Hope of orphans, and unfathered fruit, for summer and his pleasures wait on thee, and thou away,*" he said, extending his arms in an expansive gesture as if pantomiming the words he spoke, "*the very birds are mute.*"

The old man laughed as if he had told a joke. But the joke was lost on Black Wing. The wing-thief knew the tongue of the white eyes and, when in his own body, could speak it as well or better even than many of them, but when it came to old Whiteskin's wordplay, Black Wing could simply not follow. He could recognize most of the words, but the construction of the sentences was strange, unlike the speech of any other the wing-thief had ever encountered.

"That is you, isn't it, Black Wing?" asked the old man. "Been a while since we've crossed paths, but I'm pretty sure that's you."

"Who are you talking to?" said the girl from the back of the Shadow Wolf. "All I see is a big bird in that tree."

"Quiet, child," said the old gunslinger. "We'll resume our trek directly."

For the moment, Black Wing wished he were in the body of a crow instead of an eagle. A crow didn't have the eyesight of an eagle, couldn't fly as high or as fast, but a crow could talk. Not always well. Some words were difficult to form, but with effort, he could find enough words to communicate. But an eagle could only screech in acknowledgment.

"What brings you out this way?" asked Whiteskin. "Searching for something? Someone perhaps?"

The eagle screeched.

"Not looking for me by chance, are you?"

Black Wing waggled his head.

"Not me then," said the old man. "Well, I can tell you I've seen no one between here and the next mesa over. You'd likely be wasting your time to fly any farther west."

Black Wing shifted his feet, talons gripping the branch on which he perched, and screeched again.

"Wish you were in a crow and not an eagle," said the old man. "This would be easier. And I wouldn't have to deal with the screeching accosting my ears."

Black Wing bobbed his head, but refrained from screeching again.

"I wish you good fortune on your search and I regret we were unable to parley more successfully. There is actually much of which we might speak. Had I the time, I would aid you in your search, but alas, I have places to be. No time to wait for you to retrieve your body from a treetop, even if you were so inclined."

The old man placed his hat back atop his head and adjusted the magpie feather. "*Painful though parting be, I bow to you as I see you off to distant clouds.*" He smiled. "Give my regards to Antelope Eyes."

The mention of the holy man's name sent an icicle through Black Wing's heart. The Shadow Wolf walked past the old man, taking the lead. The girl stole a look up into the branches of the spruce. Her eyes locked onto his and Black Wing knew that she too had seen beyond the eagle's body and saw him for who he was. The girl swiveled as the wolf ambled on, keeping her eyes on Black Wing until the wolf passed through the clearing and again disappeared into the trees.

Old Whiteskin spurred his horse forward, following them, but just before he left the clearing he spoke out loudly, without looking up at Black Wing. "*Wizards know their times: Deep night, dark night, the silent of the night, The time of night when Troy was set on fire; The time when screech-owls cry and ban-dogs howl, And spirits walk and ghosts break up their graves.*"

The old man held up a hand and waved. "You take care of yourself, Black Wing. There's some strange medicine about and I don't have all the answers just yet. I'm taking the girl to Denver City. After that, I suspect I'll be heading south. Most likely in the direction of the old cave city. Should you or the holy man need to speak with me, you can find me there."

The old gunslinger ducked beneath a branch and followed the Shadow Wolf into the trees.

Black Wing spread his wings, lifted off of the spruce branch, and took flight. He flew high, regaining the altitude he had surrendered when his curiosity about the rider got the better of him. He looked down and found Whiteskin again, working his way down the hill. He flew eastward and watched the old man, his painted horse, and the giant wolf as black as midnight with the girl riding upon its back, until he lost sight of them.

Thirty-Five

The Manhunter

Ozymandias Hayes awoke in the dim, blue light of pre-dawn. Cora slept in the bed next to him, nestled close, her naked back pressed against his side. Hayes listened to her breathing, watched her ribs expand with each soft intake and fall with every exhalation. He smiled, then stared up at the slatted wood ceiling. He had painted it only weeks earlier. He had debated whether it needed another coat but ultimately decided against it. Perhaps he should reconsider.

It was quiet in the house. Too quiet. Was that why he had awakened? The lack of noise? He was more accustomed to the opposite. Baby Charlotte waking hungry in the middle of the night. Hungry or cold or just unhappy, her plaintive cries shattering the night's peace. Cora would rise, go to her bassinet, and lift Charlotte. She would cuddle the baby, cradling her gently, soothing her with touch and softly spoken words. Or perhaps sitting with her, rocking her back to sleep. Sometimes nursing her until her tiny belly was full of milk and, sated, she'd drift back into slumber. Hayes would always sit up in bed, watching and waiting for Cora to return.

"Go back to sleep," Cora would say. "She just needs to be comforted." Or "She's just hungry."

"I don't want to sleep," Hayes would say. "I want to watch you with her."

But this night, no restless crying, no squirming fit of anger or hunger, came from her crib. Charlotte's cries had not awakened him. He looked around, but saw nothing out of order in their small room.

He considered rising, checking the doors and windows but decided against it. There was enough pale light seeping through the curtains for him to tell that the windows were latched and the door bolted shut. There were no sounds of disturbance from within the small home or from without. All was quiet and still. Getting out of bed to double-check what he could see with his own eyes and hear with his own ears was pointless. He closed his eyes and tried to will himself back to sleep before he woke Cora.

But Cora was going to awake in a moment, anyway. This was a memory. He knew what would happen next.

Cora sat bolt upright in the bed, her eyes wide, mouth hanging open. Her head swiveled from side to side, taking in the room.

"Shhh," said Hayes. "It's okay. I'm sorry I woke you." But it wasn't okay. He knew that now. This was all a memory.

Cora jumped from the bed and ran toward baby Charlotte's bassinet. Hayes flung the blanket aside and followed after her. This was a memory. He knew what they would find. He took two steps from the bed and Cora, the bassinet, and the room all disappeared.

Hayes stood on the muddy shore of a blackwater river. A cabbage-sized ball of blue light floated over the water, pulsing softly, swirling in on itself, and casting a diffuse glow over the river bank and the birch-bark canoe resting half in the water and half on the shore. A wooden paddle in the front of the canoe.

"Back again, Mr. Hayes?"

The voice came from behind him. Hayes turned and saw the spectral woman. Her black hair was almost indistinguishable from the surrounding darkness. She held out her left hand, palm up, her little finger ending in a scarred nub just below the first knuckle, and pointed to the canoe.

"Are you ready?" she asked.

"I don't know," he said. "Am I dead... again?"

"As I said to you last time, it's more complicated than that. At the moment, your body lies at the bottom of a ravine. There's a horse on top of you. You were crushed beneath it in the fall."

"So, there's no going back this time?" Hayes asked.

"I didn't say that. I said only that your body was crushed at the bottom of a ravine. It can be restored, just as it was when you were hanged from a tree."

Hayes turned from the woman, looked at the canoe. "But I don't have to go back? I can stay. I can get in the canoe?"

"If you think it's time. If you think you're ready."

"Ready for what?"

"For what you'll find at the river's end."

Hayes turned back to her. "What will I find?"

The woman smiled enigmatically. "That's not for me to say. What you find there will depend on you. It will depend on what you are ready to find."

"But it's my decision? To get in the canoe...?"

"Or to return," she said.

"I'm not going back. There's nothing for me there."

Her smile didn't change. "Nothing?"

Hayes shook his head. "No. There's..." he paused. "Is Josiah Cooley still alive?"

"For now."

"What does that mean?"

"What do you think it means?"

Hayes looked at the canoe again, at the black water lapping gently at the bark wrapping the frame, the wooden paddle resting against the bow seat. He turned back to the woman with nine fingers.

"If he's still alive, it means I have to go back," he said.

The woman held up her hand. The ball of light floated from where it hovered over the river, bathing Hayes' face in a cold blue glow as it passed. The light shrank as it neared the woman's hand, then rested against her palm, and slowly burrowed into her flesh. Her hand glowed, pulsing with a blue radiance. The light dimmed, fading fast, and just before they were plunged into total darkness, Hayes looked at the woman's face. Only he did not see a face. He saw red and purple nebulae swirling in a horseshoe shape and twinkling stars where eyes should have been.

Ozymandias Hayes was lying on his back at the bottom of the ravine. His horse was sprawled on top of him. Still alive, though its body was broken, legs twisted, jagged white bones protruding through one thigh. The horse was quiet, but trembling. Dark blood pulsed from the arrow wound in its neck.

Hayes braced himself, wormed his way out from under the horse's bulk, and got to his feet. He was sore, bruised, and his face was scraped from a rock he had brushed on his fall down the rocky ravine, but he could stand and no bones seemed to be broken. Not now, he realized. Not anymore. His body had been restored. The moon was high in the sky, the night bright. His hand went to his holster, fingers searching for his pistol. The horse was in agony. A bullet to the brain would be a kindness. But he found his holster empty.

He reached into his boot and found the knife he had taken from Enoch Munn, the knife he had used to cut loose the reins that tethered the horses seconds before he had tumbled over the edge of the ravine. He placed one hand over the horse's eye, then quickly dragged the blade across its throat, severing the jugular vein. The horse was dead in seconds.

He returned the knife to his boot, then detached the saddlebags loaded with the maps and supplies given him by the quartermaster and slung them over his shoulder. He looked around for his pistol, finally finding it in a grassy patch at the base of the ravine. He popped open the cylinder, checked the load, then dropped it in his holster.

The incline was steep but covered with rocks and deep-rooted weeds that allowed him to grip and pull his way up. His muscles ached and burned, but he reached the top of the ravine in short order.

Josiah Cooley was nowhere to be seen. He refrained from calling out for fear the warriors who rained arrows down on them would hear. He studied the ground. It was rocky, and the soil was thin, but he managed to find the tracks left by Cooley's horse. But they weren't the only track he found. The preacher's horse had been surrounded by moccasined feet. Hayes could see where Cooley's horse had been led off the trail and up into the wooded hillside.

Hayes stared into the trees. The bright night made for deep shadows in the wood. He drew his pistol, and keeping low, followed the tracks up the hillside.

A few hundred steps later, he found Cooley's horse grazing on a patch of grass near an aspen thicket. He heard Cooley's sing-song voice, reciting scripture. He followed the sound and soon saw a light up ahead. A fire in a small clearing. A half dozen warriors in breechclouts and leggings, wearing bone armor, sat around the fire. Their faces were painted for war, each uniquely rendered in hues of red and yellow with stark symbols in black and white. Small bones were braided into their hair.

Seated in the midst of the warriors was Josiah Cooley. He had his copy of the Bible opened, reading aloud from it. The painted warriors all watched him, listening to his words, almost as if the preacher were an honored guest and not their prisoner.

Hayes wondered if, from his vantage point in the shadows of the trees, he could kill all the painted warriors before they would have time to gather their knives, bone clubs, or arrows. Could he get off six killshots before one of the painted warriors could slit Josiah Cooley's throat or put an arrow through his own chest?

Doubtful. The element of surprise might allow him to kill half of them, but once the shooting started, he didn't see a way to keep Cooley from being murdered.

As Hayes contemplated his move, Josiah Cooley raised his head, looking up from his scriptures and staring directly at him. Hayes brought a finger to his mouth, signaling for him to be quiet, but the preacher ignored him.

"Join us, Brother Hayes," said Cooley, motioning towards him.

The painted warriors all turned and looked at Hayes, but none reached for weapons. At least not yet.

Shoot them now, Hayes thought. But he hesitated.

"Brothers, this is my friend, Ozymandias Hayes," said Cooley to the painted warriors. To Hayes, he said, "I had believed you dead when you went over the edge of the ravine."

"What are you doing, Josiah?" said Hayes. "These are painted warriors."

"They are my brothers in Christ. They just don't know that yet," said the scalped man. "Come sit by our fire, Mr. Hayes."

"They're going to kill you, Josiah," said Hayes. "The moment you cease to amuse them, they're going to cut your head off and roast you on a spit."

The preacher smiled as much as his scars would permit. "If that happens, then the Lord so willed it. Who am I to question?"

"Listen to me, Josiah," pleaded Hayes. "Stand up slowly, Keep your hands where they can see them and walk to me. Maybe we can back our way out of this."

"Put your pistol away, Mr. Hayes. We are under the protection of Jesus Christ."

"No, we're not. These are painted warriors. Warriors, Josiah. Wearing paint. They are at war. What was done to you in the past will pale in comparison to what awaits you from them. Please, I beg you. Come with me. If we get out of here, I'll put you on the stagecoach in Denver City, and you'll be back in the States in a couple of weeks."

"There is nothing in the States for me. I am where I was always meant to be. This is my mission. To bring the gospel of our Lord and Savior to the savage lands. To save these people and make these lands a bit less savage."

"Please. Stand up slowly and walk backward to me."

Cooley smiled and gave his head a small shake. "If you will not join me, Ozymandias, then you should leave. Thank you for getting me here. Thank you for reminding me of my purpose. I am sorry we never got a chance to discuss what brought you to the frontier. Look to the Lord, my brother. Only he can free you of that great sadness you carry with you, that sadness that has re-enslaved you."

"Don't do this, Josiah."

"My horse is over there," he said, pointing back in the direction from which Hayes had come. "I won't be needing it. You should hurry if you're going to make Denver City before that coach leaves for the States."

Hayes made one last silent plea with his eyes. Cooley shook his head.

Hayes kept his pistol trained on the painted warriors as he slowly backed away and into the shadows.

As he found the horse and climbed into the saddle, he heard the scalped man's voice from within the aspens.

"Trust in the Lord with all thine heart; and lean not unto thine own understanding. In all thy ways acknowledge him, and he shall direct thy paths."

Thirty-Six

The Gunslinger

Hamish Frost looked out at the lodgepole pines and groves of quivering aspens steadily giving way to a field of enormous, reddish-orange boulders, some the size of small houses. The hue of the rocks created a sharp contrast with the deep, dark greens of the pines and the rich, vibrant short grasses surrounding them.

The girl named Ana rode behind him, sitting atop the Shadow Wolf. She stared curiously out at the rock-strewn field. "Why are they so orange?"

"Rust," said the old gunslinger with a laugh.

"What?" said the girl.

"Rust. Rust is why they're that color."

"Rocks can rust? How?"

"Rust is just iron that's been overexposed to the elements. These hills, these rocks, are made of sandstone. Sandstone is full of iron ore. A few million years — give or take — of sun, rain, wind, and snow, and you get yourself a mountain the color of a shovel that's been left outside for a few winters."

They rode on in silence for a stretch, slipping through the boulders as they worked their way down the hillside. At the bottom of the hill, Frost reined in his horse and twisted in the saddle, looking back at the girl. The wolf followed his lead, pausing between two large boulders. Its black fur melded with the cast shadows around it, making it near impossible to tell where one ended and the other began.

Frost smiled. *"We are such stuff as dreams are made on and our little life is rounded with sleep."*

Ana wrinkled her brow. "I don't know what you're talking about."

"You were dreaming last night. Something that frightened you, unless I miss my guess. I heard you cry out several times before you awoke."

The girl dropped her head. "It was just a dream. Don't mean nothing."

Frost nodded. "If it was indeed just a dream, then you are likely correct. Dreams mean little. But it might've been more than that. The difference between dream and vision can be a matter of experience and interpretation."

"I don't have visions."

"Mayhap you are correct. But never having such in the past is no predictor of whether you may in the future. Some people are prone to visions from birth, for others, the ability can develop later. You were unable to escape the trapper's wards until you were. And after what transpired on the mesa, I am learning there is more to you than meets the eye."

"I didn't do anything. I told you, I just picked up a rock."

"You did more than pick up a rock. You broke a medicine circle constructed by the most powerful entity I've ever come across. And you did so effortlessly and with no consequence. If you're now having visions, then we need to discuss what you're seeing. I've been tasked with securing your safe passage out of these hills. If you're being granted glimpses into the future, then I'd like to know what lies ahead of us."

"It was just a dream."

"Humor me. What did you see, child?"

The girl hesitated. "I was walking through the darkness. I was in a tunnel or a cave, I think. There was a curved rock wall all around me, over my head. Only I wasn't me. I mean, I was me, but I didn't look like me."

"You could see your face?"

The girl considered this. "No. I guess not."

"Then how do you know what you looked like? Was it just a sense of how you looked, or could you actually see yourself?"

"It wasn't like I was looking at myself from outside my body. I was seeing through my own eyes. I mean, I think they were my eyes. I think it was my body, but it was old. My hands and legs were old and all wrinkled up and spotted like..." The girl's voice trailed off.

"Like mine?" Frost smiled.

The girl nodded and held up her left hand, waggled her fingers. "You remember how the old woman only had nine fingers? How her little finger had been cut off or bit off or something?"

Frost nodded.

"In the dream, mine was too."

"Your finger was missing?"

The girl nodded. "The little one on my left hand. Just like hers. I looked at it close. It was missing from about halfway up. The end was all scarred, just like hers was." The girl looked at Frost. "You don't know why her finger is missing?"

He shook his head. "She never told me."

"Was it always that way?"

Frost thought it over and was surprised at his own answer. "I don't recall."

The girl frowned. "If I'm going to lose my finger, I'd like to know how."

"We haven't established this was anything more than a dream. What else did you see?"

"There was a light in the cave. That's how I could see my hands and my legs."

"What kind of light? Where did it come from?"

"I don't know where it came from, but it looked like the moon, only a lot smaller. I could've held it in my hands. It was floating in the air next to me. Glowing."

"Were you alone in this cave?"

She shook her head.

"Was I with you?"

"No."

"What about the wolf?"

She shook her head again, ran her fingers through the scruff at the base of the wolf's neck. "He wasn't there either."

"Who was?"

The girl was quiet for a moment. "A monster," she said.

"A monster?"

She nodded.

"What did it look like?"

"I couldn't see it good. It was walking a few steps behind me, staying in the shadows."

"But you knew it was there?"

She nodded.

"Was it stalking you?"

She shook her head. "I don't think so. It was walking with me. Like we were both supposed to be there. Like we were going somewhere together. Or at least I thought we were."

"If you couldn't see it, how do you know it was a monster?"

She looked off into the distance, swallowed hard before she spoke. "Because it ate me. It ate me alive."

Frost looked at her, his pale, heavily lined face impassive. His violet eyes wide. "You saw your own death?"

Ana nodded. "It grabbed me and picked me up, opened its mouth real wide. I could see its teeth, all yellowed. Cracked and broken. It put my head in its mouth and I didn't fight back. I could feel it closing its mouth, pressing down, squashing my head. It hurt. It hurt a lot. Real bad. And then it just stopped hurting. I couldn't feel anything, but I could still hear things. Crunching sounds. Like my bones were cracking and breaking... while it chewed."

"You could hear, but you couldn't see?"

She nodded. "I could hear it for a long time. Until it... until it finished eating me. I think it ate all of me. Every bit of me. And then I woke up."

Frost looked at her in silence, nodded his head, then put his heels to the painted horse's flanks, and shook the reins. The horse began to trot away.

"Was that a vision?" asked Ana. "Is that what's going to happen to me? Am I going to get ate by a monster?"

Frost shook his head. "No, child. Rest easy. That was no vision. It was just a bad dream. Put it out of your mind."

Thirty-Seven

The Wing-Thief

WITH DUSK AT HAND, the shadows stretching long and night encroaching, the hills and trees and rocks all merged into oneness, a single dark shape sprawling across the land. A few hours after his encounter with Whiteskin, Black Wing realized the eagle's eyes would serve his purpose no longer. The eagle's vision was unparalleled in sunlight but poor at night.

He had spent the entire day flying high above the trees, searching in all directions for the missing wife of his new brother, the war chief Bull Elk. But he had found only the old gunslinger, the girl, and the wolf. If he returned now, if he abandoned the search and reclaimed his body, he would have to face Bull Elk and admit his failure. He was not prepared for that difficult conversation. He did not want to tell his new brother that he had not found his missing wife. He did not want the war chief's hopes to be dashed, but with each hour that passed, the chances of ever finding Snow Cloud alive diminished.

Though unspoken, it was known by both Black Wing and Bull Elk that the mountain men would keep her alive only until their lusts were sated. A girl, a child, they might keep as a slave, but not a woman grown. Not a fierce woman. And only a fierce woman would wed a war chief. Black Wing knew when the white eyes had their fill of her, they would kill her. And she would be lost to Bull Elk as Antelope Eyes was lost to him. So he would keep looking. He would do what he must to find her. He would not return to his own body until he knew where she was and could lead the war chief back to her.

But first, he had to find a bird that would serve him better in the dark, a bird whose eyes were as strong in the darkness as the eagle's had been in the bright light of day. He found just such a bird in the great horned owl perched in the upper branches of a ponderosa pine. But the wing-thief was faced with a problem. He had never switched from one bird to another without returning to his own body first. He had never borrowed the tongue of a crow without first returning the wings of the sparrow. Or the night eyes of an owl without first returning the spirit of the eagle.

He wasn't even sure it was possible. And if it was, he did not know what would become of the spirits of the two birds. Would the owl's spirit supplant the eagle's inside the wing-thief's body? Would the eagle's spirit be set free from its temporary prison? Would it instantly cross the distance and somehow find its wings again? Would the eagle return to its nestlings, having lost only a day of its life, or would the spirit never find its way back to its wings? Would the great eagle be spiritless? Would its body fall from the sky? Crash lifeless to the ground?

Would the eagle and the owl swap spirits? Would the owl suddenly find itself inside the eagle's body?

Or would the eagle remain trapped in the wing-thief's body and the owl's spirit have no body to claim? Would the owl's spirit float bodyless until absorbed by the sky? When the wing-thief returned to his own body, would there be no spirit to return to the owl?

If he did this, if he succeeded in doing this, would he be killing both the owl and the eagle? What's more, if he did this, if he succeeded in doing this, would he even be able to reclaim his own body? Or would he become, in both name and deed, a wing-thief? Would he not be borrowing the owl's eyes, but murdering its spirit and stealing its body?

Antelope Eyes had told him once of an old medicine man afflicted with the wasting disease who had chosen to steal the body of a falcon and live out his days as a bird of prey, while the falcon's spirit was trapped inside the old man's body until it succumbed to the disease that had ravaged it.

Was that what he was doing? Was he stealing the owl's body, never to return it? If he succeeded in finding Snow Cloud, would he be able to return and tell the war chief where she was? Or would he be trapped forever in the owl's body?

So many questions and he had no answers. The holy man would know. Antelope Eyes would know the answers. Black Wing had always relied on the wisdom of Antelope Eyes to settle such questions, even if the holy man couched his answers in riddles and maddeningly vague responses. Black Wing had never doubted that the holy man had the answer to any question that might occur to him. But the monster Wechuge had murdered Antelope Eyes, eaten his body, and stolen his spirit. Black Wing had failed the holy man, failed to save him. That failure would haunt him for all his days. Nothing would ever erase his guilt or ease his conscience, but he could still serve the holy man by serving his brother. He was determined he would not fail Bull Elk as he had failed Antelope Eyes. He would find Snow Cloud. He would do whatever was necessary to find the war chief's wife. And he would find a way to return to his body and he would lead Bull Elk to Snow Cloud. He would reunite the war chief and his wife. This he would do for the love he bore the war chief's brother.

Black Wing swooped down, took perch in the tree near the great horned owl. The owl was startled by the appearance of the eagle. It let out a great cry and flapped its huge wings in a fierce show of defiance. Black Wing did not hesitate.

His spirit abandoned the eagle's body, jumping to the owl and forcing the owl's spirit to flee. He felt a moment of disorientation and then took a few seconds to adjust to the new body, to his powerful new night eyes.

He looked and saw the eagle's talons release from its perch. But its wings did not spread. It did not take flight. It fell, bouncing from branch to branch, making no effort to halt its tumble until it crashed into the ground at the base of the pine and lay twitching. The eagle's head was twisted at an unnatural angle. Blood smeared the edges of its beak. Its twitching ceased and the great bird lay motionless. Dead.

A wave of guilt and self-revulsion rolled over the wing-thief. He had not only murdered the eagle, but starved her hatchlings back in the nest as well.

Forgive me, little sister, he thought.

But it was a pointless thought. There was no forgiveness for him. Not in this life or the next. He was a wing-thief. He had stolen a medicine bundle from a dying old woman. Antelope Eyes had believed the gods would not condemn him for that, but he knew the truth. He had been damned from the moment his fingers had wrapped around the bundle and broken the string around the old woman's neck.

He took one last look at the dead eagle and lifted off the branch, flying low above the treetops.

Hours later, with the night receding and the sunlight breaking over the distant horizon, splaying its golden rays over the tops of the pines and quivering aspens, he found the campfire.

Black Wing took perch in an aspen near the fire. There were four men. White eyes. Mountain men wearing animal skin clothing. Their bedrolls were on the ground, their horses tied to trees nearby. The first man had sunken eyes and a weak chin, and unkempt sandy-hair poking from beneath a fur hat with a badger's eyeless face on the front. The second had a shaved head and scraggly beard streaked with gray. The third was a slight, rat-faced man with a single brow covering both eyes. All three sat staring at the fourth man.

The massive, broad-chested man with a bushy beard and arms almost as thick as his legs, stood a few feet from the fire. His buckskin pants were around his ankles and the front flap of his red undergarments was unbuttoned. His exposed phallus was turgid, swollen and purple. He held a flat, blood-covered rock in one hand. On the ground at the fourth man's feet, a naked woman lay sprawled and unmoving. Her face was covered in blood, her skull crushed. Dark matter flowed from the opened wound at her temple, seeping into the soil.

Black Wing's search was over. He had found Snow Cloud, but he had found her too late.

"What the fuck you kill her for?" The man with the shaved head asked the giant holding the bloody rock.

"I thought we agreed to keep her for a while," said the slight man with a single eyebrow.

"Bitch damned near bit my pecker off," the massive man said. He dropped the rock next to Snow Cloud's head. He gripped his manhood and showed it to the others. "Look at that. The cunt left teeth marks."

The other men laughed. The sandy-haired man slapped the shorn-headed man on the back, laughing so hard he nearly fell forward into the fire.

"You think it's funny 'cause it weren't your dicks getting chewed on," said the massive man.

These men must die, thought the wing-thief. If he were in his body, if he had his axe, he would kill them all. Slaughter them with no mercy. But his axe rested next to his body, many miles away. And even if he had his body, his axe, the white eyes were not his to kill. Their lives belonged to the war chief now. They were Bull Elk's to kill.

Black Wing would not be able to reunite his new brother with his wife, not while she still lived. But if he could reclaim his body, he could lead the war chief to this place. He could help his new brother bury his wife, see that her spirit found peace in the nightlands.

And he could mark the man who had murdered her.

Black Wing leaned forward, released the branch, spreading his wings as he fell. Two quick, silent flaps and he was on the massive man. The owl's claws ripped into the giant's forehead, hallux talons digging so deep they scraped bone, opening up bloody twin furrows from his eyebrows to the crown of his head. The giant dropped to his knees, screaming.

Black Wing released, pushing off the massive man's head with great force, wings flapping, lifting him into the sky. He heard a thunderclap and felt his wing shatter. He saw feathers exploding from the owl's body, fluttering on the night wind. He spun in mid-air, unable to control his flight as he spiraled downward, slamming into the ground. He struggled to lift himself, but the owl's body was hopelessly broken.

He saw the man with the fur hat aiming a pistol at him, firing. A puff of smoke from the barrel of the gun and the bullet tore into the owl's breast.

Black Wing heard the holy man's voice in his head. *Tell me, what do you think would happen to a wing-thief if the bird were to die while the thief was inside it?*

The owl's blood seeped from its breast, soaking into feathers, and spreading on the ground. Black Wing could feel his own spirit fading as the owl's life slipped away. Desperately, he looked up into the branches of the nearby trees, but he had little hope. Any bird would certainly have taken flight at the sound of the gunshots.

But to his surprise, there, on a low branch of a blue spruce, sat a crow. Staring at him. Watching. As if waiting.

Black Wing did not hesitate.

Thirty-Eight

The Gunslinger

Hamish Frost on his painted horse and the girl named Ana sitting atop the Shadow Wolf, rode on through the day, speaking little. As the trees thickened and the sun rose in the sky, the old man turned in the saddle and looked at the girl. He held a finger to his lips, indicating she should be silent. He pointed to a faint, wispy trail of smoke drifting over the treetops.

"No more talk," he whispered. "Don't know who might be ahead, but I want to get a good look at them before they know we're here."

Frost's painted horse moved through the trees with an unnatural quiet, each shod hoof touching down with near silence. The Shadow Wolf more light-footed still, feet almost gliding as if on a cushion of air. As they neared the source of the smoke, the old gunslinger slid off his horse, his boots touching the leaf-strewn soil without a sound. He held up a hand, palm flat, ordering the girl to stay put, then slipped through the trees toward the smoke.

A half a mile or so away, inside a thick copse of aspens, he found four rough-looking men, sitting around a campfire, drinking coffee, and eating beans from a cast-iron pot simmering at the edge of the fire. The men were loud and uncouth. Frost had been listening to their conversations long before he laid eyes on them.

Sensing something behind him, Frost spun around, revolvers appearing in his hands as if by magic. The girl named Ana stood there. In the shadows of the trees, he could see a giant silhouette and golden eyes that seemed to float in the darkness. Frost returned his pistols to their holsters and gave the girl a stern look.

She stepped to his side and peered around a tree. A gasp escaped her lips and Frost clamped a hand over her mouth. If the men around the campfire heard her, they gave no indication.

Frost looked at the girl. She had gone pale, her face a mask of fear, tears welling in the corners of her eyes. The old gunslinger leaned down, whispering in the girl's ear. "What's wrong, child?"

The girl leaned close to him and said, almost inaudibly, "I know them."

"Who are they?" Frost mouthed.

"That's the buffalo hunter," she said in a halting voice. "The big one. He's the one who killed my ma and sold me to the fur trader. Those are his men."

Frost gripped her by the shoulders, gently but firmly. "Stay put," he whispered. "Do you hear me? I mean it. Do not move from this spot. Do not make a sound. Do you understand what I'm telling you?"

The girl nodded.

Frost looked up at the wolf and nodded. "I'll be back shortly."

He moved with calculated stealth, working his way in a half-circle around the camped men. He kept low to the ground, dodging and darting between aspens and pines, making sure none of the men around the campfire saw him until he was ready for them to see him. Once he'd circled far enough to make it seem as if he was approaching the camp from the opposite direction, Frost stood straight, stepped from behind a pine and ambled towards the campfire, whistling as he walked.

The four men took note immediately, dropping their cups and bowls and drawing their weapons.

Frost looked them over and smiled. "Didn't mean to startle you fine gentlemen."

"What the fuck do you want?" said the giant bushy-bearded man that Ana had identified as the buffalo hunter. He had a blood-soaked rag wrapped around the top of his head and held a long rifle at his side.

Frost smiled. "Some of that coffee would be mighty nice."

"I know you," said another of the men, a towhead in a threadbare shirt. "You're that sonofabitch they call Whiteskin. I can tell because of that fucking bone-white skin a' yours."

Frost kept walking toward them. "I see you're the brains of this outfit."

"Give me one fucking reason why we shouldn't shoot you dead," said the buffalo hunter, drawing a bead on Frost with the long rifle. Frost wondered if it was the same gun that had killed Ana's mother.

Frost ignored the giant's threat. *"This rudeness is a sauce to his good wit, which gives men stomach to digest his words with better appetite."*

As he approached the campfire, he could see a native woman lying in a pool of congealing blood a few feet away. She was naked and her skull was crushed in. A large rock stained dark lay on the ground next to her body.

"What happened to her?" Frost asked.

"She tripped. Hit her head on the rock," said another of the men. A smallish man and an unconvincing liar. He had a weak chin and a single eyebrow that ran unbroken over both eyes.

"What was she doing here?" asked Frost.

"Sucking our dicks," said the smallish man. "If you want her, I'll sell her to you. She's a little cold, but she's got a day or two before she starts to stink."

Frost pointed at the man's head. His revolver, cold blue steel with an elephant ivory handle, appeared in his hand. There was a clap of thunder and a blue hole bloomed in the center of the smallish man's forehead, splitting his eyebrow in twain. The man's knees buckled. He crumpled to the ground and lay unmoving.

"I'll ask you again," said Frost, looking around the campfire at the other men. "What was she doing here?"

"None of your fucking business," said the giant, gripping the rifle so tightly his hands were turning as pale as Frost's skin. "Leave now or I'll shoot you fucking dead."

Frost's hands were empty as he turned to the bushy-bearded man. His revolver had migrated back to its holster. *"There is no terror, Cassius, in your threats, for I am armed so strong in honesty that they pass by me as the idle wind."* The old gunslinger smiled. "If you were going to shoot, you would've done it already. But you haven't because you know who I am. You know I can take that rifle away from you before your finger can squeeze the trigger. I'd have the barrel up your ass before you could get a shot off. Now answer my fucking question. What was this woman doing here?"

The giant's hands trembled, but he did not lower the rifle. His eyes narrowed, his face filled with rage, but no words escaped his lips.

"Ain't none of us got no warrants on us," said a stocky man with a beard and a stubbly, recently shaved head.

"Did I ask you about warrants?" said Frost.

"N-no," said the shaved pate.

"What did I ask about?"

"The w-woman. But she's a redskin, she ain't even--"

Frost's arm jetted to the level, the pistol somehow back in his grip, the end of the barrel in line with the shaved pate's face. Another clap of thunder and the stocky man lay dead on the ground.

Only the towhead and the giant remained.

Frost looked at the towhead. "This woman didn't come here of her own volition. How is it she found herself in your camp?"

"We took her," said the towhead. "We seen her washing clothes by a river south of here. So we took her."

"You took her?" said Frost.

The towhead nodded. He picked up a tin cup and tried to drink, but his hands shook so that coffee splashed and dripped to the ground. "I answered your question. I answered it true. Don't kill me."

The old gunslinger seemed to consider this. He took the cup from the towhead's hands and dumped the contents on the ground. He picked up the tin pot and poured a fresh cup. He took a sip, frowned, then tossed it in the fire. "Well, I thought I wanted coffee. It smelled a sight better than it tasted."

Frost pointed to the bloody rag wrapped around the giant's head. "She hit you with the rock? Is that why you killed her?"

"Didn't say I killed her," said the giant.

"But you did kill her, didn't you?"

"None of your goddamn business," said the giant, his rifle still trained on Frost.

"It was an owl," said the towhead, eager to please. "Swooped down on his head last night and scratched him all up."

Frost nodded, then looked into the fire.

"This woman wasn't the first you've taken, was she? You men are practiced hands at rape and murder, are you not? How many has it been? How many red women have you taken? How many settlers' wives and daughters? How many lives have you stolen?"

"I-I don't... I don't recall," said the towhead.

"Then what good are you to me?" asked Frost.

The booming crack of a gunpowder explosion rang through the trees and the towhead fell dead at Frost's feet. Blood and gray matter pooled around the dead man's head, soaking into his sandy-colored hair. Frost held the revolver at his side, a wispy trail of smoke rolling from the barrel.

"I take him at his word," the old gunslinger said, "but you keep count, don't you? You know exactly how many it's been. You remember them all. You keep their faces in your memory so you can recall them later when there's no new victim to be found."

The buffalo hunter glared at him, but said nothing.

"I want you to recall one in particular for me now," said Frost. "A year or so back. South and west of here. A woman and her child. Pretty girl. Raven hair. Twelve or thirteen years old. You murdered the mother, but not the girl. You kidnapped her. Held her as your slave. Kept her naked and tied to a tree. Beat her. Raped her. You would have murdered her as well once you grew tired of her if you hadn't first chanced across a man who made you an offer. A fur trader who took her off your hands, bought her from you. Gave you a small sack of gold dust, which was actually iron pyrite, but you were too fucking stupid to know the difference. Are you recalling this?"

"What do you want from me?" asked the bushy-bearded giant.

"I want you to have her face fresh in your mind."

By the time the buffalo hunter realized Frost's fist was coming toward him, it had already connected. The giant's nose flattened against his face with an audible crack.

The buffalo hunter staggered backward. He brought the rifle up, tried to fire, but just as Frost had promised, the rifle was suddenly no longer in the giant's hands.

Frost swung the rifle like a club. The stock connected with the giant's head, the force behind the swing so great the wood cracked and the stock splintered. The giant dropped to his knees. Blood poured from the side of his head, covering his ear, soaking into his wooly beard and dripping from his chin. The blow reopened the wounds given him by the owl and the giant's face quickly became a mask of crimson.

"You murdered that girl's mother," said Frost. "You rode up and shot her with this rifle."

Frost threw the ruined long gun at the buffalo hunter. The giant put up his hands, partially deflecting it, but the barrel struck him across the bridge of his flattened nose, sending a spray of blood spatter.

"You took that girl and you sold her to Shadrach Brown like she was livestock."

The buffalo hunter struggled to get to his feet and, failing that, tried to escape by crawling. Frost grabbed a handful of the giant's hair, dislodging the bandage around his head. He snatched the buffalo hunter's head back and threw a quick, hard punch that landed squarely in the center of the big man's throat. The buffalo hunter choked and gasped, his windpipe crushed. He reached out, tried to grab Frost, but the old man easily slapped his hands away.

The buffalo hunter went to all fours, gurgling sounds coming from his throat. Frost stepped back and kicked him under the chin. The buffalo hunter's head snapped back with a pop, then lolled to the side.

"You have her face in your mind?" asked Frost. "You remembering her?"

A revolver appeared in Frost's hand, the end of the barrel only inches from the buffalo hunter's head.

The old gunslinger pulled the trigger.

Thirty-Nine

The Wing-Thief

The crow glided to the ground, taloned feet touching lightly on the blood-soaked river bank. Black Wing had seen the carnage from the air as he flew back to the war party's camp, intent on reclaiming his body and setting the crow free. If that were even possible. He had killed the eagle when he switched to the owl's body and had gotten the owl killed by a mountain man's bullet only seconds before jumping into the crow. Whether he could now return to his body and allow the crow's spirit to reclaim its own was an open question. He had likely sealed the fate of the crow — and his own fate as well — the moment he took the crow's body.

If he was unable to reclaim his own flesh, if he was indeed trapped in the crow, at least he could use the crow's voice to tell Bull Elk of Snow Cloud's fate. He could still lead the war party back to the mountain men. He could still help his new brother avenge the murder of his wife.

Or so he had believed. He pecked at fragments of bone protruding from the mud, then hopped over a gourd-sized glob of viscera. Green flies buzzed about, alighting, sampling blood and then buzzing away to the next clump of torn and shredded human remains. Black Wing inspected the grisly sight, estimating how many warriors had been killed here. All of them, he suspected.

He recognized Bull Elk's bone armor breastplate lying in the mud. Congealing blood covered the bones. The wing-thief found weapons strewn about on the muddy ground. Arrows and axes. Spears and atlatls. Some intact, but most were broken. A fierce battle had occurred here. The war party had been ambushed. Slaughtered. Many of them as they slept. Those who had fought had fared no better. Black Wing knew his new brother, the war chief Bull Elk, was dead. All of his warriors were dead. The entire war party had been butchered here on this spot. And Black Wing knew precisely what had befallen them. The monster Wechuge had come out of the river in the night and taken them unawares.

Black Wing had seen enough of the killing grounds. He spread the crow's wings and took flight. He would reclaim his body, gather his weapons, and he would either kill Wechuge or Wechuge would kill him.

He found his body where he had left it, in a treetop, a few branches beneath the eagle's nest. The same nest from which he had borrowed the wings of the mother eagle, before stealing her life away when he switched to the owl's body.

Sitting at the base of the great tree, he could see the boy warrior Bull Elk had introduced as Slow Rabbit. At first, the wing-thief feared this was a trick. He feared this was not Slow Rabbit he was seeing, but Wechuge disguised as Slow Rabbit. A perfect trap set to ensnare the wing-thief.

However, the body sitting beneath the tree had no aura. No medicine. Each time Black Wing had seen Wechuge, the monster had an unmistakable violet glow surrounding it. Wechuge could not hide his medicine. Not from the opened eyes of the wing-thief. This was no disguise. Slow Rabbit still lived, and he sat beneath the tree, guarding Black Wing's body.

The wing-thief could hear the tonal peeps, the single plaintive note of the eagle nestlings expressing their hunger. They would live for a time, at least as long as their male parent continued to bring them food, but with their mother dead, the nestlings would never fledge. They would never fly. They would die in the nest or fall out and crash to the ground. More deaths on the wing-thief's head.

The crow alighted on Black Wing's chest and he looked into his own face. The dark eyes were open, staring into the distance beyond him. Black Wing reclaimed his body, sitting up with a gasp. He had been away from it so long it now felt foreign to him. The crow leaped to a nearby branch. It stared at him, then cawed loudly.

Black Wing had not expected the crow to survive the reclamation, but somehow the crow lived. It sat there, watching him just as it had when the owl's broken body lay bleeding on the ground. It continued to watch as Black Wing climbed down from the tree.

Slow Rabbit jumped to his feet, reaching for his axe, as the wing-thief dropped from the lowest tree limb, landing beside the boy warrior.

Black Wing held up his hands. "Calm yourself. It's only me. I have reclaimed my body."

Slow Rabbit lowered his axe. "I fell asleep. I am sorry."

Black Wing ignored the apology. "Where is your horse?"

The boy warrior pointed to an aspen copse. "There," he said.

Black Wing could see a chestnut-colored mare with white socks grazing on the short grasses ."Take your horse and ride for your home. Tell Bull Elk's mother that he is not coming back. Tell the wives and children of the other men that none of the men are coming back. Only you. The others are all lost."

"Lost? No," said the boy warrior. "They are not lost. They made camp by the river and left me to guard your body."

"I found their camp. They are all dead."

"No. They can't be." The boy warrior was defiant in his insistence.

The wing-thief took Slow Rabbit by the shoulders, shook him, forcing his attention. "Listen to me. Take your horse and ride back to your people with all haste. Stop for nothing or no one until you get there. Do you understand me?"

"I want to see them. I want to know they are dead."

"I have told you they are dead. You do not need to see. You do not *want* to see."

Slow Rabbit only looked at him with confusion.

"Stop for nothing or no one until you get home. Do you understand me?"

"I want to see them," he repeated.

Black Wing shook him. "No. Ride for your home. Do you understand?"

The boy warrior nodded.

"Say it back to me."

"Ride for my camp with all haste. Then tell Bull Elk's mother that the men will not be coming back."

Black Wing shook him again. "No! You left out the most important part. Do not stop for anyone or anything until you reach Bull Elk's mother. Do you understand me? Ride and stop for no one!"

"If they are dead, then tell me what killed them."

Black Wing released the boy's shoulders. "Knowing what killed them will not bring them back. Now ride! And do as you were told!"

Forty

The Manhunter

The hostler was a short, pudgy man with an upturned nose and heavy jowls that gave him a pig-like countenance. He stared at the emancipation papers Ozymandias Hayes had handed him, pretending he could read them.

"As you can see, sir," Hayes said. "I am a free man, not a runaway slave."

The hostler huffed and handed the papers back to Hayes. "Two dollars a night. And you muck the stall."

After being denied lodging at the city's lone hotel — as he expected he would be — he had come to the livery. He had spent many a night sleeping in a horse stall, and had expected he'd have to muck, but to pay twice for a bed of hay reeking of horseshit what he would for a night on a cotton mattress in the hotel was extortionate.

Hayes clenched his jaw, took a deep breath. "Here's a counteroffer. You take both my horse and my saddle in exchange for allowing me to sleep here until the next stagecoach departs. That's beyond fair."

Hayes had hoped to sell the horse and saddle before heading back east, but once he was paid for his delivery of Enoch Munn's gang he'd have sufficient funding to last him a while even if he gave away the horse and saddle.

The pig-faced hostler balked. "That horse been rode near to death."

"The horse was good enough for the US Cavalry. He's been ridden hard for several days, that's true, but with rest and care, he'll rebound in both health and value. And the saddle alone is worth at least ten dollars."

The stablemaster grumbled, pretending he'd gotten the worse of the deal, but nodded his acceptance and handed Hayes a pitchfork.

Hayes took off Jacob Hutchens' fine long coat and laid it atop a haystack. The hostler's eyes went to the gun on Hayes' hip. Hayes realized the hostler had likely never seen a man of color armed.

"Sheriff know you got that?" asked the pig-faced man.

"I am a federally licensed manhunter. It's my intent to inform the sheriff of my presence first thing in the morning."

"I don't want no trouble here," said the pig-faced man.

Hayes realized he should have kept his coat on, at least until the hostler had retired to his lodgings. The presence of the gun was giving the man cause to rethink their arrangement.

"Nor do I," said Hayes. "I just want a place to sleep. You'll have no trouble from me."

The pig-faced man wavered. Hayes could tell he was close to reneging on their deal.

"You've got my horse. You've got my saddle. I agreed to your conditions. I'll muck the stall and you won't hear a peep from me the entire time I'm here."

The hostler narrowed his eyes. "Not a peep?"

Hayes nodded. "Not a peep. You have my word."

The pig-faced man spat on the ground, then turned and waddled out of the barn. Hayes watched him go, then found an unoccupied stall and got to work. Once the stall was thoroughly cleaned of the soiled bedding and a layer of fresh hay installed, Hayes hung the pitchfork from a nail on a rafter and put down his bedroll. He took off his gun belt, laid it beside his bedding. A grunt escaped his lips as he sat down and pulled off his boots. He laid the knife he had taken from Enoch Munn by the boots, then stretched out on his bed of hay. He tilted his hat over his face to block the light of the oil lamps from the street outside the livery, streaming through the gaps in the slats.

He ignored the stench of horseshit, the snorting and snoring coming from the adjoining stalls, the stiff hay poking him in the back. It wasn't the accommodations he had hoped for, but fresh hay was an improvement over the rocky dirt he'd slept on for most of the past week or the hard-packed prairie for weeks before that. Hayes had learned to take sleep wherever he found it. Even if that meant in a ramshackle stall in a poorly constructed stable in an upstart mountain town that insisted on calling itself a city.

Boston was a city. Baltimore was a city. New Orleans was a city. Denver was a mining camp with too high an opinion of itself.

Hayes wasn't sure how long he'd been sleeping when he was awakened by noises coming from the alleyway directly behind the livery. Voices. Two men. One woman. Haggling, then arguing, followed by threats from the male voices, and a belligerent response from the woman. Hayes heard a slap, then cursing, and the sounds of a scuffle, escalating to combat. Fists thudding against flesh. Grunts, cries. A scream suddenly muffled. More thudding of fists.

Hayes pulled his pistol from his gun belt and got to his feet. No time for the boots. In his sock feet, he slipped from the stall, worked his way through the darkened barn, and stepped into the alley from the rear exit of the stable.

He found two men of a similar height and shared facial characteristics — roman noses, receding hairlines, and weak chins that seemed to melt into their throats. Brothers, Hayes suspected. Perhaps fraternal twins.

The woman was brown-haired and stout, on her knees in the mud. The bodice of her frilly dress had been ripped, exposing her breasts. Deep red scratch marks surrounded her throat and covered her upper chest. Her face was puffy blood poured from her nose and over her cracked and split lips. One brother stood behind her, his fists clenched and full of the woman's hair, pulling her head back and forcing her chin up. The second brother stood in front of the woman, his trousers and undergarments around his ankles as he urinated on her throat and chest.

Both men were laughing.

Hayes slipped silently from the shadows and stepped behind the second brother. Flipping his grip on the pistol, holding it by the barrel, he cracked the man across the back of the skull with the butt of the gun. There was a thudding sound and the man's head split open, blood oozing into his greasy hair. He dropped to the mud unconscious and convulsing, urine pooling around him.

The first man released the woman and shoved her face-first into the mud. Great clumps of her hair clung to his fingers. Hayes rotated the pistol in his hand, expertly cocking the hammer as the grip slid into his palm, and aimed it at the man.

But having a gun pointed at him didn't deter the chinless man. He charged, yelling and flinging himself at Hayes. Hayes fired, but his shot went up and wide as the man collided with him. The impact knocked the pistol from Hayes' hand. It sailed through the air and Hayes didn't see where it landed.

The chinless man came down on top of Hayes, raining heavy fists. He was sloppy drunk, but a scrapper, a more skilled fighter than Hayes had expected. He was also heavier than Hayes and his blows were landing with jarring effect. The days of hard riding with little sleep had taken a toll. Hayes was exhausted and unable to protect himself. He was suddenly in real trouble and he knew it.

Hayes bucked and tried to roll, but couldn't overcome the man's bulk. He felt a stinging near his biceps and looked to see that his sleeve was cut, blood seeping from a gash on his upper arm. The man had stopped hitting him long enough to pull a knife from his boot and slice Hayes to the bone.

Hayes grabbed the man's knife hand before he could strike again, but with the biceps severed he had no strength in that arm and couldn't prevent the man from pressing his advantage. Hayes could feel the tip of the knife against his chest. He looked down to see the point break the skin a few inches below his collarbone. He tried to push the knife back and away from his chest, but he didn't have the strength and the man on top of him had leverage.

The chinless man drove the knife down, directly into Hayes' heart. He didn't stop pressing until the blade disappeared, leaving the hilt resting flush against Hayes' chest.

Hayes could feel the blood gurgling up into his throat. He coughed, spraying crimson from his mouth, and spattering the chinless man. Hayes felt his consciousness waning and looked up, saw the chinless man smile, then spit in his face.

As the darkness closed in and his vision narrowed, Hayes saw a woman standing to the side of the man, looking down at him. But it wasn't the stout dove who had been beaten, pissed on, and shoved into the mud. Standing there was the spectral, ghostly woman with the beautiful face and long flowing raven hair that swirled about her head as if tossed by nonexistent winds.

Forty-One

The Gunslinger

"Why are we stopping here?" asked the girl named Ana, rubbing a hand over the top of the Shadow Wolf's head as she sat behind its shoulders.

Hamish Frost smiled at her, then climbed down from his horse. "*The deep of night is crept upon our talk, And Nature must obey necessity.* We'll make camp here."

"It ain't even dark yet," said Ana, "and we can see the town. Why don't we just go on down there? Wouldn't take more than an hour. I bet we could sleep in comfortable beds tonight."

"And what would you know of a comfortable bed, child?"

The girl shrugged. "I think it might be nice."

The old gunslinger smiled again and motioned for the girl to climb down from the wolf's back. They stood in the midst of an aspen grove on the side of a steep hill overlooking the town that sprawled beneath them. The sun sat on the horizon, sinking fast, and a gentle breeze wafted through the trees, sending the leaves to a rustle that sounded of fingers gently brushing piano keys.

"We'll go into town in the morning," said Frost. "We'll stay up here tonight."

"Why?" asked the girl.

"Because I say so," said Frost. "You need to trust me, child. It won't hurt you to spend one last night under the stars. For now, for tonight, this is where we need to be. Go get the bedrolls off my horse while I get a fire going."

The girl was still full of questions, but didn't argue and, for that, Frost was grateful. He gathered some dry wood for the fire and some bark flakings for kindling. He looked at the Shadow Wolf. "She knows, doesn't she?"

The wolf stared back at him with glowing amber eyes. Already its feet and the edges of its fur had begun to meld into the shadows.

"Did you tell her? Or did you not have to?"

The girl had surprised the old gunslinger at every turn since he'd stumbled across her, since he'd freed her from the trapper's shack, but nothing had been more surprising than the way she had taken to the wolf and the wolf to her. They had quite the bond. *"Fool. All thy other titles thou hast given away that thou wast born with."* He looked at the Shadow Wolf. "I'm a goddamn fool. The old woman told me as much and I didn't hear what she was saying. It was no coincidence I saw those warded trees. You led me there. You knew she was on that mountain. And you know who she is, as well, don't you?"

Ana returned from the horse with the bedrolls. "Is something wrong?" she asked.

The old gunslinger shook his head and looked away from the wolf. *"All's well that ends well, still the fine's the crown; Whate'er the course, the end is the renown."*

The girl began laying out the old man's bedroll as Frost expertly coaxed a spark from two dry pieces of wood and in a matter of moments, flames danced atop the gathered kindling.

The Shadow Wolf lay curled on the opposite side of the fire, its black fur like a void that absorbed the flickering light. The girl shook off Frost's buckskin coat and gave it back to him.

"You should keep it," the old gunslinger said. "It'll be a cold night."

She put her bedroll down next to the wolf and leaned against its ribs. "Don't need it. I've got him to keep me warm."

Frost nodded. He watched them for a moment, then with the fire burning brightly, he stood. "I'm going to set a few snares. With any luck at all, we'll have meat for both dinner and breakfast. You'll be safe here with him."

"I know," she said without looking at the old gunslinger.

Frost wandered away from the fire as darkness fell. He set a few snares and as he set the last one, a fat squirrel tripped his first. Frost dispatched the rodent cleanly and made quick work of skinning it and getting it on a spit over the fire.

The girl seemed preoccupied as he pulled the roasted squirrel from the spit and tore off a hindquarter for her. She nibbled, but ate little, before declaring herself full.

"You should eat," said Frost. "Tomorrow's likely to be a long day. You need your strength."

"I don't get so hungry when I'm with him. It's like up on the mesa at the old woman's house."

Frost laid his coat by the bedroll, took off his boots, and unbuckled his gun belt. He laid his floppy hat with the iridescent magpie feather on top of the guns and shook out his long white hair.

The girl stroked the wolf's ears, then ran her fingers through the thick fur at the back of its neck. After a moment of long silence, she looked up at Frost. "You want me to eat, you want me to take your coat, because you know I'll be hungry and cold without him. I know he's not coming with us. Sometime tonight, I'm going to fall asleep and when I wake up, he'll be gone. I know that's what's going to happen, but I don't know why."

"*Such as we are made of, such we be.*"

"I don't understand."

The old gunslinger sighed, poked at the fire with a stick. Finally, he said, "You and me are headed into the city. He doesn't go into civilized places."

"Why not?"

"It's complicated."

"Then explain it to me."

Frost ran a hand through his hair, pushed it out of his eyes. He paused a long time, staring into the fire. "He's not like you or me. And I don't mean because we're people and he's a wolf."

"He's not just a wolf."

"No, he's not." Frost paused again and looked at the wolf. "He avoids loud chaotic places, places where people are all congregated together."

The girl looked confused. "Why can't he go wherever he wants?"

"He comes from a different world. He was here long before people like me arrived."

"You mean people like us?"

"I'm not sure there *are* other people like you. I haven't quite figured you out just yet. But him, he's a creature of the wild. Of the mountains, the boulders, the forests, the plains. Places where the Old Gods' medicine still holds sway. He is a creature of medicine. A wild magic that's tied to the savage places. He keeps to the wild because there's no room for the Old Gods in civilized places. If he goes down there, if he goes to places like that, he'll be diminished. Do you know what that word means?"

"Diminished?" asked the girl, shaking her head.

"It means to become less than you are."

"He'd get smaller?"

"Perhaps. But it's more than that. He'd be weakened. He could be hurt. He could die in a place like that. That's why he's not going down there with us."

Ana looked at the wolf. The wolf's glowing amber eyes stared back at her. She wrapped her arms around the wolf's neck. The Shadow Wolf was so large, her hands didn't meet. She buried her face in the thick, coal-black fur and sobbed softly. "Does he have a name?"

"Wolf is his name," said Frost. "It wasn't always, but it is now. He could have been anything he wanted, but a wolf is what he has chosen to be."

"How do you know that?"

"You should get some rest. Morning will come early."

"I don't want to rest," said Ana. "And I don't want to go to Denver City. I don't want to leave you and I don't want to leave him. I want to stay wherever he is. I don't need civilized places. Let me stay with you. I'll protect him from anything that could hurt him."

Frost smiled. "I've begun to think that maybe you could. But that's not what's going to happen. That's not what is best for him and it's not what's best for you."

"How do you know what's best for me?"

"The old woman told me to put you on a coach headed east."

"I don't care what that old woman says! She can't tell me what to do. She's not my ma. My ma's dead."

"I know that."

"So why do you or her or anyone get to tell me where I belong? Or what I have to do or where I'll be safe? Why don't I get to decide?"

The old gunslinger watched the tears forming in the girl's eyes, rolling down her cheeks. He looked away from her, and back into the dancing flames of the fire. "There's nothing for you out here, child. You've seen what men do here. You've seen what men are like here, what they do to girls like you, to women like your mother. The wild is no place for you. You belong in the east. You belong in the civilized places the wolf can't go."

"I've never been east. I don't know anyone there."

"I do. I know people there. Good folk who'll look out for you until you're grown. I'm going to send them a wire from Denver City, ask them to meet you. Ask them to take you in. You'll be well-cared for. I promise you this, child."

"I don't want to go."

"I know."

"Then why are you making me go?"

Frost took a long time in answering. *"All the world's a stage, and all the men and women merely players. They have their exits and their entrances; and one man in his time plays many parts."* He smiled at Ana. "You have a destiny, child. I don't know what that destiny is, but I know in my bones you have one. So did the old woman." He pointed to the wolf. "As does he. He led me to you and the fact that he's leaving tonight after having watched over you all this way, tells me he knows his work is done. And whatever comes next, it'll be up to you to do on your own."

"I don't want to be on my own."

"I know," said Frost. "I know."

"Will I ever see you again? See him again?"

Frost smiled. "You're not done with me just yet. And ever is a long time and the world's not such a big place."

The girl tried to smile back at him, but failed. She wiped away tears and put her head on the wolf's shoulder, nestling against the thick black fur.

The old gunslinger watched her until she drifted off to sleep. The wolf stayed with her longer than Frost had expected, but sometime before dawn the giant creature faded into the shadows and disappeared.

Frost walked over to the girl and draped his buckskin coat over her.

Forty-Two

The Wing-Thief

BLACK WING FOUND THE mismatched tracks in the sandy mud downriver. One large clump of a foot and another smaller, slimmer foot that could have been that of a woman or a youth. Or a slim man. Like Antelope Eyes had been.

The wing-thief followed the tracks from the water's edge through the undergrowth and into the deeper woods, coming within a dozen steps of the tree where he had stashed his body while he searched for Snow Cloud. From this point, Wechuge could have seen the boy warrior named Slow Rabbit guarding the tree. The monster could well have seen the wing-thief's inert form in the upper branches.

But instead of attacking Slow Rabbit, Wechuge had turned, taking a looping path through the forest until arching back toward the river and the war party camped there.

Black Wing had only seen the campsite from the air, through the eyes of the crow. As he approached on foot, the smells met him first. The coppery tang of blood and the noxious mix of urine and feces assaulted his nose. At the camp's outer edges, he found broken spears, obsidian knives with snapped blades, and shattered bone clubs. Torn scraps of clothing, mats of hair attached to ragged chunks of scalp, shards of bone, and piles of entrails littering the blood-soaked ground. The rocks lining the side of the river were stained with dark streaks and spatters.

It took little imagination for Black Wing to envision what had happened. The monster had stalked the perimeter of the campsite in the darkness, making just enough noise as to alert the war party of his presence before entering the clearing and coming into the light of the fire. But the warriors would not have seen the monster's true form. They would not have seen a hulking mound of rotting flesh, a giant triangle of a head with beak-shaped jaws. Mismatched limbs.

They would have seen the holy man Antelope Eyes.

Alive. When they had been told he was dead.

Bull Elk would have been overjoyed to see his beloved elder brother. The holy man must have misinterpreted what the gods had been trying to convey. The end they had shown him must have been hypothetical, or perhaps he had simply misunderstood. The gods could be maddeningly vague in their pronouncements. This was known. Holy men were often wrong in their prophecies. Regardless, his brother was alive. Standing before him. Smiling. His arms opened and seeking to embrace.

The war chief's heart would have overflowed with gratitude. He would not have stopped to consider how it was the wing-thief had been convinced of the holy man's death.

In that moment, my words would have been the farthest thing from his mind.

Bull Elk would have dropped his weapons and rushed, with tears streaming down his face, to greet his brother.

He would have been the first to die, crushed by Wechuge's embrace. The war party would have been paralyzed by confusion. They would have had no time to regroup, to make sense of what they were seeing before Wechuge was on them. The monster would have dropped the illusion and revealed his true form to them. The war party would have scrambled for their weapons. They would have fought back, but the battle was already lost.

Black Wing took a deep breath and looked away. Wechuge could have killed Slow Rabbit easily. The monster could have climbed the tree where Black Wing's body lay immobile and murdered him as well. But Wechuge had not done so. The creature had seen them and chosen to leave them unharmed, instead it had slaughtered the war party.

It toys with me, thought Black Wing. *Taunts me.*

I faltered before when I had the chance to kill it. I let it manipulate me. Because of me, the warriors are all dead. Bull Elk, the brother of the holy man, is dead.

Because of me.

I will not falter again.

Wechuge is here. Close.

I will find it, and I will kill it.

Black Wing heard the scratchy weep of a scrub jay coming from the gnarled branches of a nearby oak. He spotted the jay, but looked away. He would take no bird to aid in his search this time. He wanted his axe in his hand when he found Wechuge.

He followed the mismatched tracks back to the shore. Wechuge had entered the river, disappeared beneath the surface once again, but Black Wing knew the monster had not gone far. Wechuge wanted this confrontation as much as he did. The creature was still here. The wing-thief just had to find it.

Black Wing followed along the river's edge, but found no exit point. He crossed at a spot where the river narrowed into shallows, flowing over and around large submerged rocks. On the opposite shore, Black Wing found the mismatched tracks in the mud. He followed Wechuge's tracks upward through the heavily wooded hills, winding through fields of boulders and a copse of aspen until the trail grew ever fainter and was ultimately lost among the detritus of the forest floor.

Black Wing paused, looked around the forest.

It toys with me. Wechuge would not be so far from the water. This is a feint. It leads me away from the river to strengthen its position.

He climbed back down the hillside. Looking across to where the flowing waters gained speed, turning into white-capped rapids as they bounced over more embedded rocks, he could see the boy named Slow Rabbit standing on the opposite bank, waving to him. Black Wing's breath caught in his throat, a pit forming in his gut.

"You were wrong," shouted Slow Rabbit over the crash of the waters. "They were not all killed."

Someone stepped from the shadows of the trees behind the boy. "Look!" The boy turned, pointing. "I found Bull Elk. He said they were attacked by a bear. It knocked him into the river. He washed ashore downstream, but unconscious. I found him wandering in the trees."

"Get away from him, you foolish boy!" yelled Black Wing. "Run now! That is not Bull Elk!"

"Of course, it is," said Slow Rabbit.

"If he fought a bear, why is he uninjured? If he fell into the river, why are his clothes not damp? Get away from him!" Black Wing pleaded. "Run! That is not your chief!"

Slow Rabbit turned to look at Bull Elk, but Bull Elk was not who he found standing behind him. A mound of rotting, mismatched body parts towered over the boy. Giant, beaked jaws clamped onto the side of Slow Rabbit's neck. The young warrior's mouth opened, but instead of a scream, only a blood-oozing gurgle escaped his lips.

Wechuge swung its massive neck from side to side, snapping its head back and forth until the boy's flesh tore loose and Slow Rabbit's body separated from his head. Wechuge shifted his beaked jaws, repositioning Slow Rabbit's head, then crushed the skull and swallowed. Blood and gray matter dripped from Wechuge's lower jaw. The creature scooped up the boy's body with one oversized hand and hurled it across the river at Black Wing.

The wing-thief dodged to the side and the boy's headless corpse slammed into a tree, wrapping around the trunk before sliding to the ground.

Black Wing pulled his war axe from the loop at his belt. But he would not throw it. It would take repeated strikes to bring Wechuge down. The wing-thief's heart raced, his teeth grinding as he waded into the surging river. "Face me!" He yelled. "Do not slink back into the water and disappear! If you want me, then come to me! Stop toying and face me!"

Wechuge left the opposite bank, striding purposefully into the water. Despite its bulk, it moved quickly and surely in the shallow rapids, reaching the wing-thief well before Black Wing made it halfway across the river.

The wing-thief swung his axe. The edge of the blade tore into the creature's belly, slicing through Wechuge's midsection. Blood the color of ink sprayed outward, then seeped from the wound.

Wechuge recoiled, stepping backward, but bringing its arm down with a whoosh of air, a club-like fist slamming between Black Wing's shoulder blades. The blow jarred the wing-thief, knocking the breath from his lungs and sending him staggering. Had he not bumped into a partially submerged boulder, he might well have lost his footing and been carried away by the current.

Black Wing pushed off from the boulder, stepping to the side just as Wechuge snapped down at him with its beaked jaws. The bite found only air and Wechuge's momentum caused him to crash into the rock. The wing-thief spun, swinging his war axe in a backhanded motion. The blade buried itself almost to the shaft in Wechuge's ribs. The creature shuddered and cried out, a sound like a tree trunk splitting.

Black wing tried to snatch the axe free, but the blade was wedged into the creature's bulk. Wechuge writhed and tossed about as the wing-thief worked the axe handle side to side until it came free. Wechuge spun, mouth opened, jaws snapping. Black Wing swung the axe again, but Wechuge extended a hand to block the blow.

The war axe struck in the dead center of Wechuge's palm, splitting the creature's hand almost in twain. Wechuge whipped its arm back, snatching the axe from Black Wing's grasp. With its beak, Wechuge clamped onto the shaft of the axe and wedged it free from its hand. The creature flung its head to the side, sending the axe sailing and splashing into the rapids.

Black Wing circled around Wechuge, reaching behind his back and slipping his knife from the sheath on his belt. When Wechuge lunged toward him, the wing-thief jabbed the obsidian blade into the creature's abdomen and twisted. The knife sank deep into the rotted flesh.

Black Wing withdrew the blade, preparing to stab again, but before he could, Wechuge grabbed him by his hair and lifted him from the water. The creature slammed the wing-thief into another boulder. Black Wing's back made a wet smacking sound on impact.

Wechuge held tight to Black Wing's hair. The creature snatched the wing-thief from the boulder and forced his head beneath the water, holding him under.

Black Wing struggled, trying desperately to get his head above the surface before the oxygen in his lungs ran out. Wechuge was too strong, its grip too tight. The wing-thief's lungs burned. He brought the blade of his knife to the base of his skull and scraped up, slicing away the hair by which Wechuge held him down. Freed from the creature's grip, Black Wing's face broke the surface and he gulped air.

He pushed off a boulder, tried to swim away, create some space between himself and Wechuge so that he might re-establish his footing and continue the fight. But the current was growing ever stronger. He could hear the roar of a waterfall near where he stood. The current tugged, pulled at him, forcing his feet from the bottom. He reached out, fingers scraping another boulder, clenching, holding on, trying to pull himself in front of the rock, escape the drag of the current.

Wechuge was on him quickly, raining down heavy blows with club-like fists. Black Wing shifted, trying to reposition himself, but in doing so, dropped his knife. It was lost from sight as soon as it hit the water.

Weaponless, the wing-thief tried to use the boulder as a shield, keep himself positioned behind it, while he plotted how to continue the fight. But Wechuge did not relent. The monster attacked the boulder, pounding it until it cracked and split, crumbling from the force of sledge-like blows.

Black Wing stepped back, the current continuing to tug at him, his feet sliding along the bottom.

Wechuge slammed a ham-sized fist into Black Wing's side. The wing-thief could feel bones shattering, the ball of his shoulder separating from the socket. He lost his footing and the current took him. He reached for another rock, fingers finding purchase. Gripping, holding tight with all his strength, as the current pulled, tugged.

Wechuge lunged, opening its jaws, snapping at Black Wing. The wing-thief's fingers slipped from the rock. The current pulled him under. Water rushed into his opened mouth, poured down his throat.

Black Wing fought his way to the surface, coughing and spewing. His nose burned, his lungs ached, one arm hung useless at his side, but he was out of Wechuge's reach. The current had separated them, carrying him downstream as he struggled to get his feet beneath him again. He saw the monster, but Wechuge made no move toward him. The hulking creature only stood and watched as the current took the wing-thief over the edge of the falls.

FORTY-THREE

INTERLUDE THREE

MY DEAREST HENRIETTA...

Major Anderson McKinney sighed and stared at the three-word salutation he had just scrawled across the top of the paper. The kerosene lamp on his desk caused the shadows in his quarters to contract, then expand with each flicker of the flame.

"My Dearest Henrietta," he spoke aloud, as if dictating the words would somehow spark his mind and spur his hand to action.

"My Dearest Henrietta," he voiced again. This time softer, barely above a whisper. Another sigh. He dipped his pen in the inkwell, though a dry pen tip was hardly the issue here, and set pen back to paper. A thick, black drop rolled from the over-filled tip and soaked into the sheet, spreading into an irregularly-shaped circle.

"Goddamnit!"

McKinney dropped the pen onto the paper in frustration, leaving a spray of blank ink and more spreading dots. He leaned back in his chair, crossed his arms, and stared at the stub of a cheroot in a ceramic ashtray on his desk. Henrietta had gifted him the tray last Christmas and elicited from him a promise that he would limit his smoking to the daylight hours. She had never appreciated his love of tobacco, going so far as to forbid its use inside their home. The ashtray had been her tacit acknowledgment that she knew the smoking would not only persist but increase outside of her presence. The promise was her attempt to mitigate it. McKinney had honored that promise.

Thus far.

The writing of letters had been coming easier for him of late, making the difficulty in penning this one all the more baffling. His marriage to Henrietta Bligh had been arranged, an anachronism in modern society, but one to which they had both acquiesced. They had spent precious little time together since their nuptials. His career as an officer of the United States Army mandated long deployments in faraway locales. None more distant than his current assignment.

He had seen their marriage as perfunctory, a societal obligation, and had not particularly minded the long separations. But her persistent letters had, to his great surprise, become a source of inspiration to him, and the letters he penned to her had ceased to be mere spousal duty and become an expression of thoughts and emotion he lacked the ability to express verbally.

Anderson McKinney had not expected to fall in love with Henrietta Bligh, but their exchange of letters during his time at this distant outpost had facilitated that very outcome. And he had decided to express that to her in this missive but had found the words damnably difficult to write.

A knock at the door jarred him from his thoughts.

"Enter," he said, crumbling the ruined paper with the three-word salutation.

A bespectacled lieutenant, a new arrival whose name McKinney had an impossible time committing to memory, pushed open the door. "You're needed on the wall, sir."

McKinney stared through the spyglass at the indistinct, shadowy mass on the horizon. It was a bright night, a large moon overhead framed against a sea of stars. "What am I looking at? Is that a bison herd?"

"No, sir," said a gangly young man with a chinless face and corporal's insignia on his sleeve. He stood next to the bespectacled lieutenant and a half dozen others, a mix of officers and enlisted men, on the narrow chemin de ronde atop the outpost wall. "Buffalo don't move like that. Not at night, leastways. They spread, meander about. Whatever this is, it's moving too fast, too straightforward. See how the formation is compact, focused?" The young man hesitated. "It looks like people to me, sir."

"Redskins?" asked McKinney.

The bespectacled lieutenant shook his head. "No, sir. They wouldn't come straight at us like this. They know we got guns.

They wouldn't face us strength to strength. They'd be marching to slaughter. Indians would set an ambush. Try to catch us unawares. They'd never let us see them coming like this."

"Who then if not red men?" snapped McKinney, lowering the spyglass. "Who else would be out here?"

"I don't know, sir," said the corporal.

McKinney sighed, turned to his lieutenant. "Guns to the wall. The order is given."

"Yes sir," said the lieutenant.

McKinney put the spyglass back to his eye, looking again at the approaching mass. As it grew closer, he could see the shadows separating, the mass splintering into shapes. Figures becoming visible through the dust and the haze. The corporal was correct. It was indeed people. But strange-looking people. Lumbering awkwardly, though moving with an unnatural quickness. Not walking, but running.

No. Sprinting.

Behind them, McKinney could see dark, heavy clouds spreading rapidly across the sky, blackening it as surely as his spilled ink had ruined his paper.

"Storm clouds?" he said, not realizing at first that he had spoken aloud.

A distant, discordant thrum filled the night air. Growing in both volume and pitch.

"Those aren't clouds, sir," the gangly corporal said. "Those are bats!"

McKinney opened his mouth to speak, but the words were drowned out by the snap of leathery wings and high-pitched, chittering clicks. The cauldron of bats — millions of bats — swooped downward, descending violently on the outpost.

My Dearest Henrietta...

Goddamn it.

Major Anderson McKinney knew he'd never get to finish that letter.

Forty-Four

The Manhunter

Ozymandias Hayes felt a tightness in his core, as if his entire person — body and soul — was caught in a vice being twisted ever tighter. He could feel a hammering from within him, an aching hollow thud that reverberated from his chest, running up his spine and ricocheting around his skull. His knees gave way, and he fell back, landing on the corner of his bed.

He knew he wasn't really where he seemed to be. He wasn't actually in the small home he and Cora — and briefly, baby Charlotte — had shared.

No. This was a memory. He had lived it before.

Was reliving it now.

This was a memory.

Hayes clutched the unmoving child to his chest. Baby Charlotte's lips were blue and her tiny body already cold.

He looked to his left and saw his wife Cora, her fists clenched at her side, standing over the bassinet. Screaming. Her eyes were unfocused, her body rigid. Her head thrown back, mouth opened wide. Screaming. Screaming from the depths of her soul.

But Hayes could not hear her screams. He could hear nothing. He didn't need to. He remembered the sound. Would never forget the sound.

This was a memory.

Hayes could feel his mouth moving, words attempting to form. But no words came. He couldn't hazard a guess what those words would have been or why he believed anything he could've said in that moment might have mattered. He could have said nothing that would have comforted Cora. Nothing that could have stopped her screams, filled the sucking void in that room, or turned back time and returned Charlotte to life.

So he rocked his dead child in silence while Cora screamed herself into unconsciousness and collapsed to the hardwood floor. Hayes made no move toward her. He sat frozen in place, looking up only when the spectral woman with flowing black hair stepped between Cora and him.

This was not a memory.

This had not happened.

The spectral woman had not been there.

He had seen the ghost woman for the first time on the night before Enoch Munn had murdered him. Years after that life-altering night in the small house in Illinois. The ghost woman had not been there then. She was not a part of this memory.

The ghostly woman stopped in front of him, reached down and gently took the dead child from his arms. She cradled Charlotte to her spectral breast. She looked down at Hayes, eyes brimming with compassion.

This was not a memory.

This had not happened.

As Hayes watched, the ghostly woman gently patted the dead child's back. And baby Charlotte squirmed in the ghost woman's arms.

Hayes opened his eyes. He could feel the sun on his face, the light streaming through the window across the room. Iron bars placed five inches apart, running from floor to ceiling, cast subtle, elongated shadows that fell across him as he lay on a small cot in the corner of a jail cell. Hayes tried to sit up, but pain arched across his chest, forcing him back down. He was shirtless and could see a blood-spattered bandage over his heart. Another encircled his left arm, just above the biceps.

Hayes forced his way through the pain and sat up. He surveyed his surroundings. The room was small, four walls composed of wooden plank wrapped around a small desk, a chair, some cabinets, a rack of rifles, and two iron-bar cages. One cage housed him. In the other, a tall man in mud-stained clothing slept on a cot. His head was swollen and heavily wrapped in bandages. One side of his face hung a bit lower than the other. Hayes recognized him as the man he had pistol-whipped into unconsciousness a few hours earlier. The brother, or so Hayes assumed, of the man who had driven a knife into his heart, killing him. The third time he had been killed.

"His brother's dead," came a voice from across the room. "And you damned near killed him, too."

Hayes saw a balding, stocky man with a heavy, dragoon mustache and thick, graying mutton chop sideburns sitting behind a small desk across the room. A wedge of pulverized tobacco pushed his lower lip almost comically far away from his gums. He wore a buffalo plaid shirt and an old leather vest with a circled gold star pinned over the left breast. He bore a vague resemblance to Hayes' late partner Jacob Hutchens, if Hutchens had lived another twenty years and fallen on hard times.

"I didn't kill his brother," said Hayes.

"No," said the sheriff. "I did. And I'd have shot you, too, if I hadn't thought you was already dead." He shifted his chaw of tobacco and spit a large brown stream that landed expertly in a spittoon beside the desk. On the desk was Hayes' gun belt and his holstered revolver.

The sheriff held Hayes' emancipation papers in his hand, studying them. On the desk beside the gun belt was an envelope containing the letter written by Major McKinney.

"Don't know how you survived having a ten-inch blade jabbed into your heart, but there you sit."

"Those are my papers you're holding," said Hayes.

"They were. But you won't be needing them no more."

"My name is Ozymandias Hayes. I'm a federally licensed manhunter. That letter on your desk is from Major McKinney of the U.S. Army. It attests to my identity and verifies that I delivered bodies to him."

"*Federally licensed.* Damn. That sounds fancy. Didn't know bounty hunters was licensed."

"If you'll allow me to send a telegram, I can — "

"Doc just left a little while ago," said the sheriff, cutting him off. "He tried to convince me to let him stitch you up. He said your wound might fester, get infected. I told him there wouldn't be time enough for that. No point in wasting good catgut on a man that's about to hang."

"I assume there is a crime with which I'm being charged?"

The sheriff looked surprised. "I don't know how it is where you come from, but around here we don't allow niggers to pistol whip white men. I think the legal term for that is assault."

"Battery," said Hayes. "Assault is the threat of bodily harm. Battery is the actual infliction of it."

"You telling me my business?"

"I'm telling you the law."

"In this town, I'm the law," said the sheriff.

"This town is a part of the Kansas territory and therefore the laws of the United States hold sway. As sheriff, you enforce them, but you don't get to make them."

"They let niggers be lawyers where you come from?" asked the sheriff, his voice dripping with mockery.

"Only if they pass the bar," said Hayes.

"Are you funning me? You want to see what happens to folks who make light of me? How about I shoot you dead where you sit? How smart you gonna feel then?"

"If you'll just permit me to send a telegram — "

"So why'd you attack them boys, huh? You looking to rob them? Thought you could take 'em both?"

"They were beating a woman in the alley."

"She weren't no woman. She was a whore!" said the man in the cage across from Hayes. He sat up, bracing himself on the cot as he did so. "He split my head open over what we was doing with a whore!" He pointed a finger at the sheriff. "And then you killed my brother!"

"I didn't ask you to interject," said the sheriff. "I saw the whole goddamn thing. I know what happened. I know who your brother is and I know who you are. You're lucky I didn't shoot you, too."

"If you saw what happened," said Hayes, "then you know they would've killed her if I hadn't stopped them."

"Were you and your brother going to kill that whore?" the sheriff asked the man in the cage.

When he didn't answer, the sheriff said "I'm asking you to interject now, you idiot. Was it your intention to kill the whore?"

"No," said the man. "At least not before we both fucked her."

The sheriff reached into his desk and took out a ring of iron keys. He stood and walked to the cage opposite of Hayes. He slipped a key into the cage's lock and turned. He swung the door open wide and motioned for the man inside to come out.

"You're free to go."

The man in the cage had to use the bars to pull himself to his feet. He looked over at Hayes. "What about him? Can I kill him?"

"Seeing as how you can barely stand, I somewhat doubt it." The sheriff waited for the man to stagger out of his cell, then walked back to his desk and dropped the keys into the drawer from which he had taken them. "Go to the undertaker and claim your brother's body and then get the fuck out of Denver City, before I reconsider and shoot you, too."

Hayes watched as the man, clearly concussed, lumbered across the room. As he reached for the knob of the door leading to the street, the door flung inward, knocking the man to the side, sending him stumbling into the wall, and collapsing to the floor.

Hayes looked up and saw an old man with a heavily wrinkled face, pale violet eyes, and flesh the color of buttermilk standing in the doorway. The old gunslinger Hamish Frost lifted his floppy hat with the magpie feather tucked into the brim and shook out his long stringy white hair. Frost nodded to Hayes, then looked from the man on the floor to the sheriff sitting behind his desk. He gave his head a subtle shake and said, *"Lord, what fools these mortals be."*

Forty-Five

The Wing-Thief

BLACK WING STARED DOWN at his broken body lying on the rocks at the base of the waterfall, mist and spray rising from the foaming white waters crashing all around his prone form. He could see his own vacant eyes, the blood oozing from his mouth and ears, his jaw dislocated, his face pressed against a large rock, polished smooth by the relentless pounding of the water.

The wing-thief had not intended to steal the crow's body, did not even realize he had done so until it was too late. He had glimpsed the bird flying overhead as he tumbled over the falls and reflexively jumped. Now the crow's body belonged to him. He wondered if he should return to his own body, accept the death he had earned.

But what would that serve? The crow's spirit had already been forced out. He had killed it as surely as he had killed the eagle while searching for Snow Cloud.

He flew upward, back over the top of the falls, searching for the monster Wechuge, but the creature had disappeared, slipped back beneath the water's surface, and made its escape.

Black Wing flew back down to the base of the falls, landing on the same boulder on which his head now rested. His body looked even worse up close. Glassy eyes, vacant stare, his face already turning pale. The blood coming from his ears was a darker color than the blood seeping from the corners of his opened mouth. Crimson mixing with streams of a gray, almost black substance. Brain matter.

The leather string around his neck had snapped. The string that held the medicine bundle he had worn ever since that day as a boy when his village had been raided, the bundle he had stolen from the old witchy woman as she lay dying in the mud. He had robbed her of her medicine, of her name, and of the wings she would've taken with her into the nightlands. The pouch had saved him, allowed him to borrow the bodies of birds, given him flight, but had damned him forever as a wing-thief.

And now the pouch was gone, taken by the rushing waters.

Black Wing knew he would not long survive inside the body of the crow. Eventually, he would grow hungry and be forced to eat as the crow eats. When that happened, he knew, his very sense of self would begin to slip away. Over time, he would forget how to be a man, what it was to be a man, and finally that he was ever a man at all. He would live on in the crow for as long as the crow lived, but all traces of the warrior he had been — the man he had been — would be lost.

If he could give life back to the crow, he would. Better to have died in the fall, he thought, than to live on but forget himself, forget he had ever existed as a man. To forget everything and everyone he had known and loved. His father, his mother, his sisters.

The holy man Antelope Eyes.

Once again, Black Wing had failed to avenge him. He had found Wechuge, faced him in battle, and been beaten. Now he would live out his days in the body of a crow, while everything he had been and everything he had known faded away.

"Are you so vain as to think your life more valuable than that of the birds in the air?"

The voice startled Black Wing. He had thought himself alone, but looking up he saw a woman standing only a few feet away. The same woman he had seen with Antelope Eyes in the clearing on that cloudless night. The woman with nine fingers who had touched the holy man's face the way a mother comforts a fearful child and then faded from view, disappearing as if she had never been.

Black Wing saw her more clearly now. High cheekbones, narrow brows, and eyes the color of sycamore leaves in autumn. Her hair fell halfway down her back, tossing in the wind as if it were a living thing moving of its own accord, so dark and inky that it seemed to absorb light. She wore expertly tanned leathers with exquisite stitching and of a design unlike any the wing-thief had ever seen.

Black Wing opened his mouth, forced air from his throat and past his beak. "W-Who?" he cawed.

The woman smiled. "We have never met. Though I have watched you from the day the raider split your head with a club and left you for dead in the mud. You do not know my name. I could tell it to you, bond us in the sharing of names, but first I would make a bargain with you."

Black Wing tilted his head. What bargain could he make while trapped in the body of a bird? Even one who could speak a few words?

"Bargain," he said. It was a question, but the crow's tongue lacked the ability to add inflection.

"A bargain, yes," she said. "I will give your body back to you." She gestured to the carcass lying on the rocks. "I will make this body whole. Mend your broken bones, stitch your split flesh back together, flush the water from your lungs, and return the light to your eyes. I will even give you back the hair you cut away to escape Wechuge's grasp. Your body will be exactly as it was before. Better even. Restored, rejuvenated, reborn." She paused. "Though there will be a cost."

"Cost," Black Wing cawed questioning.

"A high cost," the woman said. "Your body will be made whole, but you will not be as you were and you will never again fly in the body of a bird. I'm afraid I can tell you no more than that, but if you so desire it, if you will accept the cost — even not knowing precisely what that cost will be, then I can restore you to your body."

"Why," asked Black Wing.

The woman with nine fingers smiled. "It's a fair question, but one I cannot answer. If you accept my offer, you will learn."

Black Wing hesitated, tilting the crow's head to the side in a contemplative gesture.

"The holy man warned me about you. He loved you, loved you with his whole soul, and he did his best to prepare you for what is to come. But he had his doubts. He feared the path ahead would prove too difficult. He wasn't sure if this quest could be completed."

"Quest..."

"Yes. Your quest did not end when Antelope Eyes died. Nor when your body landed on the rocks. The quest remains unresolved. You will need your body to continue the quest. I can't promise you resolution, but I can give you back your body. And I can set you on the path that will lead to both answers and questions."

"Answers..."

"You will know the purpose of the quest. You will know why only you can complete it." She paused. "And when the quest ends, you will see the holy man again."

Black Wing wasn't sure he had heard her correctly. "Holy man."

"Yes."

"Cost." A question.

"Yes. There will be a high cost. The quest will be difficult. Painful. The path will lead through a place the living dare not go."

Black Wing shifted from one foot to the other.

"I need your answer," the woman said. "Will you spend your remaining days as a crow or will you resume the quest? Do you accept the cost to return to your body?"

Black Wing looked at the woman, took a long moment in forming the word, and then said, "Body."

No sooner had the word escaped his beak than he sat up on the rock, his feet dangling in the water. He bent over, dropping his head and retching. Water flowed from his nose and out of his mouth, splashing onto the rocks. His abdominal muscles spasmed and he vomited up more water, emptying his stomach. His lungs ached as he took air back into them.

He opened his mouth, stretching his jaw, feeling it move back into place. He wiped his lips, stared at the congealing blood on his fingers. He stuck his head beneath the pooling waters, let the current wash away the blood from his chin, from his ears. He raised his head, shook the water from his hair.

When at last, he felt steady enough, he stood atop the rock on which he had landed when he fell from the top of the falls. His legs wobbled and he thought for a moment he would collapse under his own weight, but he stabilized himself and remained upright. He looked at the woman and realized for the first time that she was not standing atop a rock, but on the flowing water itself. At his feet lay the body of the crow, its head bent back, the beak parted as if trying to caw at the moment life was stripped from it.

"I'm sorry, little brother," said Black Wing. His throat burned, each word like swallowing a hot coal.

"A crow lives only ten years or so," said the woman. "This one had seen that many and more already."

"I stole his life from him. It was not mine to take."

"No life is yours to take," said the woman. She held out her hand. Black Wing could see the scarred nub where her small finger should be. In her palm was the witch's bundle he thought he had lost when his body landed on the rocks. "But survival sometimes demands we take things that are not ours to take."

Black Wing reached for the pouch, but the woman shook her head.

"You will need this no longer," she said.

She untied the string and opened the pouch, emptying the contents in her hand. Black Wing had never looked inside the pouch. To open a medicine bundle was to render it powerless.

He was surprised to see the pouch's entire contents were nothing more than sand, a gizzard stone, and a single, small, downy feather. She dropped the pouch into the water, then turned her hand over, releasing the sand and pebbles. The feather fluttered briefly, then landed on the water and quickly disappeared into the roiling foam.

"Come with me," she said.

"I will need weapons."

"No," she said. "Your weapons would do you no good where we go."

"You said you would tell me your name."

The woman smiled at him. She turned and walked across the top of the white water. When she reached the waterfall, she held out a hand and the waters parted like the flap of a tipi. She looked back at him and said, "I did. And in time, I will do so."

Forty-Six

The Gunslinger

THE OLD WHITE-HAIRED GUNSLINGER stopped at the desk and stared down at the seated sheriff. The girl named Ana followed a few steps behind him. Frost could see the sheriff looking past him at the girl. Raven black hair framed a heart-shaped face with hazel eyes, too green to be brown and too brown to be green. The girl wore fur boots and a dirty smock sewn from tanned leather.

Frost dropped his hat on the corner of the sheriff's desk. "Do you know who I am?"

The sheriff's eyes drifted to the hat, then back up at the old gunslinger. "I know you."

"Prove it."

"State your business."

"Prove it," the old man repeated.

"Your name is Hamish Frost. The red men call you Whiteskin."

The old gunslinger nodded. *"Men should be what they seem.* Don't you agree, Sheriff?"

"What do you want?"

"We'll get to that after the introductions are over. Your name is Sikes? Edward Sikes, yes?"

"It's painted on the door," said the sheriff with a tone of exasperation.

"So it is. Now that we've gotten the introductions behind us, we can get to business. I am here for the gentleman you have in the cage yonder," he said pointing to Ozymandias Hayes, leaning against the cold iron bars of his cell. "He needs to be released forthwith."

"Says who?"

Frost narrowed his eyes, theatrically feigning surprise. "Why, *I* do."

"I don't take orders from you. And I can't just release a prisoner."

"Of course, you can. It's a simple matter of placing a key in a lock and releasing the tumblers. Give me the keys and I'll show you how it's done."

"He ain't going nowhere but to the gallows. I am the law here, not you. Who I jail and why I jail them is none of your goddamn business. How we mete out justice in this town is none of your goddamn business."

"Oh, but it is indeed my business," said Frost. "You see my young charge here is to be a passenger on a coach heading east and departing here shortly. Mr. Hayes is to serve as her guardian on that journey."

"I don't give a shit," said the sheriff. "That man is my prisoner and you're wasting my time. Now get the fuck out of my office, old man, before I lock you up with him and make you watch while I have a go at your girl."

"Oft expectation fails, and most oft there where most it promises." Frost sighed. "During our introductions, I asked you earlier if you knew who I was. You said you did, but it would seem you know only my name."

Faster than the sheriff's eyes could follow, the old gunslinger reached across, grabbed the sheriff by the back of his head, and slammed his face into the desk. There was a wet thud. Frost lifted the sheriff's head by his hair and then slammed it again into the desk. When the sheriff's head came up the second time, his nose was smashed flat. Blood flowed from his nostrils into his mustache. He opened his mouth and spit a mixture of blood, broken teeth, and tobacco juice that didn't land anywhere near the spittoon.

The sheriff's hand moved for his revolver, but he found his holster empty. Somehow the sheriff's pistol was in Frost's hand. The old man broke open the cylinder and shook the bullets onto the wooden floor, where they bounced and rolled away.

"The next time you reach for a weapon on me," the old gunslinger said, dropping the empty revolver onto the desk, "I'll reach for mine and we'll see who gets there first."

"I'll have your head for that," said the sheriff, vainly attempting to wipe away the blood streaming from his nose and mouth.

"No, you won't," said Frost. "And your name's not Sikes. It's Hemphill. Eugene Everett Hemphill. Ed Sikes is the nom de guerre you've been using ever since you fled El Paso. You remember El Paso, don't you Eugene? You remember what you did there, don't you? You remember why you fled? Why you changed your name?"

The sheriff's quick anger rapidly cooled, beads of sweat appearing on his forehead. "I don't know what you're talking about."

"Of course you do. You beat that woman unconscious with a cast-iron skillet and raped her on her kitchen table. And then when her son and his vaqueros came after you, you did what all cowards do. You fled the territory."

The sheriff swallowed hard, almost audibly. "I didn't do that. D-didn't do any of th-that."

"No? What say after I put my young friend on her coach I drag you down to El Paso and we'll see if anyone there remembers you. My guess is there's still a few who'd like to cut you from gut to nut and dump you in a rattlesnake den."

"Wh-what do you want?"

"*What a piece of work is man.* I've already told you what I want, Eugene."

The sheriff spat more blood and tobacco juice, then snatched open the drawer in his desk and took out the ring of keys. He flung them across the room and through the bars of Ozymandias Hayes' cell. Hayes bent and picked them up, then worked a key into the lock, and stepped through the opened door.

"If it makes you feel any better," the old gunslinger said, picking up his hat from the corner of the sheriff's desk. "You can always say he escaped and overpowered you. I think that's an eminently believable story."

Hayes walked to the sheriff's desk and dropped the keys. He picked up his gun belt and buckled it on. He lifted his papers and the letter from Major McKinney.

"I'll have the rest of my belongings, please," said the man-hunter. "My weapons. My boots, my coat, and all else I had with me in the stables."

When the sheriff was slow to respond, Frost said, "Where are Mr. Hayes' belongings?"

The sheriff spat again, anger and humiliation flaring in equal parts on his face. He pointed to the cabinet in the opposite corner. "Bottom shelf."

"He's going to need a shirt as well," said Frost. "Give him yours. It'll be an ill fit, but will serve for now."

"I ain't giving him my —" the sheriff protested but stopped abruptly when he saw the look on the old gunslinger's face. He shook off his vest and began unbuttoning his shirt.

Hayes went to the cabinet. Inside, he found his revolver and his knife, his boots, his hat, and the fine coat that had once belonged to Jacob Hutchens. Hayes pulled on his boots and rummaged through the pockets of the coat.

"You didn't happen to appropriate Mr. Hayes' coinage, did you?" said Frost, the threat of more violence dancing in his violet eyes.

The sheriff threw his shirt at Hayes, then opened another drawer and took out a leather purse. Frost snatched it from him and tossed it to Hayes."Make sure it's all there," he said.

Hayes opened the purse and perused the contents. He nodded to Frost and put the purse in the pocket of his coat. He slipped his arms into the sleeves of the sheriff's shirt, being careful not to dislodge his bandages.

Frost turned back to the sheriff. "One thing more and we'll be on our way. I left some bodies up in the Red Rocks. I need you to go get them. Four men and a woman. The men killed the woman and I killed the men. They were the gang of outlaws that have been robbing and murdering your prospectors. I hear there's a not insubstantial reward for them."

The sheriff didn't speak.

"The woman had the tattoos of a war chief's wife. Treat her body with respect. Bury her where you find her. Bury her deep and mark the grave. I would have done it myself, but time did not permit."

"No point in going after those bodies," said the sheriff. "Up in the Red Rocks, the wolves would have got them by the time you were out of sight."

Frost shook his head. "No scavenger — be it wolf, coyote, crow, or insect — will be touching those bodies. You don't need to know the details, just do as I said."

"If I bring them in, then I'm claiming the reward for myself," said the sheriff.

"You'll claim it, but you won't be keeping it. You're going to put every cent into an account I just opened in the bank across the street. That coin all belongs to this young lady." Frost gestured to the girl behind him. "Every penny of it.

Every. Penny. You cheat her and you're cheating me. And I trust you know by this point that you don't want to cheat me."

"I thought you said she was getting on the coach headed east."

"Not your concern. Bury the woman, bring back the outlaws' bodies, and then you deposit the reward into my account." After a moment of silence, the old gunslinger said, "Now, please. Scavengers won't touch the bodies, but the longer they lay, the worse the smell will get. And the more likely you are to encounter a grieving war chief."

Blood still dripping from his broken nose, and dribbling off his chin, the sheriff picked up his vest and buttoned it over his undershirt. He collected his key ring from the desk and returned it to the drawer. He squatted and gathered up the bullets that Frost had emptied on the floor.

When he stood, Frost handed his revolver back to him and the sheriff replaced it in his holster. The sheriff walked to the rack of rifles, unlocked the chain, took down one, and refastened the lock. As he reached the door of the office, he paused and took one last look back into the room. He hesitated, eyes drifting down to the long gun in his hands.

"That would be the last mistake you ever made," said the old gunslinger.

The sheriff lowered the rifle, walked out, and slammed the door behind him.

A moment after the sheriff was gone, Frost turned to Hayes, smiled, and extended his hand. "Mr. Hayes. We meet again."

Hayes shook Frost's hand. "I'm in your debt, Mr. Frost. Again."

"If you'll accept the commission I mentioned to the sheriff, we'll consider the scales balanced." Frost swept a hand toward the girl. "This is my friend Ana. Ana, this is Mr. Ozymandias Hayes. I have found him to be an honest, decent, and capable man."

Hayes nodded to the girl. The girl looked away shyly.

"I see you were injured last night," said Frost. "Are you in any condition to undertake such a journey?"

"I am on the mend," said the manhunter. "Though I will need to make haste to the transit office and purchase my fare."

Frost gave his head a slight shake. "I have secured your passage as well as hers. My apologies for the rush, but the coach is waiting."

Hayes nodded. "I appreciate your faith in me, but should it turn out I'm not able to endure the trip, then you just made an enemy out of that sheriff for no good reason."

"Corrupt, cowardly men have always been my enemy," said the old gunslinger. "Twas he that just discovered that, not I."

Forty-Seven

The Wing-Thief

The curtain of falling water closed as the spirit woman passed through and the waters resumed their natural path downward. Black Wing, following behind her, was pelted with a force so great he could hardly bear it. His knees wobbled and the pounding of the water on his head and neck made him dizzy. Once finally past the relentless deluge, he found himself standing in an expansive, dimly lit cavern.

The roar of the falling water filled his ears. He looked around the cave, but the spirit woman who had been only steps ahead was nowhere to be seen. But standing on the pathway in front of him, as if waiting, was a crow.

The bird cawed at him, flapped its wings, then took flight, heading deeper into the cavern and disappearing into the shadows.

Black Wing looked around again for the woman, waiting for her to reappear, but instead, the crow returned. Flying toward him, circling around behind him, then back down the pathway and again into the shadows ahead.

This time Black Wing followed. As he walked, the cavern grew more claustrophobic, the ceiling closer to his head, the walls almost within his reach. He could see the crow ahead, standing again on the pathway, as if waiting for him to catch up.

As he approached the crow, he could see blood smears on the bird's black beak, its eyes white and glassy. He realized this was the same bird he had jumped into as he tumbled over the falls. The bird whose body he had stolen before the woman with nine fingers had restored him to his body. This was the bird he had seen only moments earlier lying lifeless on the rocks at the base of the waterfall. Now restored to life, as he had been. How it had gotten past the waterfall and into the cavern, he didn't know.

The crow cawed at him, then took flight down the pathway, disappearing into the darkness ahead. Black Wing followed the winding path until it dead-ended at a narrow opening in the rock face. The crow was waiting for him there. The bird cawed, then hopped into the crevice.

Black Wing peered into the crack in the wall. The dim light was swallowed up completely by shadow only a few steps in. If the crow was there, he couldn't see it. He took a deep breath and squeezed into the crevice.

It was just wide enough that if he turned to his side and flattened himself against the rock wall, he could inch his way forward.

The crevice tunneled through the rock in a steadily sloping incline. It curled, spiraling ever downward, remaining so tight that he could only slink along, his body never losing contact with the rock.

He lacked any way to measure time or his progress, but after what seemed hours, he saw a faint, green-tinged light ahead. As he continued, the size of the glow increased, but the light's intensity did not.

Farther still and he discovered the source of the glow. Tiny crystals embedded in the rock and pulsing with a soft phosphorescence. He paused and pried a crystal loose from the rock. It was about the size of his thumbnail and warm to the touch as if a living thing. He closed his fist around it. The green glow seeped between his fingers, illuminating his hand.

Somewhere ahead, he saw movement. A small silhouette on the narrow path. The crow again. The bird called to him, then took flight.

Black Wing put the crystal in his mouth, holding it between his teeth, freeing up his hands to continue pulling himself along the claustrophobic path. As he trudged forward, the crystals lining the walls became few and far between. Just past the spot where he had seen the crow, the only crystal was the one he held between his teeth.

He moved slowly, methodically, never allowing the sole of his moccasin to lose contact with the rock beneath his feet. This proved to be wise. With one sliding step, his toes found nothing beneath them. He stopped. He could feel a gentle flow of air upward from the hole over which his foot hovered. He slid his foot back onto solid rock.

He spat the crystal into his palm and held it out over the opening. The path had given way to an opening so large it spanned the entire width of the walkway. The glow of the crystal cast a ring of green light that terminated in absolute darkness. He could not see the other side. If there was one.

"Where did you go?" he called out. "I am trying to follow you, but the path has ended."

His only answer was his echo. An echo meant the narrow crevice had turned into a cavernous opening.

He knelt carefully, then lay on his belly. He held the crystal out over the edge. Looking down, he could see what looked to be handholds carved into the rock face and leading up to the path on which he lay. He could not tell how far down the hole went and could only assume the handholds, if that was indeed what they were, extended all the way down. For at least the thousandth time, he wished Antelope Eyes was still with him. To offer guidance, encouragement, or just to tell him he was being a fool,

Black Wing put the crystal between his teeth, gripped the rock where the pathway ended, and wormed his way over the edge.

Forty-Eight

The Manhunter

Ozymandias Hayes stood next to the old gunslinger and the girl in the street outside the jail, watching as a strongbox was secured to the back of the stagecoach.

A short, but wiry man with a pronounced scar over his nose and a revolver holstered at his side — the reinsman, Hayes presumed — oversaw the installation of the strongbox. A shotgun messenger stood watch a few feet away, a scattergun cradled in his arms, eyes nervously panning the street. The messenger had a bearing that evoked the memory of Jacob Hutchens. A man who looked the part, but whose eyes betrayed his ineptitude.

"What's in that box?" asked the girl.

"If money go before, all ways do lie open," said Frost. "The coin of the realm, child. Mined gold headed for banker's hands in the east."

The old gunslinger took off his buckskin coat and wrapped it around the girl's shoulders. "You're not giving it back to me this time. I want you to take my coat. Keep it. It's threadbare in spots and has certainly seen better days, but I want you to have it."

"Why?" asked the girl.

"Because you don't have one. And you've a long journey ahead of you."

"Are you sure?"

The old gunslinger nodded. *"Come what sorrow can, It cannot countervail the exchange of joy, That one short minute gives me in her sight.* Think it a gift for the parting. Something to remember me by. I'm just sorry I've nothing better to give."

"I could never forget you," she said. "Even without the coat."

Frost opened the door of the coach and waited for the girl to step inside. Instead, she wrapped her arms around the old man, kissing him on the cheek.

"Parting is such sweet sorrow, That I shall say good night till it be morrow." Frost smiled, a half dozen new wrinkles creasing his alabaster face. "You take care of yourself, young lady."

The girl nodded, then said softly, "You'll tell him goodbye for me?"

Hayes didn't know who the *him* in that sentence referenced and felt a pang of guilt for eavesdropping on what was clearly meant to be a private conversation.

"I already promised I would," said the old gunslinger. "And I keep my promises."

"I know," said the girl, the tear she had been holding back now welling in the corner of her eye before releasing and rolling over her high cheekbone.

"You need to take your seat," said Frost. "We're holding up progress." He took the girl's hand in his, patted it gently, then released it and stepped back.

The girl forced a smile she clearly did not feel, then turned away from him and took her seat inside the coach.

Frost turned to Hayes, made eye contact, then tilted his head to the side. The two men took a few steps away from the opened coach door.

"Might I inveigh upon you for yet one more favor, Mr. Hayes?" asked the old gunslinger.

"Of course."

Frost sighed. "It's a considerable ask, I'm afraid."

"I am at your service."

The old gunslinger cleared his throat before proceeding. "The young lady whom I just put on the coach — her name is Ana — is fresh from a rather substantial ordeal. She is recently orphaned, and that is but one trauma among many she has faced in her short life. Civilization is coming our way, but it won't get here in time for her and the frontier is no place for a young girl. She deserves a better life than the west can offer her. She needs education and gentrification. The kind of socialization and skills that a young lady can only get in the east. That is where she belongs, not here. I would take her myself, but matters most pressing draw me in a different direction, I'm afraid."

Frost paused. "I know people in St. Louis. I've sent a wire asking them to meet her there and see to her care. As I said,

I know it is a considerable ask, but might I beseech you to not only safeguard her in transit, but in the event there is no response to my wire, should no one be waiting for her at the station, will you continue as her guardian? She will need someone to care for her until she is of an age to care for herself. May I ask such a favor of you?"

Hayes took a deep breath. The old man did not know his history. He could not have known of what he had just asked. Hayes dropped his head, staring at the ground, then slowly looked up and into the old gunslinger's violet eyes. "I will see her safely there." He paused. "And if your people are not waiting when we arrive, I will see personally to her care."

Frost smiled. "You saw me give her my coat?"

"I did."

"There is a small inner pocket. Over the breast. Inside are a few gold coins and some banknotes. It's no fortune, but enough to see that she is not destitute. I'll send more as soon as the bounties are paid on the men for which I sent the sheriff. With more to follow as I come into possession."

Hayes nodded.

"I should add," said the old gunslinger, "the girl is more than she would appear. She has what the people of the plains call 'medicine'. I have seen it made manifest firsthand. She has..." He searched for the right words. "A special nature. A great power inside her."

Hayes didn't know what to do with that information. "She has an air of familiarity about her."

"To me as well, though the source of that familiarity leaves me baffled." He tilted his head back in the direction of the stagecoach. "You took note of the shotgun messenger?"

"I did."

"Most ignorant of what he's most assured, His glassy essence, like an angry ape. I hope to be proven wrong or better yet, to need no proof, but you should under no circumstance assume his presence a comfort."

"I will keep eyes peeled."

"I give you, upon knees, a thousand thanks."

"I was in your debt before today," said Hayes. "That debt grew inside the sheriff's office. And I will remain indebted regardless of the outcome of our journey."

Frost extended a liver-spotted hand. Hayes shook it. The old gunslinger's grip was firm, strong.

"It is my fervent hope that we meet again someday, Mr. Hayes."

Hayes smiled. "I share your hope." He stepped to the stagecoach, took hold of the door, and looked back at Frost. "Until that day." He pulled the door closed behind him and took his seat next to the girl.

Forty-Nine

The Wing-Thief

THE DESCENT SEEMED ENDLESS. Black Wing's arms ached, fingers cramped. He told himself that with each step down, with each new handhold, each time he slid his foot along the rock face searching for a chiseled pocket to slip his toes into, he was closer to the climb's end. But for all he knew, solid ground could yet be hundreds, perhaps thousands, of steps away.

There was medicine at play here. This tunnel was not the product of flowing water or the shifting of the mountains above it. It had been created. It was a passage. It led to — or from — some secret place. A hidden place.

No sooner had this thought played across his mind than he heard the caw of the crow. He turned his head, letting the light of the crystal between his teeth cut an arc into the darkness. Perhaps ten feet down, he saw solid ground. Dirt, not rock. The crow stepped from the darkness into the crystal's ring of green light. The crow cawed again, calling to him.

He found another handhold, lowered himself. His foot sliding into the last pocket in the rock, before stepping onto the dirt and ending the long descent. The dirt was soft and loamy.

He felt a weakness in his legs, as if they could no longer support his weight. He reached out for the rock wall to steady himself, but the wall had disappeared as if it had never been there at all. He pitched forward clumsily into the darkness, extending his arms to break his fall, then rolling onto his back as he hit.

The ground, which had been firm seconds before, was now like quicksand. He sank into its enveloping grip. He could feel it tugging him, pulling him down. He heard the caw of the crow, but could not see the bird. He clawed for something, anything, to hold fast, but his hands found no purchase. The soil pulled him deeper. He closed his eyes, bit down on the crystal as he shut his mouth, and covered his nose to keep the fast creeping soil from his lungs.

The dirt enveloped him like a tight blanket, holding him immobile as he continued to sink deeper and deeper. He had expected his lungs to burn as he used up all the air in them. He expected he would be forced to exhale, his mouth opening in a vain attempt to draw in fresh breath. He had visions of the black loam filling his nose and mouth, choking him, suffocating him.

But the death he anticipated — his next death — did not occur. The breath he had expected to exhale remained comfortably in his lungs. He felt no need to open his eyes or remove his hand from his nose. He felt no need to breathe. After a while, he actually felt secure in his blanket of soil. He was a stone sinking to the bottom of a lake.

When the downward motion at last slowed and his descent came to an end, he found himself lying on his back, a firmness again beneath him. The black soil that had enveloped him and held him immobile released its grip and fell away, rolling off of him like water.

He opened his eyes and took away the hand that had covered his nose and mouth. He sat up. Opened his lips, letting the crystal's light reach out into the darkness. He saw a ceiling of stalactites, daggers of rock pointing down at him.

He stood. The rock ceiling was almost within reach above his head. He looked, but could see no hole through which he could have fallen. While wrapped in his blanket of soil, he had passed through solid stone.

He heard the caw of the crow and turned to see the bird step from the darkness and into the green ring of light. The crow stood on the ground, looking up at him, its head tilting gently side to side as if measuring him. Black Wing could see the still wet blood smeared on its beak.

"I am sorry. I would give you back your life if I could."

"Life," said the crow. "Life." The bird turned away and stepped back into the darkness.

He was about to follow when he heard the flap of wings and saw a blur of motion. The crow flying from the blackness, speeding directly at him. Before he could move out of the way, the crow collided with him, slamming into his bare chest. The bird's beak stabbed into him, cutting a hole in the flesh over his heart. The bird jammed its head into the wound, expanding the cut. The beak was like a knife, slicing into him. Blood flowed down his chest.

Black Wing found himself paralyzed, unable to lift his arms, to grab the crow, stop its attack. The crow's head continued to burrow into him. He could feel the beak scraping against his sternum. The wound widened, the crow digging its way into him.

He wanted to scream, but the paralysis would not permit it. He was frozen. He could only watch as the crow's folded wings, its taloned feet, and finally its tail feathers disappeared into the hole in his chest. He could feel the crow squeezing between his ribs, pushing his organs aside, pecking at his heart.

As he watched, he could see the wound closing, his flesh stitching itself back together, the wound healing, the hole the crow had made in his chest erasing itself. Even the blood that had flowed from it disappeared.

The paralysis released him. His fingers went immediately to his chest, probing for the wound. Hoping, praying, that the crow burrowing into his chest had been a vision, a waking dream, and not something that had actually happened.

His fingers could find no wound, no cut in his flesh. But as he probed, a speck of black appeared over his heart. The discoloration expanded, spreading quickly and darkening his flesh until an image took shape. The tattoo of a crow in flight blackened his chest.

He took a deep breath, tried to calm himself.

He could feel the crow moving inside him.

Fifty

The Gunslinger

Hamish Frost watched the stagecoach roll down the dirt street, a cloud of dust kicking up behind the wheels and hanging in the air. By the time the dust settled, the coach was disappearing into the glare of the sun over the eastern horizon.

The old woman had told him to put the girl on the stagecoach and his obligation to her would be complete. So why then did it not feel complete? He wondered if he had done right in abandoning Ana. Who was this girl? And why did she hold such sway over him?

He took some comfort in knowing she was accompanied by Ozymandias Hayes. He might have been a manhunter by profession, but Frost knew he was an honorable man. He had no doubt Hayes would keep his word to care for the girl and safeguard her passage. Hayes would protect her or die trying. Even so, Frost found himself wanting to follow after the stagecoach. To tell the manhunter he had reconsidered. He would see to the girl's care, after all.

Things without all remedy should be without regard: what's done, is done.

He didn't like it, but he knew he had to let the girl go. He had been given another task. The old woman told him to find the trickster. Why she had tasked him so, he didn't know. It was his hope that the trickster could provide him answers the old woman could not or, rather, had not.

But the trickster would not surrender information easily. Everything always comes at a steep price when dealing with him. With the possible exception of Snake, he liked the trickster known as Old Coyote least of all the deities he'd met.

The old gunslinger looked down the street to the livery. He knew he should retrieve his painted horse and be on his way. Assuming the trickster was where he expected him to be, he had at least two days of riding ahead of him. If he left now, he could put better than twenty miles between himself and this jumped up mining camp before nightfall.

But what difference would a day make?

The girl's mention of a comfortable bed had taken root in his thoughts. A soft pillow, a hot bath, a bottle of whiskey, and a good night's sleep. All were his to be had. And if not now, such might not be in the offing for some time to come. Besides, it would do the paint good to have a bag of oats and a brushing.

A melancholy had descended upon him. Already, he was missing the girl's company, and being apart from the wolf always left him out of sorts. Tomorrow he'd saddle up and ride south. Tonight, he'd seek solace in pampered comforts. Tomorrow, he'd concern himself with the trickster's machinations. Tonight he'd drink himself into slumber.

Frost walked down the street to the town's lone hotel. Rooms were to be had on the upper floor. The lower floor was a saloon.

He ignored the sign in the window proclaiming that weapons were disallowed on the hotel premises. He parted the doors and walked inside. A hare-lipped bouncer seated on a small stool in an alcove by the doors stood quickly and put a hand on Frost's chest, stopping him in place.

"I'm going to need your guns," he said in a marble-mouthed voice.

"O fearful meditation, where alack, Shall Time's best jewel from Time's chest lie hid? Or what strong hand can hold his swift foot back, Or who his spoil of beauty can forbid?"

The bouncer looked at Frost cluelessly.

"I know you've got your rules, son," said Frost, "and I know you're just doing a job, but you best take that hand off of me if you intend to keep it."

A slim man in a white smock came from behind the bar and rushed to the door. The bartender gripped the bouncer's arm, pulling it away from Frost's chest.

"It's alright," he said in a trembling voice that drifted into falsetto. "Mr. Frost has special dispensation. He's allowed to bypass the house rule." The bartender looked at Frost and smiled sheepishly. "Please forgive him. He's my sister's boy. He's new in town and doesn't know much."

"I can still smell the turpentine on the woodwork," said Frost. "I suspect everyone is new. The last time I passed this stretch, there was no town here at all."

The bartender forced a laugh. "The whole town sprang up almost overnight once gold was discovered. Our little establishment here has not been open long."

The bouncer looked confused. "No guns," he said. "That's what you told me. Take the guns. Nobody comes in with a gun. Don't want nobody shooting up the place. That's what you told me."

"Mr. Frost is not nobody." The bartender said, adding a hand motion for the bouncer to sit back down. The bouncer clearly didn't understand, but did as he was told.

"Come in, sir," said the bartender with a sweeping gesture. "Come in."

"Do I know you?" asked Frost.

"No, sir. But your reputation proceeds you."

The old gunslinger looked around the saloon. It was not yet noon, but already there was a faro game under way. Four men in filthy clothes and a gussied up dove of the roost in a frilly red dress sitting on the lap of one man. The game came to a halt as he walked by, all eyes on him.

He heard one man muttering under his breath about why the old fucker didn't have to surrender his irons. Frost ignored him and walked to the bar.

"What can I get you, Mr. Frost?" asked the bartender.

"I'm going to need a room."

"Of course. How long will you be staying with us?"

"Just the night."

"Very good. Anything else for you, sir?"

"I'd like a bath."

"I'll arrange a room with a tub and have the bath drawn for you."

"I'd like a bottle as well."

"We're still serving breakfast," offered the bartender.

"You don't sell booze here?"

"Of course. I just thought, given the time of day—"

"I don't want breakfast. I want a bottle." He dropped a gold dollar coin on the bar. "The best that will buy me."

The bartender smiled, took a corked bottle from underneath, and set it in front of the old gunslinger.

Frost doffed his floppy hat. "Obliged. Mind if I take a table and drink while I wait for the bath?"

"Take anything you need, Mr. Frost."

The old gunslinger took the bottle, lifted a glass from the bar, walked past the faro table and took a seat in the back, near the stairs leading up to the rooms. He uncorked the bottle and filled the glass to the midpoint. He threw back his head and swallowed all of what he had poured. He closed his eyes and let the liquid burn its way down his throat. He poured another similar amount, but before he could lift it to his lips, the woman from the faro table approached him. Her hair was the color of ditch water and her frilly dress revealed an ample cleavage.

"Hey there, darling." She smiled at Frost. Her teeth were crooked and yellowed by snuff, but Frost suspected that was no handicap in her line of work. Most men probably never got their eyes higher than her bosom.

"You want to buy me a drink?" she asked.

Frost considered this, then said, "Not particularly."

The dove stared at him, then huffed and returned to the faro table.

Frost picked up his glass and drained it, then poured another. He watched the men playing faro, the red-dressed dove floating between them, searching for her next customer. The old gunslinger sat alone, drinking until his bottle was half empty. He turned the glass upside down, then stood and dropped a few more coins onto the table. He looked to the bartender. "I trust my bath should be ready by now. I'll be checking out early in the morning."

Fifty-One

The Manhunter

THE STAGECOACH ROLLED SOUTH for about fifteen miles before turning and veering eastward. There was no road to speak of and the constant bouncing and jarring made Ozymandias Hayes feel as if they were one unseen rock from flipping and flying ass over teakettle.

The girl named Ana slept for most of the morning, seemingly oblivious to the bumpy ride. She sat beside the window, her head resting against the wooden frame. Hayes sat next to her. He could tell the girl's sleep was not restful. She fidgeted and twitched. He could see her eyes darting back and forth beneath her lids as dreams ruled her slumber. Dark dreams, from the look of it. Her face sometimes contorted as if in discomfort, nose scrunching, a frown creasing her lips, but never so much as to escape the dreams by waking.

Hayes looked across the aisle of the cabin to the short, middle-aged man in a rumpled, charcoal-colored suit sitting alone on the bench opposite them. The bench was upholstered in a red velvet-like fabric that had thus far avoided any stain. The little man had ignored both Hayes and the girl. Not even attempting to engage in small talk to pass the time.

The little man's hair was thinning, graying at the temples, and he wore round spectacles, sitting low on his nose. His entire attention since the stagecoach's departure had been focused on a leather-bound ledger propped open on his knees.

There was no one else in the cabin. Stagecoaches, as a rule, didn't embark on such long, expensive treks without all seats sold and occupied. Three in a cabin designed to seat six was unheard of. The empty seats were on account of three well-dressed men who had arrived in the company of the little man sitting across from Hayes. Seeing him, and realizing he was to be a passenger, they had balked at the very notion of traveling in such close quarters with a negro.

As a group they approached the company men and insisted Hayes be removed from the coach, else they would not board. Hayes had no doubt their demand would have been granted had the company men not feared the wrath of Hamish Frost. The wizened old gunslinger had purchased the tickets for Hayes and the girl and stood across the street, arms crossed, silently watching the kerfuffle.

The company men were in an uncomfortable situation, but held firm, explaining that all validly purchased tickets would be honored and Hayes held such a ticket. The well-dressed men, Hayes surmised as representatives of the bank to which the strongbox's contents were headed, demanded another coach. But were told no other coach was available and would not be for two days. They demanded refunds, but again the company men refused.

In the end, the four men conferred, and it seemed the little balding man in the rumpled suit drew the short straw. His three companions would wait for the next coach while he traveled on.

Hayes had long since grown inured to such displays. Truthfully, he didn't mind. Three fewer bodies only served to make the cabin less cramped and allowed him to sit more comfortably.

The girl awoke with a start, head jerking with a sudden flop to the side, and coming to rest against Hayes' shoulder. Ana opened her eyes and lifted her head. She leaned awkwardly away from Hayes.

"Having a bad dream?" He asked.

The girl only nodded and turned her attention to the window. She pushed back the curtain with a finger and stared out at the dusty plains.

"See something?"

She kept looking for a few seconds more, then released the curtain. "No."

"We should arrive at the first station shortly. They'll change out the mule team and you can stretch your legs, use the outhouse if you need to. With any luck, they'll have some johnnycakes for us."

"Why mules?"

"I beg pardon?"

"Why do they use mules instead of horses?" Ana asked.

"Mules have more stamina than horses," said Hayes. "The terrain is still rocky here. Uneven. It's a hard pull. You want mules or hinnies for that. Once the ground levels a bit, they'll switch to horses for speed. But twenty-five miles of pulling a coach is about all you can ask of either in a given day. Any more than that and you'll run them to death."

The girl nodded. "How many stations are there?"

"Twenty-six, if I recall correctly. On a good day, we'll make three and overnight at the last station each day. They'll have cots for us. We should be in St. Louis in about ten days."

Hayes thought he heard a groan from the little man across the aisle, but when he glanced in his direction, the man's eyes were down, his attention still on his ledger. At this rate, the man should have every column of the entire book memorized by the time they arrive.

Roughly an hour later, the stagecoach slowed and then came to a stop. The girl pulled back the curtain again. Station one sprawled before them. The main building was little more than a wooden shack. There was a large barn on the banks of a narrow, tree-lined creek and a row of outhouses some distance behind the main building. All of which was surrounded by a perimeter fence of split logs and twisted wire with a heavy wooden gate.

Hayes heard two quick toots of a bugle coming from the buggy whip's box atop the coach. Answered a moment later by three bugle blasts from the station.

"What was that?" Ana asked.

"Safety protocols," said Hayes. "We bugle twice to alert the station that we've arrived and to open the gates. When the station answers with three, they're acknowledging our message and telling us we have permission to approach."

"Why do we blow twice and they blow three times?"

Hayes leaned close, whispered in the girl's ear. "It's a code. One an outlaw or a bandit's not likely to know. Two says 'all is well'. But if we blow only once, we're telling them we have a problem of some sort — a sick passenger, a lame mule, a bad wheel, maybe worse. But something of which the station needs to be aware. If they answer with two — repeating ours plus one — they're telling us they received the message and will meet us with help at the gates."

"What if they don't add one?"

Hayes took a breath. "If they don't add one to our signal, they're telling the coach to stay away. Do not approach the gates and proceed to the next station."

"Why would they do that?"

"It's their way of telling us the station's been compromised."

"Compromised?"

"That it's not safe there for us."

"It's been attacked, you mean," said the little man across the aisle, looking up from his ledger. "Attacked by bandits or red men."

Hayes looked at him and gave a curt nod. He'd been trying not to say such in front of the girl.

"But the station is fortified against attack," he said to Ana. "There is a minimum of six men at every station. Armed at all times."

"Six doesn't seem many," said the little man.

"If they're handy with a weapon, it should be sufficient," said Hayes.

The little man went quiet for a moment, then said, "And if they don't blow the bugle at all?"

Hayes looked at him. "It means there's no one alive there to answer."

He turned and gave a reassuring smile to Ana, "But we heard three, so there's nothing to worry about."

The stagecoach bounced to the gates while two rough-looking men rode from the station. As Hayes had said, both men sported revolvers in leg holsters and each had a rifle sheathed on their respective saddle. The men dismounted and opened the gate. The stage coach passed through. One man accompanied the coach to the barn, while the other closed the gate and followed after.

In the barn, the passengers debarked before a hostler began the process of swapping out the mule teams. Hayes let the little man exit first, then held the door for Ana.

Standing in front of the coach, Hayes watched the shotgun messenger climb awkwardly down from the box. The messenger glared at Hayes, contempt in his eyes. Hayes stepped in front of the girl, put a hand out to keep her behind him. The messenger's lip curled into a snarl. He spat at Hayes' feet before turning and swaggering toward the main building. Hayes noted he stupidly, or perhaps arrogantly, left his shotgun resting on the seat of the box.

"I need to make water," said the girl.

"The outhouses are out back of the main building," said Hayes. "Looks like our traveling companion is presently making a beeline for one."

"I'll meet you inside the shack," said the girl.

Hayes nodded. He noticed the men switching the mule teams staring in the girl's direction as she walked.

The reinsman, a thin wiry man with mutton-chop sideburns and a prominent scar bisecting one eyebrow and running across his nose, stepped from the overseeing of the team swap and approached Hayes.

"Outpost duty is solitary work," he said in a gravelly voice. "And I can't speak to the moral character of the men here. Wouldn't let that girl out of my sight were I you."

Hayes nodded in agreement.

"I hear tell you're a manhunter," said the reinsman.

"I am."

"You any good with that iron on your hip?"

"Serviceable," said Hayes.

"What about a scattergun? You experienced with such a weapon?"

"Point and pull the trigger," said Hayes.

The reinsman nodded. "There's a double-barrel underneath a false floor in the cabin. Just pull back the rug and you'll see a lift handle," he said almost conspiratorially.

"Why are you telling me this?"

The reinsman lifted his hat, revealing a bald head dotted with stubble. He pulled the gray bandana from his neck, ran it over his scalp. "Cause I got a shotgun rider that ain't worth two shits and there's something following us."

Fifty-Two

The Wing-Thief

BLACK WING HELD THE green crystal in front of him as he walked, letting the glow illuminate the rocky tunnel. He stepped with surefootedness as if knowing the path.

The crow knows the way, he realized.

The crow he'd killed at the waterfall after his battle with Wechuge was lost. The crow that died yet, like him, lived again. The crow that had burrowed into his chest and taken residence. He could feel it still, moving inside him. The crow guided his feet, controlled his steps.

He knew he should be horrified and could not understand why he was not. He felt a strange, placid acceptance, as if a dead crow alive again and living inside him was perfectly natural.

Was this what the holy man had been preparing him for? Was this the burden Antelope Eyes feared he could not bear?

The cramped tunnel sloped gradually downward, before expanding, opening into a sprawling, domed subterranean world. Giant knife-like stalactites stabbed through the ceiling, dripping liquid sediment. A diffuse glow with no clear point of emanation bathed the cavern with soft blue light and created heavy shadows behind each rocky outcropping. Black Wing lowered the crystal but held it still in his hand. He did not need its light.

Running through the center of the cavern, he could see a river. Slow-moving, the water as dark as pitch, reflecting no light. On the muddy banks rested a birch-bark canoe, the centerline to the stern floating on the black water. A carved wooden paddle lay across the gunwales.

The spirit woman, the spectral beauty with nine fingers, stood on the shore beside the canoe. Her raven-black hair swirled about her head as if tossed by nonexistent winds.

"What is this place?" he asked.

"You ask a question to which you know the answer," she said.

He stared at the dark water, then looked into the distance, where the river rounded a bend and disappeared into the shadows.

"Where the living dare not go," he said. "This is the underworld. This is the land of the dead. The nightlands."

Her expression confirmed his statement.

"How?" he asked. "I'm not dead. You gave me back my life."

"One cannot give back that which was not lost. Your life was restored, but you died. You belong here. You are of the dead."

"I don't understand. You returned my life to me so I could go to the place I would have gone regardless? Why?"

She smiled at him. "In time, you will understand."

"I would like to know now."

"You are as headstrong as the holy man said you were."

"If I was destined for the land of the dead, why give me back my life?"

"The land of the dead is not your destination. This is but the path through which your destiny flows."

He touched the tattoo on his chest. "Was this my destiny as well? To have a crow inside me?"

She remained silent, letting his questions hang in the air unanswered.

"Why is there a bird in my chest?" He asked more insistently.

"I told you when we made our bargain that there would be changes. Nothing would be the same for you."

Black Wing angrily tapped the dark splotch on his chest. "There is a bird inside of me!"

The spirit woman smiled. "In life, you were a wing-thief. You flew on the wings of birds, borrowing their bodies without their consent. Returning them, reuniting spirit with flesh, only when they had served your purpose. Now the inverse is true. In death, the crow has claimed you. Claimed your body for its purposes."

"For what purpose? For how long?"

She smiled, but did not answer. She turned her head, looked down at the canoe. "Come. We have a long journey ahead of us. Tasks that must be performed. Your purpose, the crow's purpose for you, will become clear as we travel."

"A journey to where? What tasks must I perform?"

"The holy man said you ask a lot of questions. He was right."

"And you are as stingy with answers as he was."

She turned, and without waiting for him, stepped into the canoe, took her seat in the stern.

"You can't walk on this water as you did at the base of the waterfall?" he said.

"Too far to walk," she answered.

He hesitated. The woman waited patiently. Finally, he sighed and approached the canoe. He bent and took hold of the gunwales at the stern, made to push off from the shore.

"Hold," said the spirit woman, looking beyond Black Wing. "We have one more companion joining us."

He turned and saw the creature named Wechuge rising from the black waters and walking down the shore toward them. Instinctively, Black Wing reached for weapons that he no longer possessed. He brought his empty hands up, curling them into fists, prepared to fight.

The creature ignored him, walked past without even looking at him. Its mismatched feet sank into the mud at the shore, sloshed into the black water, then stepped over the gunwales. The creature took a seat in the belly of the canoe.

Black Wing clenched his jaws in anger, looked at Wechuge, then at the spirit woman. "I will not travel with that thing."

"Yes, you will," she said with firmness.

"It killed Antelope Eyes! It ate him! Ate his body and his spirit! It's a monster!"

The spirit woman gave Black Wing a pitying look. "These are the nightlands. We're all monsters down here," she said.

Fifty-Three

The Gunslinger

Hamish Frost found a small wooden tub, sealed with pitch, in his room. The water came to about the halfway point and was just shy of steaming. He swirled a finger in the water and found the heat to his liking.

He stripped off his clothes and tossed them on the floor by the tub. He figured he'd wash them out after his bath and hang them to dry while he slept.

He stepped carefully into the tub and slid himself into the water. The pleasing heat caused his skin to tingle. Goosebumps surfaced on his thighs, multiplying and spreading quickly over most of his flesh.

The old gunslinger eased his head back to the lip of the tub, rested it there, and let out a long, deep sigh. A breath he didn't realize he'd been holding. He could feel the effects of his rapid consumption of the whiskey and remembered why he had given up spirits so long ago. He closed his eyes, letting the water and the heat relax him. In moments, he was asleep.

He awoke to the sounds of banging on the door. He opened his eyes and shook away the disorientation. He didn't know how long he'd slept, but the water had gone cold and lost its transparency, turned a light brown from all the road dirt that had sluiced off of him.

"Who's there?" he called out.

A voice came from the other side of the door. Too soft. He couldn't make out the words.

"Speak up," he yelled. "I can't hear you."

More of the soft voice, again not loud enough for him to make out.

Exasperated, he stood. His flesh was pruned and his member had retreated. He felt a crick in his neck from craning it on the tub as he slept. He looked around and realized he'd neglected to fetch a towel before climbing into the tub. He lifted one leg and tried to shake as much water off as he could before stepping out and standing on the clothes he'd tossed to the side of the tub.

Another, more persistent, knock came from the door.

"What wound did ever heal but by degrees?" he shouted, before repeating the maneuver with his other leg. "Hold your horses. I'm moving as fast as I can."

Seeing no towels, the old gunslinger grabbed a blanket from the bed and covered his nakedness. He walked to the door and opened it.

Standing in the doorway was the bosomy woman in the frilly red dress who had propositioned him, though something in her manner had changed. "Madame?" he said. "Forgive me. *The naked truth of it is, I have no shirt.* I'm afraid I fell asleep in the bath. If you've come selling your wares, I'm afraid the answer will be no different this time than the last."

The woman stared back at him in silence, her face vacant. Her eyes twitched, then rolled back in her head, irises disappearing behind her upper lids, leaving only the whites visible in her sockets. The woman pivoted, her body turning. The old gunslinger noticed for the first time that the woman's feet were not on the floor, but hovering a few inches above it. She moved from the doorway, floating down the hallway.

"Madame?" He called.

She didn't answer. He wrapped the blanket more tightly around himself and followed after her, stepping over the threshold of the door and into the hallway. Only it was no longer the hallway of the hotel in which he stood. He found himself in the deep woods, a thick canopy of limbs and leaves overhead blocking the sun and rendering the forest floor in perpetual shadow.

The woman floated farther away from him, deeper into the woods. He hurried to follow. He knew not where he was or why he felt compelled to follow, but compelled he was.

This is a vision, he realized.

He could see an enormous elk standing in a clearing. A bull with an expansive rack of antlers, eight points on each side. The elk stood firm, not moving as the woman closed the distance between them. Frost could see the antlers begin to glow, brighter and brighter until they were a blinding white, with blue flames dancing along the points.

The woman in the red frilly dress paused, turned back to the old gunslinger, staring blindly at him. She waited as if frozen, for him to catch up. She remained motionless and did not acknowledge Frost as he passed by her.

Ahead, the giant elk with the flaming antlers stood as if blocking the old gunslinger's path. He continued forward. The elk turned, giving way as if in deference, allowing him to pass. Beyond the bull, he could see another elk, a doe with a distended, swollen belly. The doe bleated in pain, legs quivering in the midst of calving.

Standing at the doe's flank was the old woman with nine fingers, the entity who had summoned Frost to her tipi on the mesa, then trapped him in a medicine circle before disappearing. The old woman was naked and had her arm, almost to the shoulder, inside the doe, as if trying to turn a breaching calf.

The doe bleated again and shuddered. The old woman slowly withdrew her blood-slicked arm, guiding the now-turned calf through the birth canal. The doe's abdomen convulsed, legs shaking violently. The old woman continued to guide the calf out.

No, not guiding, Frost realized. She was extracting the calf, pulling it from the doe's womb.

Frost could see the calf emerge, the amniotic sac still clinging to it. The old woman pulled it free, snapped the umbilical with her teeth. The exhausted doe went to her knees, then collapsed to the forest floor. The old gunslinger looked at the calf. Something was wrong. It was small. Far too small, the legs too short. There was no fur.

It was no calf at all.

It was a child. A mewling, squalling, human infant. A girl with thick black hair.

The old woman cradled the crying girl to her breast. Only...

She was no longer the old woman. She was now the Beauty. The woman with flowing raven hair who had straddled him in the old woman's tipi, grinding against him while the mushrooms' poison held him immobile. She was the woman somehow grown from the girl-child he had seen murdered by a monstrous bat god in the ancient chalkstones during the vision in the tipi.

The beauty guided the infant's mouth to her full breast, letting it latch onto her nipple, and take her milk. Nursing sloppily while the doe who had birthed her lay on the ground and the bull with the flaming antlers stood guard. The Beauty looked up from the girl at her breast and locked eyes with Frost. "Stop wasting time and find the trickster," she said.

The old gunslinger snapped awake, his eyes springing open. He was still in the tub. The water had gone cold and lost its transparency, turned a light brown from all the road dirt that had sluiced off of him.

Fifty-Four

The Manhunter

Clouds rolled in in the late afternoon, heavy and dark, portending thunderstorms. Ozymandias Hayes could see the occasional lightning flash on the horizon, growing closer as dusk fell.

"Rain coming," he said to the girl named Ana. "But we should make the station before then."

"Do you think we'll be sleeping inside?" she asked.

They'd spent the previous night in tents outside the station house, listening to the howl of wolves and the cries of coyotes. Hayes had gotten little sleep, forcing himself to stay awake so as to keep an eye out for the girl. At each stop, he'd taken note of the stares and leers of station hands directed at Ana.

But it wasn't only her safety for which he was on guard. He'd not forgotten the reinsman's whispered warning that they were being followed. He'd kept that information to himself, but it seemed as if the girl knew or at least sensed something was amiss. She frequently parted the curtain and stared out at the passing plains as if to catch a glimpse of approaching danger.

At first, Hayes dismissed this as anxiety born of her separation from Hamish Frost. He believed she was checking the distance in hopes the old gunslinger was following behind, still watching out for her. But after a while, he realized it was something more.

"Not certain," said Hayes. "We can hope, but if it's tents again, then we'll make the best of it."

The girl said nothing, but the little man sitting across from them harrumphed. "I was told there would be a bed at each night's stop. No one said word one about cots in tents."

Hayes and the girl had learned to ignore the little man's complaints. If he was speaking, he was complaining.

"The terrain's leveled a good bit over the past couple of days," Hayes said to Ana. "Perhaps this is where we'll switch from mules to horses."

The girl nodded and peeked through the curtain again just as a flash of lightning illuminated the dusky evening with the sudden brightness of the noonday sun. For a moment, Hayes thought he saw silhouettes on the horizon, but as the flash faded, so too did the distant shapes.

Aided by the heavy thunderclouds, full-on dark arrived early, well before they reached the station gate. Only the occasional flash of lightning let them know they were still on the right path.

The coach slowed, barely moving.

"Why are we stopping?" asked the little man.

"Not stopping," said Hayes. "Just slowing out of an abundance of caution. Can't risk going off the trail in the darkness. We'll keep moving until we reach the station."

"We'd better," said the little man. "I'm not spending the night out here."

Hayes looked at Ana and rolled his eyes. She smiled.

After a passage of time no doubt shorter than it seemed, the coach came to a stop. A flash of lightning revealed a wooden gate and a row of stubby trees. The station sat a little ways beyond the gate, the light of oil lamps glowing inside the windows. The sky was spitting rain, but the deluge was still pending.

Two toots from the reinsman's bugle broke the silence.

They waited, but there was no response from the station.

Ana looked at Hayes, concern etched on her face.

"They didn't answer," said the little man.

"Quiet," said Hayes.

They heard the reinsman's bugle again. Two toots.

Long seconds passed. A blinding flash of lightning coincided with the station's delayed response. Hayes distinctly heard two toots, but then a ground-shaking boom of thunder obscured the third.

If there was a third.

"That was only two," said the little man. "There's supposed to be three."

Hayes shot the little man a stern look. "Quiet," he repeated.

"I didn't hear a third either," said Ana.

"You wouldn't have over that thunder," said Hayes.

"They'll repeat it, won't they?" asked the little man. "If there's doubt, they should repeat it."

But no further response was forthcoming.

Hayes reached down and flipped back the rug at their feet. He could see the outlines of the hatch in the false floor. He found the latch and flipped up the small door. A ten-gauge shotgun, the barrel sawed off just above the forestock, rested in the tiny nook along with a box of shells. He lifted the gun, breached and loaded it.

"Get on the floor," he said to Ana.

"What's going on?" said the little man.

Before Hayes could answer, there was another flare of lightning and he saw the red-orange burst of muzzle flash from a tree near the gate. The little man's head jerked back with the impact and then he fell over, slumping onto the seat. There was a smear of blood and brains on the previously unstained fabric. Hayes could see the exit wound just behind the little man's ear. A gaping hole half the size of a fist, raw and seeping blood and brain matter, flecked with little white shards of bone.

Hayes pushed Ana to the floorboards and knelt over her, shotgun at his shoulder, scanning the darkness for a target, for any movement outside the coach.

He heard the blast of a shotgun from the top of the coach. The messenger was responding, but firing blind, taking a literal shot in the dark.

Goddamnit, you fool! Thought Hayes. *You just gave them a target.*

There was a bevy of gunfire from the treeline. The coach rocked with the impact of the bullets. The mule team bucked, tried to turn and flee, but they were too close to the gate and there was nowhere to go. Hayes heard a body tumble from the box and hit the dirt just as the sky unloaded.

Rain in torrents pelted the coach. There was another flash of lightning and Hayes saw the shadows dance, silhouettes advancing toward them. Armed men leaving the treeline by the gate and approaching the coach.

Hayes pulled the shotgun's trigger. The ten-gauge jerked against his shoulder. He heard someone cry out in pain as the darkness reasserted itself. He breached the ten-gauge and pulled out the shell, but before he could reload, he felt a sting in his chest and noticed a new hole over the breast of the fine coat that had once belonged to his partner Jacob Hutchens.

His fingers felt heavy and unresponsive as he struggled to reload the shotgun. He heard a shot ring out and felt another sting. The shell tumbled from his fingers. He heard it bounce on the hardwood floor of the coach. His mind told him to pick it up, to reload, but his body didn't respond.

Another shot and he felt his knees buckle. He looked down at Ana crouching on the floorboards. Her face was pale, a mask of fear and uncertainty. Hayes felt the need to comfort her but knew that even if he had words sufficient to do so, he lacked the ability to speak them.

His vision blurred and he realized he was falling.

Fifty-Five

The Wing-Thief

BLACK WING DROVE THE wooden paddle deep into the dark water, leaving barely a ripple as he extracted it, pulling the canoe along the still river. He turned, looking over his shoulder at his traveling companions. The monster Wechuge sat silently between the thwarts in the hull of the birchbark canoe.

Any time Black Wing glanced in its direction, the creature would shift its form, taking on the appearance of one it had slain. One whose body and soul it had stolen. Presently, it appeared as Slow Rabbit, the boy warrior who had been tricked into leading Wechuge back to the wing-thief.

Slow Rabbit smiled guilelessly at Black Wing. Black Wing was not amused. He remembered how Wechuge had torn the boy limb from limb on the banks of the rushing river. And now it wore the boy's body as if a trophy.

Black Wing's heart ached. Slow Rabbit's death weighed heavily on his conscience. As did the deaths of Bull Elk and the entire band of warriors who had accompanied him on the search for the war chief's stolen wife.

Black Wing could have prevented their deaths. He had the opportunity to kill Wechuge on the night Antelope Eyes was murdered. The creature's back had been to him. His axe was in his hand. He had only to throw it. He could have struck down the monster, ended its existence. Saved Slow Rabbit, Bull Elk, and the others. He could have prevented all the carnage that was to come.

But he had failed to act. He had stayed his hand. Watched impotently as the creature disappeared beneath the water's surface. "When this is over," said Black Wing to Wechuge, "I will kill you for what you have done."

Slow Rabbit's face smiled back at him.

"When this is over," said the spectral beauty with the flowing black hair. "There may well be no one to stop you from trying. But for now, Wechuge travels under my protection."

"Why?" asked Black Wing. "Why do you protect it? You know what it is, what it does. The holy man protected it also and it killed him."

"Wechuge serves my purpose, as do you."

The ghost woman elaborated no further.

Black Wing looked away, turning his attention back to the river ahead. As he paddled, the cavern grew larger, the walls so distant as to disappear into the darkness. He noticed the river branching frequently, smaller tributaries breaking away on both sides, and snaking into the darkness.

"Our path continues forward," said the ghost woman, answering the question Black Wing had not asked.

As he paddled, he noticed black shapes moving from the shadows and assembling at the water's edge, as if watching their passage.

"What is that?" Black Wing asked. "On the shore."

The woman smiled at him. "When one is in the land of the dead, one should expect to see the dead."

Black Wing looked again at the dark shapes, trying to discern one from the other, but they seemed to meld together, becoming a singular, indistinct mass.

"Their bodies have not been restored as was yours," said the ghost woman, as if again sensing Black Wing's unspoken question.

"So, this is their existence? Formless shadow beings on the muddy banks of a still river? Is this the fate that awaits us all?"

"No. This is only their fate. The reward they have earned or perhaps failed to earn. These are the lost. Lost in life. Lost in death. These are they who simply existed, living and dying without contribution. For good or ill. They loitered in life. They loiter here."

"And for those who did not loiter in life?"

The woman pointed to a branching tributary. "For those, this is but a buffer between the world above and the world that awaits. Each has their own river, their own destination."

"And what awaits at the end of their river?"

The woman smiled again, her hair swirling about her head, but did not answer.

Something bumped hard against the canoe and Black Wing saw a large, fan-shaped dorsal fin break the surface of the water near his paddle, then quickly disappear again.

"We are getting close," said Slow Rabbit's face with a smile.

Black Wing ignored Wechuge and looked again at the ghost woman.

"Ask your question," she said.

"I have my body, but I am able to be here because I died."

"That is not a question."

"The monster has its body," he said, indicating Wechuge. "I can sometimes see through you, but you have your body. Are you dead as well? Were you both restored?"

The woman crossed her arms over her chest. Black Wing could see the scarred nub on her hand where her little finger should have been.

"Like you, I was born to the world above," she said. "My life was taken from me, but my body was given back."

"You are not like me," said Black Wing.

"I am more like you than you realize."

As she said these words, Black Wing felt the crow move inside him.

"But there is more than the dead to be found here," she continued.

"The living dare not come, but there is more than the dead here? What is neither dead nor alive?"

Wechuge shed the form of the boy warrior Slow Rabbit, replaced by the hulking mound of rotting skin and stolen body parts with a triangular head and wicked beak.

"It?" asked Black Wing. "It is neither dead nor alive?"

"Wechuge was born of the void," she said. "A being who belongs neither in the world above nor the world that awaits. This place, the underworld, the nightlands, is his home."

"Then how did that thing come to be in the world above?"

The ghost woman placed a hand on Wechuge's rotting shoulder. A gesture of familiarity bordering on affection.

"His condition," she paused, leaving her hand in place, "his circumstances..." she paused again. "Are my fault. Wechuge is not a thing. He is a creature of the void. He helped me once. Long ago. His service, his sacrifice, saved me. And will save me once again. He is no monster. He is what he was born to be. And he is my friend."

Fifty-Six

The Gunslinger

Hamish Frost shielded his eyes from the sunlight bouncing off the top of the mesa. From the floor of the canyon, he looked up at the bank of once habitable caves, tunnels, and hidey holes carved into the rust-colored cliff face. Three days of hard-riding had brought him to the long-abandoned dwellings.

Once this had been a place of commerce and security, of homes and schools and places of worship. A thriving community, but the entire population had fled the dwellings a thousand years before white men ever stepped foot on the continent. Disappeared without a trace, a people lost to history. Only one man lived there now.

Man? No. Not really a man. He looked like a man but the people of the plains told stories of how, for a time, he had walked the earth in the form of his spirit namesake. But Frost had only ever seen him as a man.

The old gunslinger sighed. If he was here, there was only one place he'd be. The place he always seemed to find temperamental deities, the uppermost dwelling, the highest point in the entire honeycomb of stone buildings.

Frost looked all around him. He suspected he had been spotted by now, that his arrival was no secret. He had hoped he might be spared the arduous task of climbing the narrow switchback ledges. Hoped maybe the one he sought might be so eager for company he would at least meet him halfway, if not climb all the way down.

The old gunslinger sat back on his horse, held the horn of the saddle, and waited a few more moments. It was tempting to clear his throat or call out, announce his presence, but he thought better of it. There could be things hiding in the dwellings, waiting for an unsuspecting fool like him to saunter into the canyon and supply them with a meal. Frost didn't know why this place had been abandoned, but there was good reason to believe bad medicine had been the culprit.

He grew tired of waiting for a welcome signal and slung a leg over the saddle and slid down. He left his painted horse unhobbled at the foot of the cliff. There were some grasses nearby for grazing and, though the paint might have to wander a bit to find it, fresh water, too.

Frost patted the horse on the side of the neck. "You take care of yourself. And be here when I get back." The horse dropped its head and wandered toward some thick grass in the near distance.

Frost kicked away loose dirt from the end of a narrow ledge, detritus accumulated from years of neglect and disuse, then found a fingerhold in the wall and pulled himself up onto the ledge. He steadied himself. One foot in front of the other, then repeat. Don't look down, don't look up. Eyes on the ledge and keep moving. He took a step.

In places, the pathway narrowed, either by design or erosion he couldn't tell, to barely the width of his instep. He flattened himself against the wall and inched along.

One foot in front of the other, then repeat. Don't look up. Don't look down.

The worst parts were the doorways and openings. If there was something inside, an evil spirit or some hungry creature or even a startled rat running out and getting underfoot, he would be doomed. One quick bump was all it would take to send him plummeting to his death.

The sun was near to setting when he finally reached the uppermost hole in the rock wall. His arms and legs ached from the climb, shoulder muscles twitching, fingers cramping. But he was in no position to rest. He braced himself against the edges of the dwelling's opening and, careful to keep his head from breaking the plane of the doorway, peered inside.

"There's nothing ill can dwell in such a temple," he said, taking off his hat and shaking out his long, stringy hair. *"If the ill spirit have so fair a house, Good things will strive to dwell with't."*

"Don't quote Shakespeare at me," came a raspy voice from somewhere in the darkness.

"I've ridden a long way to see you," said Frost. "I'm relieved to know you're here."

"Where else would I be, Whiteskin?"

"I apologize for disturbing you."

"Yet you disturb me, nonetheless."

"I need to parlay. It's important," said Frost.

"Are you still as white as a moon flower?"

"A condition of my birth. I'm afraid that will never change."

"I suppose not."

"So, may I speak with you?"

"I thought that's what we were doing," answered the voice from inside.

"No, I'm standing on a ledge barely as wide as my foot, trying not to fall several hundred feet and break my goddamn neck. I'd rather come inside, but I know better than to cross this threshold without your permission."

"You should know better regardless of whether I grant permission."

"Can't argue with you there. Nevertheless, I'm here and I'm asking."

There was silence for a few seconds. "No one's stopping you."

The old gunslinger took a tentative step inside the dwelling. He wasn't a particularly tall man, but if he didn't stoop, he'd be dragging his head along the rocky ceiling. A few seconds in and his eyes had adjusted to the point that he could just make out the form of a man so thin one could count bones, seated cross-legged on the floor at the back of the dwelling. He was shirtless and wore only a breechclout covering his loins. He had a band of braided buckskin around his forehead, with a few frayed eagle feathers draping from it.

"Why are you sitting up here in the dark?" Frost asked.

The trickster raised his head. "Is it dark in here? I hadn't noticed." Even in the dim lighting, Frost could see that cataracts had turned his eyes a milky white and robbed him of his sight.

"What happened to you? How long have you been holed up here?"

"I don't know. When was the last time you heard something blamed on me?"

"It's been a while," Frost conceded.

"Well, there you go," said the old trickster.

"You're wasting away. Are you hiding from something?" asked Frost.

"Not doing such a good job if you found me."

"Nine Fingers told me to find you."

"Oh, yeah? How is the old woman? She is still an old woman, right? Or did she get all young again?"

"Why did she tell me to find you?"

"Wouldn't know."

"I think you do."

"If I knew, I'd tell you."

"I'm not sure you would."

The trickster smiled. "We don't talk, me and her. She's got her reasons, I've got mine. None of us talk much anymore."

"Us?"

"Oh, you know. Crow. Jaguar. Elk. Badger. Otter. You seen any of them lately?"

"I saw Snake a while back."

The trickster harrumphed and muttered, "Little bastard."

"And I see the Wolf often."

"I notice he's not with you now. Why is that? Is he avoiding me? You know, most of us never liked him. Me and him, we never got along. Thinks he's too good for us."

"He *is* too good for the rest of you. And you and I both know you pretty much never got along with anybody."

"Fair enough." The trickster traced circles on the dirt floor with a long boney finger. "So are you going to say your piece or are we going to shoot the shit all day?"

"I need some information."

"You and every other dumb fucker on the plains."

"About Nine Fingers."

"Told you already. I don't know what she wanted."

"And I told you I don't believe you. I need answers."

"Answers don't come for free."

"I'll pay your price," said the old gunslinger.

The trickster threw back his head and laughed. For just a moment, he was more coyote than human, then his form quickly reverted to the frail old man. "Oh, will you now? You sure about that, Whiteskin?"

"I didn't climb up here just to enjoy your hospitality."

"She showed you the Beauty, huh?"

"Yes."

"You went to the mesa? Found her tipi?"

Frost nodded. "She summoned me."

"You go alone, or did you bring someone with you? And I don't mean the Wolf. I mean someone you just happened to find along the way..."

"Seems you already know the answer to that."

"Nine Fingers invited you into her tipi, showed you the Beauty, and then took you for a ride. Am I right?"

Frost didn't answer.

"How did an ancient fucker like you ever get it up?"

"She gave me mushrooms."

The old trickster laughed, lupine features momentarily flashing across his visage again. "So she fucked you, told you to find me, and then disappeared. Anything else?"

"Showed me a vision."

"Of course she did. Was this the one with the elk or the bats?"

"The bats. The elk vision came later."

"And you woke up, confused as hell, and she was gone, but you were trapped in the tipi? Inside her medicine ring?"

"Yes."

"How'd you get out?"

"The girl I found broke the circle."

"Well, in that case, we're all fucked." He scratched a few more circles into the dust. "Where is the girl now?"

"I put her on a stagecoach headed east."

"Alone?"

Frost shook his head, momentarily forgetting the old trickster was blind. "I commissioned a capable man to look after her."

The trickster let out a long sigh. "There is much I could tell you," he paused, "were I so inclined."

"Cut to it," said Frost. "What's it going to cost me?"

"Not much. Just a favor. A simple good deed for an old blind man. That's all I require."

"What's the favor?" asked Frost.

"There's a spider that's been pestering me. Since I've lost my sight, I can't see when it's around. I need you to kill it for me."

"Kill a spider?"

"Yes."

"That's all you want me to do? Kill a spider for you?"

The trickster laughed. "Did I say 'a' spider? No, no. I misspoke. I meant 'the'. *The* Spider."

Frost exhaled loudly and hung his head. "Goddamn it. You want me to kill Spider? Are you serious? You want me to kill Spider?"

"I am and I do," said the trickster in a voice of mock cheeriness.

"You realize I'm a man and he's a god like you."

"You're just a man? Is that a fact? What are you, Whiteskin, over three hundred years old now?"

"Just because I'm not dead yet, doesn't mean I can't be killed. And if I square off with a spider god the size of a buffalo, I'm going to get killed."

"You want answers to your questions. I want Spider dead. Seems a fair bargain to me."

"No," said Frost. "That's not a fair bargain at all. Even if I could somehow kill him, I've got no quarrel with Spider. He may not be the most lovable of you bunch, but I know of no reason he needs killing. He's certainly never crossed me."

The trickster pulled himself to his feet, turned his back to Frost. Swollen, mottled bruises punctuated by large red welts the size of a horse's hoof covered the trickster's backside. "He sneaks up on me when I fall asleep. He bites me. He pinches me. I've managed to fight him off every time so far, but I get weaker with every attack. Soon I won't be able to get him off of me."

"Why does he do that?"

"He's like the Wolf. He's been inside that damned body so long he's forgotten how to be anything else. He's forgotten who he is, what he is. He thinks he's a fucking spider and he's doing what spiders do! He wants to sting me to death, drink my juices, and then shit my corpse full of spider eggs!"

"I don't think spiders shit eggs."

"Fine then. When he kills me — and it's not for lack of trying that he hasn't already — then you can take comfort knowing that your morals are intact. You'll still be ignorant as fuck and a poor old blind man will be dead, but your hands will be clean."

"You're not a poor old blind man. You're a fucking god."

"Who's gotten old and blind and feeble."

"But still a god."

"Pshaw!" said the trickster. "You throw that word around like it means more than it does. I'm a god because I have medicine. But do you want to know something about medicine, Whiteskin? Do you want to know the big secret? The secret only us 'gods' know? Do you? I'll give you this one free of charge. Are you ready? Medicine is finite. It's not a river, it's a pond. There is no source you can draw from. No spring that flows with fresh medicine. There's no replenishing. Every use diminishes your supply. You got what you got and when you run out, it's all over. If you live long enough, then someday your medicine will be gone. That's why Jaguar disappeared.

That's why you don't see Badger anymore. Or Otter or Eagle. They're all gone. Their medicine ran out. That's why Nine Fingers slunk off to her tipi on top of that mountain. That's why she sends you out to do her dirty work instead of doing it herself. Her supply is low. Her medicine is running out. She's trying to stretch it, make it last as long as she can." He paused. "Same reason I'm sitting up here in the dark. We're all just holding on for as long as we can."

"That doesn't explain why Spider is trying to kill you."

The old trickster scratched at his head like a dog trying to dislodge a flea. "He's almost out, too. So he wants to take what I have left. If he eats me, he gets my medicine."

"How is that not replenishing?"

"That's not replenishment, that's simple digestion. You eat venison, you take that deer's energy and turn it into yours. If Spider eats me, he takes what medicine I've got left and makes it his."

The old gunslinger dropped his head, waited a few moments before speaking. "Where is he?"

"A dwelling down below," said the trickster. "Not far. You can't miss it. Spiderwebs and shit everywhere."

Fifty-Seven

The Manhunter

A WEATHERED BRICK WALL topped by wrought iron fencing separated the two cemeteries. Ozymandias Hayes looked out on the other side of the wall. The whites-only cemetery sat perched on a gently sloping hill, filled with ornately sculpted crypts and fine marble statuaries. He looked back to his side of the wall, the colored side. No crypts, no statues, mostly simple wooden crosses and the occasional carved headstone.

Cora stood next to him, her hand held loosely in his. Her touch was cool, her complexion pallid. Her eyes were sunken and distant. The tears that had flowed so freely for days had dried up.

This was a memory.

A sky as gray and depressing as the mood of the assembled hung heavy overhead. Prayers spoken and hymns sang had done little to ease the oppressive air. Cora watched silently as the tiny casket was lowered into the ground. Hayes bent and scooped wet dirt, then sprinkled it into the grave. He waited for Cora to do the same, but she only stood there unmoving. Hayes looked to the undertaker's men and nodded his head. They picked up their shovels and went to work.

This was a memory.

Hayes put an arm around Cora, held her close to him. He gently cupped the back of her head, pulling her face to rest in the crook between his neck and shoulder. He held her tightly, while a chill wind whipped about them, whistling as it curled and crashed against the handful of mourners gathered on that cold Illinois morning.

Cora stood frozen by the graveside as the mourners — associates from the firm and a few ladies from her sewing circle — filed past, offering well-intended, but hollow words of condolence. She said nothing. Refused to look up from the grave. Refused to move.

Hayes spoke to the parson, seeking permission to linger a bit longer in the little cemetery. The pastor not only agreed, but stayed with them, waiting in silence while Hayes held Cora and watched the undertaker's men fill the hole, forever sealing Charlotte in the cold ground.

Rain began to fall. A drizzle at first, then heavier, turning the soft dirt at their feet into mud. The pastor put a hand on Hayes' shoulder, rested it there for a moment, then gave him a silent nod, and turned, trudging his way back to the parsonage.

Hayes dropped his head, watching shovelfuls of wet dirt accumulating on the tiny casket. When he looked up again, he saw the ghostly woman with nine fingers standing on the other side of the grave.

This was *not* a memory. This had never happened. The ghost woman had not been there that grim morning.

In her arms, she cradled a squirming spectral babe. Charlotte. His child. Cora's child. The same babe whose body now rested in a pine box at the bottom of a muddy hole.

Ozymandias Hayes opened his eyes, blinking away a thin layer of mud that coated his lids. He found himself lying face down next to the front wheel of the stagecoach. Rain poured from the black sky overhead, droplets spattering the ground all around him. His chest throbbed where the bullets had sliced through, lodging in his heart and lungs. He could feel the torn organs and the muscles around them had begun the expelling of the lead lumps and stitching themselves back together, but the pain was still raw.

Someone stepped on his back, the heel of a boot pressing directly on Hayes' left wing bone. He held his breath to keep from grunting and lay still, feigning death. Another boot landed in the mud next to his ear.

Hayes watched, eyes narrowly opened, as the boots trudged through the mud, stopping a short distance away. A flash of lightning and he saw two other men. One with an arm crooked around the throat of the girl named Ana.

The flash faded and darkness returned, forcing his eyes to readjust. He could hear the bandits speaking.

"They both dead?"

"Deader 'n shit."

"You get the key?"

"Weren't no key. On either of 'em"

"Fuck!"

"Told you there wouldn't be. The bank'll be the only ones got a key."

"We'll do it the hard way, then. You at least get the scattergun?"

"Right here."

"Give it to me."

"Trade me the girl."

"I'll share, but nobody fucks until we get the box open. And we ain't doing that out here in the rain. Bring the coach into the barn. I'll hold on to the girl."

"Give me the girl and you bring in the coach!"

"Remind me why we're out here in the rain right now? Was I the one that fucked up the bugle? Was that me? How long you motherfuckers worked here, huh? And you don't know the goddamn calls?"

"I ain't the fucking bugler!"

"No, you fucking killed him. Could've at least waited 'til after the coach was through the gate before you slit his goddamn throat."

"I told you I had to! He wouldn't go along!"

"Shut the fuck up. I'm sick of your bitching. Just get the coach in out of the rain!"

His vision returned and Hayes could see a man turn, arm still around Ana's throat, dragging her through the mud, past the opened gate, and toward the outpost.

He closed his eyes to avoid detection as the two men took control of the coach. He heard the snap of a whip, the whinny of mules, and then opened his eyes again as the wheels slogged through the mud. He rolled to the side as a rear wheel passed by, the tracks where his head had lain only a second before. He kept perfectly still as the stagecoach disappeared into the darkness beyond the gate and the line of trees at the fence.

Hayes waited a moment longer, the seconds dragging by like hours. He needed to be sure the bandits were far enough away that he could rise from the mud without being noticed. The darkness and the pouring rain would aid in that task, but still he knew he would have to move slowly, carefully. Every passing second would bring the girl Ana closer to harm, but he would do her no good by getting shot down again. The bandits believed him dead. He could use that to his advantage, but only if he could avoid being seen while he put himself in position to act.

He reached down to his gun belt and was relieved to find the weapon still holstered. He got to his feet, keeping low to the ground. The rain had intensified. He shed the fine coat that had once belonged to Jacob Hutchens. The lining was soaked through with mud and rainwater. Too heavy, would slow him down. He drew his sidearm, checked the load, and made certain the barrel was unobstructed. He used the wet coat to wipe away mud from the handle and trigger guard. He re-holstered and scurried to the gate.

He leaned against a fence post and peered through the split slats. The station house was to his left, a kerosene lantern glowing in the window. The livery was to his right, though set back a ways, light coming from inside the barn.

Another flash of lightning and Hayes saw the bodies of two men in the mud by the treeline. He knew he had hit one, but didn't know he had killed two until that moment.

Hayes made his way to the bodies and squatted low. In the dim light he could see scattershot peppered both. One man's face was shredded, an unrecognizable mess of blood and tissue. Hayes searched each for weapons. The faceless man had an empty holster, but no weapon in hand. Must've dropped it when he was hit. He felt around on the ground, probing the darkness near the body, but found nothing. He had better luck with the second man. A revolver lay on the ground inches away from the dead man's hand. Hayes picked it up, broke open the cylinder, and reloaded with bullets from a pouch on the dead man's gun belt.

He looked to the station. From what he'd overheard, this wasn't an invasion. The bandits, it would seem, were the station hands themselves. These were the men of questionable character the reinsman had warned him about. He knew these outposts employed a force of six. With two dead on the ground, the three he'd seen as he lay in the mud, and — if the argument he'd heard was credible — another murdered for refusal to go along with the scheme, all six men were accounted for.

Hayes slipped from the gate and moved closer to the livery, circling around for the best line of sight. He dropped to the mud behind a scrub brush. From the lantern light inside the barn, he could see two bandits at the rear of the coach and the third standing nearby, still manhandling Ana.

The bandits hadn't bothered to unhitch the mules. They'd gone straight for the strongbox. They defeated the first lock, the lock that secured the box to the coach, easily enough. A strong pry bar and torque were all that was necessary. The second lock, the one that held the box itself closed, the one for which they'd hoped in vain to find a key, would prove significantly more challenging.

He watched as the bandits near exhausted themselves trying to leverage the box open with the pry bar. Giving up on that, the two hefted it, then slammed it onto the hard-packed dirt of the stable floor, hoping foolishly the impact might somehow jar it open. When that didn't happen, one bandit produced an ax from somewhere inside the livery and began repeatedly whacking the butt end of the ax head against the iron lock. Sparks flew with each strike, but the lock was made to withstand worse.

"Fuck!" he screamed in frustration.

"Alright, enough of this shit," said the man holding Ana. "We tried it your way. I told you there was only one way we're getting it open."

"You can use that shit if you want, but I ain't touching it."

"You scared of it?"

"Fuck yeah, I'm scared of it. If you had any brains, you'd be scared of it, too. We used it to level hills on the railroad. Hills. I seen what it can do."

"Then you know it'll open the box."

"It'll blow that box to shit and everything inside it!"

"Not if we use it right."

"And you know how to use it?"

"Told you I did when we stole it."

"Fine. But I ain't getting anywhere near that shit."

Hayes knew the railroad construction crews had abandoned black powder for blasting and leveling in favor of solidified nitroglycerin sticks. If that's what they were referring to, if the bandits were about to ignite a high explosive in an attempt to open the strongbox, then he needed to get the girl away from there as quickly as he could.

Another flash of lightning.

"Did you see something?" said the bandit with the ax. He took a few steps forward, looking in Hayes' direction, scanning the darkness.

Hayes leveled the dead man's pistol and took aim. This wasn't what he'd hoped. He had a clean line of sight on two, but not the third. Not on the one holding Ana. A shot in that direction was as likely to hit her as the man holding her.

"Is it Billy, you think?"

"Billy's dead. The nigger shot his fucking face off."

The bandit with the ax took another step toward him. The second bandit drew a revolver from his holster and stepped up.

Hayes waited, hoping the men would give up and turn their attention back to the strongbox. A flash of lightning was all it took to dash those hopes and reveal his location. He saw the eyes of the bandits go wide. He rolled to the side just as the one fired on him. He returned fire and the bandit with the gun dropped. Hayes fired again. A headshot to the one holding the ax. Both were dead, but the man holding Ana had retreated into the livery, putting the coach between them.

"Are you the nigger or the buggy whip? You sure as shit ain't the messenger. I got him," a voice from the livery shouted.

"Let the girl go," Hayes shouted back.

"I'm guessing you're the nigger. How are you not dead?"

Hayes didn't answer.

"I got a knife to the little bitch's throat. You want her? Come get her."

Hayes searched the shadows inside the livery. He could see neither the bandit nor Ana.

"Let her go and I'll let you live through this."

The bandit laughed. "Got a counteroffer. How about you throw me your gun or I cut her fucking head off?"

Hayes took a deep breath, lifted himself, and keeping low to the ground, advanced methodically toward the livery. The rain continued to pelt him. "Listen to me. Let the girl go. Give her a horse and let her go. After she's clear of the front gate, I'll throw out my gun."

"You'll give me your gun?"

"Yes."

"Just like that?"

"Just like that."

"I'll shoot you dead, you dumb fucker."

"I figure as much."

There was silence for a few seconds.

"What's the catch?"

"The catch is the girl goes free."

"And you die."

"But if you kill her," said Hayes, "then you don't get my gun, and it's a coin toss which one of us walks out of this alive. Give her a horse and you get my gun."

More silence.

"Gun first!" yelled the bandit.

"Girl first. Then you get my gun."

"Gun first!" repeated the bandit, his voice rising almost to falsetto. "Or I kill the bitch right now!"

Hayes took another deep breath. He'd reached the light's terminus. He held to the edge, letting the rain and the darkness cloak him. He held the dead man's revolver at the ready and kept his stance angled to prevent the bandit from seeing that his own weapon remained holstered. Hayes slowly held up a hand, breaching the shadows. He let the dead man's gun roll from his palm and dangle by the trigger guard. "Don't! Here's my gun." He tossed the revolver through the livery doors and onto the dirt floor. "Send out the girl!"

Hayes waited, but Ana did not appear. Instead, the bandit stepped from behind the stagecoach with the ten-gauge shotgun at his shoulder. Hayes drew his sidearm and the two men fired simultaneously.

Scattershot tore into his torso, newly healing organs shredded once again. Hayes dropped. He struggled to get to his knees, brought the revolver up, and, seeing the wounded bandit staggering toward him, cocked and pulled the trigger. The bullet tore through the bandit's jaw, twisting and distending his face. Hayes cocked and fired again. And again. Until the hammer fell on an empty chamber and the last of the bandits lay dead atop the strongbox.

Hayes turned and saw the girl named Ana, wrapped in the threadbare coat given her by Hamish Frost, stepping from under the eaves of the barn and approaching him. He couldn't tell if it was raindrops rolling down her face or tears streaming from her eyes. He struggled to form words. "Are you hurt?"

The girl shook her head. "But you are."

"I am," said Hayes, then collapsed face-first in the mud.

Fifty-Eight

The Wing-Thief

The current grew stronger and Black Wing found himself paddling not to keep the canoe moving, but to keep it steady. Ahead he could see a semi-circular shoreline covered by smooth stone, lava that had erupted from some deeper recess and cooled into walls of black rock as it flowed into the river. Green crystals, like the ones he had encountered earlier, studded the stone wall in great clusters, casting a glow out over the water.

As they grew closer, Black Wing could see that the river terminated in a swirling vortex at the base of the circular rock wall. If they continued on, they would be sucked down into the whirlpool.

"Put ashore there," said the ghost woman, the spectral beauty with nine fingers, pointing to a spot on the bank where the rocks sloped gently into the water.

Black Wing could see none of the shadowy dead figures they had seen earlier on the banks of the river. He paddled the canoe out of the current and onto the rocky shore. He climbed out, splashing into the water, and pulling the canoe to rest on the smooth stone.

Wechuge shifted his appearance, now wearing the body of Bull Elk, the brother of Antelope Eyes, the war chief whose favorite wife had been taken by white raiders. The monster stood and stepped from the canoe onto the rocks. Black Wing did not see the ghost woman leave the canoe, but she somehow stood by him on the shore.

She pointed to a spot on the rocks a few steps away. "You will need those," she said.

Black Wing looked and saw his weapons, his axe and his obsidian knife, laying on the stone floor. He had lost them when battling Wechuge at the waterfall. "You said I didn't need weapons," he said.

"No," said the ghost woman. "I said they would do you no good where you were going. But you are going somewhere else now."

"And I will need my weapons?"

The ghost woman didn't answer.

"Where am I going?" asked Black Wing.

The woman pointed to the whirlpool. "You will swim out into it and let it take you where you need to go."

"I will drown."

"Did you drown when you fell through the quicksand? When the soil enveloped you? Did you need to breathe when you passed through the rock that separates us from the world above?"

Black Wing looked at Wechuge. "Am I going alone?"

"Yes. Wechuge stays here. I have need of him."

"Where am I going? Where will it take me?"

"We will talk when you get there."

Black Wing looked at her curiously, but she said nothing else. He retrieved his weapons, slipping the knife into its sheath and sliding the axe through the loop sewn into his breeches. He waded out into the water and swam toward the whirlpool. The tug of the current carried him into the vortex and pulled him under. Despite the ghost woman's assurance, he still feared he would drown. He held his breath as the swirling waters pulled him ever deeper, down into the blackness. At some point, he could hold his breath no longer, but as the beauty promised him, he did not drown. He felt no pressure in his lungs, no burning need to breathe.

When at last the vortex released him, he found himself floating beneath calm waters. The whirlpool faded as if it had never been. He looked up and saw a dim light dancing on the surface above. He could feel the bird inside him, squirming. He kicked, pulling himself upward, until his head broke the surface. He was inside another cave. Different from the one through which the river ran. The air was not heavy and dank the way it should have been in a cave. It was fresh, soft. Even though unnecessary, Black Wing filled his lungs, enjoying the cool sensation the air brought.

He looked around for the source of the dim light whose reflection danced on the water, but could not find it. He was in a moat of sorts, a waterway surrounding a small island.

He swam for the shore, wading onto the grassy bank. His hand hovered over his axe, ready to pull it at a moment's notice. Resting at the base of a boulder, he could see a large, crude earthenware bowl. A dark liquid pooled within, congealing on the sides.

"You will retrieve the bowl," said the ghost woman, suddenly appearing beside him.

"Why?" said Black Wing, turning to look at her.

"Because you have need of it."

"What is that inside it?"

"Blood. My blood."

"I don't understand."

"I know."

Black Wing saw movement in his periphery and his head spun, tracking the motion. A creature paced in front of the boulder, as if guarding the bowl. A giant cat, shimmering and almost translucent. It was made entirely of water, he realized, as if the river had taken form, come ashore, and prowled the island.

"That is the Water Panther," said Black Wing.

"It is," said the ghost woman. "The guardian of the land of the dead, or more specifically, the guardian of the bowl."

"And my task is to retrieve the bowl?"

"Yes."

"And it's not going to just let me have it, is it?"

"No."

"How am I to take it from him?" asked Black Wing.

"You have weapons."

"I'm to battle the Water Panther with an axe and a knife?"

"No," said the spirit woman. "You are to kill the Water Panther. He will not surrender the bowl while he lives."

"Why do you need this bowl?"

"I told you. I do not. It is for you."

"What good will the bowl do if the panther kills me?"

"It can't kill you. You are already dead."

"If I do this, if I kill the panther and take the bowl, then what?"

"Antelope Eyes was right. You do ask a lot of questions."

The ghost woman said nothing more. She disappeared, leaving Black Wing alone. The Water Panther stopped, turned, and looked directly at him. It crouched, as if ready to pounce.

Black Wing slipped the axe from the loop, tested his grip, and stalked toward the Water Panther and the blood-filled earthenware bowl at the base of the boulder.

Fifty-Nine

The Gunslinger

Hamish Frost found Spider's domicile easily enough. Had he not been so focused earlier on getting to the uppermost dwelling, he might well have spotted it on the way up. Wisps of spider silk fluttered through the openings in the walls, while just inside the cave, soft strands of silk with the tensile strength of coiled wire and the girth of hemp rope covered the walls and ceilings, almost completely concealing the rock beneath them.

Frost didn't ask permission this time before entering. He resisted the urge to put a hand on his gun hilt. He was there to reason with Spider. His hand touching a gun would show weakness. Not what he wanted to convey.

He stepped carefully inside. Walking on the thick spider silk was like walking on a rope bridge. The floor was uneven and had a give to it, made it easy to roll an ankle and hard to keep a balance. Frost noticed that with each step, the room got a little darker, the ceiling got a little lower, and the walls a little closer. He wasn't in a room, he realized. He was in a burrow.

A sweet but pungent smell hung heavy in the air. He knew the source. Any thought that Spider might not be waiting for him at the end of the dark burrow evaporated.

Frost took another step, then froze. The silk underfoot was vibrating. He felt a chill run down the length of his body. He took a step backward to steady himself, causing him to be off balance and knocked aside rather than crushed by the enormous spider god charging head-on from the darkness.

Spider scurried past, but spun quickly, deftly, rounding back on Frost. He could see Spider's mouth opened, chelicerae spread wide, venom dripping from the fangs. Spider raised his two front-most legs into the air, rubbing them together violently. The bristle-like fur caused a shrill ringing sound. The stored static electricity sparked and popped with the motion of the legs, creating little mini-arcs of lightning that momentarily blinded Frost.

He shielded his eyes and pushed off the silk, tried to steady himself. His hand went automatically toward his gun, but he forced himself not to touch iron. Instead, he held his hands up and spoke loudly in as calm a voice as he could muster.

"God dig-you-den all. My name is Hamish Frost. We've met before, though it's been a while. I mean you no ill will."

Spider hesitated, lowered its legs. But before the old gunslinger could utter another word, Spider jolted forward, sweeping out with one of his forelegs. The blow struck him in the calf. A few inches higher would have taken out his knees. Still, it knocked him down and that was bad enough.

Before Frost could get back to his feet, Spider pounced on him, chelicerae clamping down on the meaty part of his right thigh. Frost cried out as the eight-inch fangs sunk deep into his leg.

He could feel the venom surging into him, mixing with his blood. Paralysis would follow soon. His leg would go numb, his knees and ankles locking into place, rendering his legs useless. The venom would spread throughout his body, shutting down one organ after another until it reached his heart and then it would all be over. Spider would eat him and then the trickster.

Frost looked up at Spider's giant, grotesque head. Eight unblinking eyes of varying sizes stared back at him. The trickster was right. The spirit Spider had once been was no more. There was nothing left but a giant, angry tarantula. And if the old gunfighter didn't act quickly, there would be nothing left of him.

He reached out and his six-guns appeared, one in each hand. He brought them up with blinding speed, jamming the barrels into Spider's eyes, and pulling the triggers. Two eyes exploded. The force knocked Spider's head backward and away from Frost. One of the chelicerae snapped off and remained embedded in Frost's thigh. He leveled the revolvers and brought the hammers down again. He kept firing until the chambers were empty. He'd destroyed Spider's eyes and made mincemeat of his head and thorax, but the angry god was still alive and squealing in pain.

Frost dropped the empty guns and grabbed the chelicerae in his thigh with both hands, pulling the fang free. Blood gushed from the wound, but he didn't have time to worry about that. He reached up and grabbed silk, pulling himself to his feet, then launched himself onto Spider's back. Using the fang as a dagger, he stabbed into Spider's abdomen, over and over again. Spider shook violently, trying to buck Frost off of him, but the old gunslinger hung tightly and kept stabbing.

Unable to dislodge Frost from his back, Spider climbed the silk-covered wall and onto the ceiling of the burrow, trying to force gravity to accomplish what he could not. Frost dangled from Spider's back, but held on firmly with one hand and kept stabbing with the other. He stabbed until the tip of the fang cracked and broke off and then he kept stabbing with the jagged remainder.

Spider grew weaker with each stab, with each pulse of blood from his wounds. The setules holding his legs to the ceiling began to give, then suddenly released. They dropped. Frost landed hard on the floor, with Spider's bulk on top of him. The silk beneath him cushioned his fall, but the weight of Spider on top of him left him stunned and gasping for breath. The broken fang he'd wielded as a dagger remained in his hand, but the hand was pinned underneath Spider's abdomen.

Spider's legs spasmed, twitching aimlessly in the air. Frost worked his arm back and forth, straining with all his might until at last, he managed to slide his hand free. He lifted the fang and jabbed it into Spider's abdomen. Again and again. Then again. And then some more.

"You can stop," said a voice from somewhere behind Frost. "He's plenty dead."

Frost paused. He could see that Spider had stopped moving, his legs retracted and curled.

"That was impressive," said the old trickster, stepping into the cave. "I didn't think you could do it. I expected he'd be munching on your bones at this point."

Frost dug his heels into the silk and wedged his way out from under Spider's carcass. He looked down at the wound on his thigh, saw that it was still gushing blood. He unbuckled his gun belt and pulled the leather strap from the bottom of one holster and re-tied it around his upper thigh, cinching it as tightly as he could.

"What are you doing?" asked the trickster. The milkiness that had covered his eyes earlier had faded.

"Making a tourniquet," said Frost through gritted teeth. "Got to slow down the venom." The old gunfighter tore the sleeve from his shirt and fashioned a makeshift bandage, tied it around the pulsing holes in his leg.

"But he's dead."

"He bit me. Injected me with venom."

The trickster laughed. "You white eyes are so fucking stupid." He walked over and knelt by Spider's corpse. With his fingers, he probed one of the great slashes Frost had created in Spider's abdomen and buried his arm up to the elbow as he fished around inside the carcass. "Think I got it."

When he pulled his hand out, he was holding a long, slender, mottled organ covered with blood and gore. He sniffed it, then wrinkled his nose and slung it back into the burrow. "Shit. That's the intestine." He reached back into the carcass and a few seconds later came out with a similar-shaped, reddish maroon organ. "Ah, that's better."

The trickster held the organ up to his mouth and took a big bite. Blood sprayed out in a fine mist, then dribbled down his wrinkled chin. He chewed noisily and spoke as he ate. "He put the venom in you. But now he's dead." He took another bite.

Frost stared at him, uncomprehending.

"He was a spirit who made a spider body for himself," explained the trickster. "And after a while, he forgot he wasn't a spider." He patted Spider's bloody abdomen. "But this, this is not a spider. This is a manifestation of Spider's will, something he made with his medicine. His venom was venom because it was an extension of his will. His medicine."

"So, is it venom or not?" asked Frost.

The trickster took another big, bloody bite. Chewed. "Oh, yeah. Deadly."

"Then I need a tourniquet."

The trickster's human form slipped for a moment and Frost saw the yellow eyes and lupine features of a coyote. Brown and gray fur. Tall ears, slender snout, and black button nose. The vision faded and the human form quickly reestablished itself. The old trickster held up the half-eaten bloody heart. "You do see me eating, right?"

Frost looked at the bandage on his leg, understanding dawning slowly. The leather tourniquet had slowed the seepage from the wound. He could feel the pins and needles of restricted blood flow to his leg, but there was no paralysis. He could move his foot, wiggle his toes. "His medicine is now your medicine."

"It is."

"The venom was deadly because Spider willed it to be so. But now the venom is yours, not his. Spider's will is no longer in play. His medicine is yours. And if you don't want me dead..."

"You're welcome," said the trickster with a flourish of his arms.

"This was the most unkindest cut of all; Ingratitude, more strong than traitors' arms, Quite vanquish'd him: then burst his mighty heart," said Frost.

The trickster shook his finger at the old gunslinger. "I told you, no Shakespeare."

"When did you get your eyes back?"

"I think you've probably figured that out by now."

"You lied to me. You were never blind. The cataracts, the wounds on your back, it was all an illusion, wasn't it? He wasn't trying to kill you. Wasn't trying to eat you."

"Does it matter?" asked the trickster, blood still dripping from his chin. "You knew who I was when you came here. Don't tell me you thought I couldn't trick you?"

Frost refastened his gun belt, then stood and gathered his guns. He reloaded before holstering them. He looked at the old trickster god, who was busily stuffing his mouth with the last few bites of Spider's heart. "He was just holed up here, same as you. Never wanted your medicine, did he? But you coveted his and I gave it to you."

The trickster shrugged.

"Why didn't you just kill him yourself?" asked Frost.

The trickster held up a finger, indicating Frost should be patient while he chewed. "Wasn't sure I could," he said after one final swallow. "If I tried and failed, he would've eaten me for sure." He wiped blood from his mouth with the back of his hand. "You know, I wasn't expecting you to actually kill him. I figured he'd kill you for sure. I just wanted you to soften him up enough that I could finish him off. Don't look at me like that. I needed his medicine."

"For what?"

"I'm getting the fuck out of here. I'm done with this place. I want to live out my days in peace. I'm going to the moon. Do you know how much medicine it takes to get there?"

"You're not going anywhere until you keep up your end of the bargain."

The trickster flashed a malicious smile. "You think you can stop me, Whiteskin?"

The old gunfighter narrowed his eyes, rested his hands on the elephant ivory handles of his revolvers. "I've already killed one god today. You want to bet I can't do for another?"

The trickster considered this, then nodded. "You make a good point. I'll tell you everything you want to know. But let's go outside first. It smells like shit in here."

Sixty

The Manhunter

Ozymandias Hayes awoke on a pile of blood-soaked hay inside the livery. The morning sun was shining through the gaps in the wooden panels of the stall. He had not died from his injuries. Not this time. At least not yet. His clothes were shredded, his body peppered with shotgun pellets, many of them buried deep in his organs. He knew he was bleeding internally. He had a high fever, was sweating profusely, and was in more pain than he could ever remember being. The girl named Ana sat by him, her head bowed. A bucket of well water rested between them, a tin dipper hanging from the side of the bucket. She had folded and propped Frost's frayed coat beneath his head as a pillow.

"I don't know how to help you," she said.

"You ...can't," Hayes croaked, his throat almost swollen shut.

"I've been dabbing your lips with a wet cloth. I tried to get you to drink some water, but I couldn't get you to open your mouth."

"I'll ...take some ...now," said Hayes.

The girl slipped the dipper into the bucket, then held it to his lips. Water spilled over his chin and down the sides of his neck. He even managed to get a little in his mouth. It hurt to swallow, but he forced the water down.

"Do you want more?"

Hayes shook his head. "You... brought me... here?"

"I had to drag you. You're too heavy for me to pick up. I dragged the bodies off aways, too, so I wouldn't have to keep looking at them."

Hayes tried to speak, but the words hung in his throat.

"I went looking for something to help you. I don't know what. Just something. Anything. I found some cornmeal in the larder. Are you hungry? I made johnnycakes."

He was, but the thought of eating forced him to suppress a retch. He shook his head. "No... no."

"I found another dead man," said the girl. "Inside the station house, but there's no one else here."

"I know," said Hayes.

The girl scooped more water from the bucket and held the dipper to his lips. She cradled the back of his head and gently lifted, helping him to drink.

Hayes swallowed. He lay back on the hay, tried to steady his breathing, manage his pain. "You... you... you need to... unhitch the mules," he said after several attempts. "Been hitched up... all night... not good... for... them."

"Already did," the girl said. "Two days ago. Had to figure out how to do it first. Took me a while, but I did it. I didn't know if it was okay to put them with horses, so I just unhitched them and let them go where they will."

Hayes turned his head, looked at her. He didn't need to speak. His expression asked the question for him. *Two days?*

The girl nodded. "I didn't know how to help you, so I just let you rest."

"Help... will... come," said Hayes.

"I know. I figure after a while, the folks from the next station will send somebody when we don't show up."

Hayes nodded. With the stagecoach missing for two days, help could well be on the way already.

"I went and got your gun," said the girl. "I gathered up all the guns, actually. Even the shotgun. I cleaned them, wiped all the mud off them. I don't know how to load the shotgun, but I loaded all the others in case we need one."

"Good."

"Do you want me to be quiet or keep talking to you?" asked the girl.

"Talk," said Hayes, closing his eyes.

"Okay." Ana was silent for a few seconds. "I'm not sure what to talk about."

"Any...thing."

She paused for a long time, then lifted her head. Her eyes were unfocused, as if staring off into a distance only she could see. "I have these dreams sometimes. I never told anybody about this but my ma and Mr. Frost. Ma didn't want to hear it and Mr. Frost said they were just dreams and not to dwell on them, but I don't think he meant it. I think he was just saying that because he thought I was scared. But I'm not scared. I'm just confused."

The girl offered him more water, but Hayes couldn't drink.

"I dream about being born," said the girl. "Only... my ma wasn't there. There was someone else, but I can't see her face. And she's not..." The girl paused again. "She's pulling me out and there's this big deer or an elk or something. I think I was inside it and somebody pulled me out. I don't think Ma is really my ma. I think that big deer is."

Hayes clenched his jaw as a wave of pain rolled through him. The girl took his hand. "I know that's stupid. I'll be quiet now," she said.

"No," said Hayes, squeezing her hand. "Talk."

The girl paused, as if not sure she should continue. "I dream about being a baby. Ma coming in from the field. Someone with old, wrinkled hands holding me, handing me to Ma. And Ma seeing me... I think for the first time." She paused again. "I dream about dying, too. I dream about dying twice. Once when I'm young like I am now and there's this monster with a head like a bat and he tears me open with his claws and my blood goes all over the ground and a flower grows up from the blood. And then I dream about dying when I'm old and my hands are all wrinkled up like the ones that handed me to Ma. And there's another monster, a different monster, and this one eats me alive. But I don't think it was just a dream. I think that's how I'm going to die. And I think the one about me dying when I'm young is a memory, not a dream. I think I've died before. I think I lived another life and I died and I came back. I know what that sounds like, but I think that's what happened."

The girl paused, helped herself to a dipper of the water. "I've had dreams about you, too. Before I ever even saw you, I had dreams about you."

Hayes opened his eyes, looked at her.

"I dreamed I saw you out on the plains at night. You looked at me, but didn't say anything. Then a bunch of bad men came and they were hurting you. They put a rope around your neck and hung you in a tree. Then me and you were in this cave and it was real dark. There was a river and a canoe. And you were trying to decide if you wanted to get in the canoe. And I told you it was your decision."

Hayes stared at the girl.

"And I dreamed about you and a woman and a little baby. You were both standing by a grave in the rain and I was holding the baby."

Hayes' jaw quivered. He tried to recall the face of the ghost woman who had followed him from that night on the plains to the muddy shores of the blackwater river. Tried to remember the spectral beauty who had held the gently squirming body of baby Charlotte at the graveside, but her features lacked clarity. Try as he may, he could not envision her. He looked again at the girl. Narrow nose. Hazel eyes. High cheekbones framed by raven black hair. Had those been the features of the ghost woman? But the spectre he had seen had been a woman grown, not a girl. He tried to age Ana in his mind's eye, to see what she might look like in ten years, twenty perhaps, but even as he looked at her, the girl's features blurred just as the ghost woman's had in his recollection.

He tried to speak but felt a surge in his throat. He turned his head and spat a gout of blood onto the hay.

The girl grabbed the cloth she had used to dab his mouth and poured a ladle of water over it. She wiped the blood from Hayes' mouth, then rinsed the cloth and dabbed his forehead. He tried to drink more water, but found he couldn't swallow, and retched it all back up.

The girl sat close to him and held his hand. His eyes closed and he drifted into slumber without hearing another word from her.

Sixty-One

The Gunslinger

The trickster sat on the narrow ledge outside of Spider's burrow, his feet dangling over the edge. The sun had dipped below the horizon and a full moon was rising, a halo of light ringing it.

"The moon's an arrant thief, And her pale fire she snatches from the sun," said Frost.

"I've always loved the moon," said the trickster. "It's cold as shit up there and lonely, but there are no giant spiders. And no wrinkled old white fuckers who want answers to questions better left unknown. You ever been to the moon, Whiteskin?"

"Of course not. And you haven't either." Frost leaned against the wall a few feet down the ledge. He had removed the tourniquet and re-tied the holster strap on his leg. The bandage was still in place on his thigh, but the seeping had stopped and the blood was beginning to clot. "I don't care where you go. As long as you give me what I've earned. As long as you tell me what I came here to find out."

The trickster sighed. "So what's it going to be? You want to know who the bat-headed one is?"

"That and more."

"Then you should sit down because this isn't a short story."

The old gunfighter looked at the narrow ledge. "I'll stand."

"Suit yourself." The trickster looked off into the distance. "A long time ago, long before the whites came, before the red people spread out and filled the land, before they split into tribes and warred with each other, before they invented gods and spirits, that's when this whole thing began."

"Skip ahead. I saw this part in my vision."

"Are you going to be interrupting like that the whole time or are you going to shut the fuck up and let me talk?"

"We see which way time doth run. Pick up the pace. I don't have time for a long soliloquy."

"Just trying to set the stage for you. Being a man of the theatre I thought you might appreciate that."

"Brevity is the soul of wit."

"You can knock off with the Shakespeare any time you like," said the trickster, shaking his head. "You want brevity? Fine. The giant with the bat head is the fucking god of death. That brief enough for you?"

"The god of death?"

"Yes. Literally. As in the ruler of the underworld and the Nightlands, collector of souls, destroyer of life, lord of bats. Though I never knew how that last one fits in, but you get the idea, right?"

"I've never heard of a god of death and I've run into just about all of your pantheon. No one's ever mentioned a god of death before."

"There's a good fucking reason for that and if you'll let me talk you'll understand why."

"Does he have a name?"

"Of course he does, but you won't hear me say it. Saying is about two steps from summoning and that motherfucker scares the shit out of me. Just talking about him loosens my bowels."

"He's still alive?"

The trickster rolled his eyes in exasperation.

"Finish the story," said Frost. "I'll hold my tongue."

"Where was I? After the fiasco with the cave, they realized the beauty had medicine no one knew about. A lot of medicine. A winter in a cave was nothing to her. Seeing that, Bat-head no longer wanted her as a sacrifice, he wanted her as a bride. Yeah, the thing at the chalkstones where they tied her up and he ripped her open wasn't a sacrifice. It was a wedding. And when it was over, he dragged his new wife with him down to the underworld, where she lived for thousands of years.

"She hated it there of course. It's dark and miserable, full of bats, the spirits of the dead and every other creepy, crawly thing you can imagine. That and her new husband was the most evil sonofabitch in existence. She never stopped looking for a way out and after a thousand years of secretly searching, she found a way.

"A tiny crack in the rock where she could feel the air from above seeping in. She made a bargain with one of the void-born creatures. If it would bore out the hole big enough for her to get through and do it in secret without getting caught, she'd take it with her to the land of the living. It took another thousand years, but the plan worked and the beauty escaped the underworld. She returned to the world of the living, but all manner of spirits and things born of the void followed through that opening to the world above.

"As you can probably imagine, the bat-headed one didn't take this too well. He was furious when he discovered his bride had run out on him. But he didn't need to find an escape route to go after her. He just tore open another hole in the earth and flew out with a few million of his closest bat friends.

"The beauty expected him to come after her and so she went to ground, hid from him in some of the most remote places she could find. Mountains, forests, anything that hid her from view.

"The bat-headed one had his bats searching everywhere and when they turned up nothing he mobilized an army to help him look. Being the god of the dead, all he had to do to compel humans to do his bidding was to kill them. Once they were dead, they were his to control. So he went on a murder campaign, killing every human he saw and putting them to work trying to find his bride.

"From her hidden place, the beauty could see what he was doing. She knew he would kill every human in the world if that was what it took to find her. A few thousand years as the queen of the underworld had not robbed the beauty of her humanity, at least not completely.

"So she left her hidden place in the mountains and returned to her husband in supplication. She offered herself to him, promising to serve him and love him and be his wife again on two conditions. One, that he stopped murdering everyone he saw and two, that they not go back to the underworld. She would return to him, but only if they stayed in the above, in the land of the living.

"The bat-headed one accepted her proposal. The underworld was his home, but he figured he could be the god of death wherever he fucking wanted, and if he missed the darkness he could always go back for a visit.

"To prove her sincerity to him, The beauty took her own heart from her chest and gave it to the bat-headed one and bade him eat. Take her medicine. He ate the heart and took her medicine. From that moment on, she did everything she could to prove her sincerity and loyalty to him. She served him and bore him many children, one each year, and prevailed upon him to not slaughter them with his touch, but to let them live and bask in his malevolence. Over the next thousand years, the mighty bat-headed one and his queen ruled the world. He kept the murdering to a minimum, only indulging himself enough to keep his reputation up.

"In that time, he grew to trust his wife and believe that she was sincere in her devotions. But this was a mistake, for the beauty was only biding her time. She had never surrendered her medicine to him, but had tricked him. The heart she had given him to eat wasn't her heart at all. She had reached past her heart and plucked one of her kidneys instead. The bat-headed one not being an expert on human body structure, never knew the difference.

"Three times in the years since she had returned to him, she had used her womanly wiles — and the medicine she had hid from him — to make the bat-headed god unknowingly sleep away an entire day. She would seduce him, drive him mad with desire, then after the lovemaking, she would use her medicine to send him into a deep slumber from which he would not awaken until the morning two days hence.

"The god of death never realized that three full days had been taken from him. So, as they neared the end of their first millennia together and on the eve of the equinox — which everyone knows is the day on which medicine is at its most potent — the bat-headed god mistakenly believed the equinox to yet be three days away.

"That night the beauty once again used her medicine to send him into a deep, deep slumber. She dragged his sleeping body to the great chalkstone cliffs where he had killed her and wed himself to her so long ago. Once there, she freed the spirits of all those he had murdered and forced to follow him. With their spirits free to leave this world and go immediately to the Nightlands, the bat-headed god of death's massive army of dead men crumbled into a pile of bones, never to rise again. The beauty knew her medicine was not strong enough to destroy her husband, not even on the equinox, so she found the same rock cavity in which she had once been imprisoned and used her medicine to polish the interior of the cave until it was as smooth and flawless as glass. She stuffed her sleeping husband inside and sealed the opening.

"With the inside of the cave so polished and slick, any attempt to use his medicine to escape would only slide off of the smooth rock. Trapped inside the polished hole with no hope of ever escaping, the body of the bat-headed one would eventually calcify and become one with the rocks around him. He would never murder again and he would be forgotten as the eons passed. At least, that was the plan.

"With her husband disposed of, the beauty gathered her hundreds of children. She had hoped that they, being half-human, might have some sympathy for humanity or at the very least be less murderous than their terrible father. After a thousand years with the god of death, she was weary of all the murder, but her children had not turned out to be what she had hoped. They were a problem that could only be solved by more murder. So she slaughtered them all.

"But she didn't condemn their spirits to the underworld. She was their mother, after all. She allowed them to remain in the world of the living. Some of them remained spirits, some of them faded away, but a few eventually learned how to use their medicine to make bodies. Some chose human bodies. Some chose animal bodies. Eagle, Otter, Badger, Snake, Jaguar, Spider, Coyote."

"Wolf?"

The trickster nodded."Still don't like him. But, yeah. He's my brother."

"She's your mother and the god of death is your father."

"Not exactly something to be proud of, but I came to terms with it a long time ago."

"Why is this coming up now?"

"Same reason Spider went crazy. Same reason I'm getting the fuck out of here after our little talk concludes. The bat-headed one has escaped his prison."

"The god of death is walking the earth?"

"And he'll murder every man, woman, and child who crosses his path until he finds his bride."

"And then murder her when he finds her," said Frost. "Take her heart in reality this time. The same way you took Spider's."

The trickster shook his head. "Are you not paying attention? Did you not hear a word I said? He's not searching so he can destroy her. He doesn't want her medicine."

"Then what does he want?"

"He wants her. She's his wife. He loves her and he wants her back."

Sixty-Two

The Wing-Thief

Black Wing bent low, moving with stealth toward the boulder and the earthenware bowl at its base. He measured his steps, keeping his eyes locked on the Water Panther. The panther stood between Black Wing and the bowl. The great water beast watched him, its head and eyes unmoving, its shimmering transparent tail swaying gently from side to side.

This is insane, he thought. *How am I to battle water with an axe?*

The Water Panther's tail stopped moving. Its body tensed. Its shimmering water form showing a distorted view of the boulder behind it.

Black Wing took a step and the panther uncoiled, charging him. It moved faster than Black Wing's eyes could follow. A silvery blur slammed into him, lifting him from his feet and sending him crashing into the dirt and bouncing over rocks.

He rolled to his feet on instinct, still holding the axe. He felt as if he had just been run over by a bison. The panther spun and was on him again before he could get out of the way. A massive paw, claws extended, raked across his chest, shredding his flesh and ripping him open.

Black Wing looked down, expecting to see exposed bone and tissue, blood pouring from the gaping wound. But he saw no blood at all. Instead, he saw the flesh stitching itself back together, the wound healing as he watched. He could feel the crow moving inside him.

He looked up and saw another translucent paw swinging at him. Black Wing dodged to his left and the paw only glanced him, tearing into his arm and shoulder. The force was still enough to send him sprawling.

As before, the wound did not bleed and immediately began to heal. Idly, he wondered how a creature made entirely of water could have claws as sharp as obsidian that sliced just as deeply. Medicine. That was how. The same force that repaired his torn flesh and allowed a crow to live inside his chest.

The Water Panther opened its mouth and roared. It lunged forward, snapping and snarling. Black Wing rolled again, bounced up, and swung his axe with all the force he could muster. The blade struck the panther behind the head and sliced through its neck with no resistance. The axe blade brought a spray of water as it exited. The panther's form rippled like the surface of a still river in a canoe's wake, but the panther was unharmed.

The battle continued for some time. The panther's claws and teeth ripped into his flesh, tearing and slicing, knocking him down, but the wounds healed just as quickly. Black Wing's axe and his knife found their targets, but he could no more hurt the water panther than he could hurt a lake by stabbing it.

The panther would not relent. It kept charging at Black Wing, biting and scratching, knocking him down. Black Wing would strike back, but neither combatant gained any ground. They were locked in a frustrating stalemate.

Black Wing wondered how this conflict could end. How could he defeat a creature he cannot hurt? The spirit woman said the Water Panther guards the bowl. That is its only task. It will not relent and it will not surrender the bowl while it lives. But Black Wing's task was to retrieve the bowl. How could he bring an end to this conundrum?

Black Wing glimpsed the bowl as the Water Panther again knocked him down, claws ripping into his back. He could see the dark liquid inside the bowl. He needed to kill the panther to get the bowl.

Or did he?

What is the purpose of a bowl? A bowl is but a container. Was his objective to retrieve the bowl or to retrieve the bowl's contents?

He rolled toward the bowl and came up with his axe high in the air. He brought the axe down with all his might. The blade shattered the earthenware bowl, splattering its contents — a thick viscous liquid — all over Black Wing.

He spun to face the charging panther, but the panther did not attack. The creature's form suddenly collapsed in on itself, water splashing to the ground, leaving only a puddle where the panther had stood.

The spirit woman appeared next to Black Wing. "Antelope Eyes was confident you would uncover the answer."

"I don't understand," said Black Wing. "You said I had to kill the panther to retrieve the bowl and yet the only way to kill the panther was to destroy the bowl. What have I accomplished?"

The spirit woman squatted and with her four-fingered hand picked up a large shard of the earthenware bowl. She stood and traced her fingers through the dark residue. She held the hand to Black Wing's face and smeared the thick liquid onto his cheeks like war paint. She covered his forehead, traced her fingers down his nose, then over his chin. Lastly, she smeared the liquid over Black Wing's lips.

"Taste," she said.

He ran his tongue over his lips.

She bent and picked up another section of the broken bowl. A small amount of dark blood pooled inside it. "Close your eyes," she said. "Do not open them until I say that you may."

He did as she commanded and he could feel the woman pouring the blood over the top of his head. He could feel it soaking into his hair, trickling down his head, then onto his shoulders and down his back. Inside him, the crow stirred excitedly.

"Open your eyes," said the spirit woman.

Black Wing opened them slowly. He and the spirit woman were no longer alone. Standing around the boulder were creatures Black Wing recognized only from the stories the holy man had told him. Spider, Badger, Otter, Jaguar, Buffalo, Eagle, Snake, Deer, and Bear.

"The gods are in the Nightlands?" he said.

"Yes," she answered.

"They are dead?"

She nodded. "They wait here."

"Wait for what?"

"If all goes well, to be reborn someday. Otherwise, they wait to fade from existence."

"Not all are here," said Black Wing. "There are some missing."

"Are there?" said the spirit woman.

"The Wolf is not here. Neither is the trickster Coyote. Old Crow is not here either."

She reached out a finger and tapped Black Wing on the dark shape in the middle of his chest. Inside him, he could feel the bird moving again. "Are you so sure?"

Black Wing looked down at the mark the bird had left when it burrowed inside him. "This is Old Crow? There is a god inside my chest?"

"Quite a way to end a spirit quest, isn't it?" The ghost woman held out a hand. In her palm was a small buckskin pouch tied with leather string. A medicine bundle. "Take this."

Black Wing took the bundle but looked at the Beauty with confusion. "You said I would never fly on the wings of a bird again."

"It's not for you."

Black Wing sensed a presence behind him. He turned and saw the old witchy woman he had known as a boy. The one felled by a raider's axe. The one whose medicine bundle he had stolen as she lay dying in the mud. The one he had robbed of her peace in the Nightlands. The old witchy woman held out a wrinkled hand and Black Wing dropped the bundle into her palm. She wrapped her fingers around it and a smile played across her lips as she faded from his view.

Black Wing turned back to the Beauty.

"There is yet one thing more," she said. "The most challenging test you will face, but you cannot face it here. It is time for you to leave the land of the dead."

"How? How do I leave?"

"Follow Wechuge. He knows the way."

"You're coming with me, yes?"

The spirit woman didn't answer his question. Instead, she said, "I promised you my name."

While Black Wing watched, she transformed from the spectral Beauty into a field of stars in the shape of a woman. A voice from somewhere within that field said, "My name is Ana."

And then the woman made of stars disappeared.

Sixty-Three

The Manhunter

Ozymandias Hayes was awakened by a ruckus from the horses and mules. Whinnies and neighs, bursts of activity, rearing and snorting. They were spooked. He forced himself to his elbows. The sun had disappeared while he slept. The girl remained by his side, still holding his hand. He couldn't tell if he felt better or worse. The pain ebbed and flowed. The ebb was almost enough to make him think he was on the mend, but the flow was excruciating. The girl, too, had been sleeping before the commotion woke her.

"What's wrong with them?" she asked.

"Hand... me a... gun," Hayes said.

The girl had a pistol hidden under the hem of her skirt. She took it out and offered it to Hayes. Instead, he grabbed a slat of the stall, clamping down with his fingers, and pulled himself to a standing position. It took all the energy he had. He was forced to lean against the stall, steady himself. He held out a hand. "The... gun," he said.

The girl held it out and he took it with trembling fingers. He pulled himself along the stalls until he reached a spot that allowed him a view of the compound. It was an unusually bright night, a large moon overhead and no clouds, allowing him to see clearly. Mules ran in semi-circles, twisting and turning, wild and out of control. The horses reared, kicked at the air as if fighting off unseen attackers.

Hayes recalled the words of the reinsman at the first outpost. *There's something following us.* He realized belatedly he had conflated the reinsman's warning with the attack on the wagon at this station. But he was wrong to do so. They were separate and unrelated. The attack had been an inside job, perpetuated by the men who worked at this outpost, meaning something else had been following the stagecoach. And whatever it was, it was here now.

Hayes heard a sound, strange and unfamiliar, but growing in volume. He looked and saw a dark cloud on the horizon, huge and approaching fast. The sound was coming from the cloud. Hayes narrowed his eyes, looked more closely. As it came nearer, he realized it was no cloud. It was bats. Thousands upon thousands of bats flying in formation, clicking and squeaking, the flap of thousands of leathery wings adding to the odd cacophony.

As the bats dropped low, skimming the top of the livery and passing over the compound, the horses and mules scattered. The storm of bats swirled over the top of the livery. The noise that accompanied them was almost deafening. The girl clapped her hands over her ears, while Hayes, holding onto the stall with one hand, his pistol in the other, could only wince and endure. At last, the cloud of swarming bats lifted skyward, blocking out the moon. The clicks and whirrs dissipated with distance.

When Hayes' eyes drifted down from the vanishing swarm, he noticed a man standing in the shadows of the station house. The man lumbered from the darkness, staggering into the open area, and approached the livery. His gait was strange. He walked almost as if his back was broken. As he came closer, Hayes could discern his face and head, his unmistakable features. Missing scalp, burned face, a painted stone where one eye should be. The Reverend Josiah Cooley.

But... how? Why? Why would Josiah be here?

Hayes tried to speak, to call out to the reverend, but his throat was too raw, too swollen, and he couldn't form the words. A moment later, he realized it wouldn't have mattered. As Cooley moved closer, Hayes could see the reverend's neck was swollen and distorted, his head sitting askew in an unnatural manner. The flesh above his collar was mottled gray and black from lividity. His neck had been broken. His head nearly twisted from his body.

It wasn't Josiah Cooley walking toward him. It was only Josiah Cooley's broken body. The good reverend was no longer inside the animated husk that struggled forward. Behind Cooley's shambling body, Hayes could see more men moving from the shadows. The fierce painted warriors he had seen sitting with Cooley around a fire. Or, as with Cooley, it was their bodies. They were ambulatory, but no more alive than was Josiah Cooley. As they came closer, Hayes could see each had been gutted, the white of exposed ribs against decaying flesh, intestines dangling from their shredded abdominal cavities. They pressed forward silently, but steadily.

Hayes didn't have time to question what he saw, didn't have the luxury of pondering the metaphysical implications. If death couldn't hold him, why should he be surprised to discover that others could slip the bonds as well? Only this was clearly different. The ghost woman had endowed Hayes with the ability to *recover* from death, to return to his natural state, wounds healed, as if death were only a brief recuperative period. Josiah Cooley and the painted warriors at his side were beyond restoration. Their corpses had been reanimated, but that was as far as it went.

Hayes raised his gun, hand shaking so severely that even resting it against the stall couldn't steady his aim.

"There's more of them," said the girl. She pointed, her arm gliding in a semi-circular motion that encompassed the compound. "They're all around us."

Hayes' eyes tracked her hand. He could see shapes moving in the darkness, becoming more distinct with each faltering step they took. A horde of dead men surrounded the station. Hundreds, maybe more, lumbering forward mindlessly, contracting their perimeter as they moved.

Hayes recognized among them Enoch Munn, the murderous outlaw who'd hanged him from a tree. The same outlaw Hayes had killed upon his first return from death, the one whose body he'd surrendered to the wolf pack that stalked him as he rode for the Cavalry outpost. He saw his one-time partner, Jacob Hutchens, his flesh blackened and melted from where he had fallen in the fire after Munn shot him. Hayes had buried Hutchens himself, but there the man stood. Or rather, the body that had clawed its way out of a grave stood before him. Hayes saw men in cavalry uniforms, among them the commanding officer, Major McKinney. There were people he'd seen in Denver City. The pig-faced hostler, the soiled dove he'd saved in the alley, the brothers who had assaulted her, and the mutton-chopped sheriff whom Hamish Frost had backed down. All of them were now dead, but reanimated and converging on him and the girl.

The horde didn't stop when it reached the twisted wire fence surrounding the compound. They kept moving forward with no heed. The wire cut into the flesh of those mashed against it by the throng, tearing clothes and shredding flesh, before ultimately the entire fence gave way and collapsed as the horde mindlessly pressed forward.

The horses and mules continued to run amuck, some of them forcing and trampling their way through the horde and, with the fence down, escaping into the night. While others were taken down by the horde, mauled and torn to pieces.

"We've ...got to... get out of here," Hayes said.

The girl stood frozen. Almost calmly, she said, "There's nowhere to go."

Hayes leveled his pistol and fired into the horde. A dead man dropped, but then got back to his feet again and shambled forward. Hayes fired again and again and again. Twice more and the revolver was empty. There was no point in asking the girl for another. He was too weak to shoot, and even when luck permitted him to hit his target, there was no effect.

Hayes dropped the empty weapon and looked at the girl named Ana. "I'm... sorry," he said. "I... failed... you."

Sixty-Four

The Gunslinger

Hamish Frost looked down at the old trickster sitting on the ledge high above the canyon floor. "He loves her?"

Coyote looked up at the full moon, a glowing ring of light encircling it. "Keep in mind he's crazy as fuck, but yeah. He loves her and wants to drag her back down to the underworld and make things like they used to be. And if he has to raze the world above to make that happen, that's what he'll do."

"I do not understand."

The trickster laughed. "I know."

"Then make it clear for me. Who is the girl I found? What is her part in this?"

The trickster looked up at Frost. "When you found her, she hid her name from you, yes?"

"For a while, but she ultimately told me."

"And what did she tell you her name was?"

"She said her name was Ana."

The trickster laughed and shook his head.

"Something funny about that?" the old gunfighter asked.

"That was the name of the girl you saw in your vision, the one who got her guts ripped out and her body dragged into the underworld. Or at least that's what the people called her. Whatever she may have been called at birth was lost when she was orphaned. But after her medicine was revealed, after she survived being shoved into that tiny cave for the winter and emerging unscathed, the people needed something to call her and so they referred to her simply as *She*."

"She?"

"That's a translation. In the language of the people it was *Ana*."

"Ana means 'she'?"

"It did, but that language is long dead. And that's not the name of the girl you found."

"Then why did she tell me that was her name?"

The trickster shrugged. "That's what she thinks it is, but it's not. At least not yet."

"Not yet?"

"I told you. It's complicated."

"If her name's not Ana, then what is it?"

"Her name is *Anaba*."

"Anaba?"

"Ana-ba," said the trickster.

"What does 'ba' mean?"

The trickster looked up at Frost again. "*Returns.*"

"She returns?" said the old gunslinger.

"Yeah. She returns."

"The girl I found, who said her name is Ana, is actually named Anaba. Which means She Returns."

"Correct."

Frost narrowed his eyes. "The old woman — Nine Fingers — is the girl who was murdered in my vision. I saw her transform into that girl. She was older, but unmistakable. Nine Fingers is Ana. NIne Fingers is She."

"No." The trickster made a face. "It's complicated."

"Clarify it."

"The girl you saw in the vision — *She* — had medicine. Powerful medicine. But she was mortal. And being mortal, her medicine would outlive her. She could've lived a hundred lifetimes and never exhausted it. And during the eons she was in the underworld with the bat-head, she leeched even more medicine from him." The trickster flashed a wicked smile at Frost. "I don't think I need to explain that one to you, do I?"

Frost glared back but didn't answer.

"Anyway, once she escaped the underworld and came back to the world above, the clock started ticking."

"She became mortal again?"

The trickster tapped his nose with his forefinger. "She had more medicine than ever before — not enough to kill the bat-head, which is why she sealed him up in a cave instead — but more medicine than a god and still she was trapped in a mortal's body. You know what that's like, right? You're only three hundred years old and you're all withered up like an apple left in the sun. Imagine being thousands."

"Still waiting on that clarity."

"You ever wonder why she has nine fingers? It's because she cuts it off."

"Why?"

"She explained all this to you in the vision. The one with the elk. What? You think doe elks give birth to baby girls all the time?" The trickster sighed and shook his head. "She cuts off her finger and puts it in a doe's womb. A little zap of lightning quickens the doe and a few months later ... she returns."

Frost's mouth hung open. "She... duplicated... herself?"

The trickster held out his arms wide. "And there it is! Comprehension! The orphan girl you saw in your vision, the original who started it all, Ana the mother of the gods, has been dead for many thousands of years. But her medicine lives on in Anaba. She Returns. Your girl is not the first. She's been doing this for as long as I've been alive. She lives. She gets old. She cuts off a finger and starts all over. When the girl comes of age, the old woman dies."

Frost shook his head. "I saw her — *She* — in the vision. And I know Ana — Anaba. They're not the same."

"Oh yeah? Describe her to me. What does she look like?"

"Which one?"

"Either one."

"She has black hair," said Frost. "Black as a raven's wing."

"Her face. Describe her face."

"She..." Frost paused. "She has dark hair. Black hair. She..."

"What's wrong, Whiteskin?" the trickster teased. "Can't remember?"

"No. Of course, I remember her, but when I try to recall her face, either of their faces, all I see is —"

"A blur?"

"Why can't I see her face?" asked the old gunslinger.

"You recognized her in the first vision. You saw that the girl you found, the girl you brought with you to the tipi, and the orphan girl in the vision, the girl the bat-head murdered and took for a bride, shared a face. Share more than that, actually. That's information you will need to do what she wants you to do, but the old woman needed you to be compliant for a little longer. Not ask too many questions just yet, so she blurred you. Told you to find me for the rest of the story."

"Why?"

"She needed to keep you in the dark until she didn't. She may have been an innocent orphan once upon a long ago, but eons with the god of bones taught her how to calculate her moves."

Hamish Frost wrinkled his brow.

"Still a little in the dark, are you? The girl you found is not the first. There have been dozens before her, but she is the last."

"Why? Why is she the last?"

"My mother knew sooner or later this day would come. She knew the bat-head would escape his prison. She planned for this. Anaba. You. Me. The Wolf. Others. We all have our part to play."

"And what is my part? Why am I out here and not with her?"

"We're about done here. She sent you here because she needed you out of the way for a while. Your presence would have complicated a few things that needed to happen."

"Where is he? Where is this god of bones and how do I kill him?" asked Frost.

"Look at you," said the trickster, raising his eyebrows. "You stab a few holes in old Spider and now you think you can do the same to the god of murder? That would be funny if it wasn't so pathetic."

"Where is he?" said Frost angrily.

"I don't know and I don't want to know." Coyote got to his feet, standing precariously on the narrow ledge. "I am staying the fuck out of this. That's why I'm going to the moon. I want to get as far away from this disaster as I can."

"You're not going to the moon," said Frost. "You're going to help me."

Coyote winked at Frost. "Nope. It's time for me to fly." The old trickster held out his arms like an eagle spreading its wings and then stepped from the ledge. He plummeted two hundred feet to the rocks below.

Frost heard the sound his head made when it struck the rocks. He leaned over and saw Coyote sprawled on the canyon floor, his legs twisted at odd angles, his skull split open and a dark liquid oozing down the side of a boulder.

Frost looked up at the moon, then began working his way down the ledge.

Sixty-Five

The Manhunter

As the horde of dead men closed in, the girl stepped to Ozymandias Hayes' side. She leaned into him and Hayes put an arm around her, pulled her close to him. Hayes noticed the girl's head twist to the left, her eyes tracking something there. He turned and saw a blur of motion, something large and dark, moving toward them with unbelievable speed. At first, he thought it was a horse. At that size, it could only be a horse. But it wasn't.

It was a wolf.

An impossibly large wolf. With fur so black it almost blended into the shadows, and yellow eyes glowing like embers.

The wolf vaulted over the line of dead men, putting itself between Hayes, the girl, and the encroaching horde. The wolf spun around and charged into the horde. Jaws snapping, teeth tearing, claws mauling and shredding dead men. Hayes saw the corners of the girl's mouth lift ever so slightly. Not so much a smile, but a sign of the sudden hope she felt.

She knows this wolf, he realized.

The wolf's jaws ripped and slashed. Where Hayes' gunshots had no effect, those dead men the wolf tore apart stayed down and did not rise. The giant wolf gashed through the horde like a tornado of teeth and claws. It seemed to Hayes the wolf could destroy the entire horde all by itself.

But then, over the wolf's snarls and growls, Hayes heard chirps and clicks from the sky, the flap of a million leathery wings. He looked up and saw the cloud of bats returning fast, coiling directly overhead. The bats darted down from the sky by the hundreds. They slammed into the giant wolf in suicide dives like a hail of arrows. Those that survived the impact latched onto the wolf's fur, biting at its ears and scratching at its eyes.

The horde of dead men regrouped, spreading out, creating a new perimeter around the wolf and the bats attacking it.

Another mass of bats descended from the sky, thousands in a conical formation touching down like a screeching, fur-covered dust devil. The mass swirled, the enormous undulating shape coalescing. It looked to Hayes as if the cone of bats were merging into a single form, melding together, morphing into something vaguely man-shaped. When at last the swirling stopped, there were no more bats. In their place was a giant, long-limbed bipedal creature with a bat-shaped head.

Hayes assumed the creature to be male, although other than the broad shoulders and narrow hips, there were no discernible gender traits. The body was naked but lacking sex organs. Only about half of the body was covered in skin. The rest was a melange of visible bone, muscle tissue, and even some exposed internal organs. The body seemed to be stuck somewhere between a state of decay and a state of rebirth. Long arms hung at its side, pointed fingernails — almost claws — glowing dully as if powered by some form of bioluminescence.

The creature's face was impossible to look away from, having no lips and no flesh on its mandible or pointed chin. One orbital socket was completely exposed, the eye within little more than a bulbous orb crisscrossed by small, pulsing veins. Patches of dark fur-like hair protruded from its scalp like clumps of weeds from a dry riverbed.

The creature stepped toward Hayes and the girl. Hayes could feel his stomach clenching, bile rising in his throat. The creature exuded malevolence.

The giant black wolf spun and leaped over the horde of dead men, charging toward the creature. The wolf put itself directly in the creature's path, shielding Hayes and the girl. The wolf pawed at the ground, snarling and swinging its great head from side to side with a frightening violence. It threw back its head and let out a howl so deep and resonant that Hayes felt waves of goose pimples roll down his arms and across his back.

The creature paused, tilted its obscene excuse for a head, and stared at the wolf. Something like a smile played across its face.

The wolf growled, a slow rolling thunderclap coming from its throat. When the creature stepped forward, the wolf charged, front paws slamming into the bat-headed creature's chest.

The creature staggered, stumbled, and fell flat on its back. The wolf landed hard on top of it. The giant wolf's head speared downward, its jaws clamped around the creature's neck and throat with a force that would have decapitated a bison. The wolf's head twisted, jerking back and forth, side to side, its teeth buried deep in the creature's throat.

The creature bucked, tried to knock the wolf off of it, but the wolf would not relent. The creature snaked a hand up and grabbed fistfuls of the wolf's fur. It ripped and tugged, pulling out great tufts of black. Another barrage of bats rained down from the sky, slamming into the wolf, but the giant wolf ignored them and continued trying to tear out the bat-headed creature's throat.

Hayes watched helplessly as the two impossible figures grappled, locked in a life-or-death battle right there in front of him. He stole a glance at the girl and saw her standing frozen, paralyzed by fear.

The girl gasped and Hayes looked back. He saw the bat-headed creature had pulled so much fur from the giant wolf's rib cage that the slick, inky flesh beneath was now exposed.

The wolf was unfazed. It continued trying to separate the creature's head from its torso. The bat-headed creature's long glowing claws broke the wolf's skin, rending the flesh. Its fingers burrowed into the wolf's side, expanding the wound. Thick blood seeped. The bat-headed creature's hand bored in, fingers pushing ribs apart.

The wolf howled in anger and pain, losing its grip on the creature's throat. The wolf stepped back, repositioned itself, and speared down again with its head, teeth snapping closed around the creature's forearm. The wolf tried desperately to pull the creature's hand free from its ribs. The flesh of the creature's arm tore, ripping away muscle and tendon from exposed bone, but still it kept forcing its hand deeper into the wolf's ribs.

Hayes saw the wolf stagger, saw its knees buckle, its hind legs going limp. The bat-headed creature's hand was buried to the wrist inside the wolf's ribcage.

The creature twisted and pulled, twisted and pulled, until it finally withdrew from the wound, holding something large and wet with red in its hand. The giant wolf's amber eyes went dull and glassy. Its jaws went slack and fell from the creature's forearm. Its great black head lolled to the side. Its body went limp.

The bat-headed creature stood, tossing aside the carcass of the giant black wolf. The wolf lay on the ground, unmoving, blood gushing from its side and pooling in the mud.

In the bat-headed creature's hand was the wolf's heart.

Hayes heard the girl let out a soft but devastating whimper.

The bat-headed creature lifted the wolf's heart to its mouth, jaws distending, its mouth opening impossibly wide. It took a large, bloody bite and swallowed. Three more bites and the heart was consumed.

Hayes could see Ana trembling with what he thought at first was fear. Then the girl stepped away from Hayes, leaving him leaning against the slats of a livery stall, and he realized it wasn't fear that made the girl tremble. It was rage.

She strode toward the creature. Hayes could see the muscles of her jaw vibrating, could hear her teeth grinding together. The girl opened her mouth, baring her teeth like an animal snarling. The sound that came from her throat was not human. It was like an explosion. Hayes could see a violet aura forming around her, pulsing with energy, roiling and rippling, distorting the air like heat radiating from the desert floor.

Hayes felt a shockwave hit him, hurling him backward, and shattering the stall against which he had leaned. He landed atop broken wood on the hard-packed dirt of the livery floor. He looked up and saw the shockwave roll through the remaining horde of dead men like a million shotgun pellets, shredding them to tiny pieces. Particles of incinerated bats rained from the sky like volcanic ash.

And yet the bat-headed creature that had just murdered the wolf stood there unfazed as the shockwave rolled over it. As the wave dissipated, the creature took a step toward the girl.

Hayes tried to stand, but couldn't. Only then did he realize he had been impaled, a splintered board sticking through his chest. He could see the stack of guns the girl had piled on the hay just out of arm's reach. He could see the ten-gauge scattergun. But he knew that even if he could lay hands on it, even if he could somehow lift it to his shoulder and fire, he had no reason to believe it would be more effective than the pistol had been on the horde of dead men. Still, he wanted to try.

He felt a darkness on his periphery and tried to force it away. He could feel the death he'd pined for earlier fast approaching. Only now he didn't want it. He didn't want to leave the girl alone with the bat-headed creature. He wanted to pick up the ten-gauge and pelt the creature's head with buckshot.

He made one last desperate effort to free himself from the broken slat pinning him to the remains of the stall. But he lacked the strength. The shattered wood sticking out of his chest remained in place.

And the darkness claimed him.

Sixty-Six

The Wing-Thief

Black Wing looked down at the shattered earthenware bowl, the remnants of dark blood clung to the broken shards. The same blood with which the ghost woman had anointed him. He walked to the river's edge, then dipped a toe into the black water. He looked back and saw the pantheon of gods had expanded. Two more stood there. The trickster Coyote. And a giant black wolf with glowing amber eyes.

The Shadow Wolf was dead. The great black wolf had been there at the beginning of this quest, comforting the girl behind the trapper's shack as he and the holy man watched. The holy man was dead and now too was the Shadow Wolf. All of them had died. But Black Wing's life had been restored that he might complete his quest. And now only one task remained.

He felt a stirring in his chest, the crow moving inside him. Old Crow was as dead as the others. Black Wing had killed him at the waterfall. He was godkiller as well as medicine thief. "Will you join them?" he asked. "Will you rip your way out of my flesh the same way you burrowed in?"

Old Crow did not stir. Black Wing waded deeper. Ahead, he could see the swirling vortex that had brought him here, spinning now in the opposite direction. He waded to his waist. When the crow still did not stir, he dove in and swam toward the vortex. The current took him, spinning him wildly before tugging him under. He closed his eyes and waited. When the vortex released him, he could see a soft green glow on the surface above. He kicked and pulled himself upward.

When he surfaced, he saw the empty birchbark canoe on the distant, rocky shore. He swam, standing only when he felt his feet brush the muddy bottom. He walked to the shore. He could feel Old Crow still inside him. He stopped and looked down at the canoe. The carved wooden paddle lay in the bow. He walked past the canoe. The rocks along the shore were covered in a thick, dark liquid.

He walked ashore knowing what he would find. The same things he had found on the river's edge where Wechuge had murdered Bull Elk and the party of warriors searching for the war chief's stolen wife. The same things he had found on the shore of the lake where Wechuge had slaughtered the holy man Antelope Eyes. He saw her shredded clothing, clumped strands of her hair attached to pieces of torn scalp. He found broken teeth and pieces of fingers. But these and blood were the only remains. The ghost woman who had restored his life was no more. Wechuge, the creature she had labeled her friend, had murdered her, then consumed her. Body and spirit.

Leading away from the shore and into the shadows, Black Wing could see heavy, mismatched, bloody footprints.

Sixty-Seven

The Manhunter

Cora did not speak a word on the carriage ride back to their little house. Once inside and with the door secured, Ozymandias Hayes helped her undress, removing the black shroud of mourning. He turned down the blankets and put her to bed. He drew water from the cistern and dissolved ten drops of laudanum into a tall glass. Cora refused to drink, but he was insistent.

"The doctor says it will calm your nerves," he said. "Help you sleep. You need rest, Cora. Please. Drink it."

She relented. Hayes took the empty glass from her and then sat in a chair by the bed. He held her hand and stroked her hair gently. She didn't look at him, didn't say anything.

"We'll get through this," he said to her.

Cora didn't respond.

"We'll get through this. I promise you." He paused. "It will take time, but we're strong. You're strong. Maybe we'll leave here. Go to England. You can visit your family. Introduce me to them all. To your aunt. Who knows? Perhaps we'll stay there. Start our lives all over."

Cora said nothing. She released his hand, rolled over and curled herself into a ball.

This was a memory.

Hayes stood and walked to the window, stared at the gray sky. A freezing rain began to fall, icy water collecting on the tree limbs, dripping from the branches. Icicles would form overnight. The cobblestones leading to the door would be slippery.

Hayes saw a figure standing on the path, staring back at him. Her dark hair whipped about her shoulders as if tossed by invisible winds. But this was not the ghost woman, not the spectral beauty, who offered him the canoe at the black river's edge. Not the woman who'd held the ghost of baby Charlotte by her bassinette and again at her graveside. Standing on the cobblestone path leading to their little house was the girl named Ana.

This was not a memory. This had not happened.

Hayes turned from the window, sat on a chair in the corner, and watched Cora sleep. The ache in his soul grew so overwhelming as to be numbing. At some point, exhaustion prevailed and sleep claimed him.

He woke in the darkness. It had been late afternoon when he'd placed Cora on the bed and sat in the chair beside her, but the sun had long since dipped below the horizon while he dozed. The room was quiet and still. He stood and stumbled to the dresser, found a box of lucifers, and lit the oil lamp. The house was cold, his breath curling into steam as it escaped his lips. He would need to build a fire before the chill woke Cora.

As he knelt to stack the logs in the fireplace, he noticed Cora was not in the same position she had been in earlier. Her head was turned toward him, her face vacant, her eyes open, staring and unblinking. Cora's arm was outstretched, hanging over the edge of the bed, palm up, fingers dangling. Her lips had a bluish cast, exactly as baby Charlotte's had when he'd found her unmoving in the bassinet.

The empty tin of laudanum lay on the floor beneath her hand.

The fire crackled. Little glowing sparks floating on the heated air rose on streams of smoke and then winked out just as quickly. On a stone near the flames sat a battered tin coffee pot. Ozymandias Hayes knew this sojourn into death had been longer than the others. Days perhaps. He had healed, both from the shotgun blast that had felled him and from having been impaled on the slat of the broken stall. Night had fallen again, the sky overhead a blanket of stars.

Across the fire from Hayes sat the old gunslinger Hamish Frost, his head bowed, long stringy white hair hanging down over his wrinkled face. His shoulders were slumped and his forearms rested on his thighs. His long, boney fingers methodically cleaned and polished a disassembled revolver with an oilcloth. The old man stared into the fire, lost in thought.

Hayes let out a long breath. Sound escaped his throat in a ragged, audible sigh. Images of Cora and Charlotte, their faces still, their lips blue, refused to leave the stage of his mind. He felt empty inside, as hollowed out as the birchbark canoe that rested on the shores of that dark river. As he stood and trudged away from the fire, Hamish Frost did not even look up.

Hayes wandered past the collapsed station house and what remained of the livery. Scattered on the ground all around him were the remnants of the army of the dead that had marched on the station. The girl's scream had obliterated the dead men. Josiah Cooley, Enoch Munn, Major McKinney, the entire horde of shambling corpses shredded, their remains littering the grounds of the outpost. Hayes stumbled past, ignoring it all. He came to the body of the giant wolf, cold and still, the gaping hole in its side exposing bare rib bones and looking like the entrance to a cave. Hayes lowered his gaze and kept walking.

He stopped only when he came to the banks of the river that bordered the outpost. On the opposite shore, he could see the upward-pointing roots of a large tree that had collapsed and fallen into the river. The trunk was only partially submerged, falling halfway across the river before its angle forced the top and uppermost limbs beneath the surface. Hayes watched as the starlight played on the water flowing over and around the trunk.

He lost track of how long he stood there staring before his knees gave way and he collapsed. He made no effort to break his fall, allowing himself to splash face-first into the river. The current lacked the force necessary to move Hayes. He became like the fallen tree on the opposite bank, merely an obstacle for the river to flow over and around.

With his head under the water, time seemed to slow almost to the point of non-passage. He opened his eyes, but saw only dark streaks as the water flowed past. He realized he did not have to rise. He could take the water into his lungs, let it choke out his breath. He could lay there until over time the water dissolved him and carried his diminished remains downstream.

But he knew that to die again would take him back to Cora. To her ashen face and blue lips, her unblinking gaze. He would see her buried next to Charlotte. He would stand alone and lost at the graveside, again watching as the undertaker's men shoveled dirt atop a box containing the body of one he loved. That was all that death held for him.

He positioned his hands under his chest, dug his fingers into the silt of the riverbed, and pushed himself up until his head broke the surface. A deep cough burst from his lungs, expelling all that had seeped in while he lay beneath the water. He stood slowly and took one look back at the river, at the partially submerged tree. He allowed himself a moment to wonder if he had made the right choice, then trudged back to the warmth of the waiting fire.

Sixty-Eight

The Gunslinger

HAMISH FROST HAD FINISHED cleaning and reassembling both of his guns by the time Hayes wandered back to the fire. The old man with the pale white flesh and violet eyes lifted the battered coffeepot from the fire ring, filled a tin mug, and handed it to Hayes. Hayes sat while Frost poured himself a cup and sipped the dark, steaming liquid slowly.

Hayes took a long, loud sip of the coffee, held it in his mouth for a few seconds, and then swallowed it down. Hayes saw now what he had not noticed earlier. The old gunslinger's shoulders were slumped. Where his back had always been ramrod straight before, it was now hunched and sloping. His hand had shaken when he poured the coffee. All the grace and agility, the vim and vigor he had displayed despite his advanced age, were gone.

Hamish Frost closed his eyes and said, *"Dream on, dream on, of bloody deeds and death."* After a few seconds, he looked up. "How many times has this been for you, Mr. Hayes? How many times have you died and come back?"

"I don't know. I've lost count."

"Was this her gift to you?"

Hayes was slow to answer. "Or her curse. I'm not sure which."

"I suspected when I found you in the jail cell. Not many men who can survive a ten-inch blade jabbed into their heart. But when I found you impaled on a stake, a good two days dead, only to have you wake up a short time later, I knew."

Hayes spread the buttons on his shirt, looked at his chest. The skin was smooth and unmarred. The wound completely healed.

"Did she appear to you as the beauty or as the old crone? Or both?" asked Hamish Frost.

"The beauty. Until this last time. Then she was the girl. Ana."

"The wheel is come full circle." The old man's chin bobbed. "They were always one and the same. A mantle passed from one manifestation to the next. She blurred our perceptions to keep us from seeing, from understanding, until she needed us to know the truth. The girl herself didn't know either."

"I would assume she does now."

"Aye. That she does." Frost took another sip of coffee and stared into the fire. "Did you see him killed? The wolf?"

Hayes nodded. "There was a... creature. A giant with the head of a bat. And a horde of walking dead men. A sky full of bats. The wolf put itself between us and them. It was protecting us."

Frost inhaled, his lip quivering. "He would have done that."

A long moment passed in silence. The old man opened his mouth to speak, then paused, took a few seconds to compose himself. When at last the words came, his voice had a tremor. "I was born in England in the summer of 1564."

The old man took another sip of coffee. "Never knew my mother. She died in my birthing. My poor father never got over it. Drank himself to death before I was yet ten years old. He was an actor and a lutist. A good one, at least until the drink robbed him of his grace. His theatre company more or less adopted me on his passing. They called it an apprenticeship, but in truth, it was an act of charity. Had I been the greatest actor in all of London, this," he pointed to his alabaster skin, "assured I would never step foot in front of an audience."

Frost tilted his head, stared up at the night sky, narrowing his eyes as if seeing his memories played out before him in the stars. "I developed a weakness for the bottle, same as my father. A problem I compounded with inveterate gambling. By the time I was twenty years old, my sizeable debts brought me into conflict with some unsavory characters. A friend — a budding playwright who would go on to some renown — helped smuggle me out of England on a ship bound for the New World. And every day for the next decade, I wished my debtors had caught up to me before I got on that goddamned boat."

He dropped his head and took a long ragged breath.

"Was your friend who I think he was?" asked Hayes.

"We know what we are, but not what we may be." A smile played across the old man's lips. "I have committed to memory every line he ever wrote, but he was dead and in the ground a hundred years before I read word one."

The old man closed his eyes and Hayes thought for a moment he had fallen asleep. But then he drained his cup and dropped it on the ground by the fire ring.

"I ultimately found my way to a place named Roanoke in the settlement of Virginia," he continued. "Hunger, disease, and the ever-present threat of hostile savages hung over us like the sword of Damocles. That sword dropped when the Croatans overran the settlement. Killed all but seven of us. Young men with strong backs. They enslaved us, put us to work in a copper mine, breaking bedrock with rock hammers from sunup 'til sundown for at least three winters, maybe four. Could have been five. I lost track of time. When the vein tapped out and the Croatans realized there was no more copper to be had, they stood us on the edge of the crater overlooking the hole we'd spent the past few years digging. Then they slit our throats one at a time and pushed us over the edge and onto the rocks below. I was the last in line. Granted the privilege of watching the others die."

The old man paused, took another deep breath. "When my turn came, I closed my eyes, said a silent prayer to a god I'd never believed in and waited. And waited...

"One moment there was a knife pressed against my throat and the next there wasn't. Everything had gone quiet. No birdsong. No chirping insects. No rustle of leaves in the trees. Complete silence.

"I opened my eyes and the Croatans were all face down on the ground. The one who had held the knife to my throat lay at my feet. He started whimpering, shivering all over, and then he shit himself.

"I saw movement in the trees, something huge and dark. I turned to get a better look and there it was. Clear as day. A wolf the size of a shire horse. Black as coal and with yellow eyes that glowed like balls of swarming fireflies. The wolf walked light of foot, making no sound. Not even leaves crinkled underfoot. He was a shadow come to life.

"He stepped over the Croatans and stopped in front of me, lowered his head, looked me in the eye. A low growl, deep and resonant like slow rolling thunder, came from his throat. My mind was telling me I should be on the ground, shitting myself like that Croatan, but I wasn't afraid. I felt... alive. For the first time in my miserable goddamn life, I felt alive.

"The wolf turned and walked back down the hill and the Croatans didn't move. They lay there, paralyzed by fear. Halfway down the hill, he stopped, turned back, and looked at me again. Those glowing eyes were inviting me to follow him. And follow him, I did. From the Atlantic to the Pacific, from the Arctic to Patagonia, and all parts in between. For three hundred years, I walked with him, living on when I should have died. His presence, his medicine, sustained me, strengthened me. Kept me alive and made me feel invincible.

"Those times we were apart, even for a few hours, I would feel myself aging. Another wrinkle on my brow. Another brown spot on my hands. When we were separated for a few days or a few weeks, my strength would fade a bit, but as soon as we reunited, it would return. His presence, his medicine, sustained me. To this day, I don't know why he saved me, why he chose me...

"If ever I had any medicine of my own, it was used up long ago. Everything I was, all the strength and speed and vigor, was on loan from him. And now that debt has been called in. He is no longer here to sustain me. The years are catching up to me fast, Mr. Hayes. I'm on borrowed time and not long for this world."

The old man stared silently into the fire for a long moment, then looked up at the stars again. *"What should be the fear? And for my soul, what can it do to that, Being a thing immortal as itself?"*

The old gunslinger turned, his violet eyes boring into the manhunter. "I am afeared I shall die in your debt, Mr. Hayes. Both for seeing the girl this far and for this last favor I will beg of you." He paused took another ragged breath. "The creature who stole the girl and murdered my friend is headed for the Chalkstones. Will you ride there with me? Will you help me kill that bat-headed sonofabitch before I die?"

Sixty-Nine

The Wing-Thief

The tracks led down a narrow winding path bordered on each side by boulders stacked so tightly together a knife's blade wouldn't fit between. With distance, the shadows grew darker, ultimately enveloping him. Black Wing could no longer see the boulders, much less the bloody tracks on the rocky soil. He slipped his axe from the loop on his belt, anger boiling inside him. Nothing would stay his hand this time. He would find Wechuge and this time he would do what he had failed to do at the lake's edge and again at the waterfall. He would do what the holy man had beseeched him not to do, what the ghost woman had prevented him from doing when the creature sat behind him in the canoe. He would end Wechuge. He would destroy the monster before it took another soul.

He paused, uncertain how to proceed. Each time Wechuge had murdered previously, the creature had fled into the water, but this time it had eschewed the dark river on which the canoe rested and instead ambled into the darkness beyond the shore. Black Wing felt the crow stir deep inside his chest and his eyes could suddenly cut through the darkness. The oppressive blackness remained but despite that, he could once again see Wechuge's bloody, mismatched footprints leading down the path and into the distance.

He followed the trail for what seemed like hours. Then hours turned to what seemed days. He continued on. Never tiring, never thirsting, never afflicted by hunger. Until at last the path ended at the base of a sheer cliff, stretching hundreds of feet upward until the shadows, like a low-hanging cloud, swaddled them in blackness.

Black Wing could see bloody smears on the rock face. Mismatched handprints where Wechuge had grabbed the rock and bloody splotches were its toes had found purchase. Wechuge had climbed the cliff.

Black Wing reached up, fingers probing the rock face until he found a handhold. He tested his grip, then dug his toes into a crack in the rock and pulled himself upward. His fingers probed again, found another handhold. His toes found another crack. He pulled himself up. And repeated. Following the monster Wechuge's trek up the cliff.

Black Wing's climb seemed to mirror his trek through the rocky maze below. It felt endless, as if he had been pulling himself up the rocky wall for hours. Then days. The rock floor beneath him had long since disappeared into shadows and, looking up, the cliff face seemed to stretch into infinity. He continued upward, never tiring, never thirsting, never hungering.

The climb took on a repetitiveness. Wechuge's bloody prints on the rock face began to all look the same. The rocks all looked the same. The handholds and footholds became familiar to him, as if his fingers knew exactly where to find them when he stretched out an arm.

Black Wing wondered if he was somehow caught in a loop. He could look down and see where he had been, but when he looked up, it seemed as if he was seeing the same. Rocks he had already climbed. Handholds he had already gripped.

Was his mind playing a trick on him? Had the monotony of the climb skewed his perception? Or was it possible he was not climbing upward at all? Was it all an illusion? Was the underworld manipulating him? The climb was no more difficult than had been the trek through the maze below, but it seemed endless. As if he was making no progress. As if he could make no progress.

His fingers found yet another familiar handhold, a crevice still slicked with the blood from Wechuge's grip, and a thought occurred to him. He had been so focused on following and finding the monster, he had overlooked what he should have immediately noticed. An incongruity that should have been obvious. Wechuge was half again his size. The creature's reach was much greater than his and yet he had been following Wechuge's path up the rock face, handhold for handhold, foothold for foothold.

He paused. He was in a stalemate, not unlike the one he had faced in his battle with the water panther. If he continued to grab and grip, pull himself upward, the climb would never end. The rocks looked familiar because they were. He was in a loop. His trek would continue forever unless and until, as with the water panther, he broke free. Until he solved the puzzle that entrapped him, he would never break the stalemate. He would be doomed to climb these rocks forever.

With the water panther, he had broken the loop and ended the stalemate by finally understanding the purpose of the earthenware bowl. The thing itself, the bowl, was not what he had been sent to retrieve. It was the blood within the bowl. It was not the object that mattered. It was the thing the object contained.

Black Wing felt the crow stir inside him and realized Old Crow had been still for the entirety of the climb. He knew how to break the stalemate. He knew how to escape the loop.

He closed his eyes, took a breath, released his grip on the rocks, and pushed off. He fell from the cliff face, plummeting to the rock floor.

It was never the object itself that mattered. It was the thing contained within it.

He felt the crow stir excitedly inside him, expanding, filling him. He felt his flesh tear, a ragged seam opening up along his spine. He felt the wings sprout from his back. Old Crow's wings.

No. Not anymore. *His* wings.

The ebony wings were as long as Black wing was tall, but these were not stolen wings. They had been gifted to him. They were a part of him now. His wings.

He extended the wings, spreading them wide, letting the wind catch beneath them. He had flown before. He knew how. He turned into his descent, building speed, flying faster than he had been falling. He shifted, wings flapping hard, stealing the downward momentum and converting it into upward thrust. The cliff face blurred as he zoomed by, flying faster than ever he had on borrowed wings.

The blackness above him retreated. A diffuse glow appeared, growing brighter until it was revealed as a beam of pure golden light. The beam broke through a narrow hole in the rocky ceiling, a shimmering shaft cutting into the darkness.

Sunlight.

Black Wing tucked his wings and shot through the gap, leaving behind the land of the dead for the world above.

Seventy

The Manhunter

Hamish Frost led the way, riding atop his painted horse as they crossed the windswept plains. In the late afternoon, the sun broke through the clouds, burning off the last of the gray cover overhead. A tumbleweed bounced along the short grasses sprouting from the hard-packed earth. Ozymandias Hayes watched the tumbleweed roll until it collided with a thick sage bush, halting its progress as the two became entwined.

Hayes rode a horse he had taken from the outpost, one of the few that had not been slaughtered by the horde of dead men or fled when the fences came down during the chaos of the attack on the station. He had loaded the gear and equipment they had commandeered from the outpost onto another horse and tied that horse's reins to his saddle, much as he had done when ferrying the corpses of Enoch Munn's gang to the cavalry fort.

He kept a close eye on Frost as they rode. The old man sat slumped in the saddle, occasionally attempting to correct his posture, make it appear as if he was strong enough to continue riding on his own. Hayes could tell the old gunslinger's strength was fading fast, even though he stubbornly insisted he was strong enough to ride. At least until the moment Frost fell from the saddle and would have landed beneath the horse's hooves had Hayes not hurried to his side and caught him.

Hayes reined in, brought all three horses to a halt.

He helped Frost straighten himself. The old gunslinger adjusted his floppy hat and sat, breathing heavily. With his head down and between ragged breaths, he said, "Won't happen again."

"You'll have to ride with me from this point on," said Hayes.

Frost gave his head a slight shake. "I can still ride."

"No, Mr. Frost. I'm afraid you cannot. And the next time you fall, I might not be able to catch you. I fear we're not making good enough time as is. We can't afford to go any slower. You'll have to ride with me."

Frost looked to Hayes and gave his head another shake. It seemed to Hayes as if even that small action required an inordinate amount of energy. "Too much weight," said the old man. "And too far still to ride. We'll kill your horse before we get there."

Frost reached slowly behind him, fumbled around for a moment before lifting a coiled length of rope from the saddle. "Tie me to my horse."

"Are you certain?"

"No time for debate. Do it," said Frost.

Hayes took the rope and climbed down from his horse. He looped it around Frost's waist and secured it to the saddle. He tied Frost's boots to the stirrups. "Your center of mass is above the waist. I'm going to have to tie your hands around the horse's neck or you'll still be just as likely to fall."

Frost nodded. "Then do it."

Hayes tried not to think of the assault on the old gunfighter's dignity he was perpetrating. With Frost secured to his horse, Hayes tied the painted horse's reins to the side of his own saddle, opposite that of their pack horse. He looked to Frost for acknowledgment before proceeding.

"Due west until dusk, then veer to the north-northwest," said Frost in a halting voice.

Hayes nodded and put heels to the horse's flanks.

He continually looked over his shoulder as they rode, making certain the rope held and the old man remained upright. Frost's head lolled several times over the next few hours, his shoulders slumping, his body swaying, but he remained in the saddle. Hayes had his doubts the old gunslinger would live long enough to make it to their destination, much less have the strength to execute their plan. Each time the old man's head dipped, Hayes wondered if the legendary gunfighter had died.

As night fell, they were behind schedule and still well short of their destination. Hayes knew they had no choice but to continue on in the darkness. He didn't ask for the old man's consent and Frost gave no objection. The old gunslinger had pointed him in the direction to travel. Hayes was confident he could maintain the course. The night was mercifully bright and the stars would actually help him navigate. Hayes rode as fast as he dared. He still feared they would not get there in time, but riding any faster would surely kill Frost.

The night winds were cool on Hayes' face as they rode. Frost's head drifted down, the floppy hat obscuring his alabaster face. Hayes could hear a strained snoring and knew that as long as he heard that sound, he needn't worry about the old man. Hayes kept a steady pace through the night, stopping only once to water the horses at a narrow creek. And a few hours after sunrise, the Chalkstone cliffs at long last came into view.

And Hayes realized the snoring had stopped.

Seventy-One

The Gunslinger

Hamish Frost's head was up, violet eyes staring ahead to the distant Chalkstones. The old gunslinger turned and looked at Hayes. *"Beggar that I am, I am even poor in thanks."*

"I am glad you're still with me."

"Woe, destruction, ruin, and decay; The worst is death, and death will have his day." Frost took another breath. "Death can have me when my last task is done and not a goddamned second before." The old man lifted a withered hand, shielding his eyes from the sun. "My vision is failing, I'm afraid. Can you see anything from here?"

Hayes turned, shifting in the saddle, and retrieved from the packhorse the German spyglass he had taken from the ruins of the station house at the last outpost. He put the lens to his eye and extended the telescoping shaft. He twisted the eyepiece, slowly contracting and expanding his view, until the distant cliffs came into sharp focus.

"Do you see the girl?" asked Frost.

"I do," said the manhunter.

"She's alive?"

Hayes nodded subtly. "She is. Sitting atop a boulder. The creature who took her is there as well. It's just standing there, staring at the sun."

"He's got his days right this time," said Frost. "Today's the solstice and he's waiting for noon. When the sun reaches its zenith, his medicine will be at its most concentrated. Its most potent. That's when he'll act. He won't harm her until then."

"What happens at noon?"

The old gunslinger lowered his hand. "With his medicine concentrated, he'll have all the power he needs to heal himself fully, restore his body to what it once was. Then he'll rip her open. From stem to stern. He'll pull her heart from her chest and eat it while she watches. Take her medicine, same as he did with the wolf. But he won't kill her the way he did the wolf. He'll use his medicine and the power in the solstice, to bind her spirit to her body, rob her of the release of death. He'll bind her to him for all time, body and soul. All that she is, all that she was, and all that she'll ever be will become his. Forever."

Frost took a ragged breath, let his eyes wander to the saddlebags on the packhorse. "But we will not let that happen. I'm going to kill the sonofabitch first."

Hayes didn't doubt the old gunslinger's resolve, only his capability.

A blur in the sky caught Hayes' attention. He spun around and put the spyglass back to his eye, fearing another swarm of bats about to swoop down on them.

He focused the spyglass, then lowered it, not trusting what he had seen through the magnifying lenses. He clenched his eyes closed, opened them wide, and looked again. The spyglass had not deceived him.

He saw a man. A flying man.

A black-haired warrior with the wings of a giant bird protruding from his back. The flying man shifted in the air, wings flapping hard, spreading and catching the wind as he descended. He landed softly, bare feet touching lightly to the rocky soil directly in front of Hayes, Frost, and their horses.

Even without the wings, the warrior was an imposing figure. Tall and well-muscled, wearing buckskin leggings. The right side of his face, near his temple, bore a large scar, the remnant of a severe wound not properly stitched. His arms were lined with dark markings, tattoos in the form of wings, and emblazoned across his chest was another tattoo, the crude silhouette of a crow in flight. A long-handled war axe hung from a loop on a sash around his waist. An obsidian knife protruded from the sash on the opposite hip.

Hayes' hand went immediately to his sidearm, finger reaching for iron but before he could break leather, he heard Frost's ragged voice say, "Wait."

The dark-haired warrior tucked and folded the giant black wings behind him. He tilted his head to the side and narrowed his eyes. His piercing gaze silently scanned Hayes and then turned to Frost, eyes lingering on the ropes that bound the old gunslinger to his horse.

"*Hell is empty and all the devils are here.*" Frost said.

"Are you this man's prisoner, Whiteskin?" asked the warrior, hand hovering over the war axe.

"No," said Frost. "*Age, with his stealing steps, Hath clawed me in his clutch.*" He paused, swallowed hard. "I am no man's prisoner. I am captive only to circumstance. Mr. Hayes was kind enough to tie me to my horse so that I might not fall whilst I rode. He has been an erstwhile ally, dare I say *friend*."

The warrior's jaw unclenched. His face showed dawning recognition. "You are dying, Whiteskin."

"We're all dying," said Frost. "I'm just getting there a might quicker than I'd planned."

"The wolf is dead," said the warrior.

Frost nodded. "He is. Murdered by the creature who stands at the base of the Chalkstones at this very moment."

"Old Crow has given me his wings," said the warrior.

"So I see."

"Nine Fingers is dead. Antelope Eyes is dead. Both murdered by Wechuge."

"*I have too grieved a heart to take a tedious leave,*" said the old gunslinger. "You have my condolences on Antelope Eyes. But Nine Fingers' death was not happenstance. It was planned. She chose Wechuge for a purpose."

"When that purpose is served," said the warrior. "Do not ask me to stay my hand."

"Wouldn't dream of it," said Frost.

Hayes looked confused. "Wechuge?"

"A murderous creature born of the void," said the old gunslinger. "The girl told me she dreamed of her own death. Of a monster eating her alive. But it wasn't her death she saw. It was the old woman's." Frost turned back to the warrior. "Do you recall the girl I was with when you saw me in the mountains?"

The warrior tapped the dark tattoo on his chest. "Old Crow's spirit moves inside me. All that it was is in me. All that it knew, I now know."

Frost smiled. "Did Nine Fingers share her plan with Old Crow?"

The warrior nodded. "She did."

Seventy-Two

The Manhunter

Black Wing unfurled his great wings and took to the skies again. Ozymandias Hayes shielded his eyes from the blinding sun and watched as the warrior disappeared into a cloud.

"I know what you're thinking," said Hamish Frost.

"He has the power of a god," said Hayes.

"He does."

"Forgive my asking, but given the circumstances, is this the best use of those abilities?"

The old gunslinger remained tied into his saddle to keep from falling. "You'd have him take your place? Or perhaps mine?"

"I didn't say that."

"There's small choice in rotten apples." Frost took a long, ragged breath. "Though it's a fair question. He's a reborn deity and I'm a broken-down bag of leather and bones that can't ride a horse without being tied to the saddle." The old man went silent for a moment, then looked to the Chalkstones. "The Wolf was stronger than Old Crow, even on his best day. And you saw what that bastard did to the Wolf. Now that it's eaten the Wolf's heart, added his medicine to its own, it's even more powerful." Frost took a few more halting breaths. "Black Wing has his part to play. And I have mine. We hold to the plan. You just get me close. I won't fail."

Hayes nodded and said no more. They forded a small stream behind the cottonwoods and then spent the better part of an hour methodically circling around the western side of the Chalkstones. As the sun neared its zenith, they were in position. Hayes again broached the subject of charging the creature on horseback but Frost, once again, ruled it out. "That thing hears or sees us coming before we're ready for it to see us and it's *Farewell the neighing steed and the shrill trump.* Its first notice of us will be when you open up on it with that scattergun and then I'll be the last thing it ever sees."

Hayes kept his reservations to himself.

When they'd ridden as close as they dared, Hayes climbed down from his horse and then untied the ropes that held Frost to his mount. The old gunslinger was frail and winded, but bristled when Hayes attempted to help him from the saddle.

"*I am constant as the northern star,*" he said in a low voice. "I might not have been able to ride unaided, but by god I can still climb down from a saddle."

Hayes stepped back, preparing to catch the old man should he fall. He did not. Frost stepped down, then leaned against the horse to steady himself. "Forgive me, Mr. Hayes," he whispered.

Hayes shook his head. "Nothing to forgive." He untied the leather strap on the long holster behind his saddle and took out the ten gauge. He breached and loaded it, then stuffed the remaining shells in his pockets.

"Hopefully, you won't need to reload. But if you do..." Frost paused. *"Give dreadful note of preparation."*

Hayes nodded. "Indeed."

Frost lurched to the packhorse and reached into a saddlebag. He withdrew a cloth-wrapped bundle and carefully peeled back the wrapping. Inside were the bundled nitroglycerin sticks the bandits at the station had intended for opening the stagecoach's strongbox. The old gunslinger looked at the fuse protruding from the blasting cap. "How fast will this burn?"

"About twenty seconds per foot."

"Won't need this much then." Frost slipped a skinning knife from the sheath at the back of his belt and cut off more than half of the fuse. "That should be sufficient."

Hayes wasn't so certain, but what was done was done. "Keep flush with the cliff face. Get as close as you can before lighting and throwing it."

"The native hue of resolution is sicklied over o'er with the pale cast of thought." Frost narrowed his violet eyes. "I won't be throwing anything, Mr. Hayes. I am going to walk it right up to the fucker and hand it to him."

Hayes nodded. The old gunslinger had seemed on the verge of death many times since they left the ruins of the station but now, mere moments away from executing their plan, he seemed more steady. As if he had been conserving his energy, marshaling his resources for this one final act.

"I don't have a lot of possessions, Mr. Hayes." The old gunslinger bowed his head as he spoke, an uncharacteristic pose for him. Hamish Frost had always bored through Hayes with those violet eyes when the two of them conversed. "Material things never much mattered to me. Don't suspect they do to you either, but there is something..." he paused. "Something I want you to have when I'm gone."

"You say that as if you expect me to survive this encounter."

"No. I don't. You and I... we're both about to die. No point in not speaking clearly. But death will only be a permanent condition for me. You'll be back." The old man reached for the elephant ivory handles of his revolvers. "I gave the girl my coat and I want you to have my guns."

Hayes shook his head. "I can't take those."

"You can."

"I am not worthy of such a gift."

"I beg to differ."

The manhunter shook his head. "Those are Hamish Frost's guns. And I am not Hamish Frost. *This above all — to thine own self be true.*"

The old gunslinger smiled. "You know the bard."

"Not as well as you did," said Hayes. "But I know if we're both to be killed, then Hamish Frost should die as he lived. With his guns on his hip. "

Frost considered this and nodded. *"Make haste; the hour of death is expiate."*

Seventy-Three

The Wing-Thief

From several hundred feet above the prairie floor, Black Wing watched the two men inch their way along the cliff wall, coming up behind the bat-headed spirit and the girl it held prisoner. The evil spirit seemed oblivious to their presence. It continued staring up at the sun, while the girl sat on a large rock barely an arm's length from the spirit.

As he waited for the men to act on their plan, Black Wing noticed movement on the prairie floor. Another was approaching from the opposite direction. Through the eyes gifted him by Old Crow, Black Wing looked closer. He saw the Beauty, the spectral ghost woman, striding across the windswept plains. Naked, her long black hair swirling about her head. Her violet aura pulsed as she strode purposefully toward the evil spirit.

But Black Wing knew the Beauty was no more. She had anointed him with her blood, making him a worthy vessel for the rebirth of Old Crow. He had seen her remains on the banks of the dark river. Her mantle, her medicine, had passed to the girl who sat on the rock beneath him. It was not the Beauty he saw on the prairie below. It was Wechuge.

Wechuge wears her body now. The same as Wechuge had worn the body of Bull Elk when it slaughtered the boy warrior named Slow Rabbit. The same as it had worn the body of the holy man Antelope Eyes the night it came into their camp.

Black Wing heard through his newly powerful ears Wechuge call out to the evil spirit, speaking in the Beauty's voice. The words were from a long-dead language Black Wing did not know, but had heard once before. On the night when Antelope Eyes had spoken to the Beauty in the clearing in the woods the day before he was murdered by Wechuge.

The bat-headed evil spirit lowered its eyes from the sun, looked at the Beauty. The evil spirit seemed uncertain, almost confused. Its head turned, looking at the girl sitting on the rock, then pivoted back to the Beauty. The Beauty was closer now. Almost close enough to touch the evil spirit. *Wechuge was closer now.*

Words in the mystery language croaked from the evil spirit's throat.

The Beauty stopped, held out a slender hand, and placed it gently on the evil spirit's arm, caressing it with a lover's touch. The Beauty repeated the words back to the evil spirit in her soft, musical voice. *Wechuge repeated the words in the Beauty's voice.*

The evil spirit groaned, crying out in a harsh, guttural tone, more anguish than anger, then dropped to its knees before the Beauty. It bowed its head, overcome by the touch of his bride, by the voice it had longed for eons to hear again.

The Beauty stood over the evil spirit. *Wechuge, wearing the body of the Beauty, stood over the evil spirit.* The Beauty pulled the evil spirit to her, resting its grotesque head between her breasts. She traced her fingers along the creature's shoulder, caressing the back of its head, and uttering more gentle words from the mystery language.

The Beauty leaned down, closer, her lips brushing the triangular ear of the evil spirit. She whispered more words of the ancient language into its ear. Then she opened her mouth. *Wechuge opened its mouth, lips disappearing as they curled back and rows of jagged teeth sprouted from a jutting beak-shaped mandible. The jaw distended, the maw opening impossibly wide, then Wechuge's jaws snapped closed on the evil spirit's neck.*

Black Wing dove, extending his wings and flapping hard. Building speed, the wind feeling as if it would peel the flesh from his skull. He extended his arms in front of him, stretching, reaching.

The girl on the rock stood. She turned away from Wechuge's attack on her captor and looked to the sky. She looked at Black Wing, held her arms up, fingers splayed, reaching for him.

Black Wing leveled his descent and flew straight for the girl. Closing the distance rapidly as the evil spirit squirmed beneath Wechuge's crunching jaws. Black Wing reached out, his hands grasped the girl's, fingers clenching tightly around her wrists. He lifted her from the rock, then thrusting down with his wings, he pulled upward. And took again to the skies, stealing the girl named Anaba away from her captor and taking her into the clouds.

Seventy-Four

The Manhunter

Ozymandias Hayes looked up at the sky. The sun had almost reached its zenith. No more time. They had to act now. He flattened himself against the rock face, cradling the ten gauge to his chest. Two more steps, then one step away from the wall, and they would round the edge of the rock and be in the bat-headed creature's line of sight. He turned and looked to his right. Hamish Frost stood shoulder to shoulder with him, long stringy white hair hanging in front of his face. The old gunslinger stared back at Hayes, a steely resolve in his violet eyes. Frost held a lucifer in one hand, the bundle of nitroglycerin sticks in the other.

"Cry havoc and let slip the dogs of war," said the old man. He dragged the lucifer along the rock face. The phosphorus ignited with a flash. Frost held the flame over the fuse until it caught. A concentrated burst of white rained sparks as it raced down the fuse. It was burning too fast, Hayes feared. The old gunslinger had cut off too much of the fuse.

Hayes cocked the hammer of the ten gauge and stepped quickly away from the cliff. He was running as he rounded the corner, lowering the scattergun. He saw a blur of motion, something large and dark dropping from the sky. The winged warrior swooping down, and faster than the blink of an eye, grabbed the girl Ana, lifted her from the rock, and shot skyward at almost ninety degrees.

In front of him, the bat-headed god was on its knees, head bowed almost in supplication. Standing over it was a naked woman with long black hair swirling in the wind. Her mouth hung open unnaturally wide, displaying row upon row of jagged teeth that seemed to wind down her throat. As Hayes ran toward them, she dropped her head and bit, clamping onto the bat-headed creature's neck. The creature cried out in a roar that seemed to shake the very Chalkstone cliffs. The woman's head morphed into something dark, leathery and vaguely diamond-shaped, like the head of a snapping turtle. Her flesh expanded and sagged, becoming mottled shades of grey, blue, and green, as if rotted and putrefying. It wrapped its mismatched arms around the bat-headed giant, enveloping it in a crushing bearhug.

The bat-headed god struggled to its feet, fighting to dislodge the teeth and jaws from its neck. It managed to break free of the bearhug, then with its long, spindly fingers to pry the teeth and jaws from its neck. The rotting monster pounded the torso of the murder god, slamming its club-like hands repeatedly into the god's ribs and abdomen, while the murder god held tightly to the other creature's upper beak and lower mandible, pulling and wrenching them away from each other until the jaw broke with a loud popping sound.

"That's Wechuge!" Hayes heard Frost shout. "Shoot them! Shoot the fuckers! Shoot them both!"

The old gunslinger moved with surprising quickness for one who'd seemed so frail only moments before. As if the prospect of his own death invigorated him. Or perhaps it was the thought of avenging the Wolf that propelled him forward. The lit fuse of the nitroglycerin bundle was already near the blasting cap.

Hayes pulled the scattergun's trigger. Pellets sprayed from the barrel in an explosive burst, peppering the two monsters locked in combat. Hayes saw their flesh rip as the lead pellets tore through them, but neither went down. He breached the shotgun, extracted the spent shell, and reloaded. He put the scattergun to his shoulder, finger on the trigger, but did not fire.

Hamish Frost was in front of him, moving quickly toward the two warring creatures. Time seemed to slow. Hayes saw the old gunslinger's foot strike the rock, saw his ankle turn. Hayes saw the white of jagged bone shoot from the top of the old man's boot, puncturing through flesh and fabric, protruding just below Frost's knee. The old gunslinger collapsed in a rolling heap. The nitroglycerin bundle flew from his hands, bounced on the ground, and cartwheeled to a stop ten steps ahead of him. The fuse was near spent. The white burst and raining sparks were almost touching the blasting cap.

Hayes saw Frost, agony etched on his face, struggling to stand, but his shattered leg would not permit it.

Hayes tossed the ten gauge aside and sprinted forward. He passed the old gunslinger without a second glance. He bent at the waist, one hand scooping down and grabbing the bundle without breaking stride. His eyes drifted down to the nitroglycerin sticks, at the sparks landing on the back of his hand. The white burst at the end of the spent fuse.

Hayes stared at the two monstrosities in front of him. Wechuge, the hulking mass of mismatched body parts, beaked jaws, and jagged teeth. And the bat-headed giant who had murdered the wolf and led an army of the dead and a swarm of bats so immense they blacked out the sky, all to steal the girl named Ana from him.

Hayes collided with the two creatures as the burning fuse reached the blasting cap. There was a deafening boom, a blinding flash of white, and a burst of heat that consumed him.

Seventy-Five

The Gunslinger

THE SHOCKWAVE ROLLED OVER Hamish Frost like a herd of stampeding bison. He felt more bones shatter, some pulverized so fine as grains of sand. There was a flash of heat as if he'd fallen into a roaring inferno. Then all went black.

For a time.

The intense pain let him know he was somehow still alive. He could tell his hair, beard, and brows had been singed away. His clothing burned and fused to his flesh. And where his skin wasn't blackened, it was red, cracked, and blistered. With great effort, he forced his eyes open, tearing the melted eyelids apart, but his vision was clouded. Blurred. All he could see was smoke roiling and curling from the ground. Other than a persistent hum and the damnable ringing, he could hear nothing. His head throbbed. His skull was a crisscross of fractures.

But somehow he was still alive. At least for a while.

As the smoke cleared and his double vision recalibrated, he could see a shape in front of him. Long and slender, moving languidly. The bat-headed god of murder and death rose from a smoking crater gouged into the earth so deep as to expose bedrock.

Ozymandias Hayes had sacrificed himself, blown himself to bits all for naught. The god of murder and death still lived.

Though as it came closer to him, Frost could see the blast had damaged it in significant ways. The creature's head was skeletal, most of the flesh burned and blown away. One arm was missing, severed between shoulder and elbow, cauterized by the heat. The other arm was blackened but intact. Most of the flesh and thin fur on the creature's legs had been stripped away, revealing the musculature beneath. If there were broken bones, there were none that prevented it from standing or walking. Its torso had been ripped open, ribs and internal organs exposed. Frost could see the creature's pulsing heart through its bloody rib cage.

The creature lumbered forward, feet dragging in the dust as it trudged toward him. The creature sustained itself through murder. It fed on death. Frost was still alive, but if the creature finished him, his death would serve to strengthen the bastard.

But Frost could not fight back. He was barely alive. He had no strength. His bones were shattered. His body was burned, his flesh blackened and melted. The fingers of his left hand were fused together and his right hand...

Frost could move his right hand. The flesh of his fingers was melted, but not fused. He could move his fingers, bend them. His hand drifted to his leg, finding his holster. The leather was blackened and covered in soot, but his revolver was still in the holster.

His fingers trembled. The elephant ivory stock was cool to the touch, but the hammer and trigger guard retained the heat of the blast. Frost's flesh sizzled on contact with the metal. He ignored the pain and managed to extract the weapon from the holster, but found he didn't have the strength to lift his arm, much less the gun. He rested his hand on the ground and used the curve of his thigh to angle the barrel upward. The blistered, fleshy pad of his thumb peeled off as he cocked the hammer into position.

Men at some time are masters of their fates.

The creature stood only a few feet away from him. Frost's finger contracted, pulling the trigger back until the hammer fell. He couldn't hear the shot, couldn't tell where the bullet had gone, but he knew instinctively he had missed.

Closer now. The creature's shadow falling over him. Frost struggled to cock the hammer, his hand shaking, his shredded thumb sliding.

It was useless. If the explosion had not ended the abomination, then what good would a bullet do? *Sound and fury. Signifying nothing.*

He had failed. Failed to avenge the wolf. Failed Ana. Failed the girl he had sworn to protect. Failed the goddess she had become. He could only hope Black Wing had taken her far, far away. But he knew the creature would never relent. She was its bride and it would have her. It would keep searching, keep coming after her. It would recover. It would grow stronger.

Frost's murder at its hands would aid in that. The bat-headed creature would find her. It would bring her back here to this spot. On another solstice. It would rip her open and take her heart.

He had failed.

Stupid, useless old man. Your life was lived in vain. She trusted you and you failed. The Wolf chose you and you failed.

Frost didn't realize he had cocked the hammer, lifted his arm, steadied his aim, and pulled the trigger until he saw the spray of bone fragments coming from the creature's shattered rib.

The bat-headed god staggered backward.

Frost cocked the hammer, fired again. The bullet tore through the creature's exposed heart.

He fired again. Then again. Only when the hammer fell on an empty chamber did Frost stop firing.

Frost could see the bat-headed god swaying. Its knees buckled and it lurched forward as it fell, landing hard and throwing up a little cloud of dust not two feet from where Frost lay.

Even so, the bat-headed god yet lived. Frost could see it twisting, turning toward him. Its one remaining hand stretched, reaching out for him. Long fingers scratched the ground near his face. The fingers dug into the dirt, taking hold. The murder god pulled itself closer to him. Frost brought the butt of the empty revolver down on the creature's hand, but it was an ineffectual blow. The murder god snatched the revolver easily from his hand and flung it. It reached for Frost, fingers splayed, jagged claws inches from his face.

Then a slender foot stepped firmly on the murder god's hand, pinning it to the ground.

Frost lifted his eyes and saw the girl named Ana standing over them.

No. Not the girl. Not a lost child in need of his protection. Not Ana.

Anaba.

She Returns.

Anaba ground her heel into the murder god's blackened hand. She knelt and rolled the creature onto its back so that it could face her. Frost saw her lean close to the creature, saw her lips move, but he could hear only the ring and hum reverberating from the explosion. It didn't matter. Her words were not meant for him. She spoke her final message to her husband, the god of murder who had stolen her from this very spot eons ago, taken her as a captive to the underworld, forced her to become the mother of the gods.

Anaba reached a hand into the creature's chest and, with a tug, pulled out the bullet-riddled heart. The creature stopped squirming and lay still. The bat-headed god — the god of murder and death — was itself dead.

Frost watched as Anaba probed the god's heart with her fingers, finding and digging out five soft lead slugs he had deposited there and dropping them on the ground. She brought the heart to her mouth and bit into it, tearing away a bloody morsel. She set the organ atop the dead god's ribs and chewed slowly but did not swallow. After a moment, she spat the well-masticated hunk into her hand.

She turned to Frost and held the meat in front of his face. She gently pulled down his chin, parting his melted lips, and sat the lump on his tongue. She closed his mouth and tilted his head back, massaging his throat until he swallowed.

Frost retched, his body trying to force the morsel back up, expel it. But Anaba would not allow it. She held his mouth closed, massaged his throat again.

She retrieved the heart, tore off another chunk, and repeated. Frost surrendered and let her feed him, as a mother bird feeding her hatchlings. She gently laid his crushed and blackened head on her thighs. She finished the rest of the heart herself, taking large bloody bites and swallowing without chewing until all the murder god's heart had been consumed, and all of its medicine had been transferred.

The ringing in Frost's ears subsided within moments. He could hear the wind whistling. His vision cleared, the clouds overhead coming into clear focus. His blistered and burned flesh began to scab. Nerves, deadened by the blast, regenerated, bringing with them waves of ever-intensifying pain.

Anaba sat with him, cradling his head in her lap.

Seventy-Six

The Wing-Thief

Wechuge's detached legs and groin lay just to the left of the blast's epicenter. Black Wing found the rest of the creature propped against the cliff face of the Chalkstones. The blast had pocked the rock wall with bits of tooth and bone. Viscera, blood, and pieces of blackened flesh were spattered behind the creature. A concentric halo of soot was painted just above its head. Smoke and dust mingled in hazy swirls all around.

Black Wing looked down at the once fearsome, but now pitiable creature. Wechuge's abdominal cavity was split open, a jagged seam running almost to its throat exposed bone and putrid tissue. Intestines spilled out onto the dusty ground in a pile. One gnarled and blistered hand was feebly trying to stuff them back into their proper place. Black Wing could see the purple aura. The glowing sheen of medicine that had surrounded the creature previously was all but gone now, faded and dim with only the occasional pop and flash of color, like the ignition of a drop of wood oil in a flickering fire.

Wechuge's turtle-like head, though blackened and blistered, remained largely intact. Although the creature's jaw, broken by the murder god, hung loosely, resting on its chest. Wechuge lifted its head, looked up at Black Wing and tried to speak, but only harsh guttural grunts and moans escaped its throat.

Wechuge's visage shifted as the creature cycled through a series of faces and bodies. Dozens of those it had consumed, those whose lives and bodies the creature had taken to perpetuate its own survival. Most, Black Wing did not know, had never seen before, but some he recognized. Bull Elk. Slow Rabbit. The family of pioneers at the river's edge. At last, it settled on the form for which it had been searching.

Wechuge disappeared. The broken body, the pile of intestines, all of the burned and blackened creature with its misshapen turtle-like head, was gone. And in its place sat a thin man with a soft face, narrow lips, and large almond-shaped eyes. A full head of thick black hair, graying at the temples, braids with eagle feathers protruding.

The holy man.

Antelope Eyes.

Unbidden, tears formed in the corners of Black Wing's eyes and rolled down his cheeks, leaving trails in the dusty black war paint.

The holy man tilted his head, looked up at him, and smiled.

"On the day Wechuge murdered you, took you from me," Black Wing said, "you appeared to me, came into our camp, and warned me to flee. From that moment, I wanted to avenge you. To kill Wechuge for what it had done. The only thing that stayed my hand, the only thing that kept me from throwing my axe as you walked to the river, was not knowing who would feel the pain."

The winged warrior paused. "Would I be striking the monster who slew you? Or would I be striking you down? Was the face I saw an illusion cast by Wechuge? Was it some trick? Or had you wrested control from the monster for a few brief moments? Did the creature destroy you? Or had you become a part of it? Were the words you spoke intended to save me from Wechuge? Or to save Wechuge from my axe?"

Black Wing bent to look in the face of the holy man. "Are you lost to me forever? Or is there something left of you behind this facade? If I take my axe and bury it in your throat right now, would I slay only Wechuge, or would I also slay what remains of you?"

Antelope Eyes stared back at him with no expression.

Black Wing lifted the war axe from its loop in the belt around his waist. He stared at the razor-sharp blade for a long moment. He closed his eyes and took a deep breath, then tossed the axe aside.

Black Wing tucked his wings and sat against the rock wall next to Antelope Eyes. He crossed his legs and looked down at the holy man's slender hand resting on the ground by his side. Black Wing placed his hand atop it. "I have fulfilled my quest. The quest you set me on." He paused. "If you are in there, if this is the last time I will see you, the last time I will touch you, if there is anything left of you, then stay as long as you can. And I will stay with you until the end."

Antelope Eyes turned, resting the crown of his head against the cliff, and looked at Black Wing in silence.

Black Wing sat there, his hand on top of the holy man's, staring into the face of Antelope Eyes as the sun reached its zenith and began its descent toward the horizon. The shadows stretched long and the sun disappeared. The moon rose and a million, million stars filled the sky. Still, he sat.

As the sun reappeared on the eastern horizon, setting the sky afire, and splaying rays of light across the plains, the holy man closed his eyes. His shoulders slumped and his head lolled. He fell, sliding down the rock wall, away from Black Wing, until his face rested against the dusty ground.

Black Wing patted the holy man's hand one last time, then stood. He watched in silence as Antelope Eyes disappeared and the dead hulk of decaying flesh that was Wechuge returned and lay there unmoving.

Black Wing stepped away, found his war axe, slipped the handle into its loop, then unfurled his wings, and took to the sky.

Seventy-Seven

The Manhunter

OZYMANDIAS HAYES HEARD THE waters lapping gently against the muddy shore. He trudged through the darkness until he saw a soft blue-green glow ahead. He found the birch-bark canoe resting at the river's edge.

The girl named Ana — no, not Ana, her name was Anaba — sat in the canoe's bow, holding the wooden paddle across her lap. She was barefoot but dressed in clean, tanned buckskins. Eagle feathers were woven into her rich black hair. A swirling ball of light floated above her, filling the area with a soft, cold luminescence.

She smiled at him. "Hello, Mr. Hayes. Are you ready?"

"Ready?"

"To see where the river leads."

"I'm not... going back this time," said Hayes. His words began as a question, but by the time he finished the sentence, they had become a declaration.

"I know," she said. "Climb in."

"Are you coming with me?"

"For a while," she said. "You don't mind, do you?"

"I think I would appreciate the company." Hayes stepped into the water and pushed the birch-bark canoe away from the shore and climbed in, taking a seat in the stern. Anaba held the paddle out to him and he took it from her.

"Gently," she said. "The current will do most of the work for us."

Hayes put one hand on the shaft of the paddle, the other on the pommel, and pressed the blade into the black water with a slow, sweeping motion. He switched sides and repeated, letting the paddle linger a little longer with each stroke, watching as the dark waters swirled around it. The orb of light floated above them, following them.

"What of Mr. Frost?" asked Hayes. "Is he...?" He let the sentence trail off, as if reluctant to say the words necessary to finish it.

"Hamish Frost has proven more durable than even he imagined."

"He's alive?" Hayes asked with incredulity.

Anaba smiled at him. "He is."

"How?"

Anaba didn't answer. And Hayes realized he didn't need to know. The simple knowledge that the old gunslinger had survived was enough.

As they drifted downstream, the orb of light above them floated higher, shifting from cold blue-green to warm white while growing in both size and luminescence, until it swallowed up the darkness and took its rightful place in a sky of azure blue. As Hayes' eyes adjusted, he could see wisps of soft, summery clouds hovering on the distant horizon. The river water, which had been black as onyx only a few moments ago, was now clear as crystal and Hayes could see schools of small, colorful fish darting in and out amongst the green leafy vegetation that waved rhythmically from the sandy bottoms.

The river narrowed, fjording through great chalky cliffs that bracketed each shore. Overhead, Hayes could see flocks of white birds swooping gently over the cliff tops and landing in precariously placed nests along the rock face.

The river bent slowly, the cliffs receding and giving way to gentle, rolling hills covered with vibrant green grasses and grazing sheep. Craggy, snow-capped mountains lined the distant horizon. Quince trees, their unruly limbs heavy with golden fruit and fragrant lavender blossoms, dotted the landscape.

"What is this place?" asked Hayes.

Anaba didn't answer. Around another bend, a small cottage appeared, set back about a hundred steps from the river amidst a carefully manicured garden of tulips and lilies, peonies, hollyhocks, crocus, lavender, monkshood and foxglove. The roof of the cottage was a thick thatch and the facade was ancient brick covered by clinging ivy. A fence of stacked cobblestones ran the length of a well-trod path leading from a weathered but sturdy wooden dock all the way to the front door of the cottage.

A woman sat on a stone bench in the flower garden, a leather-bound book half opened across her lap. On the grass at her feet sat a baby girl in a long white dress, giggling, tiny fingers splayed as she reached for a butterfly fluttering just out of reach. The woman looked up as if sensing the approach of the canoe.

Her skin was the color of café au lait, her hair long and auburn, thick and abundant of curls.

The girl-child turned from the butterfly and looked in Hayes' direction. Excitement spread across her face and she bounced happily, pinwheeling her arms.

Anaba reached and took the paddle from Hayes' seemingly paralyzed hands. She brought the canoe alongside the dock and took hold of a piling.

"They're waiting for you, Mr. Hayes," she said.

Hayes looked at her as if in a trance.

Anaba tilted her head towards the cottage, coaxing him to action. "Go. Be with them," she said.

Hayes climbed from the canoe onto the dock. The air was rich with the scent of garden flowers. He looked to the cottage, to the smiling woman and the happy child.

Cora and Charlotte. His wife and daughter.

He turned and took one last look back at Anaba, but she had already released the piling, pushed off from the dock, and was paddling silently away. Hayes watched her go until the canoe disappeared into the distance.

He turned back to the cottage. He straightened his shirt, took a deep breath, smiled, and walked down the path.

Seventy-Eight

The Gunslinger

Hamish Frost left his painted horse to drink its fill while he knelt on the rocks of the stream and filled his canteen with ice-cold water. The snows had been heavy in the higher elevations the previous winter, and now with spring giving way to early summer, the streams and rivers were swollen with mountain runoff.

Three nights past, Anaba had summoned him in a dream. He had seen her in the night sky, her body made of stars, a pulsing red sun where her heart should be. He wasn't sure what task she would ask of him this time, but he was always eager to see her again. Perhaps Black Wing would be with her.

Frost plugged his canteen and walked back to the painted horse. As he climbed into the saddle, he saw the vultures circling overhead. At first, he thought nothing of it. It wasn't an uncommon sight, but something inside gnawed at him. Some sense or intuition told him this was different. Whatever death had attracted the attention of the vultures, had garnered his as well.

When beggars die, there are no comets seen.

Frost found the large she-wolf, her foot crushed and pinned in a furrier's iron trap. She had been dead at least a couple of days. Anger flared behind his eyes. He knelt and looked at the she-wolf, her fur a mix of gray, white, and rust, with black tipping her ears and covering her muzzle. As Frost shooed away the flies buzzing about her eyes, he noticed her teats were swollen and heavy with milk. She would likely have given birth in late spring. If she was still nursing, then she had pups no more than six weeks old somewhere nearby. Still dependent on their mother for survival, they too were likely dead at this point, but Frost needed to know for certain before he could leave.

He let the painted horse graze while he searched for the she-wolf's den. He found it about two miles away in the center of a thick aspen grove. A fallen and rotted tree, the trunk blackened and split by a lightning strike, with a cavity at the base of the stump. Claw marks in the dirt. The grass and moss around the hole were worn away by persistent entrance and exit. Frost took off his long coat, folded it, and lay it on the ground. He dropped his floppy hat atop it, then unbuckled his gun belt. He set the twin holstered revolvers with the elephant ivory handles next to the hat.

Frost got down on his belly and squirmed his way, inch by inch, into the opening beneath the stump. The tunnel leading into the den was barely wide enough for him to squeeze through, but after a while, the hole expanded and became a den. No light reached this far in, but Frost guessed the enclosure was about two feet high by perhaps six or eight feet wide.

In the farthest corner, his fingers touched fur. He had found one of the she-wolf's pups. Just as he had feared. Stiff and cold. He left the dead pup where it lay and continued his search. The she-wolf would likely have had at least four in her litter. He found another, then two more atop each other in the opposite corner. All of them dead.

Frost sighed. Finding no more, he began to inch his way back out of the den. As he did so, he heard a sound. Faint. Soft. But unmistakable. The sound of something other than him scurrying about in the den. He wasn't sure how he had missed it, but clearly he had.

He reached back in, stretching his fingers, probing the entire den. He touched fur, but this time he could feel warmth, movement. Then a sharp pain as something clamped down on his finger.

Gently, he pried the jaws open, then found the nape of a furry neck and lifted, pulling the pup along with him as he shimmied his way out of the den.

Once they were both out of the darkness and back in the sunlight, the wolf pup stretched and kicked and mewled, snapping again at Frost's fingers. It let out a high-pitched howl as Frost held it up in front of his face and studied it.

It was a male and looked to be four, perhaps five weeks old. Round face, blunted snout, short ears. But the pup was easily twice the size it should have been.

With eyes so yellow they practically glowed.

And fur as black as midnight.

END

Chapter 79

this page is a dummy

About the Author

Barry K Gregory is a reader, a writer, a husband, and a dad. He writes fantasy, horror, and comic books under his own name and crime thriller novels under the name Greg Kithe. He has several novels serializing at Amazon's Kindle Vella. He lives in Florida with his wife, three kids, and a Siberian Husky who looks like a giant red panda.

Sign up for his mailing list at https://barrykgregory.com/

Special Thanks

With special thanks to Sidney Williams, Douglas Texter, and Roland Mann for suffering through the early drafts while I figured out what the story was about.

And also my deepest appreciation to the new friends and fellow travelers I've met in the Kindle Vella community. This book was on track to be chopped up for spare parts until you entered the picture. Without your encouragement and enthusiasm, this book does not exist.

Printed in Great Britain
by Amazon